The P

John Cullimore

Copyright © John Cullimore 2024.

The right of John Cullimore to be identified as the author of this work has been asserted by him in accordance with the Copyright, Designs and Patents Act, 1988.

First published in 2025 by Holand Press.

'I will live in the world of my thought,
in the palace of my imagination'

Alfred Williams , 1913

THE PALACE OF MY IMAGINATION

Prologue

1913

It was the morning of midsummer's day. He'd awoken just before dawn with a sense of anticipation. Something was brewing in his mind, yet he just couldn't see it clearly. At such times he knew he had to head to his sacred tree, the birthplace of much of his inspiration. It was a fifteen-minute walk from the outskirts of the village to the river bank near Acorn bridge where he sought out the willow that overhung the hatchery in the river. He clambered up the trunk to find his usual seat in the forked branches and looked eastwards into the rising sun.

He cleared his mind and began to feel his way forward. His emotions were beginning to crystallise. The disappointment and desperation of work in the factory had been weighing on his mind. But here, the freshness of the summer morning and the reassurance of the countryside were a soothing balm convincing him that an unshakeable bond existed between himself and the natural world. For the first time he realised how he wanted to live, and he began to write:

There is no peace in life. It is not joy to be comfortable
And to be satisfied with anything is worse than all diseases and deaths.
I myself will not rest
I will not lie down meekly
I will arise like a giant and shake myself
I will proudly lift up my head
I will swear an oath to myself
And call all things in earth to my witness
Never to rest while my heart beats on this side death
Never to be humbled
I will excel in my labour
I will leave nothing unfinished

JOHN CULLIMORE

I will understand myself before I die, and this round frame I will search deeply
I will chisel my name (how small so ever) in the rock
I do not fear greatness. I can look into it and above it if I will
There is nothing greater than life*

He felt that was a promising start. The sun was now strengthening and shining directly in his eyes. It was time to get back to the cottage whilst the feelings remained strong, and the urge to write was irrepressible.

*   *from The Testament , Alfred Williams ,1913*

THE PALACE OF MY IMAGINATION

PART 1: AWAKENING

Chapter 1

Summer 1892

July arrived, and the grasses had grown tall. The weather had been favourable, and the sunny spell looked set to continue. Just after dawn on what promised to be the hottest day of the year, Alfred walked out from the farmyard into the fields with his workmate Sam and Jemmy, the farm's foreman.

Abundant wildflowers adorned the glorious fields with patches of riotous colour. Jemmy stooped to examine the grasses and turned to Alfred.

'Well, my boy, do you think it's ready for cutting?'

Looking down, Alfred saw that the plants were a vivid green colour, and copious seed heads were just beginning to appear.

'I do, sir.' replied Alfred.

'Well then, looks like we should be makin' hay.' said Jemmy.

After getting the go ahead from the farm owner, Whitfield, the boys were dispatched to harness the mares and couple them to the mowing machine. Having done this, they watched as Jemmy set off for the field. The horses were initially skittish and restless, presumably due to the unfamiliar rattling of the mowing machine, but after one or two circuits, during which Jemmy gently tapped the horses forward with a light willow switch, they settled into the work.

The cut grass lay undisturbed for a day, during which time the sun shone incessantly.

The next morning, a small army of casual workers appeared in the fields - primarily locals from South Marston village, including Alfred's mother, Elisabeth, some of his younger siblings, and other men, women, boys and girls. They lent their help in exchange for food, drink, and a small wage.

Elisabeth Williams felt a surge of pride as she watched her

JOHN CULLIMORE

fifteen-year-old son, Alfred, nimbly climb onto the hay cart. With a quiet confidence that belied his age, he gently guided the horse forward with soft, reassuring words, coaxing the animal through the narrow gate and into the sun-drenched field. It was as if he had been doing this all his life, and the sight of his natural ease and growing maturity filled her with a profound sense of contentment.

He was her fifth child, and she relied on him more and more since his father, Elias, had deserted the family four years earlier.

After fourteen years of marriage, Elias had left her with eight young mouths to feed - four boys and four girls. At the time, the youngest was just five months old.

Elias Williams had been a skilled and talented joiner but a failed businessman. When the going got tough, he abruptly returned to contract work in his native North Wales, making himself uncontactable and leaving them with nothing but debts from his failed enterprise and a constant struggle to make ends meet.

Despite being evicted from their home, the family rallied together and moved in with Elisabeth's parents at Rose Cottage, just fifty yards away. This move spared them from destitution and the dreadful possibility of entering the nearby Stratton Workhouse.

Elisabeth was dedicated to her children and determined to prove herself a good mother. She wanted to show the village gossipmongers—who possessed an innate prejudice against wives deserted by their husbands—they were wrong, and that the failure of her marriage was not the fault of her parenting skills.

Elisabeth utilised her domestic skills to make and sell confectionery, and her experience as a seamstress allowed her to take in needlework.

With her family accommodated under her parents' roof, she had help from her mother with the younger children.

During the haymaking and harvest seasons, there was always plenty of casual work on the farms. Alfred regularly contributed a few more weekly shillings by selling local newspapers on commission over the weekends. His elder brothers applied for work at the Great Western Railway factory, while Alfred appealed

THE PALACE OF MY IMAGINATION

to Elisabeth to allow him to finish his schooling and work full-time.

He left school at the end of the summer term of his eleventh year and began working as a casual labourer at various farms to the east of Swindon. He had been taken on at Longleaze a year ago and was happy to be working at what was generally considered the best-run farm in the region.

Elisabeth and the other farmhands used long-handled forks to spread the cut grass evenly across the field, allowing the sun's warm rays to evaporate the moisture and turn it into hay. The next morning, they turned it over to dry further and then raked it into neat rows. Alfred, Sam and Jemmy arrived with the wagon to collect it.

Alfred led the horse, and Jemmy drove the hay cart while Sam followed with the pitchfork, accumulating a mass of hay that he pitched onto the back of the wagon. This was tiring work in the heat, and as they reached the end of each row, Alfred and Sam alternated between pitching loose hay and guiding the horse. Behind them, the women and children raked any remaining loose hay.

After several passes through the fields, the wagon was replete with hay, and the team headed back to the yard. Jemmy asked to be dropped off to take another team into the fields while Alfred and Sam were told to take their load to the hay barn north of the railway tracks.

With Alfred at the reins, they made slow but steady progress towards the level crossing between Stratton and Marston, which they'd have to cross to get to the barn.

As they approached, they saw another hay wagon in the distance, on the same side of the track, with a single driver. It was heavily loaded with hay and was making slow progress. Alfred recognised the driver and horse.

'That's Tim from Priory farm, and old Oliver's pulling the wagon. He's not up to pulling that load.'

As Tim's wagon continued its lumbering progress and came within a few yards of the crossing, the rumble of a train approaching from the east became apparent. Both boys felt increasing anxiety as Tim's wagon now began crossing the track.

Just as Tim and Oliver were crossing the rails, an almighty crack rang out from the wagon which tilted to one side, shedding some of the bales onto the metals. Alfred's heart sank as he realised that the wagon was immobilised on the track with a broken rear axle. Sam and Alfred descended from their cart and hitched their horse to the nearest fence post.

Meanwhile, Tim stepped down from his wagon and was unhooking Oliver from the cart. As he struggled, the outline of the train became clear a mile or so in the distance. Tim now began to drag frantically at Oliver's reins, but his attempts to move the animal off the crossing seemed to freeze it, and the eyes of the horse became wild with fear.

'I'll go and see to Oliver!' Alfred shouted, believing the horse would recognise his voice and calm down. Sam agreed, thinking the best thing he could do would be to mount the summit of the embankment in time to signal to the locomotive driver to slow down.

He set off at a sprint, heart racing, and on reaching the top, he could see the engine in the distance, still moving with considerable speed.

He began waving his arms frantically, hoping against hope that the driver would see him in time.

Alfred rushed to Tim, stopping him from pulling on the reins and began to try to calm the horse down.

'Easy, boy, easy.' he murmured, his voice steady and soothing despite the panic rising within him. After a few seconds, the animal settled somewhat, its wild eyes starting to focus on Alfred's calm demeanour.

The train was now about a third of a mile away, and Sam began shouting to attract the driver's attention, his voice barely carrying over the roar of the approaching engine. Alfred could see the glint of sunlight on the train's metal front, as the great beast of iron and steam bore down on them.

'Tim, get clear!' Alfred yelled, shoving his friend towards

THE PALACE OF MY IMAGINATION

safety. He stayed with Oliver, coaxing the horse with steady hands and a calm voice. The massive iron locomotive was now less than a quarter of a mile away, its whistle blaring a frantic warning.

Sam, arms waving wildly, screamed at the top of his lungs.

'Stop!—Stop!'

He could see the train's driver starting to react, but it was unclear if there was enough distance for the heavy engine to come to a complete stop in time.

Tim stumbled back, watching in horror as Alfred continued to work with Oliver. With a final gentle tug and soothing words, Alfred managed to get Oliver to take a hesitant step forward, then another, until the horse finally moved off the tracks just as the train bore down on them.

With a screech of metal on metal, the brakes of the locomotive engaged, and sparks went flying, but the momentum of the train was just too great. Alfred held firmly onto Oliver's reins and kept him clear as the locomotive thundered past, ploughing unavoidably into the body of the wagon, pushing it along in front of the engine, spilling bales of hay near and wide, before gradually coming to a screeching stop a quarter of a mile further down the track.

As the train came to a halt, the engineer and fireman sprang from the cab, urgency in their steps as they rushed toward the scene of the collision. Sam scrambled down the embankment, his face pale, but his movements now carrying a sense of restored confidence.

'You did it, Alfred,' he gasped, slapping a hand onto his friend's shoulder. 'You saved him.'

Alfred, still holding the reins of Oliver, nodded, his heart pounding in his chest.

'We all did, Sam. We all did.'

The rush of adrenaline began to fade, replaced by a deep wave of relief. Together, they surveyed the wrecked wagon and the stationary train.

As the engine driver approached, his face taut with concern, he asked sharply, 'Is everybody safe?'

'Yes, thank you,' they responded in unison, their voices steady.

JOHN CULLIMORE

The driver's expression softened, and he let out a long, slow breath. 'The Lord be praised' he murmured, his tense shoulders visibly relaxed as he took in the sight of the uninjured boys, and their horse.

Oliver now seemed to have calmed sufficiently for him to be hitched to the post next to their own horse.

'Right then, if all's well with you, why don't you come down and see the locomotive?' offered the driver.

The boys accompanied the train crew to the site of the collision where they went on to assess the train and the rail track.

As they approached the steam engine, their eyes widened in awe at the sight before them.

The Atalanta stood proudly on the tracks, its imposing presence commanding attention from all who beheld it. In front of it lay the remains of the cart scattered like matchsticks, and an abundance of spilled hay.

The train consisted of the locomotive, the tender and behind these at least a dozen windowless box cars with sliding doors enclosing their cargo.

The upper body of the engine gleamed in a stunning shade of racing green, while its axle and wheels were a vivid contrast in a striking bright scarlet. Wisps of steam rose gently from the smokebox at the front, adding to the air of mystique surrounding it.

In the centre of the locomotive, a colossal driving wheel, over seven feet in diameter, dominated the design. Flanked by smaller wheels, it seemed to symbolize the power and majesty of the machine.

The name *'Atalanta'* was emblazoned in gold letters along the circumference of a red half-circle of metal that covered the driving wheel, adding to the locomotive's grandeur, and its number - 3021 - was displayed in gold letters on a rectangular black plaque on the side of the cab.

Above the drive wheels, sitting atop the engine, was a polished golden dome, nearly three feet wide. Shining like a mirror, it reflected their image standing next to the engine. The boys could

THE PALACE OF MY IMAGINATION

hardly believe their eyes at the sight of such splendour.

They stood in silence for a moment, taking in the beauty of the workmanship. It was a magnificent feat of engineering, a stunning illustration of man's inventiveness and craftsmanship.

The three boys paused outside the cab of the steam locomotive and gazed upwards. A minute or so later, they were thrilled when encouraging hand signals from the cab indicated it was time for them to climb onto the footplate.

Hardly able to contain their excitement, the boys climbed the steps into the beating heart of the majestic steam engine. Arriving there, they marvelled at the intricate array of controls, the fiery red glow of the firebox, and the rumbling sound of the coal fire beneath the boiler. Sam was smiling broadly revealing his obvious delight at being on intimate terms with the giant hissing engine.

The man who appeared to be the senior engineer asked them to recount their experience and all listened intently while they described the events.

'You've saved at least one life today lads, possibly more.' said the chief engineer.

'If it weren't for your quick actions, things could have been much worse; there could even have been a derailment. As it is the track, and the engine seem remarkably unscathed.'

He insisted on taking their names and work details, explaining that he would need to file a full report. In it, he said he would highlight their bravery and how they had averted a possible tragedy.

Sam and Alfred blushed under the engineer's praise, their eyes darting to each other with a mixture of pride and relief. Tim, however, stood apart, his gaze fixed on the ground. His face was pale, and his shoulders slumped under the weight of guilt.

'I'm... I'm sorry about the wagon,' Tim said at last, his voice trembling with emotion. 'Farmer Osney's not going to like this at all. He trusted me to move the hay safely and now look at it.' He gestured weakly toward the splintered remains of the wagon, his words trailing off.

'It's not your fault, Tim,' Sam said firmly, stepping closer to his friend. 'They overloaded the wagon. You did everything you could.'

Tim glanced up briefly but said nothing, distress still written plainly across his face. The engineer caught the boy's expression and stepped in, his voice kind but authoritative.

'Listen, lad, you needn't worry too much about that,' he said, gesturing toward the wreckage. 'The Railway company always compensates for damages caused by collisions. Just tell your boss that Jim Stevens said he should head to the offices in Swindon—they'll sort it out. He'll have a new wagon before long.'

Tim blinked, the words slowly sinking in. 'Really?' he asked hesitantly.

'Really,' Jim assured him with a firm nod. 'We'll make it right.'

The tension in Tim's posture eased slightly, though he still looked uncertain. Sensing the boys' lingering unease—and catching the flicker of fascination in their eyes as they glanced at the gleaming locomotive—Jim decided it was time to lighten the mood.

'You lot seem awfully interested in this old engine,' he said with a sly smile. 'How about I give you a proper look? Climb aboard, and I'll show you the marvels of the *Atalanta*.'

By now it was nearing four o'clock and although the boys were naturally keen to stay, Tim knew he would have to give an account of the accident to Osney before the end of the day. Likewise, Sam felt he must get Longleaze's hay wagon unloaded before suppertime.

'Alfred, you stay on here, but I'll need to get on with the hay and give Tim a lift back. I'll see you at Longleaze at six tomorrow morning. You can help me with the milking.'

The pair descended from the footplate, went back to the wagon, hitched Oliver to the rear of it and set off.

***

Jim Stevens took his place at the helm of the engine, simultaneously donning a blue peaked cap that bore the insignia of the Great Western Railway. His weathered face bore the marks of countless journeys. He started by introducing Alfred to

THE PALACE OF MY IMAGINATION

Thompson, the fireman, his face streaked with soot, and Davies, the young second assistant engineer.

Both were in full overalls and Thompson wore thick gloves. He resumed shovelling coal into the firebox.

'This is where you start your learning to become an engineer.' said Jim, pointing into the furnace.

'It's a tough job, but it's the foundation of your future.'

Alfred could sense the roaring fire in the locomotive's belly. Jim pointed out the various gauges which monitored the boiler pressure, firebox temperature, speed and brakes. Perched in front of the boiler was the glass tube which indicated the water level.

'Can I ask what this does?' inquired Alfred pointing at a small lever to the left of the steam pressure gauge.

Davies smiled and winked at Jim, replying.

'Well, if you turn that lever slowly clockwise, you'll find out. Be my guest.' said Davies, indicating the control.

Suddenly, a deafening shriek erupted from the top of the locomotive, causing Alfred to almost leap out of his skin. He had unwittingly triggered the steam valve, much to the amusement of the crew. Alfred found it equally humorous and realised he was having the time of his life.

As the laughter subsided, Jim indicated that Alfred should sit in the driver's seat and indicated a control to his right.

'Now this, young man, is the regulator, and when the temperature and pressure in the boiler are right, it will unleash the power of this mighty locomotive.'

Alfred listened with rapt attention, absorbing every word as if it were a precious gift, his eyes wide with fascination.

'It controls the flow of steam to the cylinders, which move the pistons and drive the wheels forward.'

'But driving a locomotive isn't just about pulling levers and pushing buttons,' Jim explained, his voice taking on a more serious tone.

'It requires skill, concentration, and a deep understanding of the rail network, following all the signals, obeying speed limits, and communicating with signalmen along the route. And of course…'

he added with a broad ironic smile,

'-you should be vigilant, especially when approaching level crossings or navigating tight curves.' Thompson and Davies nodded in amused agreement.

'Remember, Alfred' Jim said, placing a hand on the boy's shoulder, 'the safety of passengers and crew is always your top priority. It's a great responsibility, but it's also a great privilege to be entrusted with the operation of such a magnificent machine.'

'Why don't we go down and look at the track, see if the gang have cleared away all the debris and checked the line?'

Climbing down from the mighty Behemoth, Alfred felt dwarfed as he stood adjacent to its massive wheels.

The driver spoke with the leader of the railway gang which seemed to have appeared out of the ether. There was nothing to suggest a recent accident apart from a smattering of hay on the embankment. The gang had cleared away almost all of the loose hay and stacked it in the field below the embankment. They had then checked the track and found no major problems, but at the collision point with the wagon they had taken the opportunity to put in some extra ballast below the rail and its supporting timbers.

Alfred had never before lingered so close to the rail track, even on the rare occasions he had been at Swindon station. Staring at the metal rails he was stunned by the breadth of the track, well in excess of six feet he thought.

Jim sensed his wonder and seemed to read his mind.

'If you're wondering how wide it is, it's seven feet and a quarter of an inch,'

'This is Isambard Kingdom Brunel's last remaining Broad-Gauge railway. You're privileged to be seeing this'

'It's very... impressive.' said Alfred

'Aye, it is, but it won't be around much longer.'

'Why's that?'

'Well, they say narrow gauge railways are the way forward. Easier and quicker to build, and cheaper. Important considerations when you're constructing a network all over the land. But the old trains, like this one, go faster on the broad gauge and their pulling power's much greater. So they can easily climb up steep

THE PALACE OF MY IMAGINATION

gradients.'

With a heavy heart, the driver turned towards the locomotive.

'This engine,' he said, patting the side of it affectionately, 'has served us faithfully for years. But its days are numbered, I'm afraid. Another year at best.'

As the sun dipped lower in the sky and the railway gang were leaving the scene, Jim turned to Alfred with a smile.

'How about a ride into Swindon on the footplate, lad?' he offered, his eyes twinkling with mischief. 'It'll be a journey you won't soon forget.'

Overcome with excitement, Alfred climbed up beside the engineer, his heart racing with exhilaration as the opening of the regulator roared the engine into life. With a blast of steam and a surge of power, they set off on their journey, the rhythmic pounding of the wheels beneath them a chorus of triumph and nostalgia.

Ten minutes later as the locomotive came to a stop at the bustling station, Jim handed Alfred a slip of paper and a pen, and with a nod of encouragement said.

'Write your address here, lad.'

Alfred, with trembling hands, carefully wrote down his details.

'You and your brave friends can expect to receive something in the post in the not-too-distant future,' Jim said with a knowing smile.

'And maybe we'll see more of you in the Great Western Railway at some stage in the future? I for one hope so.'

He extended his hand to Alfred, who shook it vigorously, feeling the strong grip of a man who had spent his life working with locomotives. With a grateful smile, Alfred thanked the engineer and his crew for the experience and climbed down from the footplate, his heart still bounding with excitement.

Having completed his first journey on the footplate, he felt that he was just beginning another voyage. One of discovery into the future, inspired by the events of the day, and the camaraderie of the crew.

He knew that somehow his destiny would be linked with the

railways.

***

He had heard a lot about the GWR from George, the father of his friend Charlie, who lived next door to the Williams family in South Marston, and who was a plate layer and head of a railway gang working around the west side of Swindon. He had become something of a father figure to Alfred after Elias Williams had deserted his family, and Alfred addressed him as Uncle George.

He often ate with the Ockwell family in the evenings when his mother was working late as a housekeeper for a solicitor in Shrivenham.

George had become an enthusiastic member of the Mechanic's Institute of the GWR in Swindon, which played a vital role in providing workers with access to education, technical training, and cultural enrichment. As a result, he had built up a small library made up chiefly of reference works.

Alfred regarded George as a repository of information and frequently asked his opinion on a diversity of subjects. George welcomed Alfred's inquiring nature, and on the evening after his experience with the locomotive, Alfred was primed with questions for him.

'I love the names of the engines. I rode on the *Atalanta*, but I've heard of others, called *Achilles* and *Prometheus*. Where do they come up with these names?'

'Well, they're all characters from the Greek Myths. Heroes, heroines and Gods. *Atalanta* is one of these famous for her swiftness. She could outrun almost anyone, even the male heroes,'

'And *Prometheus* seems a very appropriate name for a steam locomotive.'

'Why's that?'

'Well, he was a Titan, a divine being in Greek mythology who stole fire from the God Zeus and gave it to mankind.'

'Really? How do you know all this?'

'Oh, just some reading I did from a book about the Greek myths. You know Alfred, there are lots of other locomotives named after these mythical figures. Maybe you'd like to make up a complete list of them? I can lend you the book if you're interested?'

THE PALACE OF MY IMAGINATION

Chapter 2

Late July 1892

> Thus I wandered free and happy,
> In the meadows past and old,
> With the troop of merry children,
> Weaving flowers of brightest gold.
> *from 'The Little Celandine' by Alfred Williams ,1912.*

Alfred had been working full time at Longleaze for over two years.

The farm lay across the road that went from Swindon to Oxford opposite the branch off to South Marston. It was a unique situation given that the main Swindon to London rail line ran parallel to the road, a mere fifty yards north of it, and the old Wilts and Berks canal with its weed infested and sluggish waters, traced a similar path just to the south.

At six a.m., Alfred approached Longleaze, crossing over the lock and then made his way towards the large, thatched farmhouse.

Sam was in the dairy to the right of the house. By seven thirty a.m. they had finished the milking and were loading the churns onto the wagon for transport later to Shrivenham station.

Sam said they needed to get down to Four Docks field, where Jemmy allocated the day's work. As they approached the gate, they saw Jemmy wearing a white smock, seated on the mowing machine with the mares already harnessed to it, giving directions to the other farm hands.

Seeing the boys approaching he called out to them.

'Off you two go to the wheat fields, and get started on weeding this mornin', then later you can take the milk churns to the station.'

Jemmy handed each of them a set of leather pads to kneel on while they worked, and a wicker basket with straps attached at the front so it could be worn like a backpack. They walked to the left of the grass field and entered another filled with young wheat plants in orderly rows. The plants were about five inches high and were fragile, with only three or four leaves.

'We need to get all the charlock and thistles out o' this field - otherwise wheat won't grow.' Sam pointed out one of the dark green charlock plants with yellow four-petalled flowers at the top of a towering spike and pulled it out of the ground.

'When we've finished this field, we'll go onto harvest the peas in the next one. And then we can stop for lunch.'

Alfred concentrated on weeding around the young wheat plants, where the charlock, with its delicate yellow blooms seemed to predominate.

Soon he had filled his first basket with weeds. While progressing through the field he noticed a profusion of other wildflowers predominantly along the edges of the field where the wheat plants thinned out. But at the entrance to the field was a carpet of wildflowers, a veritable riot of colour. Amongst them were Cornflowers, of a striking blue hue, bright red Poppies, white and yellow Daisies, rich green Clover and white Yarrow.

Amidst these exuberant wildflowers, he was struck by their subtle beauty, their leaves still adorned by morning dew, glistening diamond like and swaying in the intermittent breeze.

He was familiar with all the plant names. He'd learned many of the names from his mother who seemed to have accumulated a comprehensive knowledge of flora and fauna. He had augmented this knowledge through his farming experience, and with some books he'd borrowed from Uncle George.

As he carried on with his work, he came across a concealed structure tucked away among the thistles. Carefully woven with bits of straw and delicate grass, it cradled a family of harvest mice. His heart swelled with a tender reverence for this miniature world, and he knew he must try to preserve their sanctuary. He adjusted his course, allowing the mice to continue their quiet existence undisturbed. In a few days with luck, they would have moved on.

In that act of compassion, he sensed a growing connection with the landscape around him. Never had these intricacies of the natural world struck him in this manner, and he smiled quietly as

THE PALACE OF MY IMAGINATION

he embraced this new awareness.

After emptying several baskets, they moved into the upper field and started to harvest the early peas. There were large numbers of plump firm rounded pods and Sam showed Alfred where to cut them from the plant. Within an hour they had filled three sacks with peas and were about to move them to the other side of the gate by the field entrance.

Although they were working a good stone's throw from the rail track, Alfred heard a soft humming arising from the rails. This was followed by the unmistakable sound of an approaching train. Sam interrupted his work to view the passing locomotive.

'The track's obviously open again, and that'll be *Storm King*, London bound,' said Sam, 'which means it's twenty past the hour. They're never late, so you don't need a watch if you work here. Let's go and get the wagon.'

Impressed by Sam's extensive knowledge of railway timetables, Alfred began to tell him about the ride into Swindon on the *Atalanta*.

After lunch, they set off to Shrivenham station to drop off the milk churns next to the signal box just outside the station. This was a hive of activity as several other wagons driven by young farm labourers unloaded their milk and afterwards awaited the return of yesterday's empty churns on the inbound train.

It was clear that all the boys were acquainted, and they came together to converse. The chief topic of conversation concerned the railways. Some of them were avid trainspotters recording the details of every train that came and went. Others were keen to share stories of experiences on the railway and Sam lost no time regaling them with the exploits of the previous day relating to the collision with the cart and Alfred's subsequent ride into Swindon.

Their young audience consisted of boys from Stratton, South Marston and Shrivenham. They listened with rapt attention as Alfred recounted his experience on the footplate, and added that as a result, he had received a letter from the Jim Stevens inviting himself, Sam and Tim to attend the upcoming annual GWR garden fete, along with three booklets of tickets entitling each of them to six free fairground rides.

They agreed that those who were free on Sunday morning would meet at the disused signal box at Gypsy Lane where the Highworth branch joined the main line, for further railway related adventures.

***

Sunday arrived, and the crisp morning air carried the excitement of adventure as eight children gathered at the meeting place. Sam and Alfred immediately recognised Billy Stevens, a local lad also known for his astonishing memory of railway lines and timetables. Billy had spent countless hours studying the intricate network of tracks that criss-crossed their small world, and he could rattle off the schedule of passing trains without so much as a glance at the clock.

Beside Billy stood his younger brother George, a slight boy with a limp due to one leg being shorter than the other. Despite his physical limitations, George was full of enthusiasm and determination, always eager to keep up with the older boys. Two of George's schoolmates from Marston, Joey and James, were also present, their eager faces showing the anticipation of a day filled with excitement.

Polly Patterson, aged thirteen from Shrivenham, had also made the journey. She worked in her father's bakery and had brought along her cousin Mary Peck, also thirteen, who had recently left school and had been sent by her parents to work in the bakery for the summer. The two girls, always up for a bit of fun, were giggling as they arrived, their arms linked as they whispered secrets to one another.

Billy, ever the organiser, announced that a freight train was due in about ten minutes. George, with a grin on his face, produced a pocketful of farthings and halfpennies. George and the girls quickly began laying the coins along the rails, eager to see them flattened into bizarre, distorted shapes by the passing locomotive.

Meanwhile, Alfred sauntered between the rails, his eyes fixed on the stones beneath his feet, marveling at how they had been brought from distant beaches to serve as ballast for the iron roads.

Billy had concocted a plan for the group to retreat into the nearby

THE PALACE OF MY IMAGINATION

signal box to watch the train thunder past from a safe vantage point. The prospect of observing the great beast of steel and steam roaring beneath them thrilled the children, and they eagerly anticipated the spectacle.

However, the cheerful atmosphere was soon shattered by the arrival of a group of ragged town boys, some years older and meaner. They sauntered along the track with an air of ownership, like a band of pirates sizing up their next prize. One of the boys, a lanky figure with a cruel glint in his eye, noticed George and the girls laying the coins on the line.

'What have we here?' the tall boy sneered, snatching up the small chain of coins in one swift movement. The other town boys joined in, wolf-whistling at Polly and Mary in a way that made the girls shift uncomfortably.

George, small but unafraid, stood up to the tall thief, his voice firm as he demanded,

'Give me back my money!'

The thug just laughed, shoving George backwards. The smaller boy stumbled awkwardly, his limp making it difficult to regain his balance near the edge of the track. Alfred saw all this unfold from the corner of his eye and felt a surge of anger rise within him. At the same time, he noticed Mary wiping away tears, clearly frightened by the attention of the thuggish boys. Things were getting out of control.

Billy, known for his quick temper, was already moving toward the lanky boy, his face flushed with fury, but before he could act, Alfred stepped forward, his voice cutting through the cold air.

'If you think you're such tough guys, there's another way you can prove it,' he said, his tone challenging yet calm. '-rather than picking on little boys and bothering girls that is.'

The tall thug, who seemed to be the leader of the group, sneered down at Alfred.

'So, what's the little country boy gonna do then?' he mocked, his gang laughing in agreement, relishing the growing prospect of confrontation.

The distant sound of the approaching train grew louder, the faint hum from the rails now a steady vibration. Alfred stood his ground, his eyes fixed on the leader.

'You hear that train coming?' he asked, his voice steady. 'I'm going to lie myself down between the tracks and let it run over me. I bet you a shilling I can do it, and I bet you another shilling that you're too chicken to do it.'

The gang fell silent, their jeers replaced by uneasy glances. The tall thug's sneer faltered for a moment, uncertainty flickering in his eyes. He looked at his mates, who were no longer laughing, and then back at Alfred, who had already placed his shilling on a low wall next to the tracks and started moving toward the centre of the metals. The vibrations in the ground were stronger now, the train's whistle echoing in the distance.

The tension in the air was palpable as the train rounded the corner a quarter of a mile away. Alfred seemed to know where he was going and immediately headed to the area of the track he had inspected previously, where he promptly lay face down, trying to burrow into the layer of loose shingle that was piled there generously between the metals. The other boy approached the rails, obviously with some reservation, about twenty yards behind Alfred and lay down face up between the rails, his larger frame projecting well above the surface of the track.

In an instant the train was within ten yards of Alfred. It was a long luggage train. The boys hadn't been spotted by the locomotive crew and the train ploughed on at a slow but implacable rate.

Mary screamed as the locomotive moved above Alfred.

Further down the track, the town boy felt a surge of panic, raised himself up and dived to his left while the Behemoth was a bare ten yards away.

'You're crazy!' he shouted in Alfred's direction, backing away from the track, his voice betraying his fear.

'Let's get out of here.' With that, he turned and ran, his gang following close behind, their tough demeanour crumbling as they fled.

The train crew were suddenly alerted to the presence of the

THE PALACE OF MY IMAGINATION

children and the train's brakes were instantly applied. Roars of indignation rang out from the locomotive cab as all the children hurriedly exited the scene, little George remembering to harvest the proceeds of the bet before disappearing behind the signal box onto a concealed footpath.

Meanwhile the train had eventually stopped, the last carriage now one hundred and fifty yards beyond where Alfred had laid. He emerged unscathed, duly shook himself free, turned himself over and extricated himself, heading for the footpath behind the signal box.

Some minutes later the village children came together outside Stratton station eager to see Alfred and to hold a postmortem on the incident. As Alfred approached them, they were clearly concerned.

'You gave me the fright of my life, Alfred Williams' said Polly, Mary nodded vigorously in agreement.

Alfred looked somewhat pale, his heart still racing and his breathing rapid as he now thought what might have happened.

'Sorry'

'Are you all right? How did you know you'd be OK?' asked Billy

'I'm - fine. I'm OK.'

He made a conscious effort to steady his breathing.

'When I walked the line, I realised there were lots of loose stones between the rails, so I headed straight for that area and burrowed down there as much as I could. But I won't do that again, the noise was -' He trailed off and started gazing into space. Little George broke the silence saying.

'Well Alf, here's your money. Two shillings in total' and he handed over the coins.

After a slight pause, Alfred began to feel normal again.

'Right' he said, 'let's go to the kiosk in the park and buy some lemonade.'

Mary was still shaken but now smiling. She looked at Alfred and the other children as they headed off in the direction of the town and thought to herself; that was the bravest, but also the craziest thing she'd ever seen.

JOHN CULLIMORE

Chapter 3

April- May 1896

Alfred rose with the sun, and his first duty was to attend to the dairy herd, milking them with practiced hands. Later in the morning his attentions would turn to the crops. Life on the farm had its changing rhythms, and routines. He was fascinated by the turn of Nature's wheel and loved his responsibilities all the more thanks to their seasonal variation.

On this early Spring morning he reflected that he had been working at the farm for almost five years and looked forward to more of the same, as his affection for the land increased and his bond with Nature strengthened.

He could see himself happily running his own farm someday.

However, on this morning in late April, everything changed.

Alfred walked across the farmyard, carrying an overfilled milk churn with an ill-fitting lid, splashing fresh milk over his waistcoat. His gaze inadvertently landed on a sight that stopped him in his tracks.

There, hanging out washing with effortless grace, was a young woman of medium height, her long dark brown hair arranged in a single plait cascading down her back. She wore a cream blouse buttoned up to her neck, the fabric hugging her trim waist and accentuating her shapely upper torso beneath it. Her long skirt swayed gently in the breeze, adding to the picturesque scene.

But it wasn't just her appearance that captivated Alfred. Her hazel brown eyes sparkled with mischief, and her full mouth curved into a playful smile as she went about her task. She exuded an undeniable prettiness, and a radiance that made Alfred's heart skip a beat.

Sensing Alfred's presence, the young woman turned to him, her cheeks dimpling with a mischievous grin.

'A good day for milking, is it?' she remarked, her tone light and teasing.

THE PALACE OF MY IMAGINATION

'Not so bad,' he responded, chuckling and impressed by her cheekiness, 'but an even better one for hanging out washing.'

Her smile widened, and she leaned forward slightly, her eyes twinkling brightly.

'Well then, perhaps that waistcoat you're wearing could benefit from a good wash,' she remarked cheekily. 'If you'd care to hand it over, I'll do it with the next batch. '

He couldn't help but smile widely. He felt an instant connection with this vivacious stranger and found himself drawn by her sense of humour, her easy-going nature, and the twinkle in her eyes that hinted at hidden depths.

He took off his waistcoat and handed it over.

'It should be ready by tomorrow morning' she said. Just knock at the back door after you've finished milking'

'Thanks, I'm Alfred. I've not seen you here before?'

'I'm Mary. And I remember you from a few years ago when you lay down on the railway tracks.'

'Ah, - You'll be glad to hear I've grown up a bit since then.'

'Well, I still can't look at a train without being reminded of it,' she added, beaming a radiant smile.

'Anyway, I've come to help my sister; you probably know she had a baby girl last week.'

'Yes, I'd heard. So, you've got your hands full with the other children?'

'There's plenty to do here, that's for sure.'

'Well, if there's anything I can do,' said Alfred almost imploringly, his gaze fastened on the pretty stranger. 'I sometimes run errands for your sister, so just ask'

She looked at him for a few seconds, and decided she really did like his smile.

'Actually, there might be a few things,' she replied, thinking to herself that not only were there some tasks he could assist her with but also this could provide her with an opportunity to get to know him better.

'We can talk again in the morning when you collect your waistcoat.'

JOHN CULLIMORE

Snapping out of his temporary reverie, Alfred suddenly remembered he had to get the milk loaded up and off to the station at Shrivenham.

'Until tomorrow morning then.' he said and retreated on his way to the cart, reluctant to break off the exchange.

As he progressed down the Oxford Road driving the horse and cart laden with churns, the image of the young woman lingered in his mind, leaving him with feelings he'd never before experienced and an impression that he knew he wouldn't soon forget.

Mary's presence certainly cast the farm in a new light.

Alfred found himself eagerly returning to the farmhouse kitchen the next morning. Mary was busy preparing breakfast for the children, smiling broadly as she greeted him.

'Morning, Alfred.' she said, her hazel eyes alive with playful energy as she handed him the freshly laundered waistcoat.

'Morning, Mary.' Alfred replied, unable to suppress the grin that spread across his face as he donned his cleaned garment.

'Any of you children want to help me collect eggs and feed the pigs?' said Alfred.

'Me, me!' came a chorus of reply from Matthew, aged eight and Sarah, six.

The children, obviously familiar with Alfred's presence, eagerly asked if they could help. Alfred's heart swelled with affection for the young ones.

'Well one of you will have to feed one of the piglets from a bottle, she's the runt of the litter and not doing so well.'

'I'll do it,' said Sarah.

Mary was impressed by Alfred's compassion and easy rapport with the children. Then she added a suggestion of her own which she'd previously discussed with her sister Meg.

'Could you help me set up a stall selling our vegetables at the Highworth market on May Day?'

'I can do that. But that's a busy market and we'll need some help. Can we bring Matthew and Sarah?'

The children were clearly keen to tag along, and Mary agreed they should.

THE PALACE OF MY IMAGINATION

'We'll also need to get some flowers to decorate our stall. Any thoughts?' she asked Alfred.

'I know the perfect place.' he smiled.

The next morning after breakfast, Alfred and Mary set out on a leisurely stroll to gather flowers. As they left the farm behind, they passed through the railway arch, the sound of the distant river beckoning them forth. Turning right, they followed the gentle sound of lapping water until they reached the site of the hatches, where the water flowed swiftly through the ancient gates.

Crossing to the other bank of the river, Alfred led Mary to a spot beneath a magnificent willow tree which overlooked a large deep pool further east of the river which shimmered in the sunlight. The tree's three principal branches began a couple of feet above its base, and one of them jutted out over the pool forming a natural seat four or five feet above the bank. Here, Alfred revealed this was his sanctuary, a place of inspiration and tranquility.

As they sat in quiet contemplation, a flash of blue streaked across the sky above them - the kingfisher, a fleeting vision of beauty. Below, in the depths of the pool, Mary caught a glimpse of a silvery fish darting rapidly into the depths of the dark water.

Their reverie was interrupted by the sudden flight of a heron, startled by their presence. They watched as it disappeared into the distance, leaving ripples in its wake. Soon after, a pair of wild ducks and their brood of young ones skimmed into the safety of the bullrushes.

Leaving the riverside behind, Alfred and Mary entered the meadows, where a surprise awaited them. A group of playful fox cubs frolicked around their nest in the hollow of an ash stump, their antics a joy to behold. With sudden purpose, the cubs darted off into the woods as Alfred and Mary continued on their way.

Entering the meadow, they were greeted by a breathtaking sight—A blooming mass of fritillaries, their delicate bell-shaped flowers painting the landscape in shades of yellow and purple. Intricate markings adorned their petals, a testament to the beauty and wonder of nature.

Mary reached out to pluck a few of the delicate flowers from the earth, careful not to disturb their natural beauty and Alfred followed suit gathering them into a small basket.

'These will brighten up our stall like nothing else.' she added, her smile radiant as she imagined the colourful display they would create.

***

On the morning of Mayday, as soon as the miking was done, they prepared for the market, laying up the cart with crates of vegetables. Alfred, Mary, Matthew and Sarah, set off for Highworth on a beautiful morning.

As they travelled, Alfred's natural affinity with the children shone through, his easygoing demeanour and genuine affection endearing him to them even more. Mary found herself drawn to him even more deeply. She watched, her heart swelling with love, as she imagined a future where Alfred was not just a part of her life, but a part of her family.

In that moment, as they laughed and chatted, surrounded by crates of fresh vegetables and the laughter of children, Mary knew that she had found something special with Alfred. And as they arrived at the market, ready to embark on today's adventure, she couldn't help but dream of the future they might build - a future filled with love, laughter, and the joy of a family united.

But a cloud appeared on the horizon of her thoughts as soon as she entertained these visions of wedded bliss and family life.

It was then she recalled that her family had been engaged in mapping out her life for her, and until now she had no reason to question the way they had prepared the ground. Indeed, it had always been easier to go along with what was expected, to play the role of the dutiful daughter.

She clearly remembered her thirteenth birthday, the day her mother had said,

'Now that you've mastered the basics of reading, writing, and arithmetic at school, your father and I think it's time for you to learn skills more appropriate for a young woman.'

After the term ended, she left her school days behind and was sent to Stratton to work in her uncle's bakery, helping to bake bread during the week. At weekends, she stayed with her sister,

THE PALACE OF MY IMAGINATION

where she was taught domestic skills and helped to manage the household accounts.

Her elder sister often reminded her, 'You'll need to know these things for when you'll be a wife and mother.'

Yet, she couldn't shake the feeling that she had been brought there as unpaid help, just so that her sister could join in the weekend hunts.

The idea of marrying Adam Osney, the son of the neighbouring farmer, had been raised casually, as if it were a long-expected outcome. She had met Adam at a harvest festival last year, where they had danced together under the scrutinising eyes of their families. It was all so easy, so expected. And yet, it had never felt right to her.

Her mother and sister had been particularly enthusiastic about the match, speaking of the benefits it would bring—security, a strong family alliance, and a prosperous future. Mary had silently acquiesced, too polite and too conditioned to question the path being laid out for her. But now, with Alfred in her life, everything was different.

She realised that she didn't want to be married off to Adam, or anyone else chosen for her. She wanted the freedom to choose her own path, to follow her own heart.

But the thought of defying her family terrified her. She had never been encouraged to stand up for herself; quite the opposite, she had been raised to be compliant, to do what was expected without question. They'd expect her to just toe the line.

Alfred couldn't help noticing the fleeting shadow cross Mary's face. Just moments ago, she had been laughing and chatting with him, her eyes bright with the joy of the morning, but now she seemed distant, lost in thought. He wondered what had caused the sudden change, but before he could ask, they were already in the thick of the bustling market, setting up the stall and arranging the fresh produce they had brought to sell.

As they set out their vegetables on the stall, Alfred could sense Mary's turmoil. Her lightheartedness had disappeared. He wanted to reach out to her, to ask what was wrong, but hesitated.

Instead, he watched her carefully, noticing how she seemed to be going through the motions, her mind elsewhere.

Mary felt the intensity of Alfred's gaze, and this brought her back to the present moment.

She forced a smile, hoping to dispel the gloom that had settled over her thoughts.

Deep down, she knew that her feelings for Alfred had opened her eyes to a new reality - one where she had choices, where her future was not yet written.

Whilst the idea of confronting her family, and rejecting the life they had planned for her, filled her with dread, the alternative - the thought of losing Alfred and resigning herself to a loveless existence - was even more frightening.

For now, all she could do was push the thoughts aside, and focus on the task at hand. But the seeds of uncertainty had been planted, she just hoped they would not grow to overwhelm her.

'Is everything all right?' Alfred asked, his voice tinged with concern as he noticed the brief shadow that had crossed Mary's face.

'It will be,' she replied, her tone carrying a hint of mystery.

Alfred's brow furrowed in mild confusion, but he chose not to press further, sensing that Mary wasn't ready to share what was on her mind. For a moment, an uneasy silence hung between them, but it quickly dissipated as Mary seemed to shake off whatever had troubled her.

Her expression brightened, and she returned to the vibrant, lively young woman Alfred had come to adore. She smiled up at him, her eyes sparkling with the warmth and affection that had first drawn him to her. Whatever had caused her momentary lapse into doubt or fear was now absent, and Mary was once again fully engaged, eager to savour the day with the man she was growing to love.

Mary slipped her arm through Alfred's and gave him a reassuring squeeze. Together, they resumed their work, the earlier tension forgotten, as they laughed and chatted, enjoying each other's company amidst the noise and excitement of the market.

The market day was a success. Numerous local folk were attracted to their stall not only because it bridled with colourful

THE PALACE OF MY IMAGINATION

spring vegetables but so many people recognised Alfred and wanted to talk and be introduced to the pretty woman by his side.

A tall distinguished looking grey-haired man approached the stall. This was Doctor Muir from Stratton, who helped bring Alfred and many of his siblings into the world.

'Hello Alfred, Matthew, Sarah.' Dr Muir seemed to be on close terms with everyone on the northern and eastern fringes of Swindon.

'Please introduce me to this delightful young lady. I trust you are keeping good company with her?'

Mary blushed at the intimate reference but nevertheless could not suppress a smile and a sense of pride. Alfred was keen to observe Mary's response, then he too smiled.

After placing an order for a sack of potatoes and a bag of onions, Muir addressed Alfred in a more confidential tone, with a knowing grin.

'Alfred, I was just thinking the other day, if you ever tire of farm work, and your, er - plans change and you find you wish to, er - let's say, *need* to earn a greater financial reward,' he said in time with a raising of his bushy eyebrows and a nod in the direction of Mary.

'Then come and see me, I might have a suggestion for you.' And patting Alfred on the back and directing an indulgent smile at Mary, he ventured off down the High Street.

'Er - sorry about that,' said Alfred to Mary somewhat embarrassed by Dr Muir's clumsy innuendo. The children were obviously finding the whole exchange most intriguing.

'Maybe you should take his advice,' responded Mary dissolving into giggles.

'But Alfred, you won't leave us on the farm, will you?' said Sarah.

He replied that he wouldn't. And he believed his words. Just then he couldn't see himself anywhere else.

***

After Market Day, they began to go for long walks, relishing the intimacy of being alone together.

JOHN CULLIMORE

Alfred had always found solace in the quiet beauty of the countryside. As a young farm worker, his days were spent toiling in the fields, but it was in the vast expanse of nature that he truly felt alive. Alfred relished the opportunity to share his love of the land.

Their first long walk together was a revelation for them both. As they wandered through meadows ablaze with wildflowers and along winding paths shaded by ancient oak trees, Alfred couldn't help but share his knowledge, pointing out the different species of birds nesting in the hedgerows and identifying the various plants that carpeted the forest floor.

Mary, in turn, was captivated by Alfred's passion for nature. His eyes lit up as he spoke of the intricate world that existed all around them, as he painted vivid pictures of the creatures that inhabited their surroundings.

With each passing day, Alfred and Mary grew closer, their mutual love for the natural world deepening their connection. However, their romantic idyll was not destined to last.

Mary's sister, Meg, soon noticed the budding relationship and privately voiced her concerns to her husband. He relayed a conversation he recently had with Farmer Osney, who was still expecting an engagement to be announced between his son and Mary, even though she hadn't seen him for over four months.

Meg was worried that these expectations would be disrupted by the appearance of Alfred. Determined to protect her sister from what she saw as a risky entanglement, Meg decided to intervene.

One afternoon, she suggested that it might be time for Mary to return to their family home in Hungerford.

'The little one's eight months old now, and since I'm no longer nursing her, I can manage things on my own,' Meg said, trying to keep her tone casual.

Mary hesitated, sensing something beneath her sister's words.

'But I'm happy to stay. We all get along so well, so…,' she trailed off, a sinking feeling creeping into her chest. She could sense another reason for Meg's suggestion.

'I can't believe you'd want me to be unhappy—You must know

THE PALACE OF MY IMAGINATION

I love Alfred?'

Meg remained silent, unsure of how to respond. She had always wanted the best for her sister, and the two had never exchanged harsh words before. But in Meg's mind, what was best for Mary meant marrying Adam Osney, not pursuing this unexpected romance with Alfred, who didn't have two pennies to rub together.

Meg was fearful that the situation was spinning out of control.

'Has Alfred said anything to you …. about the future?'

'Well, no, but I just know he feels the same as I do.'

'I know it's hard for you, but unless and until Alfred says something, my advice would be to go home to Hungerford and just wait things out.'

The tears came to Mary unbidden.

'Yes, you're probably right, but I won't give Alfred up for anything.'

Meg embraced her sister, but she couldn't help feeling that her insincerity and real purpose must have shone through.

But she had achieved what she had set out to do and was content to take a step back and see how events played out.

JOHN CULLIMORE

Chapter 4

Late October 1896

From Alfred's viewpoint, the moment Mary entered his world, everything changed. Her smile was like sunshine breaking through the clouds, and her laughter echoed in his heart long after she had left his presence. He realised he had completely fallen in love with her. However, when he allowed his imagination to run wild about their future, he couldn't shake the feeling that there might be obstacles in their path.

The next morning on the farm seemed oddly silent. After milking and walking through the yard, the kitchen door remained closed, and no one appeared. Even after returning from the milk round the farm appeared forlorn and empty. After topping the lower field, Alfred could bear it no longer and just before sunset he went to knock on the kitchen door.

Meg appeared and as she saw Alfred, she lowered her eyes.

'Is Mary here?' he asked

Meg hesitated.

'She's gone back to Hungerford.'

'Why?'

'It's complicated. You probably don't know this, and I'm sorry to have to be the one to tell you, but we expect Mary to marry one of Farmer Osney's sons, Adam.'

'The parents of both families have been encouraging it for some time. Now -, well I'm not sure what will happen.'

'I don't really need her help here any longer, so we felt it was best if she went back home and let things settle down. She needs some time to think about her future.'

'Can I visit her?'

'It's all a bit raw at the moment. She feels very confused, and she's not sure what to do - It's best if you just give her some time - to herself.'

'Can I at least write to her?'

THE PALACE OF MY IMAGINATION

Meg stared at Alfred for a few seconds, before responding.

'Write your letter. Leave it with me. I'll make sure she gets it.'

Suddenly he knew what he had to do. He would write his letter, setting out his true feelings. He knew he needed Mary above anything else and it was then he realised that he would do what he must to improve his prospects.

He reflected on his position in life. If he were to secure Mary's hand, he began to think how he would sustain their lives in security together. His thoughts drifted back to Dr Muir's comments at the May market.

The next day he wrote his letter, sealed it in an envelope addressed to Mary, placing this within another envelope addressed to Meg, along with a short note. He dropped the letter into the farm's postbox. He then called in at the surgery at Stratton, leaving a note for Dr Muir.

Within a week Dr Muir had left a note for him at his cottage. He told him that he'd spoken to one of the foremen at the railway factory and Alfred should present himself at the GWR offices the following week. He should ask for Mr. Dempster.

JOHN CULLIMORE

PART 2: ENLIGHTENMENT

Chapter 5

mid November 1896

Alfred rose at five a.m. and with his elder brothers set off on the four-mile walk to the GWR factory at the heart of Swindon.

It was his first day of work. As they walked, Alfred's thoughts drifted to the conversations he'd had with his Uncle George about how the arrival of the railway fifty years earlier had transformed Swindon from a small hilltop village of barely two thousand inhabitants, into the bustling town of over forty thousand that it was now.

'Why did they choose Swindon for the railway factory?' Alfred had asked.

'Well,' George had explained, 'they needed a spot between London and Bristol to maintain and repair the vast variety of locomotives that Brunel had collected. Swindon was ideal for a number of reasons.'

As they walked along the path beside the old Wilts and Berks Canal, Alfred recalled George mentioning how the proximity of the canal had been an important factor in Swindon's favour. It enabled the transport of coal from Somerset to fuel the locomotives and provided a steady supply of water for the steam engines.

Approaching the point where the main east-west line branched off towards Cheltenham, Alfred noticed the gentle rise in the landscape.

Sir Daniel Gooch, the first locomotive superintendent at GWR, made a similar observation fifty years earlier. The steeper gradients that started just west of Swindon and continued up to Bristol made it the perfect place to change to more powerful engines which could tackle the rising inclines. For Sir Daniel, Swindon was the logical, strategic choice for Brunel's central

THE PALACE OF MY IMAGINATION

railway hub.

As the factory and the railway village came into view, Alfred felt a surge of excitement. He was about to join the great tide of workers pouring into the tunnel that led to the factory, becoming part of the workforce that had shaped Swindon into the thriving railway town it had become.

On arrival at the factory gates, Alfred's brothers went into the workshops within the complex, leaving him at the factory offices. The reception area reminded Alfred of the ticket office at the main railway station, with the office staff cordoned off behind a wooden facade perforated by small windows. At one of these was a small queue of men which Alfred joined to register his arrival.

Fifteen minutes elapsed before Alfred reached the window.

The clerk took Alfred's details and instructed him to wait while someone was called to take him to the workshops to get him started.

Soon after a young man of similar age and height to Alfred came and stood next to him. He immediately recognised Billy Stevens.

'I never thought I'd see you here. Your first day in the factory?' asked Billy.

'It is,' replied Alfred, 'and you?'

'No, I've been here a month, but I'm being moved to the Frame shop. Do you know where you're going?'

'I've really no idea.'

'Probably the Frame shop, too. Twenty old broad-gauge carriages have just been brought in for cutting down and resizing, so they'll be needing more rivet hotters.'

Just then the inner door to the factory opened and in walked a tall young man with a blackened face who approached them.

'Stevens and Williams? Follow me.'

The tall man turned on his heel and retraced his steps. The boys dutifully followed.

They headed in the direction of a workshop from the roof of which a jet-black plume of smoke issued into the atmosphere, spreading as a slowly expanding cloud which hung as a pall over the factory complex. All this added to the intensely grey subdued atmosphere of a mid-November day.

At the same time, they perceived an ever-increasing level of noise as they approached the entrance. The clanking sound of metal on metal, the intermittent screeching of saws, the loud and continuous buzzing of drills, with occasional high-pitched shrieks, the low rumble from the motion of carriages on metal rails all contributed to the crescendo of sounds of manufacturing.

Alfred felt excitement mixed with mild anxiety as he considered the prospect of entering what sounded like the centre of an erupting volcano. And as they followed a slowly moving wagon entering through the eastern door, Alfred was taken aback by the sheer numbers of men working at apparently frenetic pace in hammering, sawing, riveting or drilling. All involved in the process of remodelling the old running stock for its further use on the network.

Having penetrated this inner sanctum of toil, the boys followed their guide up a set of metal stairs which ascended the side of the workshop to a height of forty feet or so to a cabin made of corrugated metal with a faintly illuminated single window, which clung from the side of the workshop like a barnacle to a ship's hull.

Once inside the boys were instructed to sit on a low bench and await the arrival of the shop foreman who would allocate their duties. The cabin was somewhat insulated from the noise of the factory, and Alfred continued his conversation with Billy.

'You mentioned that we might be working with rivets?'

'Rivet hotting - might well be one of our jobs. You work with a gang reshaping a carriage and amongst other things, you're given a number of rivets, small metal rods, to heat up in the forges, and once they're red hot you bring them out to the gang men to do a riveted joint. But there's lots of other tasks they give you to help them out, bringing them water and such like.'

Just then the door opened, and two individuals entered. One a middle-aged man with dark hair and moustache of medium height, wearing a long black overcoat and a dusty bowler hat, followed by a boy of perhaps seventeen years, short in stature, inclining to overweight, with a blackened face, and cold blue eyes. The older

THE PALACE OF MY IMAGINATION

man's rich tenor voice carried an air of authority, augmented by his relatively slow but rhythmic intonation.

'I'm the foreman, -Mr. Dempster to you. We'll get you started presently. You'll each be allocated to a gang, and you'll be heating up the rivets for them, and doing whatever else they tell you.'

'This is Bodger,' he said, indicating the youth to his left.

'He'll show you how to hot the rivets, then he'll take you to your gang and you can start work. A few other things to note; your day starts at six thirty. If you're late, you'll be locked out for a half day.'

'Second, don't let me catch you fighting or arguing with the other lads. I won't have that, or you'll be out of here as quick as a flash. Last of all, leave your workplace tidy. Get rid of all the scrap into the wagons outside and put all the tools back in their places when your gang has finished with them.'

He looked at each boy intently for a few moments, with a smile that seemed to indicate that at the core of this disciplinarian there was a well-intentioned character.

'Right Bodger, over to you,' he said to the youth as he left the cabin.

With a quick gesture the young man pointed towards the stairs and began descending. Reaching the bottom, he walked casually towards the glowing forge and began a monotonal narrative.

'Your main job is to get the rivets ready for your gang. And this is where you'll do it.'

He picked up a pair of Iron tongs from a rack and using them picked up a rivet from an adjacent tray and walked towards the aperture of the forge.

'You see those iron plates with holes in? Put your rivet into one of the holes and wait till its red hot.' He placed the rivet into the nearest vacant hole in the plate.

'But you boys must use the holes on the far right of the plate, on the back row.'

He waited about ninety seconds until the rivet was a glowing orange colour, then placed it into a metal tray. He donned a thick pair of gloves and lifted the tray.

'Once you've taken it out, get it back to your gang as quick as you can.'

On this occasion, he threw the rivet from the tray into a barrel of water where it hissed, steamed and disappeared into the depths.

'And that's about all there is to it, but your gang men will give you other jobs. Just do as yer told.'

He indicated that they should follow and headed off into the heart of the frame shop.

Billy was left with the first gang they encountered, and Alfred proceeded to the second.

Within a few hours, Alfred felt he was among seasoned and decent men who had toiled in the factory for years. The gang of three welcomed him warmly, sensing his lack of familiarity with the harsh industrial environment and after brief introductions, Alfred was asked if he could fetch a couple of heated rivets as the gang were about to resume their reconstruction of a carriage.

Alfred returned to the forge to a much more active scene, where a group of youths were scrambling to get their rivets into the iron racks above the white-hot coals. He found a space at the aperture which could accommodate three or four bodies and began the rivet heating process. He then realised that it was more difficult than it appeared during Bodger's demonstration.

Getting the rivets into the iron plate on the innermost right side was a challenge, because of the intense heat and the distance from the aperture to the rear right side of the forge. However Alfred was tall and had relatively long arms and after an initially misplaced rivet, he managed to slot two into the plate. He waited for the heat to grow and after the recommended ninety seconds removed his rivets and returned them to his gang, who immediately requested two more of the same.

The forge aperture was unattended, and he slotted the rivets accurately into the plate. He realised he had time to cool himself down and doused his face and arms with water from the adjacent barrel.

While doing this he noted that Billy had taken his place with three others at the aperture but soon saw that he was struggling, presumably due to his relatively small stature and the not insignificant distance to the intensely hot slots on the right side of the forge. However, after some minutes he managed to place his rivet but then stepped back to allow a rather burly impatient youth behind him to do likewise.

There was a cry of frustration as the youth accused the new recruit of usurping his slots, precipitating a confrontational response.

A crowd gathered as the boy pushed Billy around, causing him to stumble dangerously close to the scorching coals. Alfred, refusing to stand idly by, with unwavering resolve, intervened by inserting himself between the bully and Billy. Standing nose to nose with him and looking him directly in the eye, Alfred spoke up.

'I'm responsible for that rivet, and *I'll* remove it. So don't blame him. And if you want to take it further, I'll happily meet you in the street outside at the end of the shift and we can fight it out.'

The bully, a brash figure from the rougher part of the new town, sneered at the boys from the countryside.

'Fuckin' country boys—bloody useless!' he shouted with venom. But Alfred, studying his tone and stance, sensed that the outburst was more bluster than threat—a signal that he was backing down. It was clear that this wouldn't escalate further than hurling insults, and the situation suddenly defused without further exchanges, the boys returning to their respective gangs.

Alfred retrieved the now white-hot rivet and laid it in the tray.

'I owe you,' said Billy, 'Given what the foreman said about fights and arguments, you took a big risk for me.'

'Well, if I hadn't, life here would never have been worth living, for me as well as you. So don't worry about it.'

Meanwhile, a boy who introduced himself as Streak slowly approached. Noticing Billy's difficulty, he suggested that Billy stand on a small step concealed behind the water barrel and use the longer tongs stored in a second rack situated to the right of the forge.

Streak seemed a friendly, well-intentioned character. He took

Alfred and Billy to the mess room at break time, and over shared moments, provided insights into the factory's dynamics, pointing out good and bad personalities in the frame shop. The boys listened attentively, grateful for the benefit of his experience.

In the following days, Alfred thrived in his gang, encouraged by his colleagues. Billy, armed with the longer tongs, adapted to the forge with a little more guidance from Streak.

The bond between the three strengthened as they faced the challenges of their new workplace, and they were not troubled further by their confrontational colleague.

THE PALACE OF MY IMAGINATION

Chapter 6

December 25th, 1896
Hungerford

Mary had been eagerly anticipating her sister's visit, looking forward to seeing both Meg and the children. It had been almost three months since she left the farm, and since returning to Hungerford, she had struggled to find motivation beyond the confines of her home. Much of her time was spent dutifully caring for her frail grandmother, Rose. Unbeknownst to Mary, Rose had sensed her unhappiness and her preoccupation with something. Mary was clearly unwilling to share her thoughts.

The entire Peck family gathered for Christmas lunch, a lively affair with six adults and twelve children filling the house with noise and activity. Amid the bustle, the sisters had little opportunity to speak privately. But as the children were eventually left in the care of their grandfather, Rose seized the moment to have a quiet word with Meg.

'What did you do to her at the farm back in the summer?' Rose asked, her tone laced with concern.

'What do you mean?' Meg replied, somewhat defensively.

'Well, all the spirit has gone out of her, and it's only since she's been with you,' Rose pointed out, her sharp eyes flicking towards Mary, who was clearly trying to put on a brave face for the children but looked deflated and withdrawn.

Meg followed her grandmother's gaze and noticed the change in her sister's demeanour. In that moment, a wave of guilt washed over her. She knew what she needed to do.

'I'll have a word with her, Gran. I'm sure I can help,' Meg said, determination in her voice.

The afternoon passed quickly. Soon it was time for Meg and the children to leave to catch the late afternoon train from Hungerford, to return home by early evening. Just as she was about to leave, Meg reached into her bag and pulled out a creased letter. She handed it to Mary, raising her eyebrows and offering a soft smile.

'I'm sorry I didn't get this to you earlier,' Meg said, giving her sister a tight hug before turning to leave.

Mary took the letter up to her room and placed it under her pillow. After saying her prayers she opened the envelope and read through it.

October 24th, 1896
Dearest Mary
As I sit down to write this letter, I am filled with many emotions, first among them being love and longing for you. I hope this letter finds you well, though I cannot help but feel sadness knowing that you have left the farm.

Mary, I want you to know that my heart aches in your absence. You brought light and joy to my working life, and without you, everything feels dull and empty. The days seem longer, the nights colder, and each moment reminds me of how much I miss your presence.

I understand the expectations placed on you by your family, and know the difficult position you are in. But, my dear Mary, please know that my love for you knows no bounds. I have loved you from the moment I first laid eyes on you, and that love has only grown stronger with each new day.

I cannot promise you a life of luxury or riches, but I can promise you a life filled with love, respect, and devotion. Together, we could weather any storm, overcome any obstacle, and build a future filled with happiness.

I know that you need time to think about your future, and I respect that. But please, Mary, do not shut me out completely. Please understand that I am here for you, now and always, ready to help you in any way that I can.

Alfred

THE PALACE OF MY IMAGINATION

Chapter 7

March 1897

Alfred wiped the sweat from his brow as he stepped out of the noisy boiler shop at the railway factory. For five months, he had toiled away in the blistering heat, helping to reconstruct railway carriages and more recently to construct the boilers that powered the locomotives.

He always maintained a fresh cheerful countenance and readily volunteered his assistance whenever his colleagues seemed in need of it. As such, he had made many friends in the workshop, and as a result had been tutored by his seniors in a variety of practical skills. They began by teaching him the most effective techniques for wielding sledgehammers and mastering the use of chisels and files. Before long, he advanced to the intricate craft of boiler construction.

No longer confined to simply heating the rivets, Alfred had acquired the skill to expertly set and hammer them into place to fasten the component plates of the boiler together. He had come to appreciate the critical timing of the work—the rivet had to be hammered while it was still red-hot. Only after this would its cooling and contraction pull the steel plates together with unyielding strength. Having completed the hammering of the rivet, he paused to register the sharp, metallic ping—a sound like the snap of a taut piano wire. That sound, to him, was a promise. The plates now bound with precision would endure the roaring heat and immense pressure of the steam locomotive in motion. In his mind, he could see the finished boiler, gleaming and proud, powering a locomotive that would thunder across the countryside, a triumph made possible, in part, by his own craftsmanship.

A week earlier, Alfred had received a letter from Mary, and as he read it, he pieced together the details of her life since their last meeting. She was living at home with her parents, spending her days doing needlework and helping to care for her frail grandmother. Although she didn't mention anything about the contents of his letter from October, nor did she bring up the subject of an engagement, Alfred couldn't shake the feeling that she wanted to rekindle their correspondence.

He was eager to share with her the details of his role at the factory, yet he hesitated when it came to revealing his modest earnings—just twelve shillings and sixpence a week. Alfred worried that this admission might weaken his standing with Mary and create a rift between him and her family.

Additionally, he had begun to feel a growing dissatisfaction with the simplicity and lack of challenge in his work. He realised that if he wanted to win Mary's affection and gain the skills necessary to advance his career, he couldn't simply wait for opportunities to come his way. He needed to act to improve his situation.

Determined to change his fortunes, Alfred made up his mind. The next morning, before the workday began, he made a point of seeking out Gus Dempster, catching him just as he was heading up to the foreman's cabin.

'Sir, could I have a word?' Alfred asked, doing his best to project his voice above the relentless clatter of the workshop machinery.

'Certainly,' Gus replied, motioning for Alfred to follow him. 'Come up to the cabin, it'll be easier to talk in there.'

Once inside, Gus closed the door behind them and settled into his chair at the desk.

'So, what's on your mind?' he asked.

'Well, sir,' Alfred began, choosing his words carefully, 'I've been thinking about whether there might be any opportunities for me to take on a bigger role?'

'Since I started here, I've gotten a lot stronger and learned my way around the workshop. To be honest, though, I'm starting to feel a bit...well, bored. I was wondering if there's anything I could do that would be more challenging?'

Gus leaned back, considering Alfred's request.

'Your gang has noticed how well you've fitted in and how hard you work. Let me give it some thought, talk to a few people, and I'll get back to you.'

THE PALACE OF MY IMAGINATION

'Thank you, sir,' Alfred said, feeling a mix of hope and anticipation as he descended the stairway and returned to his furnace duties.

The next morning, as Alfred was cleaning out the furnace, Gus approached him.

'After our chat yesterday, I have a suggestion for you,' Gus began.

'How would you like to join the metal forger's gang in the stamping shop? You'd learn all about manufacturing metal goods, and it comes with nearly double the pay you're getting now. But if you take this on, you've got to work hard and not let me down.'

Alfred's heart soared at the prospect. The stamping shop was famed throughout the factory for its skilled craftsmen who shaped large, white-hot pieces of iron and steel into wheels, engine cranks, and other vital components for trains and ships. It was an opportunity to learn a new trade, to challenge himself in new ways, and to secure a more stable future.

'I'd be honoured, sir,' Alfred replied, his voice filled with gratitude.

'Good,' Gus said with a nod. 'Meet me here tomorrow morning at eight, and I'll take you over to the steam hammer shop.'

The thought of what lay ahead filled Alfred with a renewed sense of purpose. This was his chance to step up, to prove himself, and to move closer to the life he envisioned for himself, and perhaps for Mary as well.

***

As Alfred arrived home at Rose cottage that evening, he found his mother bustling about in the kitchen, preparing their evening meal. Eager to update her regarding his promotion, he greeted her warmly and sat down at the worn wooden table.

'I've some news,' he began, his voice tinged with excitement.

'They want me to transfer to the stamping shop. To work at the forges.'

Elisabeth's eyes sparkled with pride as she listened to her son's announcement.

'Oh, Alfred, that's wonderful,' she exclaimed, beaming with

delight.

'I've always known you had a knack for hard work and dedication. It's no less than you deserve.'

As they continued to talk, Alfred's expression grew more serious as he broached the subject of the letter he had received earlier that day.

'Mother, I also received a letter from Mary,' he confessed, his voice faltering slightly as he spoke her name.

Elisabeth's gaze softened with understanding as she listened attentively.

'And what does she have to say, Alfred?'

Alfred sighed, his heart heavy with uncertainty.

'You know her family has been encouraging her to marry the son of a local farmer,' he explained, his voice tinged with sadness.

'She made no reference to any of that in the letter, but I can only assume that as she's written to me there's maybe still hope for us - I'm desperate to know what's happening.'

She reached out to squeeze his hand reassuringly.

'My dear boy, this is a delicate situation indeed,' her voice soft and soothing.

'When you write back to Mary, don't make any reference to that, just give her news of your progress, and I'm sure she'll reply. Just give her the time to figure things out.'

THE PALACE OF MY IMAGINATION

Chapter 8

April 1897 (continued)

'Mid the wild heart-throbs of labour,
Where, in the thickening gloom,
With fire and smoke the shuddering stroke
Falls like the crack of doom
from Rhymes of the forge. Alfred Williams (unpublished)

The next morning, as they approached the shed, the moderate level of noise which they had noticed on setting off had increased to a fearsome din as they entered the doors of the workshop. Alfred followed Gus through the maze of machinery and bustling workers until they reached the heart of the stamping shop.

The heat inside the workshop was intense. In a line, at its centre, stood a column of five steam hammers, and to the right of each stood a furnace. Three of the hammers were currently being readied for work, and Gus led Alfred to the hammer furthest away from the entrance.

Within the workshop, the roaring boilers had generated a thick fog of steam which hung around the hammers, and higher up in the workshop a cloud of black smoke rose from the illuminated oil furnaces creating an unpleasant stench. The roof and walls of the shed were covered in black soot. Standing next to the far furnace stood the forgeman in conversation with the furnaceman. As Gus and Alfred approached, he waved in acknowledgement.

'Joe, this is Alfred Williams, the lad I talked to you about,' said Gus, and turning to Alfred he added, 'he'll be your boss from now on.'

Joe was just below medium height, spare of build yet sinewy. His gaze was piercing and intense. He seemed like a character who would not suffer fools gladly. He eyed Alfred with a critical gaze, sizing him up with a mixture of scepticism and curiosity.

'So, you're the new recruit, eh,' he grunted, his voice gruff and gravelly.

'Well, I hope you're ready for some hard work, because we don't take kindly to slackers around here.'

Alfred nodded, unfazed by Joe's brusque manner.

'I'm ready sir,' he replied confidently, 'I'm not afraid of hard work.'

Joe gave a grunt of grudging approval, though his expression remained neutral.

'We'll see about that.' he muttered under his breath.

As Gus left them to their work, Joe wasted no time in laying down the ground rules.

'Listen to me, son,' he said, his tone serious.

'This job ain't for the faint of heart. It's hot, it's dirty, and it's dangerous. You'll be working with huge pieces of white-hot metal and heavy machinery, and one wrong move could cost you dear.'

Alfred nodded, his determination unwavering.

'I understand, sir,' he said firmly. 'I'll be careful. I still really want this job.'

Joe grunted in response, though there was a hint of approval in his eyes.

'Good,' he said gruffly.

'Today, we're making coupling rods for a locomotive'. Joe pointed to a gang of six men gathered around the steam hammer. 'There are your workmates, go and join them. The chargeman will show you the ropes.'

Alfred greeted the gang collectively and was instructed by the charge man to put on a pair of heavy boots, a cap and a thick pair of gloves.

'You're just in time to help us with the metal,' said the latter enthusiastically, indicating an iron ingot connected to a porter bar slung by chains from the crane above them. The ingot must have weighed at least four tons, one end of which hovered just outside the raging furnace. The gang assembled themselves around the porter bar and awaited further orders. Alfred also registered a man sitting at the controls of the steam hammer who was adjusting a lever sitting at its heart.

THE PALACE OF MY IMAGINATION

The furnace seemed to blaze noisily as Joe approached. Having also donned a leather apron, cap and jackboots, he proceeded to peer somewhat nervously into the aperture of the furnace, and seconds later exclaimed loudly.

'Ready, now,' to the gang and the crane driver.

The metallic rattle of the crane signaled the beginning of the ingot's transfer into the ready furnace. As the iron door was lifted, it revealed a gaping, red-hot chamber. A dozen men stood nearby, prepared to guide the massive metal bar, pushing it through the opening and into the hollow space within.

'Forward, forward, - STOP!' cried Joe

Then, the heavy door lowered again, sealing the ingot inside as the heating process began.

After five minutes, the now white-hot ingot was slowly withdrawn.

'Take it back, back, - WHOA!'

'Right, right. Now bring it to the hammer. Slowly, slowly, STOP!'

Joe joined the gang of men at the end of the still gleaming ingot as it was lined up with the drop hammer and the dies, the precision tools that shaped the metal into its required form. He gestured to the hammer driver, and at this unspoken signal the driver pressed the treadle which released steam to drive the piston and its heavy metal head upward, almost disappearing out of sight, only to return seconds later, descending with immense force to deliver a powerful blow to the metal below it, making the earth vibrate, the whole shed tremble and causing sparks to fly out from its surface in white showers.

'Quarter turn clockwise' yelled Joe, and the men responded by pulling on the chains which jingled as they rotated the bar linked to the ingot.

'Now forward a bit, STOP … Hammer!' The blows were repeated and seemed to make the metal even brighter and hotter.

After two more rotations and hammer blows, Joe, dripping sweat from his grime smeared face, applied measuring gauges to the metal mass to assess the extent to which it had yielded to the blows.

Further rotations and blows led to the ingot conforming closely to the shape desired, and after some minutes Joe called a halt, and some of the gang stepped forward to throw oil and water onto the forging.

Joe warned the gang members to step back from the hammered metal and administered another blow with the hammer, whereupon a cloud of steam suddenly appeared and simultaneously exploded with a deafening roar and a surge of flame. A volley of shrapnel like material flew in all directions from the dies as the scaly deposits were blasted off the newly forged metal, which was then severed from the porter bar by the hammer and transported away for cooling and further facing work.

The men were sweating intensely, and Alfred felt a raging thirst as they were stood down for a short break.

Alfred quietly marvelled at and was thrilled by the sheer power and precision of the process, and as he rested, his rapid heart rate gradually subsided to normal.

He gratefully accepted a drink of water from the charge hand, a seasoned worker named Jack, who had been a chargeman until a year ago. He seemed to take Alfred under his wing.

'Welcome to the team, Alfred,' Jack said, his voice tinged with warmth.

'You did well out there. But remember, you'll sweat like a pig, and you'll need to drink lots of water and take some salt to replace what you've lost. Otherwise, you won't keep up.'

Alfred nodded, taking Jack's advice to heart. He had heard stories of the extreme conditions in the steam hammer shop but experiencing it firsthand was a different matter altogether.

Jack went on to explain the unique challenges of their work environment. Unlike other workers in the factory, their team didn't have regular breaks or access to a canteen. They had to work when the heat of the furnace was at its optimum, ensuring the metal was forged to perfection.

'And to keep your strength up, you'll need to eat when you get

THE PALACE OF MY IMAGINATION

home,' Jack continued. 'There's no regular breaks for us in the forges, and the atmosphere in the factory, with its fumes and heat gradually ruins your appetite.'

A fellow worker, called Strawberry, a small thin man stripped to the waist and covered in grime chimed in with a cheerful suggestion.

'Or you can have a bacon sandwich—right now.'

He showed Alfred a shovel loaded with raw bacon which he was just about to place in the depths of the furnace. Laughter rippled through the gang at the suggestion, and Alfred couldn't help but smile at the camaraderie among his new colleagues.

The furnaceman, nicknamed Tubby, a short legged rotund, bald Welshman, offered to brew tea, producing a can of water that he placed in the neck of the furnace to heat. Alfred was impressed by their resourcefulness, realising he had been placed with a cheerful team of workers who would look out for one another.

***

JOHN CULLIMORE

Chapter 9

May 1897

In the weeks after Alfred's thrilling introduction to the steam hammer shop, he began his duties as assistant to the forgemen and furnace men.

First, he wielded the sledge hammer to break up lumps of coal which he then transported in a wheelbarrow to feed into the raging furnace.

Within a few moments, all of the coal he added had been consumed, leaving behind only a white liquid residue that oozed from the furnace like the slow-moving lava flow from a volcano. The flames consumed the contents of the furnace voraciously and required constant replenishment with fuel. The heat was awful but given his youthful stamina and by remembering to keep himself well hydrated he found he could tolerate the roasting atmosphere.

One of the forgemen introduced him to working the bar that supported and manipulated the metal prior to heating, and how to turn small ingots so that the smaller hammers could beat them into shape.

Time flew by, and after completing three rounds of forging, Alfred was finally allowed a break. Grateful for the respite, he left the workshop in search of fresh air and a quiet spot to relax. Behind the workshop, he had discovered a secluded place where he could rest undisturbed. The spot was hidden behind a stack of abandoned railway sleepers that had been piled up to form a four-foot-high wall, offering privacy from prying eyes.

Unusually the area around him was lush with greenery, an unexpected patch of nature amid the industrial landscape. Various types of grasses and wildflowers grew in abundance, their colours and forms reminiscent of the most idyllic pastoral settings. In fact, many of the flowers here could easily belong to the untouched meadows he admired in the countryside. But what made this retreat truly special was the uninterrupted view to the south. From his vantage point, Alfred had a clear sight of Liddington Hill,

THE PALACE OF MY IMAGINATION

crowned by the ancient Castellum to the west and the distinct clump of tall beech trees on its eastern edge. Beyond, the Ridgeway Downs stretched across the horizon, the chalk ridges undulating towards White Horse Hill and Uffington.

In these moments, Alfred felt fortunate. Despite the grim, smoke-filled environment of the workshop, he had access to this window into the countryside he cherished so deeply. As he sat there, a growing sense of joy welled up inside him, the kind of feeling that came from seeing something beautiful and rare in the middle of a routine day. He felt an urge to express this happiness, to somehow capture the peaceful delight he experienced in these stolen moments of solitude, though as yet he had no clear ideas as to how to voice these emotions.

Just as his thoughts began to take shape, the shrill sound of the factory hooter rang out, signalling the end of his break. With a sigh, Alfred gathered himself, leaving behind the tranquil scene, and returned to the workshop, ready to resume his labour.

As he re-entered the workshop he made a mental note to write to Mary, updating her on his progress. And as he put pen to paper that evening, he carefully followed his mother's advice, avoiding any mention of her presumed engagement or his own feelings for her.

Instead, he focused on the details of his work, the camaraderie among the men, and the new skills he was acquiring, keeping the tone light and optimistic.

***

December 1897

As time went on, Alfred became skilled in handling the forge tools. Under Jack's guidance, he mastered operating the steam hammer, learned how to precisely align the anvil block and secure the lower die, and became proficient in manipulating the porter bar with ease.

He felt elated as he became familiar with working the lever to manipulate the huge steam hammer's movement up, then down. The sense of power was slightly intoxicating, knowing he had the ability to wield an instrument exerting two hundred tons of pressure on anything that got in its way.

JOHN CULLIMORE

Likewise, he regarded his work at the forge as creative, very much on a par with that of the smiths and the carpenters. He felt a huge sense of achievement and regarded each of his finished forgings as the fruit of his creativity.

His skills developed quickly, and he was keen to take on challenges. Joe was impressed that Alfred had quickly fashioned a complicated axle box out of a crude ingot; real testament to his improving skill and judgement.

Joe was also happy to leave Alfred as responsible for one of the two hundred ton hammers and its furnace, still nominally under Barrett as chargeman, but in name only, as most of the latter's work would be with the smaller drop stampers. Joe himself would move to the adjacent large hammers, still within shouting distance if Alfred needed advice, but this was a massive vote of confidence in Alfred's ability.

Just before Christmas Alfred was appointed as Junior Forgeman.

Near the end of that year, as the workshop embarked on a period of overtime lasting through the Winter season, he reached the peak of his productivity. Work began at six a.m. and finished at nine p.m. He revelled in his new found responsibilities, and continued to walk to and from work, rejecting the idea of living in dingy lodgings close to the factory.

However, it was inevitable that with only five hours of rest between each working day, that he would ultimately begin to tire.

He tried to compensate by taking shortcuts on his journey to and from work. To do this he would follow the rail tracks towards South Marston. As the winter daylight waned, he would often be seen traversing the tracks in the darkness both mornings and evenings. Occasionally he clambered aboard a freight train leaving the sidings. Some of this was highly dangerous, but since childhood he was fond of danger, and recalled the time he had laid between the lines as a goods train thundered above him.

***

1898

There was however one other entirely unexpected benefit derived from walking via the railway, which seemed to lessen

THE PALACE OF MY IMAGINATION

Alfred's recent fatigue.

One evening in the following spring, as he was going home from work, he stumbled upon a book lying on the track in tatters, which presumably had been thrown from the train by a passenger.

He collected the scattered pages and arranged them in order. He then sat upon the bank and examined the contents. The work was entitled *'Sweetness and Light from the World's Bright Spirits'* and was an anthology put together by the editor of *Reynolds' Newspaper*.

Curiosity piqued, Alfred flipped through its pages and found himself drawn into a world of profound thought and contemplation. The classical writings of poets and philosophers alike filled its pages, each offering their own unique insights into the mysteries of life and existence.

He took the book to work, tucking it into his pocket, and read by the glow of the furnace. At weekends, he wandered into the fields, settling at the base of a towering, ancient oak to immerse himself in its pages. Occasionally, he would climb his favourite willow tree, sitting among the branches as he read aloud. The book held articles on Plato, Virgil, Chaucer, Shakespeare, Buddha, Confucius, and many more great thinkers.

He found solace and inspiration in the words of these great minds and marvelled at their attempts to unravel the complexities of human nature, and to grapple with questions of morality and purpose.

Having spent so many days immersed in the monotonous rhythm of factory life, the discovery of this book was nothing short of revelatory.

He found himself captivated by the notion that there was more to existence than the daily grind of work and survival. Memories resurfaced of Uncle George's book on mythical heroes and the list he had made of the trains named after them, and he felt the beginnings of a spiritual link with a previously unrecognised world, and a sudden passion for expressive language.

At a deeper level he gradually realised that these insights had the power to change the way he thought, the way he communicated, the way he might articulate his love for Mary— indeed, the whole way he lived. He sensed the potential to become a different version of Alfred Williams, whom up to now had lain dormant.

Keen to realise this potential, Alfred wasted no time in sharing his revelation with Mary. After finishing his night shift, he wrote to her and enthusiastically explained the powerful spiritual transformation he was undergoing.

Again, he recalled his mother's wise counsel and avoided reference to his rival, but finished by adding a quote from Walter Scott which he thought would emphasise his feelings for his beloved.

'Ever absent, ever near; Still I see thee, still I hear.'

The next morning, as Alfred made his way to work, he made a brief diversion via the village post box.

***

October 1898

Mary was thrilled to receive his latest letter. She realised Alfred was in the grip of some great intellectual revelation, but she could see that this was a positive step for him, a real chance for him to discover his true self and to pursue his deepest desires beyond the realm of the factory environment.

She was pleased that he had trusted her enough to confide in her and touched by the boldness with which he expressed his affection. The thought of accompanying him on his journey filled her with determination; as long as they were together, she felt anything was possible.

Her mind was made up. She would gather her courage, share her true feelings with her parents, and write to Adam Osney. Once everything had calmed down, she would reach out to Alfred and take the next step in what she hoped would be their shared future.

THE PALACE OF MY IMAGINATION

Chapter 10

Spring 1898-1899

It is myself I am looking for. Where is the small uniformity?
Where is the little divine something, that sure pent-up image of self?
Where is the beginning and end, the present and future of me?
The little, bright light ever burning continually?
from The Testament. Alfred Williams, 1913.

Since there was nowhere to buy books in Swindon, he booked a holiday day with his foreman Gus some weeks in advance, his plan being to travel to Oxford and return with a collection of poetic and philosophical texts.

He found the concepts of the philosophers to be truly awe inspiring, but he found the lyrical compositions of the poets held particular appeal. As he read the verses penned by poets long gone, something stirred within him - a resonance that touched his soul in ways he couldn't explain. The words danced before his eyes, weaving tales of love and loss, of dreams and desires, of the beauty and brutality of life itself.

For the first time, he realised that the essence of the world could be caught in words. He discovered that he was gifted with an unusually retentive memory and was able to quote lengthy passages from the classics of poetry.

A sudden compulsion to learn offered escape from the harsh realities of his everyday existence and seemed to harmonise with his love of the countryside and nature, adding an extra dimension to his love for Mary.

With newfound resolve, Alfred sought out the counsel of Uncle George, his mentor from childhood. They met one evening after he had finished his shift, and Alfred poured his heart out to him.

'Where should I start?' he asked eagerly, his eyes shining with excitement.

JOHN CULLIMORE

Uncle George smiled, already formulating a plan in his mind.

'Now that you've discovered the power of words, immerse yourself in the great works of literature—the classics that have endured. You've made a good start with Shakespeare's plays. Add Dickens' novels and Milton's poetry to your list. Read them with an open mind, aim to really understand them.'

A few days later, Uncle George came back with another suggestion. Through the Mechanics' Institute, he had learned about courses offered by Ruskin College in Oxford that might suit Alfred.

'Alfred, you should seriously consider enrolling in one of these courses. Ruskin College was founded specifically to help working men educate themselves when full-time study isn't an option. Take a look at this syllabus—I'm sure you'll find something that appeals to you.'

'But would I have to attend lectures in Oxford?' Alfred asked hesitantly.

'Not at all,' George replied. 'The courses can be done entirely by correspondence. That keeps the costs low, and you can pay as you go. Plus, the Mechanics' Institute offers small grants to help cover some of the expenses. I think this could provide the structure and guidance you need to get the most out of your studies.'

Alfred eagerly examined the syllabus and quickly identified a course in English literature that captivated him. He wrote to the tutor for correspondence students at Ruskin, Alfred Hacking, and received a positive reply, confirming he could begin his studies at the start of the Michaelmas term.

Diving into the major and minor poets and writers, Alfred followed the course's chronological progression, from the time of the Venerable Bede to Wordsworth. Most of the required texts were available at the Mechanics' library, allowing him to borrow them as needed. The course required him to complete one essay on a designated theme every five weeks.

As he worked through the reading list, Alfred noticed frequent Latin quotations that hindered his understanding. For the first time, he grasped the importance of Latin in the foundation of

THE PALACE OF MY IMAGINATION

Western literature. He realised that to truly delve into the roots of language and literature, he would need a solid grasp of its structure and meaning.

When Alfred discussed this with Uncle George, his mentor responded with enthusiasm.

'I suppose I should've seen this coming when you first talked about your studies,' George said with a chuckle. 'You're absolutely right. Learning Latin—and maybe even Greek—will sharpen your mind and broaden your horizons in ways you can't yet imagine.'

George suggested Alfred start with some old university primers stored in the Mechanics' library. 'They're probably still the best foundation texts you could ask for. Have a look when you're next there.'

Alfred's studies progressed steadily, even as he added Latin to his already demanding workload.

Within a year, he had read Caesar's works, dabbled in Cicero's writings, and fulfilled all the reading and essay requirements of his correspondence course. He felt that now was an appropriate time to adopt George's advice and added Ancient Greek to his timetable.

His success was due in large part to his strict regimen. Alfred rose at 4 a.m., studying by candlelight until it was time to leave for work. Arriving there early he seized the opportunity to etch a selection of unfamiliar Latin words or Greek letters onto the hood of the furnace before it was cleaned and fired, in the belief that repeated passes by the furnace during his working day would etch the writings into his memory.

At lunchtime in the works, he would often find a quiet corner to read, and after supper in the evening, he continued his studies until midnight.

His new passion did not have any impact on his work at the steam hammer. On the contrary, as his knowledge grew, he seemed to find extra reserves of energy and if anything became more productive in the factory. He was convinced that manual labour refreshed him and only seemed to increase his appetite for intellectual pursuit.

In those early years following his intellectual epiphany, he became the life and soul of the forge. His cheerfulness and positivity rubbed off on his colleagues, work flowed easily as a result, and he seldom felt fatigued.

During his dinner hour, while his colleagues chatted and munched on sandwiches, Alfred switched to the intricacies of Latin. His colleague Tubby was intrigued by Alfred's fervour and was reminded of his own uncle who was a Catholic priest who taught at a seminary in the Midlands.

'My uncle Peter spent most of his time correcting his student's Latin compositions. He loved it.'

'Well, my aim is just to read and understand ancient literature. I'm not doing any exams like they had to, so I don't need to write any Latin.'

Tubby seemed to find this amusing.

'OK, so you won't be putting any more Latin words on our furnace hood then, just Greek!' They both laughed.

***

When he arrived home on an early autumn evening, his mother handed him a letter addressed to him post marked at Hungerford.

Mary had written back to him explaining that she would be visiting her sister in a few weeks' time and suggested a meeting in Highworth on the first Saturday market day in November.

On the chosen day they promptly recognised each other in the High Street and Alfred suggested they walked to St Michael's churchyard, where they found a bench in a quiet corner.

At first, they sat in shy silence, exchanging hesitant smiles. Eventually, Mary broke the quiet, her nervousness spilling out in a flurry of questions.

'You look well, but how are you managing in that grimy factory? Doesn't it keep you from getting out into the countryside? And how do you even find time to study?' she asked, her voice tinged with concern.

'I work in the factory during the week,' Alfred said, 'and I fit in studying and writing whenever I can between shifts.'

THE PALACE OF MY IMAGINATION

Mary leaned forward, her expression radiating curiosity. 'What are you writing about?'

'It's part of a correspondence course,' Alfred explained. 'It's helping to direct my learning, and I enjoy the structure. Ultimately, I'm hoping the qualification will open doors for me—maybe into teaching or even lecturing someday.'

Mary smiled, though she regarded him quizzically. 'But I still don't know how you manage the factory work and all the studying.'

'Well, I'm methodical about it,' Alfred replied with a faint smile. 'I plan my timetable to the hour, and somehow, I thrive on the challenge. And I still have time at weekends to escape to the Downs. I just wish we could do it together' said Alfred, wishing to shift the emphasis to their relationship.

Mary's heart swelled with admiration for the man she loved.

It was time for them to be honest with each other.

'Alfred, I'm so sorry for the way things have turned out. I've missed you terribly, but I couldn't find the words to write what I was going through in a letter.'

'Mary, it's all right. I understand. But what happened? Why did you leave without a word?'

'It's my family, Alfred. They've been trying to marry me off to Adam Osney for months. My sister disapproved of us being together, so I had to go home. At Easter, my father publicly announced his wish for me to marry Osney. It was humiliating. He even promised he'd give us livestock to start a farm.'

'That's outrageous! You shouldn't marry someone you don't love just to appease your family.'

'And I won't. But for some time, I felt trapped. This is the world as they see it. But I couldn't bear the thought of being with anyone but you. In the end, I had a huge stand-up confrontation with my family telling them of my true feelings for you.'

'You're so courageous. I'm overwhelmed.'

'But we still have a problem. I'm sorry to have to mention this, but you need to know the truth. They made it quite clear that they thought you were not good enough, a mere factory worker, and I should do better.'

'Mary, listen to me. You don't have to marry Osney. We can be together, despite what your family thinks — I love you, so much Mary— and I have a plan,'

'I've settled into working at the factory in Swindon, and I've been saving a little. Enough to rent a cottage, enough to support…' he seemed momentarily lost for words , but Mary smiled broadly.

'Mary, Will you marry me?'

'Oh, Alfred! Yes, yes, a thousand times yes. And I love you too.'

Alfred took Mary in his arms, holding her tightly as they shared a moment of pure happiness and relief.

As they embraced, someone entered the churchyard via the gate from the high street. There was a flash of recognition as Isobel Osney saw the couple deep in an embrace, but her step didn't falter, and she entered the side door of the church unrecognised to prepare the flowers for the Sunday service.

THE PALACE OF MY IMAGINATION

Chapter 11

December 1899

On an unseasonably mild and sunny Friday lunchtime just before Christmas, Alfred had arranged to meet his former farm comrades for a festive drink at the Carpenter's Arms pub. Arriving slightly early, he bought himself a pint of cider and settled at one of the outdoor tables facing the road.

As he sipped his drink, he sensed something was amiss. A group of three men approached, led by Adam Osney, the heir to one of the largest farms in Wiltshire. With a reputation as an outright bully and troublemaker, Osney was flanked by two cronies, their presence casting an unwelcome shadow.

'Alf Williams, we were at school together.' Osney sat down uninvited at Alfred's table while his acolytes remained standing on each side of him.

'I remember,' Alfred responded. He also remembered that his nickname was 'Oddball' an unpredictable bully. He sensed nothing had changed.

'A word of warning, Alfred Williams.'

He paused, apparently for effect. Alfred was somewhat intrigued, smiled and looked Oddball directly in the eye as he anticipated the delivery of some threat.

'You're wasting your time with Mary Peck… she's spoken for already.'

Another pause to let the threat sink in. But Alfred didn't hesitate.

'Well let me bring *you* up to date. I've proposed to Mary, and she's accepted. At some time in the near future, we'll be man and wife.'

Osney was silent for a moment or two. A bead or two of sweat appeared on his brow and he exchanged uneasy looks with his gang members.

Osney changed tack.

'Ha, well a few months back, she told me she was mine. She

does tend to flip flop a bit. I think she might well change her mind again,' he reasoned, his supporters nodding vigorously with him in agreement.

'Rubbish,' said Alfred.

'Mary has explained all about the pressure she's been under. And she's brave enough to have made her own choices about her future.'

'A fine little speech Williams. But let me remind *you*, my family have a lot of influence in this part of the world. And you're just a factory boy—and how would Mary's sister feel if, all of a sudden, they couldn't sell their milk or their crops? We can make these things happen you know?'

But Alfred was not one to back down easily when threatened. With fire in his eyes and stubborn determination, he responded.

'Osney, you've always played at being the bully, and I see nothing's changed,' he continued, his tone sharp.

'But let's be honest- whether you're with your pathetic excuses for henchmen or not, you're about as intimidating as a toothless three-legged dog. So why don't you just *bugger off*!'

Suddenly, Osney leapt up and lunged at Alfred. However, from his seated position, he lacked momentum. His wild swing with his right arm threw him off balance, causing his hand to crash into Alfred's glass, shattering it. His punch glanced off Alfred's right shoulder, and the force of his lunge sent him sprawling onto the floor at Alfred's feet.

As Osney struggled to get to his feet, Alfred quickly retreated through the pergola into the beer garden. Osney's fall created a bottleneck, blocking his supporters and preventing them from pursuing Alfred.

Suddenly there was shouting as some new arrivals at the pub took stock of the scene and advanced towards the melee. These were Alfred's fellow farm workers, and they easily outnumbered the Osney gang. Deciding it was best to flee, Osney and friends hurried off up Old Vicarage Lane towards South Marston.

Ironic cheers followed them.

Alfred gratefully stood his friends a round of drinks, and he

THE PALACE OF MY IMAGINATION

knew the story of that evening would often be recounted on the farms around Swindon.

Though the encounter left Alfred shaken, his resolve remained unshaken. He knew then that his love for Mary was worth fighting for, no matter which obstacles lay in their path.

He wasn't keen to mention this to Mary as he thought it might upset her, although he was sure that news of the fracas would spread like wildfire through the community. But there was nothing he could do about that, and he wondered if there might be even more challenges awaiting them.

JOHN CULLIMORE

Chapter 12

1900

While Alfred was usually the first to arrive at the forge in the morning, he would also be the last to leave in the evening. While his workmates would rush out of the workshop at the sound of the factory hooter heralding the end of a shift, he would sit in front of the cooling forge, and read a passage or two of poetry, allowing his mind to clear of all the current day's challenges, in order to prepare for his journey home with positive thoughts. He came to value this time of reflection, when he could test his memory by recalling any new vocabulary he had acquired throughout the day.

One warm, sunny evening in late June, after leaving the factory, he followed the railway track heading east until he reached the hatches of the River Cole. The evening sun cast long shadows across the landscape, and the air was rich with the earthy scent of wet grass and flowing water. Feeling an impulsive urge to bathe, he made his way to a deep pool beneath his favourite tree—a secluded spot where the river curved gently, hidden from view by the railway embankment and shielded from the fields beyond by the row of towering elms along the opposite bank.

The day had been one of the warmest of the summer, and the thought of washing away the grime and sweat of the factory was irresistible. He undressed quickly, leaving his clothes in a neat pile on the bank, and waded into the cool water. As he moved toward the centre of the pool, the water rose to his waist, and he paused. Turning to face the setting sun, still hovering above the horizon, its warm rays forced him to close his eyes. Standing there, surrounded by soft ripples and the gentle hum of nature, he felt a profound sense of peace.

It seemed the perfect moment to recite a verse from Horace—he thought of the passage he had carefully translated from the original Latin during his lunch hour.

He took a deep breath, preparing his thoughts, as a cool breeze

THE PALACE OF MY IMAGINATION

stirred the reeds along the riverbank. At the far end of the pool, a small group of Canada geese rested quietly, their dark forms outlined against the glowing water. They appeared oblivious to his presence, their stillness adding to the tranquil scene. Then, with a steady voice, he began his recital, the words flowing effortlessly as the world around him seemed to pause:

'Behold! one fleeting day is gone,
Another is at hand and duly fills its place,
And every new moon hastens on,
Eager to reach its end and finish in the race.

The rhythmic cadence of ancient words echoed in the stillness, intertwining with the sounds of nature.

He was pleased that his memory of the piece was reliable and was about to continue to the next section when a pair of fox cubs emerged from their den, set in the hollowed-out stump of a decayed willow on the bank to his left. They calmly approached the water's edge and began to drink, taking no notice of Alfred. The mother followed moments later.

Alfred walked slowly to the water's edge and retrieved his clothing. The evening was still warm, and in a few minutes, he would be almost dry. Once dressed, he continued to observe the events around the pool. Suddenly, there was a flash of silver followed by a large splash in front of him as a large fish exploded out of the pool.

He lay back on the grassy bank and looked up at the twilight stars above him, feeling relaxed and at one with the scene. He thought to continue the poem, but then a soft voice, possibly a child's voice, began to recite:

'But thou are earnest and resigned,
And gifted with the charm of pleasant poesy,
Wherefore, though poor, the rich will mind
To visit thee with smiles and royal courtesy

Alfred sat up quickly and glanced around but could see no one.

JOHN CULLIMORE

It was now completely dark on a moonless night.

He then realised he had fallen asleep on the riverbank and concluded that he must have dreamed about the child. He shook his head and smiled inwardly. He had no idea of the hour, save that it was time to return home.

On calm summer evenings at weekends, he would wander out towards the downs to recite beneath the canopy of a moonlit sky, once unwittingly disturbing an individual lurking in the shadows—a poacher intent on his prey. Startled by Alfred's presence and alarmed by his recitations, the poacher's pursuit was thwarted, much to his chagrin, and he made clear his dissatisfaction. Convinced that Alfred must be deranged to recite poetry in the darkness, the poacher retreated into the night, leaving Alfred to continue his solitary walk, undeterred by the encounter.

By now, his mystical inclinations had merged with his thirst for knowledge. He was convinced that an unseen inner force was guiding him, subtly directing him toward a deeper understanding of life and his own identity.

THE PALACE OF MY IMAGINATION

Chapter 13

November 1900

After settling into factory work, Alfred had been diligently saving for months. Within a year, a more senior position became available in the workshop. He had consistently impressed both the foreman and his colleagues, and there was widespread talk on the shop floor, with many strongly backing Alfred for the promotion to a higher role.

He became a senior forgeman, in charge of three hammers and forges and received a significant pay increase. Now that his future seemed reasonably assured, he felt that the time had come to address the most important issue in his life: his marriage to Mary.

The weather seemed set fair for the weekend, and he had invited her to meet him on Saturday morning. Alfred stood atop Liddington Hill, the gentle breeze ruffling his hair as he anxiously awaited Mary's arrival. The Iron Age fort, with its ancient earthworks and panoramic views of the countryside, was one of his favourite places, and he hoped it would serve as the perfect backdrop for their conversation.

As Mary appeared on the eastern horizon, Alfred's heart skipped a beat. She was as radiant as ever, her eyes bright with anticipation as she made her way towards him. They greeted each other with a warm embrace.

'Alfred, we need to discuss some practicalities.'

'Yes indeed. Well, from the point of view of a house, the tenant in Dryden cottage has given three months' notice to the landlord, so I've registered to take on the tenancy.'

'That's marvellous, Dryden cottage will suit us nicely. But we also need to talk about how and where we have our wedding. It's a bit complicated, and there might be a slight delay in organising it.' Mary looked somewhat anxious.

'What's the problem?'

'Well, I went to see your local vicar, Reverend McFadden. He's not keen to marry us. He's a close friend of the Osney family who attend his church, and he knows I've rejected Adam's proposal. So, I don't want our wedding banns to be called in South Marston, it would be somewhat embarrassing given what's happened.'

'But can't we get married in Hungerford?'

'Fortunately, we can, and our vicar agrees to a church wedding. But he advises that because the vicar of Marston seems unhappy, we should get married by licence.'

'So, our local clergyman is showing who his true friends are.'

'It seems that way. But from our point of view, marrying by licence means we can keep our marriage plans discreet. We don't have to have banns read in Marston, and we still get a church wedding.'

***

Despite all these challenges, on a crisp autumn day in September 1901, surrounded by family and friends, Alfred and Mary exchanged vows in the quaint St. Saviour's Church in Hungerford, sealing their love and defying the expectations of those who sought to keep them apart.

They left the next day for a honeymoon in Torbay.

As they strolled along the sandy beaches and breathed in the salt laden sea air, they experienced a whirlwind of new experiences and emotions. On the very first night of their honeymoon, beneath the blanket of stars that adorned the sky, Alfred and Mary shared their first intimate moments as husband and wife. In that tender embrace, passion and love intertwined, igniting a fire within Alfred's heart that he had never known before.

Inspired by the beauty of the sea and the overwhelming love he felt for Mary, Alfred was able to express his emotions in verse. And so, with pen in hand and a heart overflowing with love, he poured those feelings onto paper, to capture the essence of their love.

THE PALACE OF MY IMAGINATION

Chapter 14

At precisely five a.m. every morning, the factory hooter echoed through the quiet streets of the town, breaking the stillness of dawn. The sound wasn't just a summons to the working population; it was a call that awakened the entire region.

For the twelve thousand workers employed within the factory's walls, the hooter's call resonated like a dark foreboding hymn heralding their return to the industrial inferno. From all corners of the town and the surrounding countryside, they converged towards the factory, their footsteps mingling with the early morning mist. It was a routine etched into their daily lives, setting the rhythm of their labour which sustained the community.

Likewise, beyond the confines of the town, the hooter held significance. Its sound travelled to distant meadows where farmers tended their herds. For them, it was the signal for the start of the day's chores. And in the quiet corners of households, housewives, listened for the hooter and would glance at their clocks, finding solace in the synchronization of their daily routines with the pulse of the town's industry.

At the factory, work was scheduled to begin at six a.m. For the workers, punctuality wasn't just a virtue, it was a matter of survival.

Within the confines of the factory, time was money, and wages were tied directly to daily output. This meant that every minute counted, especially in the early morning hours when frenetic activity enveloped the workshop. Before the furnaces could be fired up for the morning's work, the mineral deposits that had accumulated within them on the previous day had to be removed.

To expedite production, oil was used as fuel, chosen for its quick ignition compared to alternatives like coal or wood. However, the trade-off came in the form of thick smoke and noxious fumes that filled the air, a grim reminder of the sacrifices made in the pursuit of the maximum achievable daily wage.

As the men toiled around the blazing forges, their faces obscured

JOHN CULLIMORE

by sweat and soot, a new foreman, Dickie Grubb, had recently made his entrance.

Alfred's previous foreman and mentor Gus had been the victim of a heart attack and though he had survived he was still in the infirmary weakened by heart failure and had handed in his resignation. In the circumstances, Grubb's appointment had been expedited.

His arrival had been a surprise to the men on the factory floor. He was a stranger in the department, having been a fitter with the engineers, and he had no previous experience of forgings.

It was rumoured that he had been appointed because he attended the same church as one of the factory managers.

The new man began to prowl through the workshop, his eyes keenly assessing the readiness of the machinery and the commitment of the workers. Occasionally, he would jot down notes, a facade of diligence masking his intense insecurity. He was a pale thin unsmiling character of medium height. His eyes were restless, and his natural habit was to avoid eye contact in conversations with workmen.

As a consequence of his lack of familiarity with the workshop, he was at a disadvantage when it came to motivating the workforce to maximum efficiency. He recognised this but firmly believed that the secret of being successful at his post was to make the men fear his authority, thereby establishing a network of underlings who would not challenge him. He would take direction from his allies in senior management as to how to achieve the optimal output from the workshop, but he believed the key to earning their favour lay in keeping the wage bill as low as possible.

Once his cursory inspection was complete, Grubb summoned the chargemen, delivering his instructions with a commanding air. Whether the requirement was for wheels, axles, or rails his directives were issued with unwavering authority. With a dismissive nod, he would retreat to his office, where the daily bulletin awaited him.

This bulletin, meticulously prepared by Jenkins, the clerk for the Stamping Shop, outlined the previous day's events with clinical

THE PALACE OF MY IMAGINATION

precision. Proud of his efforts, he handed the files to the new foreman, eager to maintain the productive rapport he had enjoyed with Grubb's predecessor.

His report was filled with detailed statistics on the number of finished items, the times taken to complete each forging, and the times of operation of the furnaces.

Grubb, however, barely glanced at the pages, his expression hard and dismissive. He flipped through the report with an air of disinterest, giving Jenkins the distinct impression that his work was of little relevance.

For a moment, he stood there, stunned. In his seventeen years of working alongside Gus Dempster, he had never been met with such indifference. Dempster had always valued Jenkins' input, making him feel that the information he provided was valuable in boosting production.

For the first time ever, the clerk found himself wondering if it might be time to follow Dempster into retirement. Then again, on the strength of today's showing, he doubted Grubb would last long in this role. Only time would tell.

The foreman's expression darkened further as he reached the sections of the report detailing absences and workplace accidents. Two forgemen were off: one attending his infant son's funeral, and the other—Alfred—taking a holiday day. Grubb's brow furrowed; he couldn't recall approving Alfred's absence and immediately made a note to confront him upon his return.

Grubb's frustration erupted as he read of an unfortunate incident involving a worker who had slipped on a patch of spilled oil and was knocked unconscious while manipulating the porter bar. His lips curled into a sneer as he cursed the workers for their inattentiveness to their working environment.

Sensing the growing tension, Jenkins decided there was little to gain by prolonging the meeting. He excused himself, mentioning a committee meeting he needed to attend. As he left the office, he couldn't shake the uneasy feeling that things were not as they once had been in the workshop.

Grubb didn't even acknowledge him as he left. His mind was

preoccupied with calculating the likely compensation the GWR would have to pay to the injured victims, and he was annoyed further by the inconvenience of adjusting the rota at short notice, especially since it would require a visit to the shop floor to find the chargeman.

Yet, he had to admit that finding a suitable replacement might not be a bad thing, if he could find an individual who would unquestionably do his bidding and thereby extend his influence. That would be much better than having to put up with individuals like Alfred Williams who within a short time had become a significant thorn in his side.

He harboured increasing resentment towards Alfred who was popular, highly competent, and efficient; Alfred embodied everything Grubb despised.

Although Alfred had failed to recognise him at their first factory encounter, Grubb certainly remembered him. The seeds of dislike had been sown two years previously, at the Carpenter's arms in South Marston, when Alfred had stood up to his friend Osney. Grubb had been there in the background, one of his cronies.

He recalled how Alfred had refused to bow to their intimidation in the matter of Mary Peck's affections, and the arrival of his colleagues had ensured that he and the remainder of Osney's gang had to scatter in humiliation from the scene.

Grubb also recalled the more recent humiliation he had felt when Alfred had dared to speak up about the lack of protective gear for the workers. Forced to acquiesce to Alfred's demands, Grubb privately seethed with anger, his authority undermined in front of senior managers. He secretly feared Alfred as he possessed superior knowledge of the forge, and he clearly could influence the men.

He was therefore determined to undermine him at every turn. As he sat in his office, surrounded by paperwork and bureaucracy, Grubb pondered his next move.

Around the furnace, the men sat and conversed as they waited for the heat to maximise. They were aware that Alfred had scheduled a day off, therefore the men's conversation naturally

THE PALACE OF MY IMAGINATION

centred on him and his relationship with the new foreman.

'Grubb, 'e doesn't like Alf does 'e?' said Tubby.

'It's simple,' said Jack, 'Grubb's out of his depth in the shop. Alf just shows him up for what 'e is… a useless bully.'

'That's why Grubb's out to get him. He's scared Alf will replace him.'

'And wouldn't that be a good thing?' said Strawberry.

'What makes you so sure 'e's against 'im?'

'They 'ad a set to. I overheard 'em talking. Alfred complained about one of the dies 'e reckons is damaged. Grubb said Alf was getting above 'imself and the chargeman Barrett would sort it.'

'an' did 'e?'

'I don't think so, but Grubb was angry when he met the chargeman. Told him he needed to get Alf in order, or it wouldn't go well for 'im.'

'After that Alf told the chargeman which die it was, but he didn't do anything about it either.' Gustavus shrugged his shoulders in a resigned fashion, then continued.

'So, Alf gave the number of the die to the engineers—After that it went quiet.'

'But Alf, 'e don't seem to want no promotion, 'e's happy at the hammer, and 'e's concentrating on 'is books, teaching himself all manner o' things.'

'Shame, he'd be better than Grubb.'

At that moment the sound of approaching footsteps alerted the men, and the conversation ceased. Grubb approached the group and barked out instructions.

'You'll only work two hammers today. We're short of men. Why isn't Williams here?'

'Gone to Oxford, to buy more books.'

'Well, that's the first I've heard of it. You send him to me tomorrow to explain 'imself. Books, eh? fat lot o' good that'll do 'im.' He marched off muttering to himself.

After his departure the men resumed their talk.

'Well, *I* knew he was takin' a day off, I was there when he asked Gus about it.'

'Poor ol' Gus, well miss 'im.'

JOHN CULLIMORE

Chapter 15

Throughout the increasingly hot days of summer, the daily grind of manufacturing continued without pause. The intense heat of the workshop became almost unbearable at the height of the season, yet the drive for production remained strong, driven in large part by the piecework system of their wages. Thus, the factory became a pressure cooker of sweat and toil, the air thick with the acrid scent of molten metal as the stifling heat of the summer sun beat down on the factory floor. As the days wore on, tempers flared, and tensions mounted among the workforce as they struggled to maximise their output despite their increasing exhaustion.

On one of the hottest days of the year, as he prepared for work at the forge, Alfred noticed that Grubb was speaking *sotto voce* with Tom Barratt behind number 1 furnace. Afterwards, Tom called the gang together for an impromptu announcement.

'Pay attention lads, - I've got something to say,'

'The situation is a bit muddled at the moment, but Management have told me this morning that the piece work rates are being lowered—by five percent.'

The men groaned as they realised they would have to work harder to earn the same amount of money. Alfred was immediately alert to this turn of events.

'But,' continued Tom, 'we're being offered overtime. You're allowed an extra quarter today.'

Alfred couldn't contain himself any longer.

'But some of the men are exhausted. In this heat they can barely manage their normal shift. We've already got two off sick. On days like this, you're running us into the ground.'

The response from the gang was muted. Some presumably relished the idea of extra money; some were too frightened to respond. Others seemed merely apathetic and unresponsive.

Barrett pressed on with his suggestion.

'Of course no one can insist on you doing overtime, but if you agree to work extra today, you can have extra work for the rest of

THE PALACE OF MY IMAGINATION

this week.'

'But what if we don't work extra today?' asked Alfred.

'Well, then you're not allowed any extra later in the week.'

Alfred was incredulous. But again, there was silence from the rest of the gang. Barrett sensed he had prevailed.

'So, if no one disagrees, the shift will finish at nine tonight.'

Hearing no opposition, Barrett sidled off in the direction of the workshop entrance, and the gang dispersed, leaving only Alfred and Jack still sitting by the furnace. Alfred suspected he was going to report back to Grubb.

'You don't get it, do you Alf?' said Jack, when they were finally alone.

Alfred seemed perplexed.

'Once upon a time, Tom Barrett had dreams of rising through the ranks, but he's fallen prey to the promise of easy money.'

'What are you saying?'

'You see, the factory has devised a cunning scheme to exploit hardworking men. Unbeknownst to them, a portion of our team's earnings is siphoned off to line the pockets of Barrett, and I think Grubb too.'

'Barrett is allowed a ten percent monthly bonus if he meets the targets set by Grubb. While that's all perfectly legitimate, nevertheless that bonus comes from the earnings of your team. It's your money really.'

'But the real issue is that Grubb gets to set the targets and the pay rate. No one in the office questions him as long as the workshop is meeting demand. And if there's overproduction, no one seems to care, so long as the wage bill doesn't vary too much between workshops.'

'So, basically, it's a case of *what the eye doesn't see, the heart doesn't grieve over*,' said Alfred.

'Exactly. And I'd wager Grubb's getting a cut of Barrett's ten percent. The two of them are more than happy to look the other way while they're pulling a fast one on their workmates. And we can't even show that what they're doing is a crime!'

'But the men will get sick, production will fall and then the plan will backfire.' said Alfred.

'But that doesn't matter to them. If push comes to shove, they'll just get new hands. There's plenty of people seeking unskilled work.'

'But surely they just can't get rid of those who take time off sick, especially when they're overworked?'

'Don't you believe it Alf! You've not had time off sick—yet—but mark my words, if you do your whole future rests in the hands of your foreman and the managers.'

'But the doctors surely have a say?'

'Well, yes, but they don't have the last word. After the doctors declare you fit for work, you have to have a meeting with the managers. They call it a *back to work interview* but it's more of an inquisition. And it gives them an opportunity to dismiss you, if your record shows a history of poor attendance. So, they insist on input from the foreman before you return. The foreman has to send them a written slip.'

'But surely the foreman can't override a doctor?'

'Ha, It's a bit more subtle than that. I happen to know this, because one of the clerks who left work recently let me in on what really happens. They've developed a sneaky, underhanded system of communicating with each other —it's disgraceful.'

'If the foreman wants to keep you on, he simply returns the slip, stating you've been out sick but are now back to full health,' he explained.

'The key detail is that he adds a specific pen mark to the slip, something the managers are trained to recognize as a sign of his confidence in you.'

'However, if the foreman doesn't want you back, he returns the slip without any extra mark.'

'And if the workman who is dismissed asks to look at the slip, he won't recognise anything derogatory in it.'

Alfred was stunned and was speechless for a few moments. But then he started to think out loud.

'What you've told me. It would discourage me from taking time off sick. I suppose I would just plod on until I was incapable of

THE PALACE OF MY IMAGINATION

getting to work.'

'Precisely, and that's what they want. And my guess is that you're probably one of those who would be a victim of the whims of our foreman—He is clearly not on your side.'

'So, what you're saying is that greed and corruption are rife here, and we workers are powerless to change it.'

'You're right, but it strikes me you're able to stand up and fight for what's right, and I think you should. And deep inside I think you want to. It's your character. Having said that, you need to be careful, for the time being at least.'

'Of course I'll be careful, but I'd like to have a say about those piece work rates.'

'Well, if you're really interested, you could put yourself forward for the Works Committee—its official name is the Conciliation Committee,' Jack said. 'The managers set it up to show they're open to hearing about problems in the works and ideas for improvement. I reckon it's also their way of discouraging men from joining the unions that are starting to appear in Swindon. I'm not sure if anything useful has come out of it yet, but you might just shake things up!'

'Well, nothing ventured, nothing gained,' Alfred replied with a grin. 'I wouldn't mind giving it a go. There's a whole list of things I could raise.'

'Right, then. Why not put yourself forward? I'll second your application. But you'll also need approval from one of the staff. If I were you, I'd steer clear of Grubb—for obvious reasons—but you might want to speak to Jenkins, the shop clerk. I'm sure he'd be more than willing to help.'

Taking Jack's advice, Alfred arranged to speak with Jenkins. When they met, Jenkins was happy to approve Alfred's nomination and asked if there was anything Alfred needed to know before the next meeting.

Alfred thanked him and said he'd follow up with any questions.

***

A week later, Alfred entered the foyer of the recently renovated Mechanics institute. Walking to the right of the central staircase he crossed the new Reading room into the Council room where the Conciliation committee was to take place. In the centre of the room was an ornate U-shaped table, with seating for 12 members.

Alfred was somewhat taken aback as he recognised the committee chairman, the legendary George Churchward, the de facto Locomotive Superintendent at Swindon works. He suddenly felt a huge weight of responsibility as he realised he might be debating with one of the most influential men in Swindon's history.

Alfred was ushered to his seat in the central part of the table by none other than Jenkins, the works clerk, who gave him a brief smile of recognition. The chairman called the meeting to order and asked the members to introduce themselves. Alfred saw a familiar face directly opposite him, and became aware that this was Henry Byett, the accounting manager of the Stamping shop.

The first item on the agenda was an announcement from the Vice chairman that the directors had approved the introduction of reduced-price rail tickets for workers and their families. Murmurs of approval emanated from the committee members for what was perceived as a generous concession. Jenkins delivered the second item—an upbeat announcement confirming that the annual shutdown would take place from 7th-14th July of the following year. The workforce would be encouraged to take a free return railway trip during this time to Weymouth.

Alfred felt that these rather benign announcements had been carefully timed to create a calm atmosphere, as from here onwards, the more controversial factory issues would surface.

The next item on the agenda was listed as 'Representations from the Stamping shop on the adjustment of prices for recent forgings', and Alfred's name was printed next to it.

'Mr. Williams, would you like to tell us what it is that concerns you' said Churchward, his manner somewhat challenging. He stared intently at Alfred while maintaining a neutral expression.

'Thankyou sir for this opportunity. I feel that piece work pricing has become an issue since we had an order for a large number of coupling rods at the beginning of Summer. What started as a

THE PALACE OF MY IMAGINATION

reasonable price for the work, was reduced without any explanation. These items require a high degree of precision...'

'Mr. Chairman, the principle of piece work is long established here,' interjected a thick set heavily bearded man to Alfred's right. 'The piece work system motivates the men and encourages them to be efficient and innovative. I don't see what's special about this issue,' he concluded gruffly.

'If you'll allow me to continue, I'll explain the peculiarities in this case,' said Alfred remembering to address himself to the chairman.

'Go on,' replied Churchward.

'The first thing to say relates to timing. Piece working does motivate the men, but during the sweltering summer months, the men are exposed to dangerously high levels of heat at the forge, but they're reluctant to slow the pace of production for fear of losing their wage.'

'The number of serious accidents has risen significantly as the men are indeed motivated, but too exhausted to execute their tasks safely. Likewise, the quality of the finished product is inferior, as they concentrate more on speed rather than quality. So, in this particular circumstance, piece working is self-defeating.'

As he delivered these words he saw some nodding of heads around the table, and sensed he had their attention. 'Don't stop there,' he thought to himself, as he proceeded directly to his next point.

'Mr. Chairman, one of the members said piece working encouraged us to be innovative. And that is indeed the case. But we can't improve production unless someone is prepared to listen to our ideas. Given the increased demand for work of high specification, it's vital that our equipment functions optimally.'

'I attended a lecture here recently here about new steel alloys, which can increase the lifespan of the dies and make them less liable to fracture and cause accidents. I've pointed this out to my overseer, but I was told I was 'getting above myself' and so nothing has changed.'

As Alfred said these words, he acknowledged that his

relationship with Grubb would be irreversibly damaged once they were relayed to him, but then, he reflected, these issues had to be faced.

'Isn't there an argument for a factory wide 'Ideas box' that would be regularly read by management?'

The silence persisted, he registered a few more nods, and it was clear that the committee were hanging on his every word. 'Press on,' he thought to himself.

'I have one more issue to raise then I'm finished; It relates to the work on coupling rods. This requires high levels of skill and significantly more resources and time than producing items such as axles and rails. We need more dies; more fuel and more men for this heavy work. The original pricing of this work was fair, but the sudden reduction of prices imposed on us doesn't seem justified, as it doesn't reflect the costs of production, or the skill required. Mr. Jenkins has kindly produced some figures on the time and materials required.'

Jenkins nodded enthusiastically and proffered the file to the committee secretary.

'And these seem to confirm my impression.'

Momentary silence, eventually broken by Byett.

'Mr. Chairman, I'd like to thank Mr. Williams for his contribution. I propose we should consider these issues further, outside of the committee, taking on board the views of the foremen and chargemen involved. I do agree it is important that the safety of our manufacturing processes is seen to be unimpeachable, and the point about workshop injuries is a fair one under the circumstances'

Churchward looked around at the members of the committee.

'All those in favour of Mr Byett's proposal say 'aye.'

A chorus of 'ayes' followed.

'Thankyou Mr Williams. We will now proceed to the next item on the agenda.'

THE PALACE OF MY IMAGINATION

Chapter 16

1906

Alfred was a man truly divided.

He had continued with his strict regimen of study alternating with work and then further study. Since they had married, Mary had watched his rigorous schedule with some concern, wondering how long he could sustain such a lifestyle. Yet she never objected, recognizing how positive Alfred seemed about his progress. Besides, they always found time on weekends to enjoy long walks on the downs or quiet conversations by the fireside—moments that strengthened their bond amidst the whirlwind of Alfred's intellectual pursuits.

However, it was clear to her now that Alfred's dedication had begun to take its toll.

After more than six years as senior forgeman his once vibrant energy waned, replaced by a weariness that seemed to seep into his bones. His determination to fill his dinner breaks with learning had led to increasing isolation from his colleagues, a price that Alfred felt was worth paying as his solitude seemed to increase his capacity to learn, and his literary addiction led him to crave it more and more.

During the colder months, when he could no longer enjoy his favourite outdoor spot, Alfred asked to take his meals in the workshop instead of joining the others in the newly built mess hall, which exacerbated the situation further. Alfred found a disused railway carriage in one corner of the shop and retired there during the dinner hour.

His once friendly colleagues now regarded him quizzically and began to think him aloof and conceited, and felt abandoned by his solitary pursuits. Grubb had sensed this rising resentment and sought to capitalise on it.

Alfred usually started his day by inscribing Greek letters and other phrases he wished to learn onto the hood of the forge. While

JOHN CULLIMORE

his colleagues had previously been mildly amused by this, Grubb had always resented Alfred's presumption that he could adorn factory equipment with graffiti and saw an opportunity to act.

Grubb decided to pay an early morning visit to Alfred's forge. Sure enough, the hood was decorated with fresh chalk marks displaying a series of bizarre hieroglyphics that he could not decipher. He was determined to find Williams and have it out with him.

However Alfred had gone over to the engineering shop and in his absence, the foreman grabbed hold of Strawberry, who was just preparing an urn of tea.

'Get a wet cloth and get rid of that funny writing.'

'But them's Alfred's letters.'

'He's no right to deface our equipment like that, so if you know what's good for you, do as I say now.'

Strawberry fetched a bucket of water and started to erase the chalk marks, while Grubb retreated with an air of quiet satisfaction.

The next morning, Grubb was doing his usual morning inspection and noticed that the letters had been re inscribed on the forge. He re-issued his threatening instructions to Strawberry.

'Get those letters rubbed off, and after doing that take a brush and apply a coat of grease to the hood. That'll stop any more of this nonsense.'

Again, Strawberry complied. However, later that evening after the shift had finished and all was quiet, Alfred stayed a little longer than usual, and proceeded to thoroughly remove the grease, and reapplied the text to a clean hood, but this time he used white paint.

The situation erupted the next morning.

'Williams! - Get those letters removed from the hood, NOW!

'No, I won't.'

'Then I bloody well will!'

'Do as you please, but I assure you as often as you do, they'll be back on the forge the next morning'

Grubb snapped, hurling the most foul abuse at Alfred. At that precise moment however, one of the works managers, Henry Byett

THE PALACE OF MY IMAGINATION

appeared a few yards from the forge. On seeing him Grubb was instantly silenced.

'Sorry to interrupt your—meeting. I just wanted to speak to Williams about the replacement of one of the hammers.'

Grubb cringed inwardly as he realised that managers were avoiding him and going directly to Alfred for technical advice. He made a hurried exit, and the gang members set about preparing the forge while Alfred answered Byett's queries.

Since the Conciliation committee meeting, Henry Byett had liaised with Alfred concerning technical issues on several occasions. He recognised his through familiarity with the workshop and its processes, and that he could communicate in a straightforward yet articulate way. He had heard the gossip about Alfred's quest for self-education and found this intriguing.

Despite Alfred's apparent victory over Grubb, he had misgivings. The petty-minded foreman would continue to try and make his life difficult, that was obvious. But he was worried that Grubb would focus his intimidation on the rest of the gang, who might be less able to defend themselves.

Dinner hour arrived and Alfred took himself off to the disused carriage. He felt no appetite, only the gnawing stomach discomfort of dyspepsia, and therefore found it difficult to concentrate on his reading. After a couple of minutes, he had fallen asleep. He woke with a start as the hooter confirmed the end of the break, and he started back to the workshop.

***

The following weekend Uncle George dropped into Dryden cottage. Stepping into the confines of Alfred's home, he was struck by the sight of his pale, gaunt appearance.

'Alfred, you've lost weight, you look very pale,' he said.

'And he won't eat, he's got chronic indigestion,' said Mary. Alfred certainly seemed to be experiencing some discomfort. 'And he's not sleeping,' she added for good measure.

'Alfred, I think you're overdoing it. And by the look of it you need to see a doctor. Take some time off, go and see Dr Muir.'

'I hear what you're saying, but I don't want it all to slip right now. I've got my poetry collection to finish, and a couple of essays to submit to Ruskin College.'

'But it looks to me like you're driving yourself into the ground. Have a break from work, *and* study, for a few weeks at least.'

Alfred sighed and he took Mary's hand. 'I know I've been pushing myself too hard, you know how important this is to me, but it keeps me going when the factory work seems overwhelming. But I want you to know that I couldn't do any of this without the support you've given me, and I'm really sorry if you feel you're taking second place to my obsession with learning.'

'But you're both right' said Alfred, 'I've been a bit selfish, and something needs to change.'

George nodded. 'I care deeply about you both,' he said, 'so please don't take offence when I say this, Alfred. You need to find a balance, to find joy and fulfillment outside of the factory walls. Maybe now's the time to be thinking of a new start?'

This immediately captured the couple's attention.

'There's a post advertised in the Mechanics Institute. A position that might suit you. It's a job as a librarian at an Oxford college. The wage isn't bad, and you'd be given university accommodation. I think you should apply.'

Mary nodded with some enthusiasm, and Alfred began to imagine an alternative future.

***

Alfred felt much better after a weekend's rest from the factory. His indigestion had resolved, and he'd been invigorated by a walk on the Ridgeway path. He decided to apply for the librarianship.

The following evening, he spoke with his Oxford tutor by telephone from the Mechanics Institute. He asked if he would act as a referee. Hacking was pleased to hear of Alfred's plans and delighted to supply his reference. He thought the post would be ideal for him and wished him luck. Alfred submitted his application the next day.

Hacking duly sent off a glowing testimonial, praising Alfred's thoughtful and original literary style and the excellence of his essays.

THE PALACE OF MY IMAGINATION

However, despite his best efforts, Alfred's application was unsuccessful. Although on the outside he seemed unperturbed by the rejection, on the inside he was disheartened.

During his lunch hour at the factory, Alfred had drifted into a deep sleep, only to find himself in a dreamscape where he encountered an ancient enigmatic sage. The scene unfolded in the setting of a Roman villa. Alfred stood behind the sage, who was draped in a flowing robe, staring intently from a balcony at a vast sea stretching out before them, tranquil and endless.

Then Alfred spoke, lamenting his own failures and questioning his self-worth. However, he noticed that the sage remained silent, seemingly oblivious to his words. He began to repeat himself, but his voice was drowned out by a tremendous noise, as if the earth itself was roaring in response. Across the sea, from a distant mountain peak, a violent eruption was underway. The sky darkened as ash and fire spewed forth, and the ground beneath them seemed to tremble with the force of the explosion.

Just as the chaos reached its peak, Alfred jolted awake. His heart pounded as he realised he had dozed off during his break and the deafening roar he had heard in his dream wasn't from a volcanic eruption but from the real-world explosion of one of the boilers in the workshop.

JOHN CULLIMORE

PART 3: ACHIEVEMENT

Chapter 17

1908

Despite the dysfunctional relationship he had with his works foreman and a growing sense of isolation from his colleagues at the forge, Alfred was still respected as a skilled Hammerman. At the same time the passion for learning continued but had been augmented by a burgeoning creativity.

He realised that he had original thoughts worth recording and now had the intellectual ability to bring them to life.

He had penned several poems, each a reflection of his deepest passions and connections. Some were dedicated to his love for Mary, capturing the tenderness and devotion he felt for her. Others expressed his profound admiration for nature and the landscapes of his homeland, weaving his sense of belonging and spiritual connection to the land into vivid, heartfelt verses.

Now, as he spent his lunch breaks gazing from his quiet patch of greenery outside the workshop toward the rolling Downs, he found himself able to channel his emotions more freely into evocative lines of poetry. The beauty of the countryside inspired him, allowing him to articulate in verse the serenity and awe he felt while taking in the view of Liddington. He carried a notepad in his pocket, and now withdrew it, to capture his latest inspiration.

'O, thou bonny high hill
I covet no other.
Our secrets we tell
For we love one another'

He had discovered that once he had the inspiration for one or two opening lines, the rest would follow naturally during his period of study at home.

THE PALACE OF MY IMAGINATION

As he headed back to the forge, he reflected that his studies in Greek had also progressed significantly, reaching a point where he could now translate some of Anacreon's *Odes*, merging his intellectual growth with artistic expression.

Through his reading of periodicals, he had become aware that submissions were being sought by the Author's Association for a poetry anthology. He had sent off four of his original works to its editor for assessment, of which two of these were translations form Greek and Latin. However, the two original poems he had submitted had received a favourable review by the poet Sidney Colvin and were chosen for inclusion in the work *New Songs* published by Chapman and Hall.

That evening Uncle George dropped in with a copy of *Reynold's Newspaper*.

'Just sit yourself down and listen to this review of your work in the anthology.'

After a brief pause, George began:

'"*This is the work of a man who has a clear vision of the things he writes about, and not one who looks at the world through half closed eyes or through a distorting lens."*' He paused. 'But the best bit comes at the end: "*It is the kind of writing which will live.*"'

'He goes on to single out your first poem, *'The Prayer for Rain'*, as the best one in the book! Well done Alfred, you're now officially a poet.'

'But that's not all,' said Mary, 'have you seen this?' She held out a copy of the Daily Mail to Alfred.

'They're calling you '*the Hammerman Poet*'.

Alfred read through the article and gave a wry smile.

'They talk as though they have just witnessed a rare type of animal for the first time, parading me around like some sort of sideshow act,' Alfred muttered, his brow furrowed as he leafed through the newspaper clipping.

George, however, saw opportunity where Alfred saw exploitation.

JOHN CULLIMORE

'Nonsense, my boy,' he exclaimed, his eyes twinkling with ambition, 'this publicity could be the key to unlocking your true potential.'

With a plan forming in his mind, George made a suggestion.

'You need support. So, use the momentum from this publicity to reach out to a powerful patron. And I think I know just the man—Lord Edmond Fitzmaurice. His estate is in Wiltshire, he has connections in Parliament, and a good track record of supporting the arts.'

'We'll send him a selection of your finest poetry, and dedicate it to him personally,' George continued.

'With his support, we can then at least be certain of publication, an essential step towards you receiving the recognition you deserve.'

'You mean financial support? It costs a lot to publish.'

Alfred was initially hesitant, unsure if the path his uncle proposed was the right one. Yet, deep down, he knew that his words had something meaningful to offer. He also felt that poetry had limited appeal in the industrial setting of Swindon and therefore he should try to reach the widest possible audience.

'I'll write to Lord Fitzmaurice tomorrow,' said Alfred, grinning.

'Oh, and there's one more thing for you.' Mary handed him a letter postmarked London. He opened it, read through it and smiled to himself.

'Are you going to share this news?'

'I've been invited to a poet's meeting…in Holborn, they want me to read some of my work.'

THE PALACE OF MY IMAGINATION

Chapter 18

1910

Alfred found himself thrust into the spotlight when his remarkable journey of self-education captured the attention of newspapers across the nation. From the confines of his workplace, he had pursued knowledge with unwavering dedication, going on to develop his skills as a poet to the point of national recognition.

In February, Alfred received an invitation that would mark a turning point in his life. Reuben George, the esteemed secretary of the Swindon branch of the Workers' Educational Association (WEA), and Mayor of Swindon extended an invitation for Alfred to speak at their forum. It was an opportunity to share his story of self-education and to inspire others on their own paths of learning.

The lecture hall buzzed with excitement on that cold February evening. The air was charged with anticipation as members of the Institute and curious townsfolk filled the hall. The stage was adorned with simple decorations, and the dimmed lights lent an air of solemnity to the occasion.

As the clock struck seven, Mayor George stepped onto the stage, greeted by a round of applause. Dressed in his finest attire, and adorned by chains of office, he radiated an air of authority and warmth. Clearing his throat, he addressed the eager audience.

'Ladies and gentlemen, esteemed members of the Workers Educational Institute, it is my great pleasure to welcome you all this evening. Tonight, we have the privilege of hosting a remarkable individual whose journey of self-learning and literary prowess has captured the attention of our nation.'

A murmur of anticipation rippled through the crowd as Reuben George continued.

'Our guest speaker this evening is none other than Alfred Williams, whose remarkable story serves as an inspiration to us all. From the forges of heavy industry to the heights of poetic creativity, Alfred's journey exemplifies the transformative power of education and determination.'

Applause filled the hall as Mayor George gestured for Alfred to join him on stage. Alfred, clad in a simple yet dignified attire, stepped forward, greeted by a warm reception from the audience.

Alfred recognized Uncle George, a reassuring presence, sitting in the third row from the front, smiling proudly in Alfred's direction.

'Thank you, Mayor George, esteemed members of the institute, and fellow citizens of Swindon,' Alfred began, his voice steady and resonant. 'It is truly an honour to stand before you tonight. My journey, like many of yours, has been one of perseverance and self-discovery.'

'Swindon is extremely fortunate to have this institute which provides educational resources for the working man. For this reason and given that my recent notoriety has arisen as a result of my own programme of self-education, I thought I would talk to you on the subject of *'How to study'*, in the hope that what I say may be useful for all aspiring students in Swindon working to improve their knowledge.'

'But first I think it's important to pose the question, why study? And I'd like to hear your views. So can I pose a general question?'

'What has the process of studying done for you?'

'Don't be shy - there are no right or wrong answers here, it's just your views I seek.'

A hand went up.

'It's provided opportunities for me in terms of my profession, and I suppose it's helped me to be more organised and much better at critical thinking.' said a voice from the middle of the hall.

'Thankyou' said Alfred as he made a quick note on his lecture pad.

From the centre of the room came another voice.

'As you may know, I'm blind, and without having studied braille…well, where would I be?' Alfred recognised Lou Robins, an old and trusted friend.

Alfred smiled, thanked him and made a further note.

'I'm one of the factory engineers. We've just had delivery of

THE PALACE OF MY IMAGINATION

new fire extinguishers recently, and I've had to gen up on those.'

'Thank you for all those comments. Clearly your reasons for learning are professional and practical, or pragmatic or related to varying everyday concerns you have about your lives or your environment.'

'And of course I acknowledge these are very important reasons to study. I too, learned my work at the forge for practical and professional reasons. But for me there's another dimension to studying which I want to share with you.' Alfred paused briefly and drank a little water.

'For me the act of learning has transcended the mere acquisition of information for the purposes we just mentioned.'

'For me, learning has become a deeply enriching and transformative experience.'

'Again, for me, the impact of learning is as inspiring and as valuable as viewing beautiful works of art.'

'Does this surprise you?'

Many of the audience smiled, some nodded, some shook their heads, but it was clear they were captivated by Alfred's opening words.

'Now, if you believe my contention that the process of study can do this, it explains rather well why I do what I do'

'Assuming then you approve of the concept of 'study,' we should discuss the right and wrong ways to approach it. Firstly, the right way.'

'Let's take the example of a Surgeon, who must study his craft in order to be able to operate on humans safely and quickly. His skill has been refined through specific education involving essential anatomical and physiological sciences but also repeated practice over time in a variety of settings. This is just one of a world of examples of what we can call 'cultivated facility' which is developed rather than innate.'

'What about the wrong way to learn something? Let's say you want to learn to speak French. You decide that you can gain all you need to know from books. You proceed laboriously through a textbook from cover to cover. But your efforts are doomed to failure. You may have learned grammar and vocabulary, but you haven't had any opportunity to apply the knowledge to create original new sentences.'

'So, in this instance, a more strategic approach is needed.'

'Let's just consider the word "study." This is derived from a Latin word "studium." Do any of you who may have studied Latin remember its meaning?'

Nobody replied but there was some audible sighing and some shoulder shrugging, and expressions of mirth.

'It means zeal or purpose. We should probably call it *Motivation*. And this is the first thing we should think about.'

'Motivation is necessary to get you to work, and especially in those times when you struggle your way through difficulties, motivation gets you through.'

'So, ask yourself, "What is my motivation?" —because you need a clear purpose. Either voice it to yourself or, better still, write it down.'

'My motivation to study Latin, was initially somewhat vague. Indeed, I was advised to study the language by someone in this audience who thought it might facilitate my understanding of literature. And when I did go on to studying English Literature of the 16th and 17th century, I discovered it was beset with Latin footnotes, so obviously it would be a good idea to study this to be better informed.'

'But sometime after this, my motivation became much clearer and much more powerful. What I was really desperate to do was to read Caesar's accounts of the invasion of Britain in their original form. I wanted to be there with him as he recounted setting foot on English soil. That newfound motivation completely transformed my approach to studying. What once felt like tedious drills in mastering grammar suddenly became key steps in unlocking doors to understanding—a depth of insight I could hardly have imagined before.'

'Having decided on your motivation, the next things to consider are: starting points and time. Start slowly. If you need a book, buy the smallest and simplest text, which should preferably be of an

THE PALACE OF MY IMAGINATION

introductory nature. Please don't invest in elaborate volumes.'

'Don't strive for rapid advancement. Look upon your sojourn as analogous to climbing a distant hill. When you start on your journey, it looks very high. But if you proceed unhurriedly, the ground rises imperceptibly and your energy levels are not seriously depleted, and as you advance further the summit appears more and more achievable.'

'And when at last you stand on the summit, you think it was very easy after all, and wonder why you ever had any doubts as to climbing it,'

'But do give yourself time, and go gently or as some would say 'gently make haste' or if you love the Latin like I do, the correct translation is '*Festina Lent*e.''

'Don't go too fast, or you'll be overwhelmed.'

'Set yourself realistic goals. If necessary, ask for advice on these from a tutor. And of course, if you get stuck with anything, ask for help. You don't need me to tell you that here at the institute, your queries may not be totally resolved, but I feel sure you would be pointed in the right direction to achieve the help you need.'

'A few final pieces of advice:'

'Exercise the memories you have recently learned; otherwise, you won't retain them. I believe it was Aristotle who said, "We are what we repeatedly do." Thus, excellence is not an act, but is achieved through habit.'

'If you can, do these acts of mentally reverting to your subject as often as you can. Start to cultivate a habit of doing this.'

'Consider giving yourself a timetable of study and stick to it. Have a momentary reflection on your subject matter before delving into it, and reflect again, as a summary on finishing.'

'Choose a quiet secluded setting for your learning, where you can receive the intensity of the message, and thereby immerse yourself in a world of thought. If you like, living contentedly in the palace of your own imagination.'

The audience responded warmly to this imagery, smiling and exchanging murmured remarks.

'Try to enjoy the act of learning. If you derive pleasure from the learning process it will inevitably feel easier, and you will achieve more.'

'And last of all—keep at it. You must allow for the fact that there will be days when you feel drained of enthusiasm, or distracted by some concern you may have unrelated to learning. We are not always fit to learn, so don't chide yourself on such days. However, if you do feel the motivation, take that opportunity and cultivate it as you would a plant.'

'I hope my talk has fired you with enthusiasm for learning, and I sincerely hope that I haven't come across as too dogmatic. These are my personal views, and my methods may not work for everyone, but they worked for me.'

'I'd be very interested in hearing things that have helped you in your quest to improve your knowledge which I may not have mentioned.'

'On that note, I will stop talking and welcome any comments or questions you may have.'

Alfred stood at the lectern, feeling a mix of relief and satisfaction after delivering his speech. There was a brief moment of silence that seemed to hang in the air.

But then, like the breaking of a wave, the silence was shattered by a swell of warm applause. The audience, obviously moved by his words, erupted into enthusiastic clapping, their appreciation palpable in the air. Alfred couldn't help but smile as he stood there, basking in the moment.

Reuben George, approached Alfred with a broad grin, extending his hand in congratulations. 'Well done, Alfred,' he said, his voice carrying over the applause. 'That was a most entertaining and thought-provoking speech.'

He nodded in acknowledgment of Reuben's words, feeling a sense of accomplishment wash over him.

Reuben then turned to address the audience once more, his voice commanding attention as he spoke.

'As there don't seem to be any spontaneous questions,' he said, 'I suggest we allow Alfred to join us for refreshments with the committee. And let me say, we look forward to the next time

THE PALACE OF MY IMAGINATION

Alfred addresses the WEA.'

The applause continued as Alfred made his way off the stage, feeling buoyed by the warmth and appreciation of the audience. As he mingled with the members of the committee, exchanging pleasantries and engaging in lively conversation, he couldn't help but feel grateful for the opportunity to share his knowledge and insights with such a receptive audience.

George proceeded to introduce Alfred to the committee members. Firstly, his old friend Lou Robins, known for his keen intellect and warm spirit. Lou had once toiled alongside Alfred in the factory, but the onset of blindness had instigated his journey from shop floor to shopkeeper and campaigner for the disabled in Swindon. Alfred was delighted to renew his acquaintance.

Next, he recognised Henry Byett, with whom he had had previous dealings in the factory. Henry was the accounting manager from the office at the factory, and he had been the first to respond to Alfred's question to the audience at the start of his presentation. His quiet demeanour belied a keen intellect and a deep appreciation for the power of education.

There was no need to introduce Uncle George who took him into a warm embrace.

'I was so proud of you, Alfred' he said, a slight moistness in his eyes belying his emotion.

And then there was Reuben George himself, a towering figure in Swindon's social and educational circles. Though he made his living as an insurance salesman, George's passion for education and social reform had earned him a place of respect and admiration in the community. Furthermore, he was well connected with members of the aristocracy and other influential figures, and George was already thinking to himself how he could exploit these contacts in the promotion of Alfred's literary career.

And as the evening came to a close, these four influential men convened in private to discuss Alfred's future. They resolved to lend him their support and guidance, recognizing his potential to inspire and uplift others through his words and actions.

JOHN CULLIMORE

Chapter 19

April 1910

Because of a scaling back of activity, the factory had implemented short time working and so was no longer operating on Saturdays. Alfred found himself faced with an unexpected reprieve.

On his first free Saturday morning for some years, Mary and Alfred embraced the opportunity to venture out on a sunny morning. With Alfred carrying a wicker basket containing a picnic, they set off to ramble across the rolling hills, the crisp morning air filling their lungs.

By mid-morning they had climbed to the ancient Iron age fort on the crest of Liddington Hill, and now seated on a blanket, they shared their meal of eggs, bread and cheese as they gazed over the fertile plains to the north, the idyllic view stretching miles to a clear blue northern horizon.

'We should do this more often,' said Mary.

'I could ask them to let me have every Saturday free, but it would mean less money.'

'Well, it can only be good for you to spend less time in that unhealthy place. And it would give you more time for your written work. Besides, we can manage with a bit less,' said Mary.

'By the way you've not told me about the meeting in London, how did it go?'

'Not quite as I'd hoped. I arrived late and had to leave early. They still hadn't got round to calling me up when I had to leave for the last train back to Swindon.'

'So, a waste of time then?'

'No, I met some interesting people. Particularly the Daily Mail reporter, who wrote the newspaper article about me. He had a very interesting idea. He suggested that I should write a book about working in the GWR factory. He believes the public would be very interested in an informed account of the working conditions inside

THE PALACE OF MY IMAGINATION

the factory. And he said he could more or less guarantee it would be published.'

'But haven't you got enough on your plate with your poetry and your learning?'

'Well, the fact is, I started writing about the factory soon after I joined. It's all there in my diaries; it just needs organising. And it carries an important message worth sharing.'

'But is it the right thing to do? You might upset some important people.'

'You're right, love, it's a warts-and-all account. I couldn't publish it while I'm working there. I'd be sacked immediately, and I daresay we'd have to leave the area. There'll come a time for it, but not yet. It's something for the future. I'm going to stay in touch with the reporter.'

'But I do have some good news,'

'Lord Fitzmaurice has replied to my letter. He seems to like my poems. He congratulates me on being included in the recent poetry anthology. And more encouragingly, he's been in touch with one of the directors of a new publishing venture and has encouraged them to publish a complete volume of my poems.'

'Alfred that's wonderful.'

'And what's more, Lord Fitzmaurice has selected the poems he feels are worthy of publication and has offered himself as guarantor.'

Mary looked a little puzzled.

'That means, if the book makes a loss, he will cover the excess costs to the publisher.'

'Well, if that isn't a huge vote of confidence in you, I don't know what is!'

'All I have to do, says Lord Fitzmaurice, is choose a title for the volume.'

'So, what do you have in mind?'

'I'm going to call it *'Songs in Wiltshire.'*

***

Just as Alfred had begun to relish his newfound freedom, and enjoy some early literary successes, the factory announced that full-time work would resume after three quiet months. Disheartened by the thought of returning to the grind, Alfred mustered the courage to approach management with a bold proposition—he would willingly take a pay cut if it meant he could continue to have Saturdays off.

He was pleasantly surprised when Henry Byett agreed to his written request. However, when Grubb heard of this, he resolved to seize every opportunity to curtail Alfred's freedom and summoned him to work the following Saturday.

'These furnaces need cleaning out,' said Grubb 'and when you're through with that, the hammers need lubricating. I've called in Gustavus to help you, and one of the boys.'

Alfred bit back his indignation as he realised that one of the furnaces on Grubb's list hadn't been used for the last four days and was already primed for forging. And the second furnace should have been cleared yesterday evening, but Grubb had taken the unusual step of sending the workers home straight after the last forging. Alfred now understood the cynical motive behind this decision.

Alfred saw Gustavus making his way from the entrance to the workshop. Alongside him was one of the furnace boys, Teddy.

He was surprised to see Gustavus as he had heard that he had been recently admitted to the GWR Medical Fund hospital. His breathing seemed slightly laboured and he appeared gaunt and pale.

'You don't look as though you should be back at work,' said Alfred.

'Well, the doctor has said I can return to work, but I still feel exhausted. One of the children has been ill so I've not slept much. Of course, Grubb knows what the doctor has said and he's insisting that I come back, so I've not been given a choice,' replied Gus hoarsely.

'Grubb owns the house I live in, and I've not been able to pay him rent in the last two weeks as I've been ill. He's threatening us with eviction if I don't pay him by the end of next week. So, he offered me a double shift. It should give me enough to get him off

THE PALACE OF MY IMAGINATION

my back.'

'But who's looking after your children?'

'I've got a nice neighbour who'll look in on them in the late evening and early morning. They should be fine.'

Alfred sympathised with the plight of the weakened man. His wife had died tragically a few months previously from an infection after a difficult childbirth. Gustavus was having to be mother and father to his three young children and clearly wasn't coping.

Like Alfred, Gustavus was one of the workers whom Grubb loved to terrorise. Although a few of the forgemen had begun to resent Alfred and his attitude towards them, Gustavus was not one of those. And this loyalty to Alfred was in all likelihood an additional reason to single him out for victimisation.

'Look Gus, I'll do all the heavy work, and Teddy can empty the barrows. Why don't you make a brew for us, and then you can take your time changing the oil on the hammers. With a bit of luck, Grubb won't stick around after this morning, so you should be able to take it easy from the afternoon. Oh, and I'd be happy to look in on the children for you this evening on my way home.'

It was nearly six o'clock and the shift had almost finished. Fortunately, Gustavus was able to leave at five. That left Alfred and Teddy to do the clearing up.

After finishing Alfred walked out of the factory in the direction of the bicycle shed, with the small figure of Teddy trailing behind him. He was no more than ten years old, an inch or two short of four feet tall, covered in grime and hobbling with each step.

Concern etched across his face, Alfred stopped in his tracks and turned to the boy.

'What's the matter, lad?'

The boy looked up at him with weary eyes, and tears glistening in the corners.

'It's me boots, sir,' he said, his voice barely a whisper. Alfred's heart sank at the sight. He knelt beside the boy, his own exhaustion momentarily forgotten. The boots were completely soleless and Teddy's feet were red raw.

'Tell me, Teddy, where do you live?'

JOHN CULLIMORE

The boy hesitated, then spoke in a soft, trembling voice.
'Crombie street, sir.'
'Well, you're in luck, I've got my bike here, and if you're happy to sit on the crossbar I can give you a lift home.'
Teddy gratefully accepted.
Hoping to be able to give the little wretch something Alfred reached into his pocket, only to find it empty. Guilt washed over him as he realised he had nothing more to offer the boy.
'I'm sorry, Teddy,' he said, his voice heavy with regret. 'I wish I could help you more, but I'm afraid I'm penniless at the moment.'
Teddy nodded understandingly, his eyes downcast.
'It's all right, sir. I'm very grateful to you for taking me home.'
They set off on Alfred's bike with the boy perched on the crossbar. He was tiny and light as a feather, so pedalling was no problem for Alfred.
Determined to make a difference, Alfred racked his brain to try to find a way to help Teddy. Though his pockets may have been empty, his heart was filled with compassion.

***

'You look so tired, and so deflated, What's wrong?' asked Mary.
Alfred recounted the story of his day, focusing mainly the issue of poor Teddy and his injured feet.
'As we were cycling to his home I asked about his family situation. His father passed away last year, and his mum's always out working, charring in the day and working in a public house in the evenings. His elder sister does most of the childcare in the day for the baby and also in the evenings for the two younger sisters who are at school. Teddy has to work to support his family.'
Alfred felt a lump form in his throat he recounted Teddy's struggles. He couldn't imagine the burden the child carried on his young shoulders, and he couldn't shake the image of the boy's tear-stained face from his mind.
Mary looked thoughtful.
'Just one moment,' she said.

THE PALACE OF MY IMAGINATION

She disappeared out of the back door and soon after Alfred heard a shrill knocking on his neighbour's door.

Alfred sat back in the armchair feeling weary to his bones, and just as he was drifting off to sleep, the door opened, and Mary entered clutching a small pair of boots and smiling broadly.

'Fortunately, Uncle George had a spare pair of his son's boots which he'd hung on to. He insisted we took them.'

'Good old Uncle George,' said Alfred. 'I'll drop them off at Teddy's house first thing in the morning.'

'And while you're about it you can take some eggs with you, our hens have been laying nonstop, and we've more than enough for ourselves.'

Alfred was pleased that he could help in some small way, but then sighed heavily, and began staring into space.

'Is everything else all right?' asked Mary, sensing Alfred's unease.

'It's that damn factory and what it does to people—especially that poor little boy. I feel wretched about it. Some days, I'm not sure how much more I can take.'

'You know how I feel about it,' Mary replied. 'And you were so much brighter and healthier after a few weeks away from the place.'

'I know,' he said, rubbing the back of his neck. 'It's taken a toll on me, no doubt. The smoke, the stench, the heat—it's all relentless. But it's the monotony that gnaws at me the most. Wears me down bit by bit.'

'But Alfred, you've always found ways to escape. You have your beloved countryside right here, on your doorstep.'

'I do,' he admitted, his voice softening. 'And I'm grateful for it—more than I can say. But it doesn't feel right to enjoy that freedom knowing how trapped my workmates are. They spend all their time in that shed, and it's like the place swallows them whole. Any passions they once had—their ambitions, their interests—it's all dulled by exhaustion and the need to scrape by.'

Mary hesitated. 'So, they've lost all their spark?'

Alfred sighed. 'Not all. Some still find solace in things like sport or gambling,' he said carefully, his tone more reflective than dismissive. 'But for most, the factory leaves little room for anything else. And it's not their fault. They're too worn down to think beyond survival.'

'But isn't that why the Mechanics' Institute is there? Couldn't education open doors for them?'

'For a few, maybe,' he said, his expression pensive. 'But what they need more than books is adequate rest and leisure time. And they need to feel secure in their jobs, to know they're more than just cogs in a machine. Instead, they're forced to bow and scrape to overseers who treat them like expendable parts.'

'What about the unions?' Mary pressed, 'Surely they can help?'

'For the skilled workers, maybe—engineers, fitters, the ones with higher wages and more bargaining power. But the unskilled workers? There's no one fighting for them. And even the unions that do exist are divided, with some members more interested in tearing the system down than improving lives in the here and now.'

Mary frowned. 'It sounds like there are problems on all sides. Some of your overseers sound cruel, but are the workers truly as apathetic as you say? Maybe they just lack the confidence—or the opportunity—to speak up, like you do.'

Alfred looked at her, surprised by her insight. 'You might be right,' he admitted after a moment, 'I've made suggestions, but I know I don't fit the mould. I'm one of them, yet... not quite. Maybe that's why they don't listen—or why they resent me for trying.'

Mary nodded. 'You're exceptional, Alfred, and you see things differently. But that also makes you stand out. It's no wonder some might feel threatened by your ideas, even if they're good ones.'

Her words struck him, and he fell silent, gazing at the floor. Mary watched him carefully, wondering what was going through his mind. He finally looked up, a wry smile tugging at the corner of his mouth.

'You've given me something to think about,' he said quietly. 'Maybe... maybe I need to find a better way to reach them. Less like a lecturer and more like one of their own.'

It was a rare moment of humility, and Mary felt a flicker of hope

THE PALACE OF MY IMAGINATION

that Alfred might begin to bridge the gap between himself and his fellow workers. Yet, deep down, she couldn't help but wonder if he could ever truly adjust enough to find lasting contentment in his current world.

'Oh, Alfred,' she said gently, 'you can't fix everything on your own. But you need to think about yourself too. If the factory is wearing you down this much, maybe it's time to consider something else. You've worked on the farms, and that didn't seem to suit you. So, is there anything else that calls to you, my love?'

Alfred leaned back; his brow furrowed in thought. For a moment, he seemed far away, as though turning over a hidden corner of his mind. Then, gradually, a smile spread across his face—broad, almost boyish.

'I think you may have just given me an idea.'

JOHN CULLIMORE

PART 4: DISAFFECTION

Chapter 20

Summer in the forge was indeed the most challenging time of the year. On a hot sunny day, the added difficulty of labouring by working furnaces, boilers and white-hot metal took its toll on the workforce. Many men collapsed in this environment and their fellows had to carry them out of the workshop to be revived. Those who suffered less acutely from the excess heat were frequently seen hosing each other down or jumping into tanks of water standing near the furnaces. No one in Alfred's gang could escape the conditions.

When Alfred took his turn as hammer driver, even though he was a little further away from the heat than his other colleagues, the smoke and fumes from the oil and grease placed in the dies to cleanse the metal drifted directly towards him and gradually rose up from ground level irritating his eyes and air passages.

On sweltering summer days like this, the challenge of controlling the heat applied to metal became even more difficult. The intense temperatures raised the risk of accidents, as the margin for error narrowed with the increased danger of overheating. In the stifling heat of this Saturday morning, the atmosphere in the factory felt especially oppressive as the day shift prepared to relieve the exhausted night workers, who were just finishing their final forging.

It was a routine transition, but the conditions made everyone uneasy. As Alfred's team readied themselves to begin their first forging of the day, a sudden, deafening explosion shattered the already tense air. The blast came from one of the adjacent large hammers, sending shockwaves through the workshop. In an instant, the factory was thrown into chaos.

Without a moment's hesitation, Alfred dropped what he was doing and sprinted toward the source of the sound.

When Alfred arrived, he was confronted with a chaotic and grim

THE PALACE OF MY IMAGINATION

scene. A man lay motionless on the ground, unconscious and bleeding, surrounded by jagged metal fragments scattered across the floor. His heart sank as he recognised the figure—it was Joe. Panic gripped him, but there was no time to hesitate. He and Jack immediately rushed to Joe's side.

The sight of Joe's injuries was horrifying. A large, gaping wound marred the upper right side of his neck, and from the back of his head, a mass of grey tissue, bone, and clotted blood was visible. The severity of the damage was shocking, and it was clear that Joe was gravely injured.

Working carefully, they turned Joe onto his side, and Jack quickly slipped his coat beneath his head for support. Alfred, fighting the rising dread in his chest, grabbed a towel and pressed it firmly against the wound at the base of Joe's neck, trying to stem the flow of blood that was pouring out. Every second felt like an eternity as they waited for skilled help to arrive, aware that Joe's breathing was becoming increasingly irregular.

Some of the gang had run off to summon the ambulance men from the offices.

Despite the severity of the situation, no one else appeared to have been injured severely in the blast, although two others who had been in the vicinity of the hammer had suffered minor injuries and appeared shocked and disorientated.

Seconds later the foreman arrived on the scene, summoned by the explosive blast.

Grubb reacted in a characteristically autocratic and distinctly unhelpful manner.

'Stand back all you men. He needs air. Get back, you're suffocating him!'

The gang stared incredulously at Grubb, but the pair administering first aid refused to budge.

'You'd better move now, or I'll get the hose on you!' cried Grubb almost hysterically.

Although many of the men shifted uncomfortably at Grubb's bizarre reaction, still none moved away or broke the silence.

At that moment the ambulance men arrived with a stretcher.

JOHN CULLIMORE

Grubb was reluctant to stand aside until one of the ambulance men angrily told him to give them room. As they lifted the injured man on to the stretcher, they insisted that Alfred maintain the pressure on the wound and that he accompany them on the transfer to the infirmary. Grubb now stood some yards from the casualty and the ambulancemen. He was seething with anger, his authority summarily ignored by all and sundry.

The stretcher party left and most of the men followed the rescue party on their way out of the workshop.

It soon became clear what had happened: during the forging process, one of the dies had exploded upon impact with the hammer, sending searing metal shards flying in all directions. Joe, unfortunately, had been the closest to the blast, and a large fragment had struck him with full force.

Grubb stayed near the forge and surveyed the scene. Blood and small metal fragments were spread wide over the floor adjacent to the steam hammer. He examined the fractured upper die which showed an irregular deficiency, although its identification number was still recognisable on the part of the surface that remained intact. A few feet from it lay a sharp pointed fragment, about nine inches in length, weighing five or six pounds, lying in a pool of clotted blood.

He felt uneasy as he recalled an argument with Alfred about a damaged die. The chargeman Barrett had also been involved, and some of the gang had probably overheard them.

He'd got the die in question moved from Alfred's furnace to another and thought no more about it.

He picked up the fragment with a rag and stopped to think. But after a few seconds he decided to cast the fragment into roaring flames of the adjacent furnace. He reasoned that, as with the lethal fragment, he could make the whole situation melt away.

He would tell the chargeman and gang to keep quiet if they were asked anything. Most of them depended on him for their accommodation, overtime work and promotion, so they'd probably toe the line, having too much to lose to speak up. Thus, he reassured himself that in the event of any subsequent inquiry,

THE PALACE OF MY IMAGINATION

he would be immune from any criticism.

At the infirmary the news was grim. Within minutes of arrival Joe was pronounced dead.

***

Some days later, production at the steam hammer resumed, with Alfred reluctantly assuming the role of Senior Forgeman-elect. And while his position hadn't been verified contractually, the team clearly looked to him for guidance in the wake of Joe's passing.

The following week, the senior manager, Henry Byett toured the steam hammer shop with foreman, Grubb.

He observed closely the efficiency and output of Alfred's team and was impressed by Alfred's grasp of his responsibilities. However, Grubb, with a look of hatred on his face, expressed reservations about Alfred's leadership.

'Williams is young and naturally brimming with self-confidence, but he assumed the responsibility of leadership without consulting anyone, and production hasn't exactly been high since the accident.'

'Well, I suppose somebody had to assume responsibility after that terrible accident, and it appears from here that Williams and his team are performing very well,' replied Byett.

'Yes, but I would have expected production to be back to normal by now, but it just isn't,' Grubb responded glumly.

'It's probably because Williams goes too easy on the men, you'll never keep the wage bill down if he's in charge.'

Byett recalled that Alfred had impressed the directors at the time of the Conciliation committee, and he was also conscious of his growing reputation as a scholar and poet.

'I'm surprised to hear you say that about Williams. It strikes me he is clever and inventive. He seems like the sort of individual who could improve manufacturing processes, and spot natural efficiencies. We consider such changes as more important than simply pegging back wages.'

'Nevertheless, I have a man in mind who I believe is more experienced and would be better suited to the role.'

Byett was somewhat taken aback by Grubb's attitude and felt he should speak directly to Alfred.

'We were all very sorry to hear about Joe, and you seem to be running things well from where I'm standing, but I'm hearing some concern that it may be somewhat early to consider further promotion for you. Recent events seem to have had an impact on output.'

'I understand your concerns, Sir and it might help if I explain a few things,' replied Alfred, who seemed grateful for the opportunity to talk over the tragic events.

'On that fateful day as he lay dying, Jack and I were with him in his last minutes in the infirmary. Joe handed me letters to be taken to his wife and to Mr. Churchward,'

'Like many of us, he'd prepared these, in the event of just such an accident. It was then that Joe suggested I could be his immediate successor, urging us to waste as little time as possible in getting things back on track.'

'I delivered the letters that day. Firstly, to his wife Bess. She was so upset, and insisted I read Joe's letter which was such a heartfelt loving tribute to his wife and family.' Alfred paused as the sad memory of the encounter was relived.

'And that took me up till lunchtime.'

'Then I went to Mr. Churchward's office and explained everything. I saw his secretary who said she'd get back to me in due course. She called me in on the following Monday morning while we were preparing the furnace, and Mr.Churchward passed on his sympathy. He said he'd read Joe's letter and in it, apparently, he did urge that I be considered for promotion at some stage. He thanked me for my efforts and said the directors would consider this in due course, and that I should feel optimistic about my future career in the factory.'

'He also said that the team should take the Monday off as a sign of respect for our fallen comrade.'

Later that day, Byett took Grubb to one side saying.

'Well, I for one am entirely satisfied with Williams' answers. His conduct and his obvious ability seem exemplary.'

'Well indeed, sir, I am pleased to hear you say that, for it is not

THE PALACE OF MY IMAGINATION

pleasant to think that a workman might have neglected his duties,' replied Grubb in his characteristic sneering and disingenuous tone. 'Nevertheless, I would still recommend Tom Barratt as my first choice as the next senior forgeman.'

Grubb quickly excused himself and went off to inspect another part of the workshop.

Byett sensed Grubb's hostility towards Alfred and decided to explore this further.

'Can I ask, Alfred, if you are satisfied with Grubb as your foreman?'

'Well sir, in the sense of him carrying out his foreman duties conscientiously, I can't criticise him. But from the point of view of being a comrade? No, I am not satisfied with that relationship. We had a disagreement concerning the shortage of protective gloves for my workmates, and some equipment issues. It's clear to me he's never liked me since then.'

'Would you be able to work with Barrett as your immediate senior?'

'I'm afraid I don't know him well sir, he seems mainly restricted to the drop stampers. But if the company appoint him then of course I will do my utmost to work as part of his team and hope to go on improving.' Alfred declined to add that Grubb and Barrett were clearly in cahoots in a nefarious scheme.

'But would you accept promotion if you were offered it. I happen to know there is a post becoming available in the boiler shop?'

Alfred thought about this for a moment and responded.

'It's most flattering to hear you raise the question, Sir - However, since my poetry and writing have taken off, I'm considering all my options at the present time, but for now I'm happy to stay where I am.'

Tubby began waving at Alfred as the heat of the furnace reached optimal levels.

'I'm sorry but I must go and supervise the next forging. Thanks for talking to me—I'm always at your disposal, Mr. Byett.'

Watching him go, Byett felt sure that Alfred would be right for the job of Senior Forgeman. He certainly didn't understand Alfred's reticence. Likewise, he didn't fully understand Grubb's attitude, but given the situation he didn't believe he was in a position to override his recommendation for Barrett.

A pity, he thought, but having read Alfred's published poetry he felt sure that it was only a matter of time before his literary talent and growing celebrity would lead him to a much brighter future outside the factory.

After finishing his forging, Alfred sat and reflected for a moment. He realised he hadn't given a full explanation to Byett when he asked about promotion. The reality of it was that his newfound literary ability was of overriding importance to him, and he wanted the rich vein of creativity that he had found to continue flowing, acknowledging that it had only happened in the context of his work at the forge.

He had also been told that the sales of his first poetry book had provided enough return to cover all his expenses, so he did not need to call on his patron to cover any financial loss. Perhaps he might get better rewards with subsequent efforts?

Despite the victimisation by Grubb and the isolation from his workmates, he still felt his current situation was one he should persist with if he could.

He thought back to his last conversation with Mary.

'You've got your beloved countryside on your doorstep,' he recalled her saying, after he had lamented the toxic oppressive environment he and his workmates suffered in Swindon.

He seemed to have concluded to his own satisfaction that urban life was associated with all that is noxious, not only in terms of the factory environment but what he saw as the corrupting effect it had on the quality of urban dwellers' lives outside work.

He felt sure that the rapid expansion of the railway network had contributed to the decline of rural traditions, replacing them with new forms of entertainment like cinemas and music halls, which he struggled to appreciate. While he respected his fellow workers' right to enjoy themselves, he couldn't help but feel a pang of regret as he saw wages spent on activities he personally found

THE PALACE OF MY IMAGINATION

unfulfilling, such as gambling on horse races.

On the other hand, his recollection of rural life was of a simpler, more wholesome, noble and virtuous existence.

Yes, their work was hard, but wasn't it true that few rustics seemed to live with the despair and helplessness suffered by town dwellers?

As he pondered these contrasting worlds, here was the germ of an idea. A work that would contrast his experiences in the factory with his nostalgic longing for life in the villages.

He would describe the people, their traditions, their history.

Wasn't this a worthy subject? Especially as the world was changing quickly, as the towns and cities expanded, rural lifestyle was threatened.

He had had some success with poetry, but he now realised this was a hard sell, and perhaps it was time to change tack, in an attempt to reach a wider audience. He resolved that his next publication would be a prose work. And what better subject could he choose than that of life in his own village, South Marston.

Chapter 21

Spring 1912

With the factory temporarily shut down, Alfred found himself with an unexpected stretch of free time. He saw this as an opportunity to launch the project he had long contemplated:
His account of life in the village.

He was uniquely qualified for this task, which would be more than just a collection of observations. It would be his own life story intertwined with the essence of South Marston, the village where he was born and raised, hence he could speak with unrivalled authority.

He decided that the book would cover various aspects of village life:

Its setting, traditions, noteworthy characters, and the rural industries that sustained the village. He began by sketching out an outline, planning to describe the picturesque setting of South Marston at the foot of the North Wiltshire Downs, and the rivers, railways, canals and roads that traversed it would receive a full description.

He thought how he could use the view from the platform in his sacred tree to launch into a lyrical description of the flora and fauna and the wildlife he had encountered in the district. He relished the idea of describing how the appearance of the countryside and output of the land varied as the seasons changed.

He would go on to describe village fairs, harvest festivals, and the annual celebrations that brought the community together, and the customs and traditions that had been passed down through generations as well as the various industries that sustained the rural economy, from farming and milling to weaving and carpentry.

As he wrote, Alfred realised that this book was not just about the village, his love for home, and his deep connection to the land; it was also about his own beliefs and how his experience of working in heavy industry had shaped them.

Alfred sincerely believed that the life of a rustic was the ideal existence. In contrast, he viewed those who lived in towns and cities, toiling in grim industrial surroundings, as little more than modern-day serfs. In his book, he resolved to pose a crucial question:

Was enduring such a poor quality of urban life worth the meagre benefit of a few extra shillings per week?

He felt a small ripple of pleasure as he noted that his writing would challenge the status quo and encourage a broader reflection on the true value of life. By highlighting the stark differences between rural and urban living, he was convinced that his readers would consider the intangible benefits of a simpler, more fulfilling existence.

He would craft passages depicting the serenity and inherent rewards of life in the countryside and contrast it with the harsh reality of industrial labour.

His rural descriptions must be vivid and enchanting, filled with the scents of blooming flowers, the sounds of chirping birds, and the sight of rolling green hills.

THE PALACE OF MY IMAGINATION

In the weeks that followed, Alfred derived significant satisfaction and pleasure from writing his book, which he had decided to call '*A Wiltshire Village.*'

Within ten weeks, he had renewed old acquaintances, made new ones, and learned considerably more about the village he loved.

He warmed to his theme, not only with his powers of description but also with his commitment to honesty.

He did not shy away from controversial issues, such as his belief that local farmers were not paying enough to their workers, and the story of the penniless old rustic whom, exhausted of financial resources, was literally dragged from his cottage to the Stratton workhouse, where he died a few days later.

Yet, the overall picture of life he painted was a rosy one, filled with the charm and simplicity of rural existence. Alfred's deep affection for the village was evident in every page.

He was keen to have Mary's assessment of his manuscript before sending it to his publisher. One evening, as the sun was setting and casting a golden hue over the fields, he handed her the thick sheaf of papers. Mary, seated by the window with her knitting, looked up and smiled.

'Here it is, Mary,' Alfred said, his eyes twinkling with a mix of excitement and nervousness. 'I've finished the manuscript. I'd love you to read it and tell me what you think.'

Over the next few days, Mary immersed herself in Alfred's writing and when she had finished the manuscript, she found Alfred in the garden, tending to his beloved roses.

Mary paused, looking deeply into Alfred's eyes.

'It's beautifully written, Alfred,' she said, handing back the manuscript. 'you've captured the essence of the village perfectly. It's heartfelt and so evocative.'

'Thank you, that's encouraging,' responded Alfred, a hint of relief in his voice, 'but from the look on your face, I think you have more to say.'

'Indeed, I do, but before doing so, I want to say again that it's a unique piece of work, and I'm sure Duckworth will publish it.'

'But?...,' asked Alfred, a broad smile spreading across his face.

JOHN CULLIMORE

'Well, I think you idealise life in the countryside,' Mary said gently. 'There is a lot of poverty and hardship in the village, and I feel you're underestimating it. You know how we've all struggled to get by.'

'Even your own experiences pushed you to seek work in the town. There are many families here who can't put food on the table for their children. Many of them don't have good sanitation in their cottages. Many of their children don't survive childhood.'

'And as regards the working life of a farmhand, that's just so uncertain. It's very seasonal: they can be laid off at a moment's notice, and they're completely at the mercy of the landowners. They have no security.'

Alfred nodded slowly, absorbing Mary's words.

'You're right, Mary. I've seen those struggles myself. Maybe I got carried away by my affection for the village and wanted to paint it in the best possible light.'

Mary continued.

'I found the chapter about the workhouse to be one of the most powerful and heart-rending in the book. But you seem to remain curiously neutral about the workhouse. Aren't you missing an opportunity to say something important?'

Alfred looked thoughtful.

'I wanted to let the facts speak for themselves, to allow readers to draw their own conclusions.'

'I understand that,' Mary said gently, 'but your disapproving view of the iniquities of town life and heavy industry comes across strongly in the book. Yet, it seems a paradox that you don't see the need to speak out against the injustices and cruelty of the workhouse system?'

Alfred was silent, though he saw that Mary had a point.

'Also, I think you can expect some negative reactions from the village, particularly from the vicar—you're sticking your neck out there. But as I said earlier,' continued Mary, smiling 'it's a wonderful piece of work and you can be proud of what you've achieved.'

Alfred submitted the manuscript to Duckworth a week later.

THE PALACE OF MY IMAGINATION

They responded within two weeks, confirming they would be delighted to publish it.

At the beginning of October, one hundred copies of the finished work arrived at Dryden Cottage, and all the published periodical reviews were encouraging.

Alfred was reinvigorated by the whole process and benefited from a new vein of inspiration by quickly composing another volume of poetic works.

By the end of the year, over five hundred copies of '*A Wiltshire Village*' had been sold and the positive reception from both critics and readers continued. Reuben George, Lou Robins and Henry Byett had written to him congratulating him on his efforts, and Uncle George had been first in to get a signed souvenir copy.

Having succeeded commercially with the book, Alfred found himself facing one unusually hostile reaction from within the village itself.

The local vicar, Reverend Angus McFadden, who had previously distinguished himself in Alfred's life by refusing to allow him to have his marriage banns read or his wedding celebrated in South Marston, had a close friendship with the Osney family. Their son had been rejected by Mary in favour of Alfred, which fuelled McFadden's disdain.

On a Sunday morning a couple of weeks after publication, the Very Reverend McFadden ascended the short stone stairs to the pulpit, towering above the congregation. He had been the vicar of Marston for over twenty years and wielded considerable influence in the local community.

McFadden had always felt justified in using his position of authority to publicly correct what he considered to be poor moral behaviour among his flock, and, with a complete lack of discretion, used his sermons to publicly shame those whose indiscretions and absences became known to him.

In short, he was a bully, exerting a strong negative influence on the simple villagers. He considered many of them to be misguided and had no qualms about the potential to cause harm to reputations and relationships, and to increase divisiveness within his community. Indeed, he was fully aware that such conduct only seemed to increase his hold over his congregation.

Clutching a copy of Alfred's book about the village and wearing a thunderous expression, McFadden rose to the pulpit.

George Ockwell, seated in the middle of the congregation, noticed the vicar's manner and felt his heart sink. Many of the villagers attending the service recognised the book. Some of them had been characterised in its pages and revelled in their minor celebrity, while others felt resentment at being left out.

George suspected that McFadden's apparent dissatisfaction was likely related to the chapter on the South Marston church and Alfred's portrayal of what he considered the over-paternalistic attitude of the vicar, as well as the dour, severe nature of his sermons.

Not only that, but Alfred's exposé of the Stratton workhouse had almost certainly ruffled feathers as McFadden was chairman of the management board.

'This book,' McFadden shouted, brandishing Alfred's work, 'about our village, is an affront to this village and to God.'

His voice boomed through the church, reverberating off the stone walls.

'I will not dignify the author by speaking his name in the house of God.'

'He should be filled with shame, for he has committed a mortal sin in publishing these ungodly observations. You must not read this book. To do so will corrupt you!'

Sweat glistened on McFadden's brow as his tirade continued, his volume rising with every sentence.

'If I see that any of you maintain possession of this demonic work, I will declare you to be in league with evil' thundered McFadden from the pulpit, his voice echoing through the shocked silent church.

The congregation shifted uncomfortably in their seats. As the vicar gazed down at them accusingly, few could meet his inquisitorial stare.

'And this is by no means the end of the matter,' McFadden

THE PALACE OF MY IMAGINATION

continued with righteous fury.

'There are two copies of this heretical work in our village that I know of,' he said, resting the book on the edge of the pulpit and pushing it away as though it were the source of infinite evil, 'this one and a second copy, which I erringly placed in the village reading room before I had fully appraised its contents.'

He paused, letting the weight of his words sink in.

'Suffice it to say, I will dispose of these offensive publications, in public, tomorrow. I advise any of you who possess a copy to bring it to the library at three o'clock, and I will gladly destroy it with the others.'

McFadden paused for dramatic effect before concluding.

'In the name of the Father, Son, and Holy Spirit.'

He then descended from the pulpit, his movements sharp and determined, resuming the service with a perfunctory air. His mind was clearly elsewhere, consumed by his mission to eradicate the offending book.

Communion was much abbreviated, and few came forward in the tense atmosphere. The congregation remained subdued; the usual reverence replaced by a palpable sense of unease. As the service ended, McFadden exited through the rear door, slamming it behind him with a force that matched the intensity of his unchecked temper.

The villagers left in a state of disquiet mixed with relief. They dispersed, quietly whispering among themselves about the vicar's furious condemnation and the book's impending death sentence, but relieved not to be the current focus of the cleric's ire.

After the service, George stood at the exit from the churchyard gazing out at the quaint village of South Marston. He could hardly believe what he had heard in the sermon. The autumn sunshine cast a warm glow over the narrow lanes and thatched cottages. But despite this idyllic setting, George's mind was troubled. The vicar's vehement reaction to Alfred's book and his proposal to remove it from the village library had struck a chord in him. He couldn't stand by and watch Alfred's right to free speech be trampled upon, and his reputation tarnished.

JOHN CULLIMORE

George grabbed his hat and coat, heading for the door. He knew exactly who could help—Tom Bradshaw, the editor of the Wilts and Glos Standard—Tom lived in the nearby village of Shrivenham, and George recalled that Tom habitually visited the Barrington Arms after the Sunday morning service. If he set off now, he might well catch him there.

***

At just before three o'clock on the following day, McFadden made his entrance to the South Marston library. He was accompanied by two individuals whom George Ockwell vaguely recognised but couldn't quite place.

Smiling broadly and clutching one of the copies of '*A Wiltshire Village*,' he and his party strode past the three other individuals, one of whom was George, grouped together outside the reading room.

McFadden and his party entered the reading room and seized the remaining copy of Alfred's book. As they exited, McFadden addressed the party outside.

'You are all welcome to come to the churchyard where I will dispose of these volumes.'

The party of six individuals now proceeded down the lane towards the church, with McFadden striding purposefully ahead. George winked at the two men who had been standing with him outside the library. As they reached the churchyard, George observed that McFadden had erected a small brazier emitting a glaring heat from red-hot charcoal fire placed a few yards in front of the church entrance.

As McFadden went inside to collect the other copy, he didn't pay much attention to the gardener who seemed to have been cleaning up the churchyard, stacking loose branches and leafy vegetation in a pile about five feet high at the side of the church to the right of the brazier. A small group of passing villagers lingered outside the church, curious to understand what was happening in front of them.

McFadden emerged from the church door now clasping two copies of Alfred's book. He paused by the fire and addressed the

THE PALACE OF MY IMAGINATION

six individuals.

'Are there any other copies you wish me to dispose of?'

A thin woman of about fifty years of age with a pale wrinkled face dipped into her handbag and walked forward to offer the contents to McFadden.

'Thank you, Mrs. Osney,' said McFadden with a smile, and she returned to stand next to the man who was clearly her husband. In that instant, George recognised the parents of Adam Osney.

Suddenly, everything made sense.

As McFadden made his apparent ritual sacrifice of the three books to the flames, the two individuals accompanying George moved off to the side. At the same time, the gardener raked the pile of vegetation to one side to reveal a camera ready assembled on top of a tripod.

With impeccable timing, as the books began to smoke and burn, one of the men slipped behind the camera to capture an image that included the flaming books, the vicar, and the Osneys.

'What the devil is going on?' erupted McFadden. He stepped back from the brazier, glaring at the camera and then at George.

The second of the as yet unidentified men stepped forward, his expression calm yet firm, and addressed McFadden.

'We're here representing the *Wiltshire and Gloucestershire Standard*.'

'Just ensuring that your actions are documented, Reverend. We believe it's in the public interest to report what's happening here today.'

The Reverend's face turned an even deeper shade of red.

'This is an outrage! How dare you undermine my authority in this sacred place!'

'Undermining your authority?' said the reporter raising an eyebrow, 'or simply holding you accountable for your actions? Don't the villagers deserve to know who stands against them and their stories?'

Mrs. Osney's face turned pale, and she tugged at her husband's sleeve, whispering urgently. Mr. Osney, equally unnerved, nodded in agreement, and they began to edge away from the group, clearly uncomfortable with the sudden turn of events, as the camera shutter clicked to record a second image.

McFadden, seeing his supporters wavering, tried to regain control.

'This is blasphemy. You cannot use the house of God to spread dissent and lies!'

'Some believe that burning books is the real blasphemy, Reverend,' replied the reporter, his voice steady, 'especially those books that recount the true stories of the people of this village.'

The small group of spectators, sensing the tension and the shifting power dynamics, began to murmur among themselves.

The vicar's eyes darted around, looking for an escape.

'This is not over,' he hissed, 'I will not tolerate this insolence.'

'Then we'll see how the public react.' said the reporter as the villagers continued to stare, shocked by the confrontation and the presence of the camera, documenting everything.

McFadden, realising he had lost the crowd, turned on his heel and marched back into the church, slamming the door behind him. The brazier continued to burn, but the symbolic power of the flames had shifted.

We won't let anyone silence true stories, thought George.

The reporter, the cameraman and the gardener, who was in fact also a junior reporter from the Standard, bid their farewells to George, advising him to watch for an article which should be in the next day's evening edition. George asked the reporters to pass on his thanks to their boss Tom Bradshaw.

***

Two days later, Alfred was horrified when George Ockwell presented him with the previous evening's edition of the Standard.

There, on the second page, below the headline *'Vicar Burns Controversial Book About Wiltshire Village,'* was the unmistakable image of McFadden, standing above what were clearly burning books. Below this ran a brief article explaining the vicar's objections to Alfred's book, as well as a summary of the unanimously positive reviews it had received in the national press. It concluded that the author, who was unaware of the events at the

THE PALACE OF MY IMAGINATION

church, was not available for comment.

Alfred stared at the article in disbelief.

'How did this happen?' he murmured. George shifted uneasily, his hands deep in his pockets.

'Well, McFadden was determined to make a spectacle of it,' George replied, 'But what he failed to appreciate was the interest of the story to the press.'

'But how did they find out?' asked Alfred feeling a mixture of anger and fear.

'I'm afraid I'm to blame for that,' confessed George. 'The story was bound have reached them somehow, but I felt it was better to be in control of the situation, rather than you having to react to it unexpectedly.'

'But isn't this going to cause even more trouble?' asked Alfred.

Suddenly the door opened, and Mary entered the room, her eyes widening as she saw the tension etched on Alfred's face.

'What's happened?' she asked, sensing the gravity of the situation.

Alfred handed her the newspaper, his heart heavy. As she read the article, her expression shifted from confusion to shock and then to anger.

'How dare he!' she exclaimed. 'He had no right to burn your book.'

'I know,' Alfred agreed, his distress obvious.

'I need to set the record straight. Maybe I should write directly to the editor. There's nothing I've written in that book that isn't anything more than opinions honestly expressed.'

Alfred paced the floor impatiently, while George remained seated and calm. After a brief pause, George responded.

'I would suggest you do nothing. You've absolutely nothing to be ashamed of.'

Alfred stopped pacing and sat down opposite George.

'In my opinion, a little controversy surrounding the book can only be a good thing. The publicity you've obtained is bound to be reflected in sales, you mark my words.'

'Well, I feel unhappy about the ill feeling generated.' responded

JOHN CULLIMORE

Alfred.

'But McFadden has behaved dishonourably and made a fool of himself, and that comes across in the article. He made no attempt to communicate his feelings to you and slandered you from the pulpit without actually naming you.

'He is beneath contempt, and he is the one to bear the shame. And what's more, this is the second time this so-called man of God has made life difficult for you. With a bit of luck, the story may be picked up by the national press, and then sales would really rocket.'

Alfred appreciated the truth of what George said, adding,

'You are right, George, but I'll not seek to inflame the situation further.'

'That's typical of your generosity, Alfred. There are many who would seize such an opportunity.'

Mary placed a comforting hand on Alfred's shoulder. 'You have always been honest and fair in your writings. The village knows that. Let this blow over, and truth will prevail.'

In the days that followed, the story did indeed gain traction beyond the village. Letters of support poured in from readers across the region who had read about the incident in the press. Sales of *A Wiltshire Village* surged as people became curious about the book that had sparked such a reaction.

Alfred, though still uncomfortable with the controversy, began to focus on his next project.

George's words had indeed proved prophetic. The controversy surrounding the book had boosted its popularity. Alfred received invitations to speak at regional literary events, and his work gained recognition far beyond the confines of South Marston.

One afternoon, George met with Tom Bradshaw, who revealed that there had been some interest from *The Times*, which seemed keen to run with the story. However, at the last minute, the interest evaporated. Bradshaw explained that he had come to understand that the editor of *The Times* had been leaned on by a high-ranking cleric in the Church of England to drop the story.

On seeing Alfred, George was incredulous.

THE PALACE OF MY IMAGINATION

'Can you believe it, Alfred? They must have felt threatened.'

'It's troubling, but I'm not surprised. The Church wields a lot of influence. Still, I'm relieved. While the added publicity would have been beneficial for book sales, I'm not comfortable with my work being used to sensationalise or attack individuals, even someone like McFadden.'

George sighed.

'I understand your perspective. But I still think people should know the truth.'

One day, some months later Alfred received a letter from an unexpected source. It was from Mrs. Osney, the same woman who had handed McFadden her copy of *A Wiltshire Village* to burn. She wrote to apologize for her actions, explaining that she had been influenced by McFadden and regretted her involvement. She admitted that after re-purchasing and re-reading the book properly, she found it to be a heartfelt and honest portrayal of the village.

Alfred showed the letter to George, who smiled.

'See, Alfred? Your integrity shines through.'

***

The success of the book induced him to consider a further prose work.

Next, he would extend his attentions to a locality rather than a single village. Yes, the area to the south, downland throughout, of unsurpassed beauty. He was aware that the villages of the region were some of the most ancient settlements in the land. They had been populated since prehistory and followed down the centuries by early Britons, Romans, Saxons, Danes and finally English. And all had left their traces in the villages at the foot of the Ridgeway Path, the *Villages of the White Horse.*

He felt a magical surge as he recognised the gift of fresh inspiration. The first thing he would need to do would be to borrow one of Uncle George's maps.

JOHN CULLIMORE

Chapter 22

January 1914

As the weeks passed, he began to feel the strain of leading a dual existence. The stomach discomfort he had been experiencing grew worse, a physical manifestation of the stress and isolation he felt at work. And since the controversy with the Vicar, many in the village had avoided his gaze.

Eventually Mary sent for Dr. Muir when the pains became more severe and seemed to settle just below his heart.

The doctor surveyed his patient critically. He seemed a shadow of the vigorous young man he had last seen a year ago. Dark shadows sat beneath his sunken eyes. His pallor was marked, and he appeared to have lost a good deal of muscle from his limbs. He was acutely tender in the upper abdomen. Dr Muir's verdict was damning.

'Alfred, I believe you have a stomach ulcer. As a result, you're anaemic and you may be having some slight internal bleeding. I can give you some medication and I'll talk with Mary about a suitable diet, but I see no alternative to insisting that you give up work in the factory. The fumes and the smoke are destroying your digestive system, and probably your lungs.

'My boy, you should *not* return to the GWR. Should you wish it, I will write today to your overseers.'

'But if I leave the railway works now, we won't have enough to live on. Earnings from my books still aren't sufficient to feed and clothe us.'

'I know it's a difficult decision for you, but my belief is that if you continue there, you'll be dead within six months.'

So this was the bitter truth. He stayed off work and wrote to his acquaintances. It was then that his two most steadfast companions, Reuben and Lou, stepped forward with unwavering support. Understanding the gravity of Alfred's predicament, they pooled resources and dispatched a generous cheque for twenty pounds, urging him to seek solace and respite by the tranquil shores of the

THE PALACE OF MY IMAGINATION

seaside alongside his beloved wife, Mary.

Amidst the soothing embrace of the ocean breeze, Alfred and Mary found refuge from the tumult of their worries. The azure expanse of the sea at Ilfracombe stretched before them, offering a sanctuary of tranquility and renewal.

Day by day, as the gentle rhythm of the waves lulled their troubled spirits, Alfred felt the burdens upon his shoulders begin to lighten, and hope kindled anew within his weary heart.

Yet, upon his return to the smoky embrace of the factory, the oppressive weight of labour bore down upon him with renewed ferocity. Despite his fervent attempts to persevere, his strength waned, the stomach pains returned, and his health faltered once more. Each day became a battle against exhaustion, each breath a struggle against the suffocating grasp of industrial toil.

Finally, with a heavy heart and trembling hands, Alfred made the agonising decision to sever ties with the factory that had been both his livelihood, and his undoing. Though he had no real choice in the matter, he felt a pang of anxiety as he made his way to Henry Byett's office. Sensing Alfred's unease, Byett suggested they head to an empty boardroom where they could speak in private.

'I can't stay here any longer,' Alfred began softly. 'I wanted you to be the first to know,'

Henry nodded, listening intently as Alfred continued, 'I'm under doctor's orders to leave. It's all in here,' he said, handing over Dr. Muir's letter.

Henry scanned the note, then looked up with concern. 'I'm so sorry to hear that, Alfred. I'll take care of the necessary arrangements.' After a brief pause, he added, 'Honestly, I sensed this day would come. I'm grateful you came to me directly... your priority now is, of course, to get well. But Alfred, you're meant for something greater than this factory.'

Henry's voice softened. 'It's a real loss to see you go—you'll be hard to replace. But I look forward to reading more of your work as a writer. That's where your true talent lies, and I hope we can keep in touch. If there's any way I can help, please let me know.'

Alfred, feeling relieved and touched by Byett's sincerity, shared a few of his ideas for possible future projects. As they wrapped up, he rose to leave.

'Thank you for everything, Mr. Byett,' Alfred said.

'Nonsense,' Byett replied, extending his hand with a warm smile. 'It's I who should thank you for all your hard work. And from now on—call me Henry.'

As he left the office, Alfred made one final stop at the furnace, where he paused in quiet reflection.

With a sense of quiet defiance, he etched a single word in capitals into the iron plate above the flames:

VICI.

Though the Latin word may have seemed cryptic to some, to Alfred, it held profound significance. It was a declaration of victory— resilience and ultimately triumph in the face of adversity. With that silent testament to his indomitable spirit, he bid farewell to the factory that had first shaped him but then began to consume him.

*****

But now, the future looked very uncertain. And even more so since the Great War had broken out at the end of July. He left the factory on 3rd September. Two weeks later, Mary handed him a letter, postmarked Swindon. He opened it and read the contents. He suddenly felt his chest constrict. He placed the letter on the table and walked out into the garden.

Mary followed him.

'Are you all right?' she asked. 'Im fine.' he replied. She returned into the house, picked up and read the letter. It was from Gustavus.

'Dear Alfred,

I thought we ought to inform you of this news, before you read it in a newspaper.

Our old foreman Grubb met with a fatal accident last week. Although none of us liked him, we regret the manner of his passing.

You may not realise this, but there had been an inquiry into the

THE PALACE OF MY IMAGINATION

death of Joe, and the issue about the faulty die and Grubb's failure to dispose of it had surfaced. The men had all been asked questions by the enquiry about Grubb and all of them had complained about him. The upshot of it is that he was asked to resign. This was obviously too much for him, because the next day it seems he threw himself off a railway bridge near Shrivenham as an express train was approaching.

We are sorry to have to give you this news.
We all hope you are recovering well after leaving the workshop. Please send regards to your wife Mary

Yours sincerely,
Gustavus

JOHN CULLIMORE

Chapter 23

Autumn 1914

Alfred sat at the kitchen table staring through the window out into the garden. The late afternoon sun filtering through cast a warm glow over the room. The garden was bathed in the golden light of summer, but inside, Alfred felt a chill that seemed to seep into his bones.

It had been two months since he left the factory, and as the days passed, he found himself sinking deeper into a state of despondency. The outbreak of war had cast a shadow over the country, but here in Swindon, there was yet little evidence of the conflict raging on the continent. Instead, the most palpable change was the surge of anti-German sentiment that seemed to permeate every corner of society, seen most prominently in the content of the daily newspapers.

Alfred, too, had been swept up in the fervour, composing poems denouncing the enemy and extolling the virtues of patriotism. But as he put pen to paper, he couldn't shake the feeling that his words lacked authenticity, that he was merely parroting the sentiments of others rather than speaking from his own heart.

He attributed his lack of genuine inspiration to his poor health and the restrictive confinement to the cottage, which deprived him of the long walks through the countryside that had always invigorated his creativity.

Despite still receiving praise for his recently published works, *Villages of the White Horse* and *A Wiltshire Village*, Alfred felt a growing unease about his future. The acclaim felt distant, and his uncertainty gnawed at him.

However, towards the end of the year, new ideas began to take shape in Alfred's mind. His manuscript of his time in the Railway factory was gathering dust, but now was the time to finalise and submit it. He hoped this might help draw a line under his factory experiences and help him move on.

THE PALACE OF MY IMAGINATION

He also thought back to when he had started to write his book about South Marston. He had spent many evenings in the company of rural dwellers, listening to their tales and their songs passed down through generations, purely through oral tradition. He realised these were the true collective memories of the people, and that their stories deserved to be preserved as a vital part of the region's heritage.

And so, Alfred decided that after revising his Railway factory manuscript, his next project would be to compile a record of these stories from the region all around the Upper Thames Valley. It would be a monumental task, requiring him to travel far and wide, but he was committed to completing it.

But first, he knew he had to focus on his recovery. For months, he had been plagued by feelings of anxiety and a lack of appetite, but now, as the days grew shorter and the air took on a chill, he felt a renewed sense of energy coursing through his veins, and now that he was able to resume a normal diet, his appetite improved.

***

He revised his manuscript, naming it *'Life in a Railway factory'* and submitted it to Duckworth in May. To his delight, within two weeks, they responded with a positive reply. They expressed their willingness to publish the book and proposed an interview with a journalist from *The Times* for an article to coincide with the book's release, likely scheduled for November.

Alfred met the journalist in the conservatory at the rear of Goddard's Hotel in the Old Town area of Swindon. The setting was tranquil, with sunlight filtering through the glass panes, illuminating the lush greenery within. Alfred hadn't expected such a young interviewer, but the reporter greeted him warmly and with evident enthusiasm.

'Hello Mr. Williams, I'm Edmund Harper, thanks for seeing me.'

'I've never read anything like your work on the factory, Mr. Williams. I found it riveting. But it has provoked a lot of questions which I feel sure our readers would appreciate hearing your response to.'

'Fire away,' said Alfred with a welcoming smile.

'First of all, I wondered why you had written a book about a factory. All your previous work was either poetry, much of which was inspired by nature, or prose about the life and traditions of the countryside.'

Alfred paused for a moment, collecting his thoughts.

'I like to write about what I see and experience. Although I've only just submitted this work, I actually completed it four years ago. I wasn't able to publish it while I still worked there, for obvious reasons.'

'On the whole, it's a simple and faithful account of my experiences and the effect it had on me. I felt that the world might like to hear about it, I thought it offered something original.'

The young reporter made some notes before continuing,

'But it's more than just a descriptive work, is it not?'

'Well, yes, indeed. It's about how groups of factory workers react to their environment and to their overseers. I have merely put forward my own opinions and interpretations.'

'Indeed,' responded the reporter, leaning in with interest. 'You describe the environment of the factory as "oppressive" and "closed in." You talk about the polluted atmosphere, saying that it is "dark, sombre, and repellent," and you discuss the working environment as being dangerous and unregulated. This is much more than just description; there's real emotion in those words.'

'I wonder if you'd respond to that and perhaps say how such a centre of heavy industry could be any different? I mean, is it so different in the industrial Midlands or on Merseyside, the Clyde, or in the Welsh valleys?'

'These are, of course, my personal observations,' Alfred replied thoughtfully, 'and my opinions, likewise, are personal and subjective. But I don't say these things to condemn the factory.

'Far from it—I spent many happy times there, and while working in it, I was able to educate myself and transform my existence. On the other hand, the cumulative effect of working for many years in such an environment does pose hazards to one's health.'

THE PALACE OF MY IMAGINATION

'I stand by my comments on the dangers posed by the rather toxic environment in the GWR, which is completely unregulated. I therefore think that they should aim to reduce the average number of weekly hours worked by the men and improve the safety of that working environment.'

The journalist nodded, scribbling furiously in his notebook.

'Your insights are indeed compelling, Mr. Williams. However, the thing that seems to offend you most is not the factory environment, or the dangers posed. It is the autocratic attitude of your immediate superiors, the factory foremen. You say they won't tolerate suggestions for improvement coming from educated workmen, such as yourself, and so make life difficult for you and your colleagues'.

'Isn't this predictable, given that you are a man of considerable intellect dealing with those less gifted in this respect? Aren't you really just a fish out of water, if you'll forgive the expression?'

Alfred's eyes narrowed slightly as he considered the question.

'What I would say,' he began, choosing his words carefully, 'is that the kind of petty narrow-mindedness displayed by these officials is totally reprehensible and unjustified. They should be working towards improving the productiveness of the factory and inspiring the men to work effectively in a safe environment.'

'Instead, they do the opposite. They suppress good ideas, don't care a jot about the wellbeing of their charges, and exploit their underlings through relationships built on fear.'

The young journalist's pen moved faster as Alfred's voice grew more impassioned.

'Many of the workmen depend upon the approval of the foreman to be given overtime work. In many cases, these foremen also happen to be landlords of the accommodation in which they live. There are many of these controlling characters in the factory, who are really just there to build their own empires based on intimidation, and they don't care a hoot about industrial production.'

The journalist looked up from his notes, eyes wide with interest.

'This is explosive stuff, Mr. Williams. You're describing a

system of systemic abuse and corruption that goes beyond mere inefficiency.'

'Exactly,' Alfred agreed, leaning forward. 'They create an atmosphere where innovation is stifled—unless they can claim the good ideas coming from the factory floor as their own and so ingratiate themselves with management. And yes, I've witnessed that,' he said with feeling.

'Workers are constantly on edge, afraid of losing their livelihoods or even their homes. It's a vicious cycle that perpetuates itself, making it almost impossible for any real progress or improvement to occur.'

The journalist changed tack.

'So, these overseers have unchecked power. You are also very outspoken about the iniquities of the piece-work system, which seems to exploit the workers, as the payment rates can be unilaterally reduced according to the whim of managers.'

'Aren't these situations where supporting the working men's organizations, their unions, to defend them and to negotiate on their behalf would be sensible? Yet you seem reluctant to do so.'

Alfred considered this for some time before replying,

'Well, the unions in Swindon are still not officially recognised by the GWR. And the unskilled workers suffer particularly from a lack of representation. In my time I did my bit in speaking out at the Works Conciliation committee, and they did listen to some of my arguments. But generally speaking, I don't approve of the unions. They are bitterly anti-Christian, Republican to a man, and some of their members are simply out to destroy the system.'

The journalist raised an eyebrow, intrigued by Alfred's response. 'Yet you talk sympathetically about labour unrest in your book... if I may quote directly. You say—

'The very fact that working men are rousing themselves and showing a masterly interest in problems of labour and are prepared to fight fairly and bravely for better conditions should be a source of satisfaction to everyone.'

'Aren't you being somewhat inconsistent?'

Alfred sighed, acknowledging the complexity of his views.

THE PALACE OF MY IMAGINATION

'Yes, I suppose my position is a little illogical,' he admitted. 'My political views are moderate; my precise position is hard to define. I suppose I've always been more concerned with the rights of the individual, rather than the materialistic aspirations of groups representing capital and labour.'

'That's an interesting perspective' replied the young journalist, nodding understandingly.

'It's been a pleasure talking with you, Mr. Williams. You should see something in the next *Times Literary Supplement*.'

Alfred shook the journalist's hand, feeling a mix of relief and apprehension. As he left the rear of Goddard's Hotel, he couldn't help but reflect on the contradictions within his own beliefs. Despite these reservations, he knew that his experiences and observations had the potential to spark important conversations about the future of the political system in Britain. But of course, this would require that the right people read the book and took notice of his comments.

Come October, there were a series of positive reviews in the press, not just confined to the *Times Literary Supplement*. Publications like *The Chronicle* and *The Globe* lauded Alfred's *Life in a Railway Factory* as a groundbreaking work that illuminated the often-overlooked lives of factory workers. They praised his vivid descriptions and his deep empathy for the working class.

However, the response from the Great Western Railway Magazine was hostile and damning. They accused Alfred of exaggerating the hardships and misrepresenting the working conditions. Undeterred, Alfred insisted on and was given the right to reply. In his response, he reiterated the independence of his views and the authenticity of his experiences and emphasised the need for better working conditions and fair treatment of the workforce.

Despite the media coverage and some mild local controversy, the book sold less than a dozen copies in Swindon over the ensuing six months. The local community, tightly knit and wary of criticism of their primary employer, was hesitant to embrace

Alfred's work.

Many factory workers, although quietly appreciative of Alfred's efforts, feared reprisal from their superiors and kept their distance.

However, by mid-December, Alfred was ready to embark on his next quest. Armed with nothing but his bicycle and a notebook, he set out into the countryside of the Upper Thames Valley, eager to capture the voices of the past before they were lost to time.

THE PALACE OF MY IMAGINATION

PART 5: DISPLACEMENT

Chapter 24

1916

By November, Alfred felt fit enough to enlist in the army, eager to contribute to the war effort. He reminisced about his childhood weekends spent walking up to the Downs to observe the military exercises above the village of Bishopstone. The sight of heavy artillery being manoeuvred to the hilltops by teams of horses and fired by well-drilled soldiers had always fascinated him.

Alfred was keen to understand the workings of these formidable weapons and, given his background in metalworking in the forges, he believed he would have a natural affinity with ordnance.

With these thoughts in mind, he presented himself at the recruitment centre in Devizes, determined to be assigned to the Royal Field Artillery regiment.

His journey began at Winchester barracks, where he embarked on his training as a member of the 328th battery of the RFA.

He was billeted with other Wiltshiremen who were also aspiring Gunners. He was very pleased to renew his acquaintance with Streak, his former teenage colleague in the GWR. Alfred introduced himself to the two new faces—Tripp and Winston, the latter being their supervising corporal.

Tripp was a little younger than Alfred and hailed from Stratton just west of South Marston, where he had worked as a bricklayer. His wife had left him in late 1914, having ran off with one of the builder's he worked for, whereupon Tripp volunteered for the army. Streak was a little younger than Alfred, around thirty-two, and unmarried. As his nickname suggested he was tall and slender. Since leaving the GWR in 1906 he had worked in his family's butchers' shop in Chippenham. Seeing an opportunity for travel and adventure, he had volunteered for the services in 1915.

Winston was the same age as Alfred. He had been a police constable in Swindon but became widowed in early 1914. He had been totally desolated after his wife had died after haemorrhaging after childbirth, but the child survived. Winston wasn't able to look after three children and continue working. Therefore, he and his children had moved in with his parents, and when war was declared he decided to enlist.

The first few weeks of Alfred's training were intense and demanding, with days starting as early as five a.m. Each morning, he and his fellow recruits were at the ready, performing maintenance tasks on the eighteen-pound gun, followed by practice firings that honed their skills.

Afternoons were spent attending to the horses—cleaning out the stables and receiving instruction in horse riding. Alfred embraced these challenges with enthusiasm, finding satisfaction in the physical demands and the camaraderie that developed among the men.

The months raced by, and despite the dank and dreary conditions of the army huts, Alfred discovered a newfound sense of purpose in his role.

In early September 1917, he managed to write a quick note to Henry Byett, capturing his experiences:

328th Battery, RFA
Winchester
4/9/17
Dear Henry
'Having an extraordinary time, but very little free time—even to wash! Certainly, no time to write anything. Working like a slave, but I must admit, the Army is spiffing. How any man could last in a factory after being in the Army defeats me.

I'm responsible for one 18-pound gun, ensuring all its maintenance is up to date. Scoring of the barrel has to be done every day, even at Christmas, so that it's always ready at a moment's notice.

But I've still found time to fit in classes on gun laying and even squeezed in a week's musketry. I think we'll be on the move fairly soon.'
Alfred

THE PALACE OF MY IMAGINATION

Henry realised that Alfred was obviously thriving in the structured environment of the Army. He was pleased that, at last, he felt a sense of belonging and purpose that was clearly lacking in his later years in the factory. Henry thought it was somewhat sad and ironic that it had taken the outbreak of a World War to restore his enthusiasm and wellbeing.

JOHN CULLIMORE

Chapter 25

As Alfred and his fellow gunners waited in Winchester barracks for their next posting, uncertainty hung in the air like a thick fog. Alfred, Tripp, Winston and Streak had been billeted with two other gunners, Andrews, a trawler fisherman from Stonehaven, and Davies, known as Taffy, an ex-coal miner who had married a Swindon girl and worked in the GWR. The men had been allocated to what the sergeant called the 'Eastern draft,' but he was not yet able to speculate on the exact implications of this term.

'Fall in the battery,' called Sergeant Evans, 'Eastern Draft to the rear.'

'What do the papers say about the war today,' asked Tripp, 'will it be over by Christmas?'

'Stop talking when on parade,' chided the Number 1 officer but the banter persisted in hushed tones.

'Well, it says here in Old Moore's almanac that the war will be done by Christmas,' added Tripp in a whisper.

'Must be right then,' smiled Alfred.

'Eastern draft to the stables. March 'em down there Number one,' shrieked Evans. They set off for their regular duties feeding, watering and grooming the regiment's horses.

'Apparently the sarge thinks were going East, could it be India?' asked Tripp, 'and if it is, what do we do when we get there?'

'Might get torpedoed on the way,' came the laconic Scots brogue of Andrews, his words a sobering reminder of the dangers that lurked beyond the safety of the barracks.

'Nothin' definite has come through about our posting. Could be Egypt, Palestine, East Africa, even Mesopotamia,' said Davies.

'Well, if we go there, you can sit-down under the trees of the Garden of Eden' joked Andrews.

After their morning chores, they gathered for breakfast, their conversations filled with speculation and apprehension.

They'd been told that it definitely wouldn't be France, and Alfred couldn't shake the feeling of relief that they would be

THE PALACE OF MY IMAGINATION

spared the horrors of the trenches. He had recognised that the war was lately becoming nothing more than a contest between massive guns. Now, even sixty pounders were being brought up to the front line, and the battlefield had seen a corresponding steep increase in casualties of Royal Garrison artillerymen.

Some of the men, chiefly the younger ones were disappointed at the prospect of going East and would have preferred to be in the thick of the continental fight. They questioned why they had been trained as gunners if they were to be sent somewhere where there was only a remote chance of firing their weapons in anger. However, Alfred sensed that no posting came without its own set of challenges.

Sergeant Evans had suggested to him that he thought it would be India, but the Colonel's speech had offered little clarity, leaving them all to wait anxiously for orders that seemed to be perpetually delayed.

The men of the battery came from a wide range of geographic and social backgrounds. English, Scots, Welsh and Irish were all well represented, and the draft was made up of teachers, artists, bank managers, other professionals, as well as labourers and street hawkers.

There was also marked disparity in the ages of the men and notable variability in their physical stature. Given such variation, Alfred found it difficult to visualise them as an efficient unit. He thought it likely that they would be exposed to challenging situations where teamwork was vital and that they might be found wanting.

At the start of September, the men were offered a few days of leave, and Evans strongly urged them to take advantage of it. He warned them that once the call to mobilise came, it would be sudden and for far-off lands, with no time for goodbyes. Alfred wasted no time deciding—he hadn't seen Mary for nearly ten months, and his mother was unwell, possibly nearing the end of her life. This might be his last chance to see her.

***

Upon arriving home, Alfred found Mary looking downcast.

JOHN CULLIMORE

'When do you have to go back?' she asked as soon as they embraced.

'The day after tomorrow,' he replied, feeling an overwhelming sense of emptiness.

Mary shed a few tears but quickly composed herself, wiping her eyes and saying.

'You must go and see your mother right away. Her heart is failing, and she's getting weaker by the day.'

'Of course, we'll go right now. But how are you, my love?' Alfred was concerned about her thinner appearance and wondered how she was managing on her own.

'I'm all right. Lou and Abigail Robins have been so kind. I often stay with them and sometimes help out in their shop. It keeps me busy, and they're good company. But Alfred... where will you be sent?'

'Rumour has it... India.'

At this, Mary couldn't hold back her tears.

'I know it's hard, darling, but at least it's not front-line combat. We'll be reserves for an Indian regiment that's in Europe, so I'll be safe, and I will come home—eventually.'

Despite his words, Alfred knew they didn't provide the comfort Mary needed. When he left two days later, all he could do was bury his own distress beneath a mask of forced normality.

As the sun rose on the morning after Alfred's return, a palpable tension hung in the air of the army barracks where Alfred and his fellow soldiers resided. Rumours swirled like leaves in the wind, with whispers of impending orders and imminent departures.

In the army, secrecy was paramount, and strategic announcements were divulged only at the last possible moment. So, when the rumour mill began churning, Alfred knew better than to put too much stock in hearsay.

It wasn't until Monday evening that the order finally came down from command. Gathered in the mess hall, Alfred and his comrades listened intently as Sergeant Evans delivered the news: they were to proceed by train to Devonport, but didn't add anything else. So, their voyage would indeed be by sea.

THE PALACE OF MY IMAGINATION

With the order confirmed, preparations went into overdrive. Kit bags were packed, and letters written to loved ones.

At dinner, Evans made the announcement they had waited weeks to hear 'The next parade for the *Indian* draft is zero five thirty. Full marching order with kit bags ready.'.

So there they had it, a voyage of seven to eight weeks by the Sergeant's estimate.

That evening they were paid up to the date, and afterwards as they gathered for dinner, Evans delivered another directive: They were to conserve their pay as much as was practicable, as they wouldn't receive any more until they reached their destination in the subcontinent. It was a sobering reminder of the long voyage that lay ahead, a journey that would test their mettle and endurance.

JOHN CULLIMORE

Chapter 26

27th September 1917

Just after dawn, Alfred stood on the dock, his eyes fixed on the towering silhouette of the SS Balmoral Castle, its entire length brilliantly illuminated from bow to stern. Once a symbol of luxury, the liner now bore the unmistakable signs of wartime adaptation. The bold, irregular black and white stripes painted across its hull gave it an almost surreal appearance, like a colossal, floating puzzle. Andrews gestured towards the heavy gun mounted on the stern, a stark reminder of the perils they might encounter in the channel.

'Well, boys, if the Germans come for us, we'll be ready to give them a taste of their own medicine,' Andrews remarked with a grin.

Alfred made a mental note to inspect the gun later. It looked to him like a 4.5-inch howitzer. If that was the case, he knew he and his team would be more than capable of making it roar to life if the need arose.

On boarding the steamer, men were allotted to specific decks and messes. The ship would transport sixteen hundred troops, as well as three hundred passengers in first and second class, and an equal number of crew.

There were four decks for troops and Alfred's unit were allocated to deck two, which was above the lowest deck. This deck, which was formerly for cargo, but which had been converted to meet the needs of wartime, was situated in the forward section between the forecastle and the first funnel. They found themselves in an area roughly sixty feet square, into which five hundred men were being crammed. They sought out mess number twenty-five.

Eighteen men formed each mess, identified by a numbered table. They were instructed to stow their gear on racks above the tables. They would be overcrowded like bees in a hive. To add insult to injury there was a terrible stench throughout deck two. The men tried to relieve this by opening port holes, but it quickly became

THE PALACE OF MY IMAGINATION

apparent that they had all been screwed shut.

Washing facilities were at the aft end of deck two, and all latrines were situated in an open deck below the bows and stern.

A breakfast was served, which consisted of a mutton stew with one potato. It was barely edible, and the tea served alongside it tasted like dish water. As he pushed the inedible potato around his plate, he saw Sergeant Evans approach the table.

'How goes it men?' he asked as his expression seemed to register something unpleasant.

'Sarge, what is that smell?' asked Tripp.

'I've no idea, but it's utterly foul.'

'We can't get the portholes open, so it lingers,' said Andrews.

'We'll have to wear the gas helmets if we've got to sleep in here tonight.'

Evans said he'd investigate.

Curiosity had been gnawing at Alfred's mind since he boarded the ship.

'Sarge, why does the ship have the peculiar markings all over it?'

Evans chuckled, a wry smile playing at the corners of his lips.

'Ah, that's what's called 'razzle dazzle' camouflage,' he explained, 'it's meant to confuse the enemy's U-boats lurking in the Channel. So when they look at us through their periscope, the pattern of stripes disrupts the ship's outline, making it difficult for them to work out how far away we are, and likewise they can't judge our speed or our heading accurately.'

Alfred nodded, absorbing the explanation of this strange but ingenious tactic, designed to protect the ship and its precious cargo of troops.

Nevertheless, Alfred's comrades went on to voice concern about the dangers of sailing through U-boat-infested waters. Evans, a seasoned veteran, offered a reassuring smile.

'Don't worry, lads,' he said. 'We'll be sailing in convoy with naval vessels armed to the teeth. The new convoy system has been in place for three months now, and the number of ships lost has plummeted since it started. We'll have a destroyer or two watching our tail.'

JOHN CULLIMORE

'Anyway, I need to tell you all to be on deck by eight thirty tomorrow, for roll call and fatigues.'

Dinner was served at twelve, a slight modification of breakfast with mutton, potatoes and peas and a slice of duff. The mutton had flavours which conjured images of the bilges and only the duff proved edible and was at least filled with sweet raisins.

The gunners were severely restricted in what they could do, only being allowed to walk around the narrow precincts of the dock, and the promenade decks. After a tea of plain bread and butter, hammocks were drawn, and the true extent of overcrowding was revealed. There was no option but to stay in deck two as sleeping on the outside deck was forbidden. Somehow the night passed with all five hundred men crammed into the abominably smelling deck. Daylight brought some welcome relief from the appalling atmosphere of deck two, although many men awoke with a headache.

The Hammocks were stored and while this was occurring, a couple of seamen came and opened the portholes. This helped the rank smell to dissipate and led to a welcome lowering of the temperature on the deck.

The next morning, fatigues consisted of unloading the officers' luggage from the rail wagons and hoisting supplies from the quartermaster's stores.

Later that morning the moorings were cast, and the ship proceeded a mile or so into the outer harbour, where the anchor was lowered.

The portholes were to remain open until six p.m. and permission was given for men who wanted to sleep on the port promenade deck. While the deck would be a hard surface for sleeping, the option was taken by Alfred and his comrades who proceeded there with hammock, blanket, and greatcoat and the night yielded a brief but more refreshing sleeping experience.

The next morning revealed that the Balmoral Castle was surrounded by a large group of ships including a destroyer, several other transports and cruisers, and one vessel painted in a variety of shades of green, applied in varying patterns of lines, patches and

THE PALACE OF MY IMAGINATION

curves giving rise to a bizarre appearance that some of the men likened to a spring cabbage. Yet another variation of razzle dazzle camouflage.

Signs of preparation for leaving were numerous. Various flags were hoisted, and the ships of the convoy began to exchange signals. Another auxiliary cruiser appeared five hundred yards off the starboard bow and during this time the Balmoral castle slowly pivoted to lie with its bows pointing seawards. Soon after dinner, a tender drew alongside to deliver the mail and the men were provided with life vests and informed of their lifeboat stations.

Tea was to be served at four thirty p.m., and they proceeded to deck two for bread, butter, and strawberry jam which proved as unpalatable as all the previous fare. While eating, Alfred became aware of movement, and the gunners rushed up the gangway to the deck. On reaching the top they found they had steamed several miles and were cruising through the open sea. The shoreline was now indistinct.

There was a rosy twilight, and the moon had risen directly astern of the ship. The Balmoral Castle lay at the centre of a convoy led by cruisers and destroyers with the rest of the ships spread out to the left and right.

At six p.m., canvas screens were lowered along the entire length of the promenade decks to conceal the lights from the saloon, cookhouse and bakery.

Sergeant Evans emerged from the gangway and joined the men observing the moon lit waters and the array of signals between the craft of the convoy.

'It's a grand sight is it not?' he said.

'It's reassuring, safety in numbers I suppose,' said Andrews.

'They'll be with us in the channel. And it's a calm bright moonlit night and the sea is flat, which is good. Because if there are any U-boats out there, the convoy will probably spot them before they can fire on us.'

'Can't they use torpedoes when they're submerged?' asked Tripp.

'They have to be no deeper than periscope depth, a few yards, so they can see and aim at us. But all U-Boats have to surface at some stage to recharge their batteries, so that's another reason to have good lookouts on the cruisers. Anyway men, if I were you, I'd get an early night and some sleep while the sea is flat. It might be different tomorrow when we're in Biscay, which could be a lot rougher.'

Clearly many of the other soldiers had anticipated the Sergeant's advice, as when the gunners retuned to deck two there was no available space for hammocks, and there were few available blankets. Andrews had found a spot on the floor where he spread his hammock and offered to share the space with Alfred. He had also obtained an extra blanket.

Alfred woke early the next morning feeling cold and slightly nauseous. He was conscious of much more movement beneath him as the ship rode the swell, and there was much creaking of the frame of the vessel as it yielded to the changed sea conditions.

He decided that further sleep was beyond him and thought he would go and get a cup of tea from the canteen in the stern of the ship, thinking that a walk and a blast of fresh air in the open might settle things down.

On deck, the sky and the sea were slate grey and there was a heavy swell. He observed four or five men leaning over the rails, their faces down, and another sat down on the promenade deck, head in hands. Tripp was one of the men leaning over the rail.

'Good morning, Tripp, early start this morning?' asked Alfred.

'And you too,' he responded, 'You feeling all right?'

'I'm off to get some tea, do you want one?'

'No thanks' he replied and resumed his position over the ships rail and began to retch.

He reached the canteen and drank a cup of tea. He thought he would bring one back for Andrews but moments later found himself in the same situation as Tripp, and after a few stops at the rail, he launched the now cold cup of tea overboard along with the rest of his stomach contents.

On returning to the mess, he could not face breakfast. He was not alone. Most of the men were similarly afflicted and

THE PALACE OF MY IMAGINATION

unsurprisingly all parades were called off. The men spent the rest of the day sat or lying down, and there was utter silence.

The swell decreased somewhat after one p.m., and it brought a concomitant reduction in feelings of nausea. Soon, Alfred felt well enough to consider updating his diary, only to be interrupted by a loud booming sound coming from the starboard side, and slightly astern.

Alfred's heart raced as the distant explosion shattered the calm of the sea. Gripping his diary tightly, he bolted upright, his eyes scanning the horizon for any sign of danger. The sudden commotion on deck sent a shiver down his spine, and he knew instinctively that trouble was brewing.

With nimble hands, Alfred swiftly fastened his lifebelt, his fingers deftly tying a secure reef knot. The blare of the ship's alarms pierced the air, drowning out all other sounds as mild panic rippled through the crew. Orders were shouted, and Alfred found himself being directed to his assigned boat station along with his comrades.

Out at sea, the convoy was thrown into disarray as the leading cruiser veered sharply to the left, its powerful engines churning the water into a frenzy. Two destroyers flanked the convoy, their guns trained on the yet unseen threat lurking beneath the waves. Alfred strained his eyes, searching for any sign of a periscope, but the vast expanse of ocean offered no clues.

Multiple explosions echoed in the distance, and Alfred's heart sank as he appreciated the severity of the situation. The convoy surged forward, leaving behind the destroyer engaged in the skirmish. Tension hung thick in the air, but after a few anxious minutes the men were stood down from their boat stations, their nerves still on edge from the encounter.

Seeking solace from the chaos, Alfred and his comrades sought refuge in the familiar confines of the cookhouse, the aroma of brewing tea offering a brief respite from the turmoil of the open sea. After two or three cups, most of the men went below decks for a welcome rest after a tension filled day. Alfred took the opportunity to update his journal while the events of the day remained vivid.

***

Over the next twenty-four hours, the weather steadily improved, and the once tumultuous seas gave way to a calm, almost serene, expanse. The relentless seasickness that had gripped the men had faded, replaced by a collective sense of relief. But even with the tranquil waters and clear skies, the memory of the submarine attack still cast a shadow over their thoughts. Despite their curiosity, the men received no information about the events surrounding the supposed submarine attack. It was as if the incident had been swept under the rug, a minor detail in the wider story of the war.

The next morning, Alfred emerged from his cramped bunk, the memories of the U-Boat encounter just two days earlier still vivid in his mind. As he stepped onto the deck of the troop ship, he instinctively scanned the horizon, hoping to catch sight of their former escort. To his surprise, the Balmoral Castle was now alone, surrounded only by the vast expanse of sea.

A sense of unease crept over Alfred as the reality of their situation sank in. They had likely passed through the most dangerous part of their journey, where the threat of submarines and mines had been at its peak. Yet, despite this, he couldn't shake the uncertainty—had they really left those dangers behind? or were they still lurking just out of sight, waiting for another opportunity?

The thought lingered, casting a shadow over the morning as he pondered what lay ahead.

Over lunch in the mess, Alfred brought up his concern with Sergeant Evans.

'Sarge, now that we've lost our protection, what are the chances of running into a lurking U-Boat?'

Sergeant Evans took a moment before replying.

'Well, considering we're about three hundred miles northwest of Cape Finisterre, it's not impossible, but the likelihood decreases with each passing day. It'll probably be at least another week before we can breathe easy on that front. But even then, I've heard

THE PALACE OF MY IMAGINATION

there are still a few German surface ships prowling the Atlantic, looking for trouble.'

Tripp, listening closely, couldn't help but comment,

'That's a sobering thought.'

'Actually, I'm glad we're having this conversation,' Evans continued, 'because it reminds me—the ship's gun crew is looking for a couple of trained gunners to join them as reserves, just in case we need to defend ourselves, and one of the naval ratings gets sick or injured. So, anyone keen to volunteer?'

Without hesitation, Alfred raised his hand. After a brief pause, Tripp broke the silence, saying,

'Well, there's no point in having done all that training if we're not going to put it into practice. Count me in too, Sarge.'

'Right-o, that's sorted then,' Evans said with a nod. 'I'll let them know to expect you. The team will be at the gun tomorrow morning at nine, so go along and introduce yourselves.'

That evening, as the sun dipped below the horizon, Alfred made his way to the stern and stood beside the now silent gun. He took a few moments to familiarize himself with its controls, his fingers tracing the cold metal as he reflected on the events of the past days, and after a few minutes of quiet contemplation, he turned his gaze out over the endless sea.

The ship's wake caught his eye, a shimmering silver path stretching out behind them, leading back toward the distant northern horizon. The rhythmic motion of the waves and the fading light created a mesmerising scene, drawing Alfred into a calm, almost meditative state. As the gentle engine rhythms of the ship combined with the cool evening air, a wave of drowsiness began to settle over him. His thoughts turned to the comfort of his bunk, and he found himself longing for uninterrupted hours of what he hoped would be a refreshing night's sleep.

***

Early the next morning, Alfred and Tripp strolled towards the stern when they spotted two crew members inspecting the deck mounted gun.

'Good day,' Alfred said, introducing himself and Tripp.

JOHN CULLIMORE

'We're the volunteer gunners. Is there anything we can help with?'

The older man in charge looked up and extended a firm handshake.

'Ah yes, Sergeant Evans said you'd be along. Pleased to meet you and thank you for joining us. I'm Carruthers, Gun Captain, and this is Able Seaman Fellowes. Your timing is perfect as we're just about to carry out some routine checks and maintenance on the gun.'

'Is it a Howitzer?' asked Alfred. Carruthers smiled and shook his head pointing to the large naval gun, its metal gleaming in the sunlight.

'Infact it's a Quick firing 4.7-inch Mark Four, and it's been redeployed from an old battle cruiser.'

'We did all our training on field guns, eighteen pounders, twenty-two pounders' said Tripp.

'Well, all artillery works on the same basic principle, but since this one is firmly fixed to the deck, it's got a bit of a different setup. See this cradle? When we fire, the gun doesn't just slam back—it moves along these slide rails, which absorb the recoil and keep it steady for the next shot. And of course, being at sea, this gun faces conditions that field guns don't experience. The relentless salt, spray, wind, and high humidity can really take their toll on the metal. If we don't keep it in prime condition—cleaned and lubricated —it won't be much use when we need it.

'How often do you have to check it?' Tripp asked.

'Daily inspections for obvious problems are a must,' Carruthers replied. 'We do a complete cleaning and lubricating once a week. Of course, if sea conditions are particularly harsh, or after any firing, we might need to review it more often.'

'Can I ask what this piping is for' asked Alfred pointing to a length of tubing emerging from the deck, with a flared end made of brass.

'That's a speaking tube. We can communicate with the bridge through it. And there's a whistle attached, for calling them up if need be.'

THE PALACE OF MY IMAGINATION

Carruthers, impressed by the interest shown by the pair then added.

'I'll leave you with Fellowes here who will demonstrate how we service the weapon, and then Fellowes if you wouldn't mind talking to them about how we store and retrieve the ammunition.'

'Aye aye, sir,' he responded.

'That should be enough for your first session. And then tomorrow please join us for some practice firing.'

Alfred's eyes lit up at the prospect.

***

Three days later, they were steaming south, their position due west of Madeira, making good progress in the fair weather. Alfred, Andrews, and Tripp were strolling along the starboard deck just before midday when they came across a group of sailors gathered at the starboard rail, gesturing toward a point about twenty degrees toward the stern. One of the sailors was peering through a pair of binoculars.

'What can you see?' Tripp asked the man with the binoculars.

'There's a ship about four miles out,' the sailor replied. 'Looks like a banana boat, but it's moving quite fast, which is odd.'

'Why's that?' Tripp inquired.

'Well, these tramp steamers usually don't do more than about eight knots, but she must be doing twice that.'

'Maybe she's carrying perishable cargo, and she's in a hurry to get home,' another sailor suggested.

'Could be, I suppose. But she's flying a Norwegian ensign, which is the other strange thing.'

'Mind if I take a look?' Alfred asked.

'Be my guest,' the sailor said, handing him the binoculars.

Alfred focused on the vessel, which seemed to be gaining on the Balmoral Castle. Through the binoculars, he noticed that the ship's course had shifted, bringing it closer. As he watched, the Norwegian ensign began to descend toward the deck, and he wondered why. The sailors also noticed the vessel's change in course and glanced up at the bridge, where two or three officers were clearly watching the craft as well.

JOHN CULLIMORE

'They've taken down the Norwegian flag.' Alfred observed.

'Right, that's it. I'm going up to the bridge to find out what's going on,' one of the seamen said, turning to head toward the bridge.

The approaching vessel was now just three miles away, directly on the beam of the Balmoral Castle. One of the other sailors was peering through the binoculars when he suddenly cried out.

'That's no banana boat; it's a German raider!' As the alarm for boat stations blared, he thrust the binoculars into Alfred's hands before sprinting towards the stern.

Alfred quickly focused on the approaching ship and saw the truth for himself. The vessel was indeed flying the German ensign and was unmistakably armed, with guns mounted amidships on each side. Alfred could now see sailors on deck removing what were false bulwarks to expose even more guns situated forwards on each bow and a single gun at the stern.

Realising the danger, Alfred and his colleagues hurried along the deck towards the stern, knowing that was their assigned station in an emergency.

As they moved, it became clear that the German ship was on a collision course with the Balmoral Castle. They felt the deck shift beneath them as their ship altered course hard to port, its engines roaring to life in a desperate bid to outrun the enemy and present the smallest possible target to the attacker behind them.

Despite the Balmoral Castle's increased speed, the German raider was steadily closing the distance. Alfred recognised Carruthers, Fellowes, and their colleagues rushing aft toward the gun, urgency in every step. As the gap between the two ships shrank to just two miles, the raider fired its first shell. It exploded seventy-five yards off the starboard rail, sending up a massive plume of water that drenched those on the starboard decks.

The gun crew was nearly at the stern when disaster struck. A second shell exploded nearby, blowing off the davits of the rear starboard lifeboat. Tragically, Carruthers and Fellowes were caught in the blast, struck down by flying debris. Alfred and Tripp saw them fall and reacted instantly, manoeuvering around the

THE PALACE OF MY IMAGINATION

wreckage to join the remaining gun crew. The ammunition had been brought to the surface, but the crew was awaiting their Captain and shell loader.

Thank goodness he and Tripp had done two practice firing exercises with the team, thought Alfred, and they now had a working familiarity with the ammunition and firing of the weapon. Exchanging a few words with the gun crew, Alfred assumed the role of Gun Captain, positioning himself to the left of the gun. He looked over the stern at the rapidly approaching vessel. Tripp stood by the breech, ready to help load the first of the forty-pound shells.

Meanwhile the German vessel fired another shell which had landed in the sea on the port side of the Balmoral Castle.

Alfred picked up the voice tube and blew the whistle to alert the bridge.

'Gunner Alfred Williams here. I'm stepping in as Gun Captain in view of the injury to Carruthers,' he reported crisply. 'Please give me a bearing and distance to the enemy craft.'

After a few tense seconds, a voice on the other end provided the necessary information. Alfred adjusted the gun's traverse slightly to the left, then fine-tuned the elevation using the data he'd been given. The pursuer was now about two thousand yards away. He nodded to Tripp, who swiftly loaded the shell into the breech, while one of the seamen promptly closed it.

'Fire!' Alfred ordered. The gun roared to life as the shell shot towards the raider. Almost simultaneously, the bridge responded by altering course further to port, beginning a series of zigzag manoeuvers designed to confuse the pursuing ship.

A thunderous explosion erupted from the pursuing vessel. Glancing up, Alfred saw that his aim had been precise, and the shell had struck home near the port bow. Within seconds the German ship was listing to port, her bow dipping slightly as she lay broadside to the stern of the Balmoral Castle. Appreciating that this was a moment of vulnerability for the enemy, he knew he had to act quickly.

He waited as the Balmoral Castle completed her turn to port, and as the ship straightened out on her new course, Alfred requested another bearing and distance from the bridge. He adjusted the gun's traverse to bring it back toward the centreline and fine-tuned the elevation.

With a nod to Tripp and the breech operator, Alfred watched as the next shell was swiftly loaded.

'Fire!' he ordered. The gun roared once more, and Alfred's aim proved true once again. They saw a blast erupt from the central part of the German ship, followed almost immediately by a second explosion as the blast wave swept toward the stern. Smoke and flames began pouring from the ship's centre.

'That's the stuff to give 'em!' Tripp shouted; his voice filled with adrenaline.

The German vessel was struggling, its momentum fading as it listed more heavily to port. Despite sporadic attempts to fire from a smaller gun near the bow, the shells splashed harmlessly into the sea, falling well short of their target. Alfred, always alert, noticed a distinct increase in the rumble of the Balmoral Castle's engines. The ship responded immediately, surging forward and altering its course once more to throw off the enemy's aim.

As the Balmoral Castle gained speed, an officer from the bridge quickly made his way to the stern where Alfred and the remaining gun crew were stationed. His face reflected a mix of urgency and cautious optimism.

'Excellent work, men,' he called out, raising his voice over the roar of the engines and the distant thud of gunfire. 'the raider's losing ground, and we've got a real chance to put some distance between us.'

The officer turned to Alfred, who remained focused at the gun, hands steady on the controls.

'We've been in contact with Gibraltar,' the officer continued, 'and they're looking to see who they can send to assist us. But until then, it's on you to keep that raider at bay while we make our escape.'

Tripp, standing nearby, peered over the rail and remarked,

'The ship seems to be leaving them behind.'

THE PALACE OF MY IMAGINATION

The officer nodded.

'That's the hope. The captain believes we can squeeze a few more knots out of her. She can do twenty at a push. But be warned, if the Germans manage to repair the damage, they'll be back in pursuit. It's a heavily armed ship, and it can obviously shift, so we can't afford to relax just yet.'

With a curt 'Carry on, men,' and a sharp salute, the officer turned and headed back to the bridge, leaving Alfred and his crew to their task.

The Balmoral Castle pressed forward, cutting through the waves as the gap between her and the raider remained steady. Although Alfred's shells had damaged the German vessel, it was evident that the blows hadn't been fatal. The enemy had seemingly managed some makeshift repairs, allowing them to continue the pursuit. However, the distance between the two ships held at over three miles.

Alfred had noticed that the wind speed seemed to have picked up quickly. Wave heights were increasing markedly and the sea state which had been relatively smooth during the missile exchanges was now moderate. The Balmoral Castle, now steaming close-hauled, experienced a noticeable pitching of the deck with each strong gust. He knew that if they needed to fire the weapon under these conditions, it would be much more challenging. Meanwhile, the German raider occasionally fired a shell, but they all landed harmlessly in the water, far short of the Balmoral Castle.

Over two hours had passed since the initial exchange of fire, and the Balmoral Castle pressed on through increasingly rough seas. The gunnery team remained at their station, eyes fixed on the enemy ship which continued to shadow them. Despite the mounting tension, they maintained their focus and vigilance.

Tripp soon noticed a growing crowd of crew members gathering along the starboard rail, pointing excitedly towards the horizon. Plumes of smoke had appeared in the distance, and within minutes, it became clear that two destroyers were rapidly closing in, slicing through the waves like determined predators.

The ship's klaxon blared across the deck, a sharp and urgent

JOHN CULLIMORE

signal that reinforcements had arrived. Cheers erupted from the men on deck, who waved enthusiastically at their rescuers. The destroyers, moving at nearly thirty knots, sped past the Balmoral Castle on the starboard side, zeroing in on the German raider. As they approached the enemy ship, the furthest destroyer unleashed its first salvo, missiles streaking through the air towards the struggling German vessel.

A wave of relief swept over the gunnery team. They began congratulating each other, their earlier tension dissolving into raucous cheers as they joined in the jubilant celebration.

Later that evening, the weather had settled, and Alfred and his comrades gathered on the port bow, the sun setting behind them in a blaze of orange and gold. He could just make out the faint outline of land on the horizon.

'If I'm not mistaken, that's the coast of Morocco,' said Sergeant Evans, squinting into the distance.

'When do we reach our first port?' Tripp asked, his tone carrying a mix of curiosity and impatience.

'Not for some time yet. Sierra Leone is still a couple of days off, I'd say,' Andrews replied.

'After today, I could really do with a good night out,' Tripp remarked with a sigh.

Alfred, hearing this, found himself reflecting on the day's events, still surprised at how instinctively he had responded during the heat of battle. He was relieved to hear that Carruthers and Fellowes had survived and would recover from their injuries.

'Well, you're not getting that night out just yet, Private Tripp,' said Andrews with a smile. 'But the captain has issued the battery with a very nice bottle of rum as a token of appreciation for your actions today. So, when you're ready, we could head below and have a little toast.'

'Or two,' Tripp added with a grin, clapping Alfred on the back enthusiastically.

THE PALACE OF MY IMAGINATION

Chapter 27

After a month at sea, they arrived in Cape Town.

Alfred, like a thousand other artillerymen, was desperate to go ashore.

After breakfast, the men were finally paid, and with a surge of excitement, Alfred and Tripp found themselves free to explore Cape Town for the day. After weeks at sea, it was a welcome relief for Alfred to take the railway which linked the docks with the town and to then stroll through this elegant coastal settlement, nestled as it was beneath the protective presence of the cloud-capped Table Mountain.

Cape Town had a fine pier and a magnificent esplanade bordered by a variety of tall ferns, flowers and tropical plants, with many vacant benches which provided a scenic and relaxing environment. The waters of the harbour were a perfect caerulean shade of blue which seemed to emphasise the tranquility and expansiveness of the bay.

The wide streets, grand buildings, and bustling shops were impressive, and Alfred was struck by how familiar it all felt. He didn't feel that he was in a foreign country despite being thousands of miles from home, the scene before him was reminiscent of a much more exotic version of an English seaside town.

As they approached the heart of the township, Alfred wondered how the soldiers would be received by the locals, but his doubts were to be rapidly dispelled.

They had been advised to head to the Soldiers' Institute, and upon arrival, they were welcomed into a grand hall buzzing with animated conversation. Soldiers mingled with enthusiastic locals at numerous circular tables. Along the hall's edges, tables were heaped with food, and a small army of female volunteers were busy serving sandwiches, scones, cakes, and tea to the soldier's filing past.

'How much is it to eat here?' Tripp asked as he queued up and addressed an elegant, middle-aged lady who seemed to be overseeing the operation.

'This will cost you nothing, my dear,' she replied warmly. 'You are honoured guests of the township. Please, eat and drink as much as you like, and find a seat at one of the tables. We've arranged some entertainment for you.'

With plates piled high with delicious treats Alfred hadn't seen in months; he and Tripp were directed to vacant places at a table already filled with friendly locals and two other soldiers.

'Please, join us.' said a woman of about fifty. Her hair was pinned up in a neat bun, and she was dressed elegantly in an ivory blouse and a long navy skirt, her neck and wrists adorned with tasteful jewellery.

After a round of introductions, the woman introduced herself as Audrey Botha, the wife of the mayor of Cape Town, and she offered them a warm gentle smile.

'We can never do enough to thank you brave men for fighting on our behalf,' she said.

Alfred, grateful for the hospitality, replied, 'I wasn't sure how we'd be received, considering the memories of the Boer War and whether any ill feeling lingered.'

'Oh, not at all from our community,' Audrey assured him. 'We're proud to be part of the Empire and to be fighting the same enemy. There were some mixed loyalties among the Afrikaners, true, but things have settled since the rebellion was quashed a few years back.'

'Has the war affected your family personally?' Alfred asked, intrigued.

'Yes, indeed,' she replied. 'Our two sons are in the South African Mounted Infantry. They fought in the Southwest Africa campaign.

'One was wounded at the Orange River, but he's recovered and has left the army, but our other son, William, is just about to board your ship. He's heading out to fight in German East Africa. You may run into him. Are you bound for Kigali?'

'No,' Alfred said, 'we're headed for India, for garrison duty. But I'll be sure to look out for him.'

THE PALACE OF MY IMAGINATION

Audrey smiled and handed Alfred a card. 'Well, Alfred, when you're finished here, feel free to stop by any shop on your way back to the ship. Just show them this, and you won't need to pay for a thing.'

On their return to the docks, Alfred and Tripp made good use of their soldier status. They enjoyed a complimentary haircut and shave, and each was gifted a cigar. Tripp couldn't resist ducking into a fruit and vegetable store, emerging minutes later with a small sack of oranges, also free of charge. He generously shared them with their comrades once they were back aboard the Balmoral Castle.

The ship remained docked in Cape Town for what felt like far too short a stay - just two brief nights. As the morning of the 28th of October dawned, Alfred found himself standing on the rear deck, watching the city fade into the distance. His eyes lingered on the sight of Table Mountain; its flat, imposing peak framed against the sky. A deep sense of longing washed over him as he gazed back at the bustling township nestled beneath the mountain's shadow, wishing he'd had more time to explore its wonders.

The sheer, monumental form of Table Mountain, wrapped in the wisps of clouds that clung to its summit, seemed almost otherworldly. In his mind, Alfred could easily imagine that this place was a seat of the gods, a timeless sanctuary standing watch over the land, bathed in the radiant light of the southern sun.

***

Despite encountering rough seas off East Africa, the Balmoral Castle docked at Durban on the morning of the second of November. The men received a similar welcoming reception in Durban, but in addition, they enjoyed free travel on the city's trams, and many venues offered free teas and suppers to the promenading troops.

The city of Durban, with its warm climate and bustling harbour, provided yet another striking contrast to the cold, damp, and often grim conditions the men had left behind in England. Alfred marvelled at the vibrant colours of the local flora, and the lively atmosphere of the markets. He found solace in these moments of respite, which allowed him to temporarily forget the horrors of war that might be awaiting him.

Eager for adventure, Alfred and his colleagues seized every opportunity to explore their surroundings and soon found themselves drawn to a mysterious event—a séance— advertised on a weathered poster plastered on a lamp-post.

Curiosity piqued, Alfred, Tripp, and Andrews made their way to the address indicated on the poster. The location was a disused house just outside the town, nestled in a leafy suburb. It was a rather foreboding Victorian-era villa that looked as though it might indeed be haunted by the spirits of its former inhabitants. The large double entrance doors were wide open, leading into a high-ceilinged hall with a wide staircase directly in front of them. The hall was in complete darkness, and an eerie silence hung in the air.

At this point, the resolve of Tripp and Andrews seemed to falter, and they decided to return to the town, leaving Alfred to continue alone. Looking up at the source of a dim light at the top of the stairs, Alfred felt a mixture of trepidation and excitement. He ascended the steps cautiously, each creak of the wooden stairs echoing through the silent house. Upon reaching the top, he entered a dimly lit room and was greeted by the sight of about forty individuals. Their faces were illuminated by the flickering candlelight, casting long, shifting shadows on the walls. The room was adorned with symbols of the occult, and mysterious artifacts were scattered haphazardly across the floor, adding to the unsettling atmosphere.

At the centre of the room stood the medium, Madame Beatrice, an elderly woman with piercing eyes that seemed to see into the depths of one's soul. She exuded an aura of wisdom and mystique, and her presence commanded immediate respect. After introducing himself, Alfred was ushered to a place of honour on the right side of the medium, his status as a soldier in khaki earning him special recognition.

The seance began with a solemn prayer and a collection for Madame Beatrice, followed by a period of reverent silence. Then,

THE PALACE OF MY IMAGINATION

as the room fell into a hushed stillness, the participants joined hands in a circle, their collective energy pulsing through the air.

Madame Beatrice turned to Alfred, her eyes glinting with a knowing twinkle.

'Welcome to our brave soldier.' she said softly.

'Do you seek a connection with the other side?'

Alfred nodded vigorously, his heart suddenly thumping.

And with whom would you wish to speak?'

'I would dearly like to speak to my mother. She passed away shortly before I left England.'

'What was your mother's name? And do you have an object that belonged to her?—something she held dear?'

With trembling hands, Alfred produced a small locket from his pocket. Inside was a photograph of his mother, her kind eyes and gentle smile captured forever. He handed it to Madame Beatrice, who handled it with reverence.

'Her name was Elisabeth.'

'What questions do you have for her?

'Well, as a soldier, I know I'm certain to meet danger, but—will I survive this war?'

'And if I do, what should I do in the future?' he asked, his voice trembling.

'Those are good questions,' said the medium as she took both his hands in hers.

'Now focus on your mother,' she instructed, 'think of the bond you shared.'

Alfred closed his eyes, the image of his mother vivid in his mind. He heard Madame Beatrice begin to speak in an unrecognisable language in a low murmur, as she conjured a spell that seemed to tear at the fabric of reality.

The room grew colder, and the candles flickered wildly. After a few tense moments, the medium became silent, her eyes now closed, while the grip on his hands increased. Alfred was still uncertain whether he was in the midst of a well-crafted charade, but the medium's response was undeniably disturbing.

The rocking motions of Madame Beatrice increased further,

whilst her grip on Alfred's hands alternately relaxed and tightened. A tall black woman, presumably an assistant, moved to her side as the intensity of Madame Beatrice's movements reached a crescendo.

Suddenly her neck extended, and she emitted a dull moan. After this she appeared to go limp, leant forwards, her head resting on Alfred's left shoulder, and became silent. The assistant was clearly prepared for this and supported the medium.

Gently disengaging her from Alfred, she sat her down and wrapped her upper torso in a loose blanket. She gently mopped her brow and lifted her head which had fallen onto her chest.

Slowly Madame Beatrice seemed to recover, her tone and posture were gradually restored and her eyes opened. She smiled.

The assistant provided Madame with a glass of water, followed by a small glass of brandy.

The medium took Alfred's hands in hers.

'Alfred, your mother came to me,' she said, smiling reassuringly at him.

'She realises you face great trials ahead, but your strength lies not in fear, but in the resolve of your heart. The war's end is uncertain but know this—you must walk forward without allowing terror to cloud your path. You are meant for more than the battlefield.'

Alfred swallowed, his chest tightening. He had always feared that war would swallow him whole, but hearing these words gave him a strange sense of calm. He steeled himself as the medium resumed her report.

'As regards your destiny, I see that you were born to create Alfred. Your words bring light to the darkest places. When the war is over, your duty will not be on the battlefield, but in the hearts of those who need to heal. Write for them. The world will need voices like yours to rebuild what has been lost.'

Alfred's emotions nearly overwhelmed him. He felt a wave of warmth and a profound sense of connection, but the weight of his grief mixed with unexpected relief left him awed into silence. He sat quietly for a moment, his heart full, before finally whispering.

THE PALACE OF MY IMAGINATION

'I really can't thank you enough.'

Madame Beatrice's eyes flickered with a knowing look.

'Your mother has one more message for you,' she said softly.

'She sees a figure surrounded with a wreath of ivy.'

Alfred furrowed his brow, somewhat perplexed by the cryptic image, but the sense of peace he had felt moments ago remained, overriding any confusion. He nodded, choosing not to dwell on the meaning, trusting that it would reveal itself in time.

The medium then reached across the table and handed back the small locket Alfred had offered, her voice tender as she added,

'And know this—your mother is at peace.'

With a deep breath, Alfred took the locket and placed it back around his neck.

'Thank you,' he said again, his voice stronger now, as he stood and nodded toward Beatrice.

He left the séance, stepping into the night air, and made his way back to the ship.

***

'You look as though you've seen a ghost,' said Tripp.

'Well, something very strange took place in there, but I'm not sure what to make of it.'

'Any predictions you'd like to share?' asked Tripp.

'Nothing that made much sense,' replied Alfred. 'I'll reserve judgement on it for now.' Having said that he suddenly felt exhausted and headed for his bunk.

Nevertheless, the experience of the séance had left him feeling unexpectedly uplifted. The image of the ivy wreath remained etched in his mind, and he had pondered on it. As a classical scholar he was aware that wreaths of ivy evoked themes of poetic inspiration and the eternal nature of art and beauty. He recalled the other words conveyed through the medium, channelling the spirit of his mother. The message had been unambiguous: *—to be brave was to prevail.*

This insight resonated with him, and he resolved to adopt it as his future mantra.

***

JOHN CULLIMORE

On the evening of the sixth of November, they left Durban and began to sail across the Indian Ocean. They had now transferred to the SS Caronia, a former Cunard liner taken over by the government. However, despite being almost twice the size of the Balmoral Castle, it was no less overcrowded and oppressive with four and a half thousand troops aboard.

To make things worse, the sun shone relentlessly after leaving Durban. The winds dropped, and the temperature soared during the daytime. Alfred spent most of his time trying to find a shady spot on the forward upper deck beneath the lifeboats.

However, he and his comrades were forced rather cruelly into performing physical jerks during parade in the afternoon, at the peak of the blazing afternoon sun. Although wearing khaki shorts and a helmet, his legs became severely sunburned and blistered in places. This caused considerable discomfort, necessitating the bandaging of his left lower leg for some weeks after.

The days blurred together as the heat sapped the energy from the men. The air below decks became stifling, and tempers occasionally flared in the oppressive conditions. Alfred found some solace in writing letters to Mary, describing the voyage and the privations they faced. He knew she would worry about him, and therefore he chose his words carefully, aiming to reassure her, even as he felt the strain of the journey himself.

On the morning of the tenth day at sea, Alfred stood at the railing of the SS Caronia, his gaze fixed on the horizon where the waters met the sky as the vessel steamed towards Bombay.

The soldiers had been briefed that they were entering a perilous stretch of sea, mined by German forces. Minesweepers and admiralty vessels would be waiting to lead them in convoy from an assigned rendezvous point, and while this offered some reassurance, it was believed that some of the mines had become detached from their moorings raising the threat level further.

As they neared the meeting point, the Caronia slowed to a halt, joining several other ships in the area, all of which were smaller than her. Alfred watched as the smaller craft grouped together waiting to be piloted through the treacherous waters ahead.

THE PALACE OF MY IMAGINATION

On reaching the rendezvous, an Admiralty vessel came alongside and requested that Caronia lowered her anchor. They were advised that the convoy would set out the next morning along the perilous maritime corridor.

That night, as the Capstan and anchor were now being used, the forward area was closed off. Tripp realised that he would have to move his hammock as far astern as possible, and Alfred followed suit. He found a situation on the port side hatches where he stowed his hammock, coat and blanket.

The next morning as Alfred stood looking out at the sea over the starboard deck rail, the tension in the air was palpable. The convoy of ships, including the twin minesweepers and the Admiralty cruiser, had commenced their journey through the mined waters. The Caronia was at the centre of the formation, with smaller vessels ahead and astern.

The sense of apprehension was made more acute by the sight of a steamship flying an Australian flag off the starboard bow. Its course was parallel to the convoy, seemingly oblivious to the danger lurking beneath the waves. But then a few minutes later, the vessel changed its course, presumably with the intention of joining the rear of the convoy. However, within minutes as she drew ever closer, disaster struck and a deafening explosion rocked the approaching vessel.

Alfred watched in horror as the steamship listed to starboard, its fate sealed by the force of the blast. Without hesitation, orders rang out to launch the Caronia's starboard lifeboats and begin a rescue operation. Alfred and his comrade, Tripp, took up their previously appointed station at lifeboat C, anticipating action.

Alfred could now see men on board the afflicted vessel jumping into the sea. In addition, he could see what appeared to be a mass of logs floating on the sea and coalescing together to give the appearance of a small island at the starboard side of the bow. This cluster of drifting material was being carried with tide and wind in the direction of the Caronia.

The Australian vessel was evidently going to sink, and its stern had begun to rise up out of the sea, the inactive propellers becoming visible and the ship's bow almost completely submerged. The urgency of the situation was clear, and when Sergeant Evans called for eight volunteers to man Boat C towards the sinking vessel and aid the rescue efforts, Alfred stepped forward without hesitation, his sense of duty overriding any fear.

But as he glanced over at Tripp, he noticed his friend remained silent, his expression unreadable. Alfred felt a pang of disappointment, but he knew that each man had to make his own choice in such perilous circumstances. Similar preparations were made with five other lifeboats ranged along the starboard side.

With smooth efficiency the crew and the volunteers swiftly mobilised the lifeboat from its secure position on the davits. Thick ropes strained as they bore the weight of the craft as it was carefully manoeuvred over the rail, guided by the hands of the men.

The boats were lowered sufficiently for the crew to board. There would be eight oarsmen, an officer and two other men who would act as lookouts. When they were inside the vessel, the ship's crew lowered the boat to the ocean surface.

Alfred was allocated to the second row of oarsmen, on the port side, and took his seat facing the stern of the boat. He and his comrades turned their attention to fitting rowlocks to the gunwales and then the oars were carefully lifted and fitted, while the officer and the lookouts stored spare life jackets and lengths of line.

The ropes were freed and the crew cast off from the liner, rowing with a steady rhythm set by the officer coxswain at the stern. Alfred's boat was the second of six to leave the side of the Caronia, the others followed in quick succession, and the small fleet of vessels advanced through the waves. Fortunately, the wind was light and the sea state was generally calm. About a half mile separated them from the sinking vessel.

The angle of the ship was now more acute, the stern rising about thirty yards above the sea surface, as some unsecured deck machinery slid into the sea. The listing to starboard increased further as men continued to pour over the side. No lifeboats seemed to have been launched from the steamer.

THE PALACE OF MY IMAGINATION

She finally rolled onto her starboard side and was now clearly on the point of sinking. The funnels collapsed into the sea, and seconds later, a dull echoing roar rang out as the entire vessel plunged into the depths and vanished from view. The scene was chaos incarnate. Alfred's boat was now about four hundred yards from where she had gone down, the intervening sea being occupied by the island of timber floating towards them. The lifeboats changed course somewhat, steering to avoid collision with this island of dangerous material, and yet, amidst the horror, there was a glimmer of hope as they spotted survivors amidst the floating debris.

The lifeboat rocked against the waves as Alfred and his crewmates worked quickly to aid those in need. The officer's orders cut through the clamour, directing four of the oarsmen to maintain a safe distance from the treacherous floating debris, while simultaneously the rest of the crew set to rescuing as many souls as possible.

Alfred's heart raced as he reached out to haul a man aboard, his hands shaking as he gripped the slippery clothing. The man's eyes held a mix of relief and fear, a silent acknowledgment of the peril they had narrowly escaped.

As they continued their rescue mission, Alfred couldn't shake the sight of some lifeless bodies bobbing in the water, some displaying signs of fatal head trauma. The brutality of the disaster was confirmed by the expressions of horror displayed on some of the dead men's faces.

Alfred's boat rescued twelve men from the waves, and as they turned their attention to the last man, he observed him rising and falling with the swell, securely held in the centre of the life preserver that kept him afloat. The lifebuoy was emblazoned with the name of the lost ship in capital letters: the *SS Ivy Glen*.

Alfred and his neighbour at the oars worked quickly and efficiently to get the man over the side of the lifeboat. He was still clutching the lifebuoy as he came into the boat. They wrapped him in a warm blanket. Alfred reached for a flask of brandy, pressing it into the man's shaking hands. The man was too exhausted to speak, but his eyes shone with gratitude as he lifted the brandy flask in salute to his rescuers.

Alfred's neighbour, a burly sailor named Jack, patted the rescued man on the back reassuringly.

'You're safe now, mate,' he said. The man took a small sip of the brandy, the colour slowly returning to his cheeks as the warmth of the spirit spread through him.

'SS Ivy Glen,' said the man his voice hoarse from the cold and the strain. 'we were hit... just an hour or so ago - I thought I was a goner. Thanks. I'm Jack O'Connor, from Freemantle'

Alfred nodded, understanding the magnitude of what the man had endured.

'You're a long way from home.'

The lifeboat continued its steady course through the choppy waters, the crew keeping a vigilant eye out for any other survivors from the Ivy Glen. The sun was directly overhead, as the rescued man drifted into an uneasy sleep, clutching the lifebuoy tightly as if it were a lifeline to his past.

Alfred allowed himself a moment of respite. He leaned against the side of the lifeboat, chest heaving with exertion as he surveyed the scene. The once mighty ship was now nothing more than a memory, swallowed by the unforgiving depths.

On their way back to the ship, Alfred was reminded of his night in Durban at the séance with Madame Beatrice. The harsh reality of the day's events sent a shiver down his spine as on the one hand, he recognised the accuracy of her prediction, although on the other hand he smiled to himself as he recognized that he had somewhat misinterpretred her remark relating to the wreath of ivy.

As the lifeboat drew closer to the ship, Alfred found himself lost in thought. The sea's rhythmic lapping against the boat's hull seemed almost hypnotic, a counterpoint to the whirl of his thoughts. He couldn't help but ponder the nature of fate and destiny, and the inexplicable threads that seemed to weave their way through his life.

The eerie chill lingered, even as the crew hauled the lifeboat aboard and the survivors were taken to the ship's infirmary. Alfred

THE PALACE OF MY IMAGINATION

stood on the deck, gazing out at the vast expanse of the ocean, the events of the morning replaying in his mind. Madame Beatrice's words had proven to be more than mere curiosity— and he began to consider whether she had infact provided him with genuine insight into the course of his future.

JOHN CULLIMORE

Chapter 28

November 1917. Roorkee, India.

After enduring a gruelling 56-hour rail journey north from Bombay, Alfred found himself among a battalion of exhausted men in the city of Rorkee. The landscape they had traversed varied from vast plantations of tea and cotton to imposing mountains and desolate tracts of dried mud and rock. But despite the hardships of the journey, Alfred couldn't help but marvel at the picturesque sight of Roorkee as they approached. A grand aqueduct, its pink brick structure enhanced by the setting sun behind it, extended majestically over the river, while the bustling array of rooftops and minarets added to the town's charm.

Upon their arrival the battery pitched their tents, finding temporary respite from their travels. In the days that followed, they were allocated to bungalows with three men sharing each. Alfred found himself with more than adequate leisure time, thanks to an undemanding timetable of regimental duties, allowing him to indulge in his passion for observation and writing once more.

Acknowledging Alfred's clear initiative and leadership abilities during the lengthy sea voyage, Andrews had suggested that Alfred be promoted to the rank of Bombardier upon arriving in India. In this role, he would oversee his group during field expeditions. One of the first of these assignments took them beyond the camp, into the countryside, for artillery practice near the village of Sohalpur.

As they made their way through the rural landscape, Alfred couldn't help but be struck by the tranquility of the surroundings.

As the sun dipped below the horizon, it cast golden hues over an area of rich vegetation bordering the Upper Ganges canal, the designated halfway point in their journey.

First and foremost, the canal, of mid nineteenth century construction, served to irrigate the agricultural land in the region between the Ganges itself and the Yamuna River. Regions that were formerly desert had been transformed into rich and fertile areas and many towns and villages had sprung up as a result of its

THE PALACE OF MY IMAGINATION

construction.

Alfred and his comrades prepared to make camp for the night. They had chosen a spot where the tow path was lined with mango trees and led directly to a small clearing. The chosen site lay above an area of dense vegetation. It was in this latter area, that one of the soldiers, Tripp, had found a secluded but inviting corner between some bushes and an area of tall grasses in excess of ten feet high.

'Is it wise to camp there?' Alfred asked, his voice tinged with concern.

'It looks like that could be an excellent covert for many creatures; snakes, jackals and wolves to name but a few.'

In response, Tripp brushed off Alfred's worries with a dismissive wave of his hand.

'Ah, don't worry yourself, Alfred,' he replied nonchalantly, 'I'll be fine here.'

Reluctantly, Alfred conceded. With some reservation, he joined his comrades in arranging their belongings in a circle around the base of a large mango tree, their shadows dancing in the fading light.

As darkness settled over the camp, the soldiers gathered around a flickering campfire, their faces illuminated by its warm glow. They shared stories and laughter, finding solace in each other's company despite the uncertainty of their surroundings. In due course they bedded down for the night.

It was difficult to sleep. Alfred couldn't shake a sense of foreboding. The rustling of the wind through the trees seemed to whisper of unseen dangers lurking in the shadows, and the distant howls of wolves and the rhythmic ya-ya-ya sound of hyenas sent shivers down his spine. However, sleep came eventually, and some tranquil hours passed until Alfred was jolted awake by the sound of urgent whispers and panicked voices.

It was the twilight just before dawn. Disoriented, he scrambled to his feet, his heart thumping in his chest. Tripp, his comrade, came running towards the encampment, his expression grave.

'What's going on?' Alfred asked, his voice filled with concern.

'Something's out there,' Tripp replied, his eyes scanning the dawn sky beyond the flickering firelight. 'I heard rustling in the bushes, and then I saw eyes—glowing eyes. And growling—I was scared stiff. And then it pulled my blanket away. So, I just ran for it. Maybe it was a tiger?'

Alfred reacted immediately.

'We need to defend ourselves.'

He and his comrades hurriedly armed themselves, a sudden surge of adrenaline coursing through their veins. Cautiously, the group entered the dense thicket, rifles at the ready.

However, instead of a tiger, they were startled to find a native man emerging from the underbrush. His animated gestures and rapid speech in Hindi made it clear he had something urgent to share. Jugal, one of Alfred's Indian guides, stepped forward to translate.

With his eyes on the array of weaponry, the local man spoke in a flurry of agitated Hindi, but Jugal responded calmly, his tone reassuring.

Alfred noticed that Jugal's words were beginning to have an effect; the man's tense demeanour began to relax, and soon both men were smiling. A few sentences later, they were laughing heartily.

Alfred, intrigued and impatient, turned to Jugal, who was still chuckling.

'Well? what's so amusing?'

After a few more moments of shared laughter with the local man, Jugal managed to compose himself. In heavily accented English, he explained.

'Sahib, this man is local farmer. He was returning to village from market yesterday night after buying ox. In early hours of morning, he was walking with ox along path when he saw soldier's feet sticking out of bushes onto path.'

Jugal paused as another wave of laughter passed between the pair.

'So, he take ox down into fields so not disturb soldier. He let ox graze in the field, and he go to sleep under mango tree.

THE PALACE OF MY IMAGINATION

'But, ox come back to path and start chewing on soldier's blanket!'

By now, the entire battery was in fits of laughter, while Tripp's face grew redder by the second. The laughter continued, augmented by the relief that their fears had been unfounded. Alfred was pleased to see that despite feeling initially embarrassed, Tripp was now joining in with the general merriment.

After a hearty breakfast, the battery resumed their journey to Sohalpur, their sleeping mats rolled up and strapped to their backs as they followed their native guide.

The path led them through fields of swaying wheat and dense forests of towering sugar cane. They rested at lunchtime in an ancient fort and waited for the heat of the day to dissipate before resuming their march.

As the sun approached the horizon, they finally arrived at the outskirts of the village.

The local populace, having been alerted to their arrival by the village authorities, awaited them on the brow of a nearby hill. Alfred noticed women at the village's edge, gracefully balancing *chatties*—clay vessels filled with water—on their heads as they fetched water from the well.

The soldiers wasted no time and set about their campsite preparations. Having experienced the extreme cold of the evenings, Alfred tasked some men with finding firewood, but before they could scatter, a native approached, bearing a hefty faggot of wood. With a nod of gratitude, Alfred directed the men to set up the campfires.

The following day, Alfred took the opportunity to explore the village. Its narrow streets wound between mud-built houses, their roofs thatched with dried grasses and maize stems. The layout was haphazard, with alleys leading to more alleys and irregularly shaped compounds scattered throughout.

Within these compounds, Alfred observed a menagerie of livestock—oxen, cows, donkeys, pigs, goats, sheep, and poultry— roaming amidst the villagers. Humans, too, mingled among the animals, navigating the mud and filth that permeated the air.

The village emanated the earthy scent of the countryside, mingled with the stench of cesspools and cattle excrement. Stacks of dried ox dung, shaped into fuel cakes, were piled against walls, ready to be used for cooking and heating.

In one of the compounds, Alfred's gaze fell upon a gruesome sight: long-snouted pigs feasting on the carcass of a rotting goat, while nearby, pariah dogs squabbled over the scraps. The scene was a stark reminder of the harsh realities of rural Indian life, where survival often depended on making use of every available resource. Undeterred by the grim spectacle, Alfred pressed on, further exploring the village's labyrinthine streets. He observed the local industries at work, with many engaged in spinning, weaving, and sugar-making. Naked young boys played in the dusty lanes, their laughter echoing through the air as they chased each other with playful abandon.

Meanwhile, older girls and women sat diligently at their spinning wheels or looms, weaving coarse sheets and blankets from locally grown cotton. Their skilled hands moved with unerring precision, producing fabrics that would be used both within the village and sold in nearby markets.

As Alfred continued his exploration, he noticed groups of older men seated on *charpoys*, or traditional woven cots, engaging in animated conversation and puffing on their hookahs. Their weathered faces spoke of a lifetime of toil and hardship, yet there was a sense of camaraderie and resilience among them.

Although there was no grand temple in the village, Alfred was touched by the presence of a small shrine dedicated to the local Devi. This simple yet reverent structure was nestled beneath the shade of an ancient banyan, where a pair of villagers were offering prayers, seeking blessings for their families and crops. Standing at the shrine at sunset in the coolness of the evening, he couldn't help but think of Mary and found himself offering up a silent prayer that she was well.

As the battery settled in, preparations for cannon firing practice

THE PALACE OF MY IMAGINATION

commenced. Targets were set into the dried-up riverbed, and the soldiers began their drills with mechanical proficiency. Villagers gathered on the brow of the hill to watch the spectacle, their curiosity piqued by the unfamiliar sight and sound of military exercises.

However, their initial fascination quickly turned to alarm as the thunderous roar of the cannons shattered the tranquility of the village. Some, unaccustomed to such loud noises, recoiled in fear, while others stared wide-eyed at the source of the deafening blasts. The situation took a surreal turn when an aeroplane appeared in the sky on the second day of the drills. For some of the villagers, who had never seen such a contraption before, the sight of the aircraft was met with awe and wonder. But as the plane circled overhead, its engine roaring, a sense of dread began to spread among many of the onlookers. In their fear-stricken minds, some interpreted the arrival of the plane as the coming of a new and vengeful deity, sent to punish them for their perceived sins. Some of them, so overwhelmed with fear, dropped to the ground, prostrating themselves and pressing their faces into the dust.

The scene was one of panic and confusion, where superstition blurred the lines between reality and imagination, leaving the villagers terrified of the unknown forces that had invaded their world.

Later that evening, as the camp settled down, Alfred couldn't shake the guilt that weighed on him. The arrival of his battery had brought such distress to these simple, unassuming people, and the thought troubled him deeply. He imagined how he would feel if a foreign force suddenly appeared and shattered the peace and security of his own home with weapons of unimaginable power. The empathy he felt contrasted sharply with the indifference of his comrades, who seemed largely unconcerned by the villagers' terrific fear.

What disturbed Alfred even more was the realisation that some of his fellow soldiers harboured a disdainful view of the natives, seeing them as little more than subhuman. This blatant lack of compassion troubled him to the core, and as he lay in his bunk that night, sleep eluded him.

***

Alfred had begun to appreciate that India was a land rich in culture yet fraught with dangers. It was just after Christmas in 1917, and despite the festive cheer, a sense of ennui began to seep into his soul. As he grew more accustomed to the challenging environment, thoughts of the perils lurking in every corner plagued his mind.

The threat of mosquitoes, whose bites could bring forth malaria, loomed large. He also pondered the venomous sting of scorpions, the relentless attacks of other insects, and the possibility of encountering deadly snakes while traversing the countryside. Even the presence of jackals and pariah dogs added to his sense of unease.

In moments of maudlin reflection, Alfred contemplated the fate that awaited him should misfortune befall him in this distant land. Would anyone mourn the loss of a British soldier who perished in India?

However, amidst these dark thoughts, a glimmer of intrigue emerged. Alfred noticed a line of people moving along the canal in the direction of Hardwar. Alfred asked Sergeant Evans where the line of people was headed.

'They're pilgrims, heading towards some sort of religious festival in Kelair.'

'Isn't that a few miles along the canal?' asked Alf.

'Straight along the path for five miles or so,' confirmed Evans. Alfred decided there and then that he would join the procession to the festival. He had the whole day free of duties, and the weekend lay ahead. The moon was full, and his way home in the evening would be well illuminated along the tow path.

Though Evans was sympathetic, he reminded Alfred of the rules. 'Remember, you were told on parade not to fraternise with the natives, you'd better hope the Colonel doesn't hear about this. ' Tripp was convinced Alfred was taking a risk by attending the festival.

'You'll be the only European, and if you get into trouble there'll

THE PALACE OF MY IMAGINATION
be no one to get you out of it. '

'I realise that, but when we arrived in India, an old soldier gave me some useful advice. Provided one behaves properly, treats people with respect, doesn't stare inappropriately at women, and keeps out of their holy places, there really shouldn't be any concern for one's personal safety. But having said that would any of you care to accompany me? It could be an interesting day.' His offer was met with silence and averted eyes. Nevertheless, he decided he would trust to good fortune and set off to join the procession.

As he joined the canal path, he reflected on the conversation he had had with Sergeant Evans. He felt that the directive of non fraternisation served only to augment the harsh unsympathetic attitude of his colleagues towards the natives, and this was coming across in many of the day-to-day interactions between the soldiers and the locals.

Alfred had also realised that he would learn nothing about India's culture and its people if he were to shut himself off from Indian society and this would be a total abandonment of his principles.

He believed that true understanding could only come from engagement and interaction, rather than from behind the confines of misguided military regulations.

Alfred was pleasantly surprised by the easy camaraderie of the Muslim pilgrims as they journeyed towards Kelair. There were groups of well-dressed individuals, who realising that he was British, were keen to use their knowledge of English to discuss topics such as the weather and the prospects for the festival. He learned that the festival was to celebrate *Eid*, which marked the end of Ramadan, the holy month of fasting, a time of joy and celebration after a month of spiritual reflection and fasting from dawn to sunset.

The good humour among the pilgrims and their friendly reception dispelled any lingering doubts he may have had about attending.

JOHN CULLIMORE

As Alfred continued on his way toward the bustling festival, another younger stranger approached him with a polite smile.

'Hello, sir. May I walk with you to the festival?' the young man asked in fluent, unaccented English. He was adorned in traditional attire—a long black coat, a vibrant red waistcoat, and a fez perched proudly atop his head.

'It would be a pleasure,' Alfred replied, impressed, 'and where did you learn to speak such excellent English?'

'Thank you,' the young man responded with a nod, 'I attended university in Delhi, where all our instruction was in English. I still use it often in my father's export business, where I handle all the necessary translations. By the way, I am Hassan bin Ahmed, and very pleased to meet you.' Alfred responded by introducing himself in return.

'But tell me, sir, what brings you to India?' asked Hassan.

'We're here mainly as reserve forces, I believe,' Alfred answered. 'Many of your own soldiers have been sent to Europe and Mesopotamia to fight for the Empire, for which we are, of course, very grateful.'

As they walked, Alfred learned more about his companion.

The young man hailed from the city of Roorkee and carried with him a prayer rug, beautifully adorned with intricate floral designs and scenes from the Quran. In a basket by his side was a live cockerel, destined to be sacrificed at the festival in honour of his recently departed mother.

Alfred found himself fascinated by the young man's devotion to his faith and was eager to learn more about Islam. His companion shared insights into his religious beliefs, explaining his commitment to abstaining from alcohol and pork, as well as strictly following Halal practices when consuming meat. He spoke of his future with hope, expressing his desire for marriage but noting that he did not see himself having more than one wife.

As their conversation turned to the customs of the festival, the young man offered Alfred some friendly advice.

'Sir, as you have recently arrived in India, forgive me if I offer a word of caution. No man attending this festival should stare at

THE PALACE OF MY IMAGINATION

any woman, as it could lead to trouble for you—and later, blindness would be the inevitable result.'

Alfred appreciated the young man's concern and smiled.

'You need have no worries there; I had a discussion with colleagues about that very subject earlier today. But thank you for mentioning it again.'

The two continued their walk, the atmosphere around them growing more vibrant as they neared the festival grounds. Alfred felt a growing sense of connection with his companion, appreciating the insights into a culture that still seemed unfamiliar though intriguing.

Soon they had arrived at Kelair, and Hassan went his own way to seek out the Imam who would supervise the sacrifice of the cockerel.

Alfred stood for a moment, taking in the scene before him. The surge of people arriving at the fair was staggering. He estimated there must be around twenty thousand pilgrims, representing all sections of Indian society. Most notable among them, he spotted aristocrats, their regal presence unmistakable, as well as prosperous-looking merchants with their wives by their sides, some of whom walked unveiled, adorned in sumptuous silks of crimson, saffron, and magenta.

He noticed smiling bands of young men walking arm in arm, their laughter mingling with the buzz of the crowd. The fairground was alive with activity, with stalls set out in the form of a bazaar. Here, veiled women in white robes could be seen bargaining for goods, their voices rising above the din of the market.

Amid it all, musicians played stringed instruments and banged on drums, creating a non-stop cacophony of sound that seemed to fill the air. Alongside them, other entertainers dotted the fair, offering a variety of spectacles.

Alfred watched as jugglers performed their feats, sword swallowers showcased their skills, and fakirs passed through the crowd, demonstrating rigorous acts of self-mortification including walking upon sandals studded with sharp spikes and lying on beds of nails.

JOHN CULLIMORE

Having made his sacrifice, the young Muslim rejoined Alfred as he continued to navigate through the bustling fair, and was keen to add an informed commentary to the events Alfred was witnessing for the first time. They moved through the crowd, unable to ignore the sight of numerous beggars scattered across the bustling paths, some with deformed and twisted limbs. A group of them lay prone on the ground, reaching out for alms. Hassan approached the beggars, signalling for Alfred to follow.

'It is our duty,' he said softly, 'to give alms to those less fortunate. Charity is a pillar of our faith.'

He dropped a few coins into their hands, and Alfred, moved by the scene, followed his gesture, offering some of his own.

As they walked further, Alfred noticed many others who appeared diseased or on the verge of death. He was struck by the fact that such sights did not cause alarm or disturbance among the festivalgoers. Hassan explained.

'We offer *Dua*, prayers for the sick and dying, asking for their comfort, peace, and mercy from Allah. This not only helps them, but Allah will reward us for our compassion.'

With a moment of quiet reflection, the young man closed his eyes in silent prayer. A serene smile crossed his face as he turned back to Alfred.

'Now, let's find something to eat,' he said, lightening the mood.

As soon as he said this, Alfred felt a pang of hunger. His gaze landed on a nearby booth serving chah, and food from which emanated a tantalizing aroma. Hassan noticed Alfred's interest and guided him towards the stall.

The stall holder gestured towards what appeared to be cakes as he uttered the word '*Malpua.*'

'They are made from wheat flour, butter, and sugar, and fried in ghee over red-hot charcoal. Do you want to try?' asked the young man.

Smiling enthusiastically, Alfred handed a few coins to the stallholder signalling with his fingers that he wanted portions for both of them.

Once cooked, they were promptly rolled up and served wrapped

THE PALACE OF MY IMAGINATION

in large, dried leaves.

As he took his first bite and sampled the rich warm sweet flavours, he couldn't wait to tell his comrades back at camp that there really were some native dishes worth savouring.

The pair continued to explore the bustling bazaar stalls. Alfred found himself amazed by the diverse array of artisans and craftsmen showcasing their skills. Potters moulded intricate clay vessels. Basket makers weaved complex designs. Smiths and ironmongers shaped metal into useful tools and drapers displayed vibrant fabrics. The fair was a feast for the senses. Native jewellers and herbalists also caught Alfred's attention, offering unique wares and remedies.

Alfred felt pleasantly surprised that despite being a foreigner amidst an exclusively Muslim crowd, the pilgrims he encountered expressed only curiosity and a mild degree of surprise. He enjoyed the event all the more thanks to his well-informed young guide. There was no impression of hostility or impediment as they continued their exploration of the fascinating scenes, mingling with the crowd and immersed in the vibrant atmosphere.

As the sun began to dip below the horizon, casting a warm glow over the fairground, they were drawn to the balcony of the mosque. From there, a white-robed muezzin emerged, his voice ringing out as he called the faithful to prayer with a familiar chant.

'Lā ilāha illā Allāh.'

'He is saying that there is no God but Allah,' said Hassan.

As evening descended and the fairground came alive with the glow of lanterns and torches, he noticed tents and marquees erected across the grounds. Peeking into some of them, he glimpsed luxurious furnishings, quality carpets, and costly hangings, evidence of the wealthier pilgrims' accommodation. Outside these tents, groups of these well-to-do individuals sat, conversing and smoking hookahs, while the poorest among them sought rest on any available patch of bare ground.

Realising they had circled back to the canal; Alfred felt a wave of fatigue wash over him. With the full moon casting its silver light upon the landscape, he decided it was time to make the ninety-minute walk back to Rorkee. Sensing he was ready to depart, Hassan insisted that Alfred take a simple torch made of wood and cloth to light his way.

Grateful for the considerate gesture, Alfred accepted it and thanked Hassan for his guidance. He bid adieu to the young man and the vibrant festival, still in full swing, revitalised by the experience, and pleased that he had the resolve to venture into something his companions were hesitant to embrace.

THE PALACE OF MY IMAGINATION

Chapter 29

'O Whither, like a shattered bark that glideth,
Bereft of sail or oar,
Wend'st thou thy course?
What God thy journey guideth
Unto what unknown shore?'
On the body of a Hindu, floating down the Ganges. Alfred Williams ,1926

In March 1918, Alfred received orders to transfer from the hill station to Cawnpore, a city three hundred miles to the south. The climate in Cawnpore was significantly hotter, and upon arrival, Alfred found himself struggling with a severe bout of fever and bloody diarrhoea, which the regimental medic diagnosed as dysentery. The heat was oppressive, reminding him of his old job in the railway factory, where the flames and heat of the oil furnaces were similarly relentless.

He was confined to his bed for a week. At first, he could tolerate nothing by mouth apart from water and a little Kaolin and tincture of morphine. Then he slowly began to recover. He was unfit to join his comrades on parade, but as his strength returned, he rejoined the morning parade from seven until nine in the morning, though he was assigned light regimental duties for the following month. Alfred attributed his full restoration to fitness to a diet consisting almost exclusively of mangoes. For some weeks this was the only foodstuff he could tolerate and which he considered safe to eat.

His light schedule allowed him afternoons and evenings to himself, which he used to explore the bustling city of Cawnpore, a welcome contrast to the isolated hills of Rorkee.

Cawnpore's modern amenities fascinated him. The trams made it easy to navigate the city, and the large public gardens, filled with orange trees, mangoes, and limes, provided a fragrant escape from the heat. The Ganges River, a mile wide at Cawnpore, captivated

JOHN CULLIMORE

Alfred with its vast, flowing waters.

A week later, Alfred and Tripp were patrolling the outside perimeter of the camp together on evening guard duty. On the northern side of the camp was a large area of open grassland and scrub stretching to a small copse about half a mile distant. As they reached this area, they heard a low hiss from the vicinity of some dry bushes about four feet from where Alfred stood.

Looking to the right the men were stunned by the sight of a King Cobra with its hood completely open, in strike mode, rearing some eighteen inches above the ground. Paralysed by the terror yet mesmerised by the beauty of this deadliest of all snakes in India, Alfred stood stock still. He knew it was futile to turn and run and nor could he draw out any weapon as the cobra slithered closer and engaged eye-to-eye with Alfred, almost hypnotically. Tripp began to react and fumble with his rifle.

'Dont move.' said a calm voice.

A medium-built Indian gentleman, dressed in the purest white dhoti and shirt, stepped forward, holding two slender sticks.

He addressed the cobra softly, calling it '*Nagaraja.*'

The cobra remained motionless, and the man continued speaking in low, soothing tones. After what felt like an eternity, the snake slowly retracted its hood and turned slightly. With lightning speed, the man in white secured the cobra's head in a precise pincer grip using his sticks. He beckoned to some local boys who seemed to be accompanying him, and they promptly brought him a mud pot covered with a cotton cloth.

With gentle urging, the man coaxed the cobra into the pot, swiftly wrapping the cloth around the mouth and tying it securely. He muttered that he would release *Nagaraja* into the nearby forest, where it could reunite with its family.

Alfred and Tripp were awestruck by what they had witnessed.

'Sir, we can't thank you enough for what you did,' said Tripp, his voice filled with gratitude.

The man in white smiled warmly.

'I'm pleased to help. These boys fetched me when they spotted *Nagaraja* in the area. I was a bit concerned when I saw you

THE PALACE OF MY IMAGINATION

approaching where they had seen it.'

'Thank goodness you were here, sir. Allow me to add my thanks as well,' Alfred added, as both soldiers introduced themselves.

'And whom do we have the honour of addressing?' Tripp inquired.

'I am Ramananda, though some call me *Pandit*. I teach Sanskrit at the high school in Cawnpore.'

'I understand that *Pandits* have deep spiritual knowledge, does your teaching include this?' Alfred asked, his curiosity piqued and his excitement growing.

'It does,' the man replied with a gentle nod. 'In addition to my teaching, I also work with your British officers as a translator. So, I'm quite familiar with your barracks.'

Alfred couldn't contain his enthusiasm.

'Sir, I've dabbled in scholarship myself. Would it be possible to meet with you at the barracks when you have some free time? I'm very interested in learning more about Sanskrit and the philosophies of the Hindus.'

The man smiled warmly. 'I would be delighted. As it happens, I'll be at the barracks tomorrow. Meet me outside the officers' mess at seven pm.'

Alfred's eyes lit up. 'Thank you, sir. I look forward to it.'

With a final nod of acknowledgment, the Pandit turned and walked away, leaving Alfred and Tripp to marvel at the unexpected encounter.

'A *Pandit*, eh?' said Tripp, 'D'you think he could help me fix my dodgy handwriting?'

***

The following week *Pandit* Ramananda was planning to officiate at one of the may Hindu funerals which had occurred in Cawnpore due to an influenza epidemic which was sweeping the country.

Alfred had read in the newspapers that the illness had originated in the United States and spread around the globe and had been nicknamed the 'Spanish' flu. He had been aware that some of his military colleagues had been similarly affected, though none he knew had died.

Ramananda suggested Alfred join him at the funeral to witness and learn from the rituals, and the family involved had no objections. As they entered the town, they met the funeral procession headed toward the burial ground.

The body, wrapped in a white cloth, lay on a bamboo bier. A lone drummer at the front kept a slow, steady beat, guiding the mournful march. Four relatives of the deceased followed behind, walking ten paces, then pausing for ten seconds, a gesture filled with sorrow. Two young boys carried the bier, the boy in front carried a lantern, while another boy followed, holding a small earthenware jug of water.

In the shadows of the trees, a menacing presence lurked. Jackals and wolf-like pariah dogs, drawn by the scent of the decaying corpse trailed the cortege, hoping to feast on any carrion left behind. They lingered at a distance, a grim reminder of the cycle of life and death in these lands.

At the burial site, Alfred watched as vultures and dogs competed for remnants of earlier cremations.

On arrival, the body was gently placed on the ground amidst several still smouldering heaps of ashes. An ox cart arrived bearing wood, and several fair-sized logs were laid in parallel leaving a central space which was filled with twigs and small branches. Ramananda joined the mourners, and after the shroud was removed, began the ceremony.

Ramananda sprinkled holy water on the ground before the body and began chanting. The corpse was anointed with oil from a small vessel that he had brought, and the corpse was then lifted on to the logs. More twigs, dried wood, and grasses were added until the pyre stood three feet tall.

The deceased's personal items—his clothes, his hookah, and the bier—were placed on the fire, which was lit using coals brought from the family hearth. As the flames grew, the chanting intensified. A young man, likely the eldest son, took responsibility for tending the fire, stirring it with a bamboo pole and adding oil to keep it burning steadily.

THE PALACE OF MY IMAGINATION

As the fire consumed the body, and the head of the corpse became obviously seared, the young man struck it with a pole, causing the skull to crack open. Overhead, vultures circled impatiently, some swooping down to snatch pieces of the burning flesh as the body was consumed by flames.

Lost in the macabre spectacle, Alfred noticed that Ramananda was now standing next to him.

'We call this ceremony *Antyesti*,' Ramananda said quietly. 'It honours the deceased and ensures their spirit's safe passage to the afterlife.'

Alfred nodded, still absorbed in the ritual.

'By performing certain rites and giving gifts,' Ramananda continued, 'the penalties of sin can be avoided.'

Alfred shifted slightly, listening more closely.

'It's crucial for a son to perform these final rites for a parent,' Ramananda added, his tone serious, 'a Hindu without a son risks falling into eternal damnation.'

Alfred found that the Pandit's explanations transformed the scene from one of grim curiosity to a profound cultural experience, and for the first time, he grasped the deep cultural and religious importance of having male children—and why daughters, in comparison, were often regarded with less significance.

As the flames danced and the chanting continued, Alfred felt the urge to learn even more about the timeless traditions of the land and its people.

After bidding farewell to the bereaved family, Alfred and Ramananda made their way back toward the barracks. The streets were filled with the sombre sight of numerous funeral processions, a clear indication of the epidemic's devastating toll. The bazaar's narrow alleys and the paths leading to the *ghats*, the steps leading down to the river, echoed with the steady beat of drums and the melancholic sound of horns, a haunting backdrop to the mass of mourners.

As they passed one particularly heartbreaking scene, Alfred noticed a father carrying the lifeless body of his infant child. The sight brought the harsh reality of the epidemic sharply into focus.

Continuing their walk along the wide, muddy banks of the Ganges, they came across an unsettling number of bodies being placed directly into the river. Troubled by this, Alfred asked Ramananda why so many were not being cremated.

Ramananda sighed, his expression heavy with sorrow.

'These families are poor, and the epidemic has claimed so many lives. Wood for funeral pyres is now very scarce, and to make matters worse, I'm sorry to say that the British army has requisitioned much of the available supply for its own purposes. The fuel is also rationed, leaving many unable to afford the traditional cremation.'

Alfred was stunned.

'That's appalling,' he replied, feeling a rising sense of anger and shame. No one in the camp had spoken of this situation, and it weighed on him to learn that the army, *his army*, had contributed to such hardship making the depth of the suffering surrounding him completely unfathomable.

The sacred *ghats*, leading down to the Ganges, were overwhelmed with mourners.

The river, low and steadily subsiding due to the dry season, revealed a grim landscape. Hundreds of bodies floated in the shallows or lay lodged upon sandbanks, their final rest unmarked and unattended. The sight was enough to turn Alfred's stomach. Above, the sky was thick with vultures and crows, gorging on the exposed human remains. On the ground, swarms of pariah dogs had been drawn from the city by the smell of decomposition, their eyes glinting with hunger as they prowled the riverbanks. At night, the grim feast continued as jackals and hyenas seized the smaller carcasses of infants and children, dragging them far out onto the sandbanks.

The scale of the deposition had forced the authorities to establish a special clearing station on the bank opposite the *Massacre Ghat*. This station operated continuously, a sombre assembly line for the dead. Alfred stood transfixed by the scene: a long train of oxcarts, each filled with bodies, waited in a grim procession for their turn. As the oxen patiently bore their load, the bodies were unloaded

THE PALACE OF MY IMAGINATION

and prepared for their final journey.

A brief but poignant religious ceremony preceded each committal. Sacred water was poured upon the corpse, a final act of purification. The body, now placed on a bamboo bier, was taken by four bearers who waded into the stream. The leading bearers, beat the water with the palms of their free hands. Ramananda explained that this was an attempt to ward off crocodiles and any evil spirits or demons that might be lurking nearby, a symbol of the enduring faith of people amidst overwhelming despair.

Alfred watched as body after body was floated into the river, the serene flow of the Ganges contrasting starkly with the tragedy it bore witness to. He felt a deep sense of sorrow and helplessness. In Alfred's view, the veneer of civilization had been totally stripped away, revealing a raw, primal struggle for survival and dignity in the face of disease and death.

Ramananda, sensing Alfred's inner turmoil, gently sought to offer a spiritual perspective to help him process the immense tragedy surrounding them.

'Alfred,' he began, 'this is indeed a profound loss for many families, and no one can deny the sorrow felt by those grieving. But understand that everything in this world is fleeting, even life and death itself.

'In our tradition, the soul transcends these temporary states. As the *Bhagavad Gita* says, for the soul, there is neither birth nor death. It is eternal and indestructible; it is not slain when the body is slain.'

He paused for a moment before continuing.

'Most of these souls will continue their journey, being reborn and moving closer toward *moksha*—liberation from the cycle of birth and death. But to truly cope with this grief, all those affected must practice detachment.

'That doesn't mean becoming cold or indifferent; you must still show compassion to those who are suffering. But by cultivating a spiritual outlook, you accept both joy and sorrow as part of God's divine play.'

Alfred listened intently, beginning to understand the wisdom behind Ramananda's words, though he struggled to reconcile the situation—particularly how the actions of his own army were compounding the suffering for so many.

***

After having spent the previous evening witnessing distressing scenes at the riverside, Alfred felt somewhat apathetic and had little appetite the next day. Initially, he attributed his feelings of malaise to an intense emotional reaction to the horrifying sights of bodies being committed to the Ganges.

However, by evening, he was sweating profusely and experiencing severe chills. The camp medic, upon examination, diagnosed Influenza and he prescribed aspirin, bed rest, and plenty of fluids, excusing Alfred from further military duties. Alfred was told to isolate himself from all contact with others for a week, while his food would be delivered to his bungalow.

If his symptoms got worse, he was to report promptly to the Military Hospital, which apparently was already full with many of his colleagues with the most severe symptoms.

As Alfred lay on his makeshift bed in the oppressive heat of the Cawnpore camp, the relentless sun made it difficult for him to stay cool. His body ached, and the sweat-soaked sheets did little to alleviate his discomfort. The dry, dusty air seemed to sap what little energy he had left.

After a couple of days of fitful sleep and delirious dreams, he began to improve. The shivering subsided, and the fever gradually broke. Alfred found himself with some time on his hands as he recuperated. He decided to write letters home, attempting to reassure Mary and his other correspondents that despite him having experienced poor health, he was now recovering and was optimistic about his time in India.

He picked up his pen and began to write to Mary, describing the beautiful yet harsh reality of India. He detailed the poignant scenes by the Ganges and the sorrow he felt for the people who had lost loved ones to both the epidemic and the relentless heat.

As the days passed, Alfred's strength slowly returned. The agonising heat persisted, but the mornings were relatively cool,

THE PALACE OF MY IMAGINATION

and the sounds of temple bells in the distance, the calls of street vendors, and the rhythmic clatter of the city's daily life refreshed him. He found shade during the hottest part of the day and felt able to take short walks around the camp in the early evenings.

One evening, as the sun dipped low and the air cooled, Sergeant Evans gathered the men for an important announcement. The Indian troops from one of the northwestern stations had been deployed to Europe, leaving a need for replacement troops.

Sergeant Evans addressed the assembled soldiers with his usual gravitas.

'Men, we need twenty volunteers to deploy to a place called Ranikhet, to man the garrison. Ranikhet is the home of the Kumaon Regiment, and some of its troops are in France, but many are currently fighting for the allies against the Ottomans.'

'You'll be there as a backup for them. The air is cooler up there, and the work will be less frenetic compared to what's expected here. If anyone is interested, step forward.'

'Sounds too good to be true. What's the catch Sarge?' asked Tripp.

'There's no ulterior motive here Private Tripp' responded Evans 'the only things to consider are first, there's a long rail journey and three or four days of marching up into the foothills of the Himalayas. Then, when you arrive there you'll be under canvas until the accommodation is sorted. And thirdly, if men are to be deployed to Palestine or Mesopotamia, it will be the men at Ranikhet who will be in the vanguard of that mobilization.'

Alfred thought for a few moments and then felt a stirring of hope. Instinctively, he knew this would be the right move for his health. And at this moment a full recovery was what what he craved most. The camp doctor, who had been monitoring Alfred's recovery closely, had already suggested that a change of scenery and a cooler climate could only benefit his convalescence. Alfred stepped forward without hesitation. Somewhat to his surprise Tripp, Andrews and Streak followed him into the line of volunteers.

Over the next few days, Alfred prepared for the move. His

belongings were packed, and farewells were exchanged with comrades he had grown close to during his time in Cawnpore. The journey to Ranikhet would be long, but Alfred felt ready for the challenge. The thought of the crisp mountain air and the tranquil surroundings raised his spirits.

The journey to Ranikhet was arduous, but with each passing mile, the air grew cooler and the landscape more verdant. As they ascended into the foothills, Alfred felt a sense of renewal. The sights and sounds of the bustling city were gradually replaced by the tranquility of the mountains.

THE PALACE OF MY IMAGINATION

Chapter 30

Ranikhet is soft and fair, With the pine-scents in her hair
On her breast a rose is worn with a ravishing perfume,
And a rhododendron bloom- Richer than the skies at morn.
So all my heart with love is set; I'll live and die for Ranikhet
from Monsoon Time, by Alfred Williams 1926

Alfred arrived in Ranikhet after five days on the move. Nestled in the lap of the Himalayas at an altitude exceeding six thousand feet, this hill station was made up of three major ridges; the Alma, the Deolikhet and the Chaubattia, all three being interconnected by upper and lower roads. Ranikhet appeared to Alfred as a serenely beautiful, isolated earthly paradise.

The name Ranikhet translates to the 'Queen's Meadow,' and legend has it that a thousand years earlier, the Kuryati king had built a palace here for his beloved queen, who had fallen in love with the area's enchanting beauty.

As his battery marched beside the steeply inclined, pine-covered slopes, Alfred could hardly contain his awe. The crisp mountain air, fragrant with the scent of pine and wildflowers, invigorated his senses. In the distance, seeing the village of Ranikhet for the first time, the settlement was spread over the slopes of a ravine and nestled among chestnut and deodar trees. The ravine plunged steeply downward below the village revealing several cultivated terraced plots, dotted with stone dwellings, where the locals grew maize, vegetables and wheat.

The slope descended further into a vast, cup-like hollow that opened out before a range of blue hills, which ascended to the silvery heights of the snow-capped peaks of the mighty Himalayas, fifty miles away.

His first weeks at Ranikhet were spent in spellbound reverie. No parades or duties of any kind were allocated to Alfred's unit in the first ten days after their arrival from the plains. The tranquil beauty of Ranikhet, with its serene landscapes and majestic vistas, felt like a world apart from the tumultuous experiences of his past. Gazing southwards in the clear dust free atmosphere of morning and evening, he could just make out the gleaming towers of Delhi three hundred miles away.

Looking to the north the hill terraces around Ranikhet rose to twelve thousand feet but they were still dwarfed by the wall of sublime peaks which reached twice the height and shimmered in the pale blue of the northern sky.

His health improved rapidly, and he was entirely free of episodes of feverishness. Within two weeks, the men had been moved from tents into the permanent quarters of the camp. These stone buildings, with low iron roofs, offered cool accommodation for all the men, and the broad eaves provided shade from the intense sunlight and the rains. The camp quarters also boasted a messing area with a reading room. Utilitarian bed frames were provided, along with a plentiful supply of coconut coir, ensuring each man had a comfortable bedding surface.

The urge to write, the surest sign of his mental well-being, returned with startling intensity. Within weeks, he had written a dozen new poems, and every day seemed to bring new inspiration.

As Alfred resumed writing, influences arose from the distinctiveness and beauty of his new surroundings. Rising just before dawn, he would hike up the hillsides, watching as the first light pierced the eastern horizon, gently illuminating the landscape. The dewy pines sparkled as the morning mist rose, and the ethereal calls of birds reverberated through the valleys, adding an almost mystical quality to the scene. As the sun climbed, the vibrant colours of blooming rhododendrons would catch his eye, painting the landscape in hues of red and pink.

In the evenings, he would take another walk as the sun began its descent, a cool breeze drifting down from the mountains, carrying with it the scent of wildflowers. These quiet moments of reflection in nature lifted his spirits and ignited his creative energy.

His sense of well-being was such that he began to dream vividly, and in one of them his spirit soared up from his earthbound body into the serenity of the heavens, and he looked down on the

THE PALACE OF MY IMAGINATION

panorama of the Himalayan landscape.

He felt that his recently penned poems possessed a newfound depth and clarity, free of the rigidity which he had lately perceived in his earlier work.

Before arriving in Ranikhet, Alfred had found himself frustrated by the occasionally crude language and narrow-mindedness of some of his colleagues. But the tranquility of the landscape, the gentler climate, and the improved living conditions at camp allowed him to let go of this irritation. His writing, once tinged with frustration, now reflected this deepening sense of peace and wonder.

Gradually, he started to appreciate the company of his fellow gunners, finding in them moments of camaraderie and even humour that he hadn't noticed before. He smiled to himself, recalling the events of the past few days.

'I swear, Alfred, you've been grinning non-stop since we left camp this morning. What's gotten into you?' asked Sergeant Evans, raising an eyebrow. 'You used to be the quiet one, always with your nose buried in that notebook.'

Alfred chuckled softly.

'Maybe it's just the hills, sir. A bit of fresh air does wonders. Feels like I'm a different person.'

'Fresh air is it?' chimed in Tripp, smirking as he gave Alfred a playful nudge. 'Or maybe it's that local brew you've taken a fancy to. Especially after last night's little... *incident*.'

Alfred grinned. 'Not every day you walk into the mess and find a hyena waiting for you.'

Andrews burst out laughing.

'You screamed like a girl, Streak!' The men started chuckling, their laughter contagious.

Streak crossed his arms defensively.

'I didn't scream! It was staring right at me, baring its teeth! What was I supposed to do—invite it for a drink while you lot cowered by the door?'

Alfred, still chuckling, added,

'Honestly, Streak, you did the right thing. Running would've only made it chase you. And fortunately your shrieking was enough to scare it off!'

'It's a miracle any of us were even standing, given how much we'd had to drink,' Andrews remarked, 'still can't believe a hyena wandered in while we were up on the terrace.'

'Yeah,' Streak agreed, shaking his head, 'probably best if we don't leave any food lying about next time. We should clean up before we turn in tonight.'

The laughter continued, and Alfred couldn't resist a grin.

'Well, it certainly made for an unforgettable night. That's not something I'd ever expect to see back home.'

Sergeant Evans gave Alfred a knowing smile.

'It's good to see you enjoying yourself, Williams. The old you would've been scribbling away in a corner. But now, you're definitely one of us.'

Alfred shrugged with a smile.

'I suppose I've learned to see things a bit differently. But don't worry, Sergeant—that story will make its way into my diary—eventually.'

Evans raised his canteen, grinning.

'Here's to more nights like that—minus the hyenas, preferably!'

The men raised their canteens, laughter echoing once more through the group.

***

In the mess reading room, Alfred found copies of the periodical, '*The Englishman,*' which had a wide circulation in the British expatriate community. Considering the recent marked increase in his literary output, he decided to submit some of his new poems to the editor, along with a brief letter explaining his background and recent experiences in India.

By early June, the heat in Ranikhet had become insufferable, and all eagerly anticipated the coming relief of the monsoon season. The approach of the monsoon was heralded by the development of large white and purple cumulus clouds that accumulated in the skies in the late mornings. Occasionally, a storm would come from the west, obscuring the view of the snow-clad peaks to the north

THE PALACE OF MY IMAGINATION

for the first time. The bell-like boom of thunder echoed across the now invisible mountain tops, while the air remained calm, and the lofty pines stood motionless. Occasionally, the storm would break directly over the valley, and rain would pour forth, its large drops beating loudly on the iron roofs of the camp. But after some minutes, this would pass, and the sun would return.

By mid-June, the real monsoon had arrived, bringing dense torrents of rain traveling northwestward. The valley became filled with fluffy white clouds, and the mountain wall disappeared within its mantle. Storms arose every day, and flashes of lightning occurred ceaselessly, annihilating the jet blackness of the moonless nights. The cooler environment and surging appetites encouraged the approach of many large cats to the village, which nightly roamed the streets of the bazaar unchecked. The tradition of maintaining nocturnal fires and the continuous beating of drums was reinstigated to discourage their approach.

However, it was almost two months later that the most significant predator, a tiger turned man-eater, began to prey on the local populace.

In the streets of the bazaar, the soldiers sensed an air of tension, fuelled by the rumours that had circulated for a couple of days.

It was said that a tiger had been prowling the area for some days and had claimed the lives of two natives in its relentless hunt.

Before arriving in Ranikhet they had first heard about the beast in the village of Bhowali , and now it seemed it had been responsible for the deaths of over fifty individuals in the area of Naini Tal and Almora.

Sergeant Evans and Jugal, the unit's native guide, sought out the village head to gather more information.

Their worst fears were confirmed when they learned that two young women grass-cutters had been attacked on the previous morning. They were accustomed to going out from the village in the early morning in order to retrieve grasses for sale in the bazaar. The tiger, having accustomed itself to their whereabouts, lay in wait from early dawn, pounced upon them and bore one of them off screaming into the forest.

JOHN CULLIMORE

While discussing this with the village headman they encountered an unexpected figure: a man clearly of European descent who introduced himself as an expert hunter. He had been called in to deal with the rogue animal. He had arrived that morning and had spoken with the community leaders. He was keen to appraise them of the situation, and to assess the potential for obtaining assistance in his goal of dealing with the fearsome threat.

Later that evening, gathered around the campfires, the men were called to order by Evans, his voice solemn. Alfred could sense that an important announcement was forthcoming and braced himself for the news.

'Lads,' Evans began, his tone grave, 'we're facing a serious threat here. A tiger has been attacking locals and is still at large, and it may be that we can help put an end to its reign of terror. I'd like you to listen to Mr. Jack Barnett, who has been sent here by the Indian authorities. He will tell you more about it, and how we might be able to help.'

'Lend him an eighteen pounder and some ammo!' suggested Tripp, eliciting a few guffaws.

'If that's what's decided, then I'll put you in charge of the gun, Private Tripp.' responded Evans who then gestured to Barnett to take the floor.

'Hello men, I'm Jim Barnett.I was born and raised in the hills of Kumaon in Uttarakhand , but as you've probably deduced I'm of British extraction. My father came here, from London as a railway engineer thirty-five years ago, just before my birth, and it's a strange coincidence that he did his apprenticeship in Swindon! I also became a railwayman, but in the last few years I've become increasingly involved with a peculiarly Indian problem. By which I mean tigers that prey on humans.'

There was a collective sharp intake of breath, Alfred and his comrades listened intently, but their apprehension seemed tempered by Barnett's relaxed confidence.

'I know this isn't something you want to hear, but unfortunately while we're in this region it's not something we can ignore. I've been hunting down rogue tigers over the last ten years. I travel all

THE PALACE OF MY IMAGINATION

across the subcontinent, and I'm doing this for the Indian government. And right now, right here in Ranikhet, there's a killer on the loose.'

He paused for a moment, allowing his words to sink in before he continued.

'What's important to know about such tigers, is that they didn't want to become man eaters. Healthy tigers like to hunt and catch their food, and their normal diet *doesn't* include humans. But a tiger that has become sufficiently impaired or disabled, either by wounds it has suffered, or by old age, has to take the easier option of preying on human flesh.

'Yesterday morning two young women were killed by a tiger. They were on the edge of the forest gathering grasses and they were attacked. I followed a trail of blood into the forest. I also found some bones as I penetrated further.'

A low murmur of horror rose from the men as they absorbed the graphic detail.

'There've been fifty-five victims of this animal in the last few months. And for the last few nights, this tiger has been stalking the lower road that leads into the village. You may hear it roaring tonight.

'So the first thing I suggest—which is for everyone's safety—is that we construct an observation platform and we keep it manned with two armed men on watch through the night. The village headman says the timber is available for this, and with three or four of you helping we can get this up before we retire for the night.

'I also suggest that we keep the campfires burning all night. The villagers are doing a similar thing.'

'Now, I know I can't insist on your help and I won't sugarcoat it—hunting down a rogue tiger is no easy task. But, with our combined skills, and some determination, we are very well placed to deal with this threat.'

'The government of India have offered me one thousand rupees to end this horror. But I'm not interested in the money. If you're prepared to help, I'll donate the money to your battery sergeant, to make life easier for you while you're stationed here.'

'I do have a plan to deal with this creature. The plan is more likely to succeed if you're involved. But right now, I won't go into it any further. I'll stop talking and let you decide how you wish to proceed. I'm happy to answer any questions you may have.'

After Barnett's speech, the soldiers gathered around in small groups, discussing the proposal. Tripp, ever the materialist, was the first to speak up.

'He's offered us a thousand rupees if we help. How much is that in English money?'

'Well,' replied Alfred, 'I'd say it's about fifteen hundred pounds. But that's really not the point. My vote would be to help. We've got plenty of men, rifles, and ammunition. We might even get some practice with the 18-pounder you mentioned.'

Andrews, the practical Scot, nodded in agreement. 'Aye, attack is always the best form of defence. Let's help the locals by ridding the area of this demon once and for all.'

The rest of the platoon murmured in agreement, their resolve strengthening as they considered the plight of the villagers and the challenge ahead.

Sergeant Evans, sensing unanimous support, stepped forward.

'It seems we're all in agreement, Mr. Barnett; So, we are at your service. Maybe you could outline the rest of your plan?'

Barnett's eyes lit up with gratitude and resolve.

'Thank you, Sergeant. Here's what we need to do...'

He laid out a detailed map of the area which pointed to several key locations where the tiger had been sighted, mainly at the edge of the forest below the road where a series of steep ravines emerged into a flatter crescent shaped area. Barnett gave a broad outline of his methods, describing how he would ensure the villagers were safe, then entice the tiger with live bait and subsequently stalk it. After this he suggested what weaponry would be required.

But first of all help was needed to build the platform and he called for volunteers. Tripp immediately put himself forward, believing that his skills in construction would be of value.

THE PALACE OF MY IMAGINATION

'My next request is a significant one. In view of the fact that one of my hunting colleagues has gone down with fever, and a second has gone abroad, I would appreciate it if two of you would come with me on the trail of the tiger.' Again, there was a collective intake of breath.

'I should say that I need good marksmen, or those of you who are used to hunting game with rifles.'

Initially there was silence. Some of the men gazed in Alfred's direction. He had distinguished himself a few days earlier obtaining the highest scores in a field firing and bayonet training exercise. He duly raised his hand. As did Streak, who was also a proficient rifleman and adept hunter of game in his native Wiltshire.

'Excellent. If you two men would care to join me in an hour's time, we'll do some reconnaissance.' said Barnett.

Alfred and Streak headed to inspect the rifles and ammunition. While Barnett used a .275 caliber Rigby, he had recommended to Alfred that a larger caliber would be more suitable for the soldiers. In the camp armory, they found several Holland & Holland rifles in .375 caliber with ample ammunition. They selected these and signed them out with the duty sergeant.

Taffy and Winston would be responsible for maintaining the campfires through the first half of the night. While this would not discourage the tiger from approaching, at least they would be able to track its movements and summon Barnett if it made a serious attempt to enter the village.

Andrews and Winston would be on first watch on the platform.

Barnett instructed the Headman of the village that no one should venture out the following day.

Later that evening, Barnett, Alfred and Streak walked to the site where the girls had been attacked by the tiger. They were accompanied by one of the villagers, who was leading a young male buffalo.

On arrival at the site of the attack, Barnett scraped away a little earth at the base of a large mango tree, exposing one of the roots. He tied the buffalo to it with a length of rope and the native lay down some hay for it to eat.

The gravity of the situation hit Alfred as the group retreated from the solitary buffalo tied to the tree, realising it was a deliberate lure to attract the tiger.

The night passed uneventfully in the camp, but when Alfred and Streak joined Barnett at the ravine entrance the next morning, the buffalo was no longer there. A small quantity of clotted blood marked the base of the tree, and some light impressions of the tiger's footprint were visible in the soft earth. The rope that had bound the buffalo had been gnawed through. Barnett gazed up the narrow, heavily wooded valley, and the men followed him along the trail of flattened vegetation indicating the direction the tiger had taken with its kill.

The ravine stretched southwest for about three hundred yards before curving to the left. High, rocky ridges bordered the eastern and western sides of the steep valley. Beyond the bend, a stream flowed, and farther ahead, the land rose steeply through dense undergrowth, extending as far as the eye could see.

Barnett signalled for silence and cautiously led the way, his rifle ready. The morning sun cast long shadows, and the thick foliage severely limited visibility. After crossing the stream, they spotted the buffalo lying beneath a sapling, partially eaten. Barnett gestured for the men to form a close single file. They advanced quietly, each step deliberate, staying alert to any sound or movement in their surroundings.

Suddenly, a rustle in the bushes broke the silence, and in an instant, the tiger appeared. Alfred was stunned, his breath catching at the sheer size and raw power of the creature that had emerged just six feet from where he stood. The tiger's presence was overwhelming. As it surged past the men with shocking speed, it let out a deep, menacing growl—a low, guttural rumble, like a revving motorcycle engine, that vibrated through Alfred's chest and left him momentarily breathless. The air around him seemed to shift with the animal's movement, carrying the pungent, musky scent of the tiger's fur.

The animal was imposing, stretching at least seven feet in length

THE PALACE OF MY IMAGINATION

and likely weighing a solid three hundred pounds. Its movements were fluid and powerful, each step revealing the ripple of thick muscles beneath its coat. As it darted effortlessly in front of the line of men, its striped coat seemed to coil and stretch in a rhythmic, concertina-like motion, the orange and black stripes almost blurring as it bounded up the ravine. Within seconds, it vanished into the dense undergrowth beyond, leaving a heavy silence in its wake.

It took several minutes before Alfred's heart stopped pounding and he could breathe normally again, still reeling from the awe-inspiring encounter.

On inspecting the buffalo's carcass, it was clear that much meat remained on it, and Barnett took this to indicate that the tiger might return. However, with respect to hunting the beast, the surrounding terrain offered no suitable trees where the men might set up a hide from which they might fire on it.

'Well men, we've learned one thing from today, we're actually dealing with a tigress'

'How can you tell?' asked Streak.

'It's basically down to my experience of pug marks,' answered Barnett. 'And I've seen enough of them now to conclude it's a female. She basically has a narrower, longer foot, making the overall track slimmer.'

Given the practical difficulties due to the terrain, Barnett reluctantly decided it was best to leave everything as it was and return the next morning to reassess the situation.

At dawn the next day, Barnett and his team returned to the area of the ravine beyond the stream. The buffalo had vanished, and drag marks traced a path along the valley floor through a maze of low shrubs and bramble. The valley remained flat for about a hundred yards before the ground began to rise once more. As they moved deeper into the ravine, its walls closed in around them, steep and jagged, forming a natural funnel that channelled them along a rocky path into an eerie corridor of rock and shadow. The air grew damp, heavy with the scent of decaying vegetation and something darker—an acrid tang that lingered in their nostrils and made them tense with anticipation.

They climbed a small rise, the path levelling out just enough to give them a view of a narrow clearing ahead. It was a grim tableau. The ground was strewn with bones—scattered remnants of past kills, their surfaces gnawed clean and sun-bleached, a haunting reminder of the tiger's dominance here. Some of the bones were small, likely deer or other forest prey, but a few were larger, and unmistakeably human, a sad testimony to the victims recently claimed by the beast. And there, half-hidden in the underbrush, lay the fresh remains of the buffalo. The carcass was splayed open, its flanks torn with deep slashes, the meat freshly stripped from its bones. The ground around it was soaked in dark, clotted blood, that stained the soil. Flies buzzed in thick clouds, disturbed by the men's approach, filling the air with a sickly, cloying hum.

But the tigress itself was nowhere to be seen.

'She's a clever beast,' Barnett murmured, examining the bones, 'she's seen us. She knows we're after her. So, she'll be extra cautious.'

Beyond the grim clearing the valley opened out into a bare rock-strewn area where thick ferns covered the lower half of the hillside. On the eastern side, the valley wall rose sharply above the ferns to meet bare ridges while the western side retained its cover of vegetation.

Barnett stood staring at the high valley walls for a minute or so, his mind weighing up all the options. Alfred broke the silence.

'A penny for your thoughts, sir?'

Barnett gave a wry smile.

'Indeed, but let me turn the question to you, Alfred; How do you see the situation?

After a few moments thought, Alfred made a suggestion.

'Well, it looks to me that the tiger isn't yet finished with its kill, so she's likely to return. We need to be here waiting for when she does.'

'I agree with you, but the problem is deciding where we wait. Ideally, we'd have a hunting platform in a tree above her approach. But there's nothing suitable here.'

Streak pointed to the ridge off to his right.

THE PALACE OF MY IMAGINATION

'There are a few trees up there—maybe four hundred yards from here. If we come back tomorrow with live bait, a goat perhaps, and leave it below those trees?'

Barnett nodded, considering Streak's suggestion.

Just then, the party heard the unmistakable call of the tigress from further down the valley.

Alfred could sense Barnett's mind at work. A look of dawning realisation crossed his face, and he reached a decision.

'I believe that tigress is searching for a mate. That mating urge is almost as strong as hunger. We can use that to bring her to us.'

Alfred and Streak exchanged a glance, both somewhat mystified and slightly perturbed by the thought of further close contact with the beast.

At that moment, the tiger let out another call. Barnett immediately responded to it by cupping his hands around his mouth and, taking a deep breath in, answered the call across the valley.

Alfred was impressed not only by the volume and the authenticity of Barnett's tiger imitation but by the hunter's wily strategy. The men listened intently. A minute or so later, the call was again answered.

'We're on,' said Barnett 'and she seems to be heading this way.' Barnett surveyed the terrain, his experienced eyes scanning the western side of the valley and the trees growing out from the ridge.

'We need to head for those trees. It's going to take a couple of hours to climb up there, but once we're there we can set up hunting platforms. We've got plenty of rope, and if we start now, we'll be settled in by five o'clock.'

The trees grew out from edge of a steep bank a few yards below the apex of the ridge. Their trunks, spaced about ten yards apart, extended over the ravine while their upper branches were intertwined, providing a natural network of cover.

The first tree had a sturdy branch emerging about eight feet up the trunk, projecting up and out over the ravine thirty feet below. Barnett noted its potential but focused on the second tree, which was more substantial and featured a large natural seat ten or so feet off the ground. He suggested that Alfred and Streak use this tree as their refuge and helped them climb up before handing up their rifles and ammunition.

Barnett supervised as Alfred and Streak slung two strands of rope between some reasonably substantial branches just below the level of the seat to support their feet. This arrangement provided a secure platform for the two men, who would have a good view of the ravine below.

Satisfied with the setup, Barnett moved to the first tree. He climbed up and began to assemble his ropes into another simple but effective hunting platform. He tied three strands of rope between branches, creating a stable perch from which he could monitor the area and take a clear shot if the tiger appeared.

During the assembly of the rope platforms, the tigress continued to call, and Barnett responded, but as the sun settled over the horizon, the tiger's calls ceased. The group were still able to converse as they were only separated by a few yards. Barnett suggested that Alfred and Streak took first watch focussing on the ravine as it descended, where the tiger was most likely to emerge, and to alert him if they saw anything by whistling.

Alfred's watch passed uneventfully, and despite the tension in the air, he and Streak managed to drift in and out of sleep, even in their upright positions. Just before dawn, Alfred was startled awake by the sudden sounds of skittering and squawking. He noticed small birds fluttering up from the underbrush, and two jungle fowl, clearly frightened, hurried past the tree and disappeared into the valley below. He let out a soft whistle to alert Barnett.

As the sound left his lips, he heard it—a low, guttural snarling, accompanied by the unmistakable crunch of heavy footsteps. A large figure emerged behind them; its presence confirmed by the shadows dancing at the edge of Alfred's vision.

Barnett silently motioned for them to stay still. Then, for the second time, they saw the tigress, its orange and black stripes blending into the dim light, as it began stalking around the base of the tree. She looked magnificent and powerful, her muscles rippling beneath her coat. Alfred's pulse quickened as he realized just how close the predator was.

THE PALACE OF MY IMAGINATION

The tigress stopped, and for a moment, it seemed to size up the tree. But sensing the hunters above she immediately sprang up the slope to their right, disappearing into dense vegetation. Alfred's heart raced as he observed just how close the animal had approached their position.

'Do you think she might come at us from above?' Streak whispered nervously. Barnett shook his head.

'Not a chance,' he replied quietly, 'she won't risk a jump from above, not with that thirty-foot drop into the ravine on the other side.'

The jungle fell silent once more. The rest of the night passed without incident, though the men found sleep elusive.

'I can hear cracking sounds down over to the left,' muttered Streak at one point, his eyes darting into the darkness.

'That's a good sign,' Barnett reassured him. 'She's gone back to her lair to feed on the buffalo. You can rest easy for now.'

Despite their nerves, exhaustion eventually claimed them. But as dawn's first light touched the bare eastern ridge, Alfred's soft whistle brought them back to full alertness. He pointed silently into the ravine, where the underbrush rustled with movement.

In the dim light three or four Sambar deer were bolting up the ravine, and now their sharp barks of alarm rang through the valley.

Barnett gave the alert.

'I think she's on the move, look over to the left.'

Within seconds, the tigress appeared. She moved through the foliage with an unhurried grace, presumably satiated from her recent meal of buffalo meat and not yet ready to hunt.

'Be ready with your rifles, chaps, ' said Barnett.

The tiger began to canter across the flat stretch of the valley, a blur of raw power and grace. Within seconds, she was directly below the trees, continuing her ascent up towards the end of the valley.

Barnett took aim and fired. The shot struck true, but clearly it wasn't fatal. The tigress bellowed a thunderous roar, spun around, and in an uncontrollable fury charged straight toward the tree where Alfred and Streak were stationed. Barnett aimed and fired. This time, the shot struck near the top of her head, causing her to flip backward over her tail in a dramatic arc. But as soon as she hit the ground, she sprang back up, her relentless advance toward the trees undeterred.

'Fire when you're ready,' Barnett said calmly, his voice steady despite the tension. At that precise moment, the rising sun crested the ridge opposite them, its blinding rays flooding their eyes and momentarily dazzling them as Alfred tried to focus on the advancing target, feeling the weight of the moment.

Barnett fired first, but the rifle only clicked—no explosion. The tigress sprang, and as Alfred tightened his finger on the trigger, time seemed to stop.

Suddenly, he was no longer in the jungle but back in South Marston, approaching the sunlit gates of the village churchyard. Ahead, Henry Byett and Reuben George walked at the back of a line of people, their figures leading him through the old lych gate, both turning occasionally to look at him. But then, the familiar place transformed—the churchyard now buzzed with a lively bazaar. The path was lined with stalls, the air filled with animated voices, the pungent smell of spices and the sounds of livestock, and children darting between the groups of people.

The scene was vividly Indian, but strange. Both familiar and yet he couldn't place it. As he walked, he realised that people were recognising him, offering friendly nods and smiling, some greeting him with a warm '*Namaste*.'

Suddenly, to his right, he heard the whoosh of a rocket ascending, followed by an explosive burst of orange sparks against the darkening evening sky. In an instant, the vision faded, and he was thrust back into reality.

Alfred and Streak had fired their rifles just in time. Their bullets struck the tigress squarely in the chest and neck, halting her in her tracks.

She collided with the lowest part of the tree trunk, rebounded down the slope and disappeared into the undergrowth of the ravine below.

Alfred glanced down and saw the trunk of the tree stained with a large quantity of blood. Barnett, wasting no time, descended quickly and having reloaded the gun's magazine, signalled for

THE PALACE OF MY IMAGINATION

Alfred and Streak to descend and follow him closely in strict single file as he led them down the slope.

The blood trail was easy to track, directing them toward a large rock about two hundred yards away in the centre of the valley. Moving cautiously, they soon heard the tigress snarling in the distance. Barnett signalled for them to halt, and after a few tense moments, they could make out her striped body lying still in the undergrowth. After a minute, the tigress struggled to her feet and resumed her slow, unsteady progress toward the rock. Clearly weakened, she paused again just fifteen yards short before finally staggering the last few steps and collapsing beside it. Her body lay motionless. They watched intently for five minutes, ensuring she was truly lifeless before moving in closer.

When Alfred and Streak reached the rock, they noticed their clothes were flecked with blood—not their own, but the tigress's, which had spattered from her wounds as she collided with the tree trunk.

Barnett, noting their bloodstained appearance, smiled.

'Well, that was a proper baptism for the both of you,' he said, his tone light despite the tension of the moment. They gazed silently at the lifeless body for a few seconds more, before Barnett broke the silence.

'Now you'll understand why I wanted you with me. Well done, chaps.'

Raising his gun Barnett fired into the air. He fired five shots at regular intervals, each echoing through the valley. Alfred looked at him curiously.

'This is my way of signalling to the villagers that the threat has been dealt with,' Barnett explained with a grin. 'Now, I think it's time for some refreshment.' He offered his flask of whisky, and they each took a turn before settling down by the rock to admire the lifeless tiger.

Alfred could scarcely believe he was here. His mind drifted to how he might capture this experience for posterity, beginning to envision a work he might create to commemorate it. Hailing from rural Wiltshire, his closest encounter with any type of unusual animal had been a fleeting glimpse of a polecat by the River

Cole—but this was infinitely more profound. He felt incredibly privileged to have been part of the hunt, and also fortunate to come out of it in one piece, bearing in mind the strange experience he'd had immediately prior to taking his critical shot.

Sure enough, the sound of Barnett's salvo of gunshots had drawn the attention of the villagers, who were now visible as they approached from the northern end of the valley. Filled with excitement, they had quickly cut down a pair of saplings and fashioned a makeshift bier using branches and creepers. With what seemed like smooth efficiency, they retrieved the tigress's body from behind the rock and began the return journey. Their first stop would be in Ranikhet, from where they would commence a tour throughout the region to demonstrate to the people that the deadly threat had been eliminated.

Back at the village, Alfred, Streak and Barnett stood solemnly over the fallen tigress. Barnett stooped to make a cursory examination of the body, and discovered a festering gunshot wound in her left shoulder. The wound was riddled with three or four sinus tracts, each oozing thin yellow fluid. From the base of one of these, Barnett carefully extracted three steel pellets.

'This must have been an excruciatingly painful wound,' he murmured, his voice tinged with sadness, 'it's no wonder it drove her to become a man-eater.'

As the reality of his actions settled in, Alfred felt a complex mix of emotions—relief that the village was safe, but also a deep respect for the life he had taken. The thought weighed on him heavily.

Streak, standing beside him, broke the silence.

'It's ironic, isn't it? Someone wounds a creature, leaves it to suffer, and in return, it comes back to hunt us.'

Barnett paused, absorbing the truth in those words.

'The locals would call it karma' he said, smiling as he stood.

THE PALACE OF MY IMAGINATION

Chapter 31

'Whoever has not tasted a mango is the poorer thereby, the loss of which could not easily be compensated in this life.... The flavour is indescribable in its exquisite delicacy. One seems to taste half the earth and half the sun in a married mystery of delicious sweetness.' *Alfred Williams , Mid Palm and Pine , 1918 (unpublished)*

Alfred and his unit departed his beloved Ranikhet on November 8th, 1918, making their way back to Cawnpore in the plains. They rode out on mountain ponies, beginning a two day fifty-mile journey to Katgodam, and spent the first night under canvas. Alfred remembered little of the trek itself; the sure-footed ponies had made this journey countless times, and he barely noticed his surroundings as the party descended towards the plains.

He used the time to reflect. He was earning a decent supplementary income from his writings in Indian newspapers and periodicals and had gathered enough information about India and its culture to write extensively or even give lectures on his return home. However, the war had not yet concluded, and he was unsure when, or even if, he would return. The prospect of returning to Cawnpore, plagued with mosquitoes and oppressive heat—one hundred and two degrees in the shade—was not appealing.

It was in this state of uncertainty that Alfred arrived in Cawnpore two days later.

***

However, It was cooler than he expected when they arrived back in Cawnpore. The men had been allocated to the bungalows on the edge of the camp, with two men in each.

Alfred spent his first day back reacquainting himself with the Ganges and the *ghats*, and in the early evening he called upon his tutor, *Pandit* Ramananda, who had been guiding him in his spiritual and intellectual discovery of the ancient Hindu philosophy.

JOHN CULLIMORE

They delved into the Vedas, ancient scriptures that Alfred found both puzzling and enlightening. Ramananda, recognizing Alfred's continuing thirst for knowledge and truth, gave him some written Sanskrit examples from the Rigveda as well as English translations of these, and also wrote down how these verses sounded using English letters.

However, Alfred experienced an almost overpowering curiosity regarding the Sanskrit characters written above the translations, sparking a strong desire within him to understand the original texts. For now, though, he chose to keep this to himself.

The evening continued with a simple but nourishing meal of dhal and rice, which Alfred savoured, finding it far superior to the monotonous camp food. He felt a profound sense of peace and fulfillment in the company of the *Pandit* , whose wisdom and serenity were a balm to his restless mind.

By nine p.m., Alfred had wandered back to the camp. Exhausted but content, he headed straight to bed. His companion Tripp was already fast asleep in the adjoining room, his loud snoring filling the bungalow. Despite the noise, Alfred was so tired that he fell asleep almost immediately, not even bothering to undress.

A few hours later, Alfred was awoken by the distant sound of ringing bells emanating from the city, which he thought was unusual for a Monday night. As he lay there, a sharp knock on the front door brought him fully awake. Heart pounding, he rose to answer it, wondering who could be calling at such an hour. Then the familiar voice of Sergeant Evans rang out.

'Williams, Tripp, great news, it's over, the war's over! Get yourselves to the parade ground, now!'

The initial confusion was quickly replaced with excitement. Alfred hurriedly pulled on his boots, and roused Tripp from his deep slumber. The two men, still groggy but exhilarated, rushed to the parade ground.

When they arrived, the scene was one of unrestrained jubilation. Men were cheering, laughing, and embracing one another. Some had started singing patriotic songs, their voices rising joyfully into the night. A spontaneous chorus of 'God Save the King' echoed

THE PALACE OF MY IMAGINATION

across the camp, mingling with shouts of 'Hurrah!' and 'It's all over!'

The sense of relief and happiness was palpable. Alfred and his comrades danced in circles, their faces alight with the expectation that they would soon be going home. Others stood in small groups, talking excitedly about their plans for the future, their voices filled with hope and anticipation.

Tripp suggested breaking out the cannon from the armoury to fire a series of celebratory rounds. The idea was met with unanimous enthusiasm, and the euphoric men of the battery hauled out the cannon and prepared it.

Each round fired was greeted with deafening cheers and laughter. The thunderous booms reverberated through the night, a triumphant announcement of peace. In total, thirty rounds were fired, each one a powerful symbol of the war's end.

As the cannon shots echoed into silence, Sergeant Evans found that Alfred had rejoined the celebrating crowd. He pulled him aside, his expression a mixture of relief and solemnity.

'Williams,' he began, his voice hoarse from shouting, 'It's true. The war is over. The Germans surrendered in France, the Kaiser has abdicated, and the armistice was signed a few hours ago. Hostilities have ceased.'

Alfred listened intently, absorbing the gravity of the news. 'The Kaiser abdicated?' he repeated, almost in disbelief.

Evans nodded.

'Yes, it happened just a couple of days ago. There was a naval mutiny in Kiel, which grew into a full people's revolt. There was no other way for the Kaiser. He's fled to the Netherlands.'

Alfred let out a breath he didn't realise he was holding.

'So, it's really over then. We can go home?'

'Yes,' Evans confirmed, a rare smile spreading across his face. 'It's really over. Exactly when we will head home, I don't know. But for now, let's celebrate. This is a night to remember.'

As the two men returned to the festivities, Alfred felt a profound mix of relief, hope, and excitement. The nightmare of war was finally ending, and a new chapter seemed ready to unfold, and he realized that he was about to reach an important crossroads in his life when he would be called upon to make some fundamental decisions.

***

Although the war was over, when he spoke with Sergeant Evans the next morning, it became clear that he still couldn't be sure when their battery would be demobilised and the journey home could begin.

'It could be several months before all this is sorted out,' Evans explained. 'Until I hear otherwise, we're to carry on as usual with our regular training and field exercises. The only thing that's about to change is that we're going back to Rorkee in two weeks' time'

Seeing the disappointment on Alfred's face, Evans attempted to lift his spirits. 'You know, you're all due some leave if you'd like to take it,' he added, catching Alfred's attention.

Alfred's ears pricked up, and Evans went on, 'Plus, there's your share of the bounty from that tiger hunt back in Ranikhet. I could arrange some funds if you're thinking of doing something with your leave.'

'How much time could I take?' Alfred asked, his enthusiasm rising.

'Well, if we say three weeks, would that suit you?'

Alfred smiled broadly and began to think about where he wanted to go.

'Just give me two or three days to get the funds sorted. Oh, and don't forget' said Evans, 'as a member of the British Army, all your rail travel is of course free.'

Having consulted the map on the wall of the mess, Alfred had decided on an itinerary which should take him to the places he wished to visit and return him to Rorkee within three weeks.

Alfred left camp at the first opportunity, managing to catch an evening train to Agra, where he arrived just before midnight. Although he arrived unannounced, he found accommodation at the Soldier's Rest, albeit on a *charpoy* in an outdoor tent. For the remainder of his trip, however, Alfred would have sufficient funds to hire local guides who were familiar with the sites he wanted to

THE PALACE OF MY IMAGINATION

see and could usually recommend suitable places to stay along the way.

Thus, within the first ten days of his leave, Alfred found ample time to fully immerse himself in some of India's most extraordinary sights.

He had marvelled at the ethereal beauty of the Taj Mahal under the moonlight, its luminous marble seeming almost otherworldly in the soft glow. In Lucknow, he wandered through the splendid remnants of Mughal architecture, captivated by its grandeur and intricate design. At Benares, he experienced the serene magic of sailing down the sacred Ganges River at sunrise, watching the *ghats* come alive with pilgrims. He observed the priests performing time-worn rituals, all bathed in the soft early morning sunlight.

Alfred embarked on the second half of his Indian adventure by boarding an overnight train of the East India Railway to Calcutta, feeling a mix of excitement and anticipation for the journey ahead. With a comfortable reserve of funds still at his disposal, he chose a first-class ticket, including a sleeping compartment, relishing the luxury it afforded him. As he settled into a plush seat in the first-class carriage, he noticed a fellow passenger who appeared to be of European descent. The moment Alfred took his seat, the man lowered his newspaper and extended his hand in greeting.

'Peter Langford—pleased to make your acquaintance,' he said with a warm smile. Alfred returned the gesture, saying, 'I'm Alfred.'

'I see you're in the forces,' Langford observed, recognizing the lightweight khaki uniform.

'Indeed, Royal Field Artillery gunner, stationed at Cawnpore,' Alfred replied., 'I'm on three weeks' leave and there are places I'd like to see before we're eventually demobilised.'

He leaned back slightly, eager to learn more about his travel companion. 'And what brings you to Calcutta?'

'I live and work there,' Langford answered, his expression brightening. 'I'm a silk merchant; manage my own firm— Langford & Co. Oriental Silks.' He offered Alfred his card and gestured slightly, as if inviting Alfred to inquire further about the trade that captivated him.

Alfred's curiosity was immediately stirred—here, for the first time, was an Englishman who had not only settled in India but embraced life there fully. Eager to learn more, he asked Langford about the expatriate experience in India. He was more than happy to share his story.

Langford explained that he had come to India from London nearly forty years earlier as a child of five, accompanying his father, who had established the silk business in Calcutta. When he was twelve, he had been sent back to England for his secondary schooling, first at Winchester and later at Oxford, where he met his future wife. She too had ties to India. Her father served in the British diplomatic corps in Delhi. After completing their studies, the couple returned together to join the family business, and they'd never thought of making a life anywhere else.

Now, they were raising three children in the bustling expatriate community of Calcutta, where the children attended British-run schools that upheld the standards of English education, and although he envisaged his sons returning to England for Higher Certificate studies and University, Langford spoke with pride about the thriving expatriate network in the city. Alfred listened intently, envisioning a life where England and India met in a unique blend of heritage and opportunity.

Langford listened intently as Alfred shared his background, intrigued to learn about his work on the railways, his recent experience in the forces and his experiences of writing which included recent articles which had appeared in Indian publications. Alfred explained that as a result of recent writings about steam hammers and drop stampers, a firm in Calcutta had reached out to discuss a potential position, which he planned to explore during his stay.

Langford seemed genuinely captivated by Alfred's story.

'I'm heading back to Calcutta myself, though I'll only be there for 24 hours before heading to Ceylon on business,' Langford said, 'otherwise, I'd have loved to host you and introduce you to some

THE PALACE OF MY IMAGINATION

key people in the community. If everything works out and you settle here, please make contact—I'd be delighted to introduce your wife to my Vanessa. She'd make her feel at home here.'

'Thank you,' Alfred replied warmly. 'I'll be sure to let you know how things go.'

'Excellent,' Langford nodded. 'At the very least, let me give you some recommendations for your time in Calcutta.'

After another hour of animated conversation, Alfred retired to his sleeping compartment with a carefully crafted itinerary for his stay in Calcutta and the stirring realization that India could offer him far more than a simple tourist experience.

Following Langford's recommendations, Alfred arrived in Calcutta, left the bustling Howrah Rail Terminal, and made his way to the nearby ferry for a short ride across the Hooghly River to the Esplanade area. Here, he planned to find transport to the address Langford had suggested. As he reached the front of the line at the carriage stand next to the ferry, he was intrigued to see a man of Chinese descent step forward, offering his services as a rickshaw puller and guide. The colourful, shaded rickshaw seemed a refreshing and effective way to navigate Calcutta's lively streets, which on this side of the river were lined with broad boulevards, imposing colonial buildings, and vibrant marketplaces.

It was a quick five-minute ride to the YMCA on S.N. Banerjee Road, which Langford had recommended as a comfortable and welcoming spot for Western visitors. The YMCA offered safe, pleasant accommodation along with dining, recreation, and the chance to meet others in a friendly, community atmosphere.

The following day, Alfred visited the headquarters of Saxby and Farmer, the engineering firm that had reached out to him. Arnold Saxby, who had been impressed by Alfred's articles, personally conducted him on a tour of the engineering shop and its neighbouring railway workshop. Though it was much smaller than the GWR works he knew from Swindon, the facility was poised for expansion, and Saxby shared a highly optimistic outlook for the railway industry in eastern India.

His optimism and enthusiasm led him to extend a generous

personal offer to Alfred.

Alfred, taken by surprise yet deeply flattered, expressed his heartfelt gratitude. Unsure how best to respond, he said he would consider the offer, discuss it with his wife, and return with an answer within a month if that was agreeable.

Alfred felt both pleased and a bit unsettled by Saxby's offer. The day's heat was building quickly, and Shu-Lin, his rickshaw driver, noticed Alfred's tension and unease. Sensing he might appreciate a respite, Shu-Lin suggested a relaxing boat trip along the Hooghly on a friend's vessel, where Alfred could enjoy the shaded decks and an ample supply of refreshments. He arranged the outing, assuring Alfred he'd return later to bring him back to his hotel.

As he drifted down the river, the breadth and flow of the waters reminded him of the Mersey at Liverpool's Pier Head. However, Calcutta's waterway bustled with a mix of picturesque local and commercial craft, including fishing boats, ferries, steamships, pleasure craft and country boats transporting goods.

As the boat made a scheduled stop at a landing stage near the Eden Gardens, Alfred heard Shu-Lin calling out to him. Turning, he saw his driver's familiar, smiling face as he skillfully guided the rickshaw along the riverbank. Once Alfred was settled, they continued along the riverside path, with the lush greenery of the gardens to his right as they headed back towards the Chowringee road before turning right towards the YMCA.

Alfred returned to the YMCA at four p.m., feeling hot and weary. He headed to his room and promptly fell asleep until seven. When he awoke, he felt refreshed and eager to explore more of what Calcutta had to offer. Outside the hotel, he had noticed some posters on the telegraph poles along S.N. Bannerjee Road advertising some kind of theatrical event, which he couldn't decipher but had piqued his interest. He asked the reception staff for details. They informed him that there was to be a trilogy of Bengali plays at the nearby Minerva Theatre which included famous Indian actors in the cast. However, they felt it would be unlikely to appeal to him as a European.

But true to his nature, Alfred was intrigued enough to convince

THE PALACE OF MY IMAGINATION

Shu-Lin to take him there in his rickshaw. As they approached, he saw a large crowd of locals queuing to enter what was evidently going to be a popular event. As Shu-Lin set him down, there was a look of concern on his face, which grew more intense as a military policeman approached and stopped to address Alfred.

'Sir, I'm not sure it's advisable for you to attend this event,' said the officer in heavily accented English.

'Whyever not?' asked Alfred.

'Well, you are obviously British soldier, and there has been much unrest. I'm sure you'll understand?'

Alfred guessed he was referring to the rising levels of civil unrest across the subcontinent coupled with an increasing clamour for Indian independence. The heavy-handed attitude of the governnment, which had adopted a regime of arrest and detention without trial was also fanning discontent.

A small group of well-dressed onlookers were now focused on the increasing tension of Alfred's encounter with the policeman, some of them showing obvious expressions of concern.

'I'll be fine,' insisted Alfred in reply.

'But sir, is this sensible?' said the policeman, while at the same time Shu-Lin nodded enthusiastically in agreement with the officer's sentiment.

But then a well-dressed local stepped forward, addressing himself to the policeman in faultless English.

'This gentleman will be fine. We've reserved a seat for him in our section, and we'll make sure he's taken care of for the evening.' Alfred's newfound acquaintance assured the policeman firmly. The officer gave a shrug, muttered something under his breath, and stepped back, evidently satisfied.

Shu-Lin, taking Alfred aside, nodded and informed him that he'd return at the end of the plays to escort him back.

With the show about to begin, Alfred's group moved through the entrance and made their way up to the dress circle, where the seats provided a perfect view of the stage below. As they settled in, there was little time for in-depth conversation, but Alfred introduced himself to the gentleman who had intervened on his behalf. The man gave a polite nod, though the bustle of the crowd and the dimming lights signalled the need for silence as the performance was about to start.

Alfred, ever curious, took in the unfamiliar surroundings and the lively atmosphere, glancing around at the patrons who filled the theatre. He made a mental note to learn more about his companion and the rest of his party at the next interval. For now, he sat back, preparing himself for what promised to be a memorable experience.

Though Alfred didn't understand a word of Bengali, the actors' physical expressions, the intensity of their dialogue and singing, and the evocative set allowed him to follow the storyline.

During the interval, Alfred reached out to the man who had come to his aid outside the theatre. The man introduced himself as Manjit Ohbrai, saying he was glad to have been of help.

'It was very considerate of you to step in,' Alfred said. 'But I'm curious—what made you speak up for me?' he asked with a glint of interest.

Obhrai smiled. 'You seemed genuinely interested in seeing the plays and experiencing our culture. It's rare to see that, so I felt it was worth lending you a hand.'

Alfred was then introduced to Obhrai's companions, all fluent in English and eager to learn more about him. They shared insights into the plays and gave him background on the celebrated actors, adding depth to his experience of the evening.

Alfred savoured every moment of the three performances and didn't leave the theatre until the event concluded at 4 a.m. True to their plan, Shu-Lin was waiting outside, having perfectly anticipated when the plays would end.

Alfred spent two more days in Calcutta, visiting notable sites including the Kalighat Temple and the Black Hole Memorial. Remembering Ramananda's suggestion, he made sure to visit Kalighat. In one of the temple's outer areas, he observed the sacrificial rituals, with goats being offered to the goddess Kali.

The Black Hole Memorial, however, was packed with tourists, and Alfred began to feel the urge to escape to a quieter, more

THE PALACE OF MY IMAGINATION

peaceful setting.

With Langford's advice in mind, he boarded an overnight train heading south to Puri. This coastal town, famed as a centre of pilgrimage, proved to be a revelation for Alfred. He strolled along the expansive beaches, swam in the sea, and witnessed the renowned Rath Yatra festival, where an enormous chariot carried the statue of the Hindu god Jagannath through the streets. Alfred was deeply struck by the vast crowds and the profound devotion of the pilgrims who had come to participate in the festival and worship at the temples.

After exploring Puri, Alfred felt a sudden weariness. Realising he'd seen enough for one journey; he decided it was time to think about returning to his unit.

He spent most of the return journey deep in thought. When he set out, Alfred had hoped that this trip would fully satisfy his urge to experience India, once and for all. But now, he understood that the timeless allure and magic of India had woven themselves into his very being, leaving him uncertain of how he could do without it. He also needed to make a decision about Saxby's offer—and find a way to explain it all to Mary. The thought filled him with a pang of guilt and a sense of duplicity he knew he'd have to confront.

By the time he arrived back in Rorkee, he felt more conflicted than ever.

JOHN CULLIMORE

Chapter 32

28 /1/ 1919
Rorkee

Dearest Mary,

As I sit to write this letter, I am struck by the realisation that it has been over a year since we were last together. This milestone seems an appropriate moment to reflect on the profound impact India has had on me and how it has shaped my current outlook. I hope you will understand if my thoughts appear somewhat tentative.

With the war having ended, I find myself preoccupied with thoughts of our life in England and how it will contrast with the India I have come to know and love. India's charm and beauty have left a deep impression on me, and I believe you would be equally captivated, though I acknowledge it would require some major adjustment on your part. (but more of that anon.)

One of the most significant changes I have experienced here is a surge in my creativity and some recognition of my efforts. I have had several poems and articles published in local periodicals, which have been well received. This has even allowed me to supplement my income, and I am pleased to enclose some much-needed funds for you, along with a selection of gifts from this remarkable country. Encouraged by the positive response, I am currently working on a book entitled *Indian Life and Scenery*, and I have received promising feedback regarding its serialisation in a prominent Indian newspaper.

Unfortunately, my accounts of life in the Gun Battery and our journey around the Cape to India have not been met with the same enthusiasm from my English publishers. This leaves me uncertain about the prospects of returning to writing in England, where past experiences in Wiltshire were marred by jealousy , bitterness and narrow-mindedness.

Adding to my concerns, your recent letter informed me that we

THE PALACE OF MY IMAGINATION

no longer have the privilege of staying at Dryden Cottage as our landlord intends to sell the property. It feels as though life is nudging us towards a different path. Often, I think how wonderful it would be if you could join me here, to marvel at the stunning peaks of the Himalayas and immerse yourself in the mystery and timelessness of India.

Beyond creativity, my philosophical outlook has undergone a radical transformation. I have delved deeply into the major religions here, Islam and Hinduism, and am particularly fascinated by how Hindus seamlessly integrate their philosophy of existence with their religious practices. This has led me to embrace a more universal perspective. I now see 'God' as an intrinsic part of ourselves and every aspect of our waking life.

Poetry seems endemic here; every third man is a poet, though not all may capture their poetry on paper. Despite the formidable challenges—the climate, pervasive poverty, and social inequalities—I believe these are not insurmountable, and that we could thrive in this environment. There is a supportive expatriate community, and I have received serious encouragement to remain in India. After some articles were published about me in the Indian press, one firm in particular, aware of my previous experience with modern steam hammers in the GWR, have been keen to canvas my views concerning the restructuring of one of their factories. Offers of introductions to work with Indian Railways and engineering firms have likewise been extended to me, and even an Indian railway factory has made a generous offer of employment.

I wanted to share these reflections with you, to understand how you might react to my observations and to gauge your feelings about resuming our life in South Marston after the war. I hope these revelations are not shocking to you, but rather that my experiences have helped me to grow spiritually and enabled me to reflect on what is particularly important in life, and for all that I still very much see you and you alone as the focus of my existence.

With my fondest love,
Alfred

JOHN CULLIMORE

South Marston
21/3/19

My Dearest Alfred,

I hope this letter finds you well. The war is finally over, and there is a sense of relief and new beginnings in the air. I have been under the weather with a chest infection, which has made these past months quite difficult, especially managing on your army allowance. The struggle to make ends meet has been wearing, and I find myself longing for some stability and comfort.

Your last letter filled my heart with mixed emotions. On one hand, I felt the excitement and passion in your words about India, and on the other, I was saddened by the negative perceptions of our life here and the uncertainties it holds.

Your experiences and reflections on India are deeply inspiring, and I can see how much the country has touched your soul. The idea of starting afresh in a land so vibrant and rich in culture is indeed appealing, though it would require significant adjustments on my part.

You mentioned your creative pursuits and successes in India, which I am so proud of. Your poems and articles being published and well received must be incredibly satisfying. It is heartening to know that you have been able to supplement your income, and I am grateful for the funds and the thoughtful gifts you sent. They have been a great comfort during these trying times.

The thought of not returning to the old ways in South Marston does not displease me entirely. The bitterness, slander, and jealousies you faced there were indeed harsh, and I can understand your reluctance to go back to such an environment.

I also have some sad news from the village—Uncle George passed away peacefully in his sleep two weeks ago. The funeral is next week, and I will attend, though perhaps you could send a note to the Ockwells.

Losing our stay at Dryden Cottage adds to the uncertainty, and perhaps this is the right moment to consider a life beyond the village.

THE PALACE OF MY IMAGINATION

You own some land at The Hook, left to you by your mother in her will. This might offer us some opportunity for development, and I wonder if you had forgotten that, but apart from that, there is nothing else here to anchor us down.

If you can envision a way forward in India, I am willing to consider it. Your work and the encouragement you have received there seem promising, and I trust your judgment on this matter.

My love, I yield to you to make the decision that you believe is best for our future. If India is where you see our dreams taking shape, then I am prepared to embrace it with you. I just ask that you guide me through a potentially difficult transition, as your support and understanding will be crucial.

Please let me know your thoughts and plans. I await your response with bated breath, hoping for a brighter and more stable future together.

With all my love,
Mary

***

On guard duty the next morning, Alfred and Tripp found themselves in a deep discussion about their future. The ending of the war had left them both contemplative about their next steps, and their differing views became quickly apparent.

'I'm fed up being in a foreign country,' said Tripp, his frustration evident, 'some people here don't even speak our language. The climate is unbearable—too hot or too wet. Everywhere is dirty, and the hygiene's appalling. Beggars follow me everywhere. It's just—uncivilised.'

Alfred listened patiently, understanding Tripp's viewpoint even if he didn't share it.

'But there's so much to love about India,' he replied thoughtfully, 'I've never seen anything like the shores of the ocean at Puri. Beautiful palm trees running along the beaches for miles, and the sunsets over the sea are just—breathtaking.

'And the Himalayas—the sight of those mountaintops fills me with inspiration—I'm not sure I'll survive without being able to see those sights again.'

JOHN CULLIMORE

Tripp shook his head, bewildered.

'You're a writer and a poet, Alfred. You need artistic inspiration. Me? I need a cosy cottage in an English village, with a friendly pub and a comely wife to welcome me home every night with a hearty supper. I've never felt comfortable among the natives here.'

Alfred smiled, a hint of melancholy in his eyes. 'But it is possible to live harmoniously here if you work at it. I've been delighted to see Brits and Europeans in Cawnpore and Calcutta mingling with the natives. Even the children of well-to-do expats wander around the bazaar in the daytime and evening. They seem completely safe among thousands of natives, and they're having a wonderful time.'

Tripp sighed. 'Maybe so, but my health has suffered because of this climate and the bloody insects, and that can't continue. You've had your share of fevers yourself, and you've lost plenty of weight since we've been here. How can you bear to continue here?'

Alfred paused, considering his answer. 'I think it's "the call of the East". It's something very strong, in fact it's irresistible. I'll just miss not wandering around among the crowds at the bazaar, and I'll miss the noise of festivals and ceremonies.

'But I suppose I'll miss the warmth of the sunlight more than anything.'

Tripp nodded slowly, acknowledging Alfred's feelings even if he couldn't share them.

'I guess we're just different, mate. For you, India is an adventure, a place of inspiration. For me, it's a trial I can't wait to leave behind me.' Alfred smiled again, this time more warmly. 'That's what makes us human, Tripp. We find our homes in different places, in different ways. But no matter where we end up, we'll always have these memories to bind us.'

As they looked out over the camp, the noise of celebration still echoing in the distance, both men relished a new beginning—whatever and wherever that might be.

THE PALACE OF MY IMAGINATION

PART 6: HOMECOMING

Chapter 33

As Alfred looked at the receding coast of India from the deck of the *Huntsgreen*, he wondered if he had made the correct decision. In his heart of hearts, he was convinced that India would be the place where he could attain his full life's potential, but in the end, he had followed the path of least resistance, which was to return to his native land.

He couldn't help but interrogate himself regarding the wisdom of his choice. He was tired. He missed his wife. In the last few months he had lived in a state of chronic poor health, with intermittent fevers and reduced vision caused by an ulcer on his eye that had scarred and left him with chronic pain. But for all that, he knew he was returning to a country that was cold, grey, and economically and socially depleted.

He was convinced that he had been forgotten as a writer in England, making it imperative that he promptly re-establish his literary reputation with new work. Yet, as he gazed over the deck rail of the cramped steamer, at the monotonous expanse of the ocean, he felt little in the way of inspiration.

His thoughts turned to Tripp, who had eagerly anticipated their return to England. Tripp's longing for the comforts of home contrasted sharply with Alfred's own yearnings. Alfred couldn't help but feel a pang of envy for Tripp's straightforward desires. Perhaps it was easier to be content with simple pleasures and a predictable life?

These feelings of negativity seemed to trigger an alert in his mind. He thought of the conversations he'd had with his tutor, Ramananda, and the wisdom imparted to him through the Vedas. In particular he remembered one of the *Pandit's* favourite sayings;

'As you think, so you become.'

This was a timely reminder that he should seek to replace those negative thoughts with thoughts of strength and truth, as only in this way would he reach his long-stated mission to discover his real self, the pure consciousness that was the source of his recurring inspiration.

Alfred knew that his journey back to England was a new chapter. He would find a way to reconcile his love for India with the realities of life in post-war England.

His writings would bridge these two worlds, capturing the essence of his experiences and the profound lessons he had learned. And in that instant, smiling to himself, he realised that in order to achieve this, he would have to return to the process of self-education.

In order to maximise the insights he had begun to gain from the Vedas, the Upanishads, the Bhagavad Gita, and other ancient texts, Alfred would have to embrace the idea of learning the archaic language of Sanskrit. How exactly he would accomplish this, he wasn't sure, but he felt certain that the knowledge gained would deepen his understanding of these profound works and help him fulfil his objectives.

He was confident that the University of Oxford, close to Swindon and renowned for its academic excellence and extensive resources, would surely have scholars well-versed in Sanskrit. The university's libraries and its distinguished faculty presented an invaluable opportunity for his linguistic and intellectual aspirations. With a determined heart, he resolved to seek out these scholars on his return.

He left the deck of the Huntsgreen and returned to his berth feeling significantly more reassured and optimistic than he had been for some time.

THE PALACE OF MY IMAGINATION

Chapter 34

November 1919

Alfred stepped off the train onto the cold, wet platform of Swindon station, his breath visible in the chill November air. His heart raced as he scanned the sparse crowd for Mary. The sight of her, wrapped in a worn woollen coat and clutching her hat against the wind, filled him with a mix of joy, tenderness and apprehension. He hurried towards her, his haversack heavy on his shoulder.

'Alfred!' Mary called out, her voice breaking with emotion as she ran towards him. They embraced tightly, the two years and two months of separation melting away in that instant.

'Mary, my love,' Alfred whispered into her hair, inhaling her familiar scent,

'I've missed you so much.'

'I've missed you too, Alfred. Welcome home,' she replied, her eyes glistening with tears.

They held each other for what felt like an eternity, as if afraid that letting go would mean losing each other forever.

They walked hand in hand out of the station. But as they left Alfred couldn't help but notice a news stand with a headline that stopped him in his tracks.

£1 million goes missing from SS Balmoral Castle.

He bought a copy of the Standard to discover that cases of gold bullion had gone missing while the liner he knew so well was in transit from Cape Town to London. Apparently, the thieves had replaced the contents of the cases with cement.

He couldn't conceive of such a sum of money and grimaced inwardly as he realised he would soon have to confess to Mary that they were now almost penniless, and when his army allowance stopped in a week's time, he would be struggling to put food on their table.

Alfred was surprised to see a large collection of motor vehicles as they exited the station, significantly more than when he had left in 1917.

JOHN CULLIMORE

Behind the steering wheel of one of these vehicles sat Adam Osney. He had parked opposite the station, in front of the Great Western Hotel. Adam was a frequent visitor to this part of town, known for its darker side, where it was easy to find what he sought. Women of easy virtue were his target, and they were plentiful when you knew where to look.

Osney had profited materially during the war years. The war had created a huge demand for food to supply the military and civilian populations, and Europe itself, where so much farmland had been transformed to battlefields. The continent had clamoured for his exports. Osney had even managed to increase output using Prisoners of War as cost-free labour.

Consequently, Adam's lifestyle was transformed, and he used his recently found wealth recklessly to provide himself with luxuries and to indulge his crude passions. The prostitutes were drawn to the prosperous-looking driver of a new vehicle like moths to a flame.

He was becoming addicted to this lifestyle, yet if anything, his desires raced ahead of him, and he was never satisfied.

While scanning the streets outside the station, Osney was taken aback as he saw the familiar couple exit the station.

There was Mary Peck, his old flame, with her writer husband Williams. She looked somewhat gaunt but still possessed a subtle beauty that he found arousing. Williams in contrast appeared to be a shadow of his former self, thin, pale, and dressed in a threadbare, shabby suit that looked sizes too large for his diminished frame.

Adam still felt anger that Williams had bettered him and stolen Mary away. And now, he felt a sharpening of desire as he followed the retreating form of Mary along Oxford Road.

He wondered; now that he was a different person, why would she not be impressed with his success and wealth, as other women certainly were?

Surely it was worth one more try. After all, he had nothing to lose.

***

Alfred and Mary headed east along the road towards the village he

THE PALACE OF MY IMAGINATION

had once called home. The streets around Swindon station were dull and grey, a stark contrast to the vibrant colours of India which he had left behind.

There was little traffic on the road as they left the town, and the old Wilts and Berks Canal which ran parallel to it, appeared stagnant and devoid of craft. The locks were in a severe state of disrepair, with piles of displaced bricks spilling on to the tow paths and into the brackish water.

A thick film of green algae rested on the surface upstream of the lock, some of it still showing signs of frost from the previous night. The fields appeared barren and grey. It was too cold for the cattle who were now sheltered within the barns in anticipation of the long winter ahead.

As they approached South Marston, he couldn't help but notice how much smaller and more rundown it appeared compared to his memories.

His first thought was that, come spring, he would have to begin working the land he owned in the hope of growing produce—fruit and vegetables— to help to sustain them and generate some income.

Inside the cottage, the fire was struggling to keep the cold at bay. Alfred set down his bag and looked around the small, modest living room. The place felt cold and unwelcoming, a far cry from the warmth and beauty he had experienced in India.

'How have you been managing, Mary?' he asked, taking her hand in his.

'It's been difficult, Alfred. The weekly allowance from the army barely covered living costs, but I received a letter this morning saying you're due a demobilisation grant, so we'll have about twenty-five pounds in capital. It will keep us going for a while, but—'

Mary couldn't complete the sentence, her uncertainty about the future belying itself.

'But now that you're back, …'

Alfred sighed deeply.

'I know, Mary. I've been thinking about that too. I'm not sure what work I can find here, but I'll do whatever it takes to provide for us. We've got plenty of land. Come Spring we could start on a market garden.'

Mary looked at him with a mixture of love and concern.

'Oh, I almost forgot, there's a letter here for you from your publishers.' She handed him the envelope.

Alfred opened the letter and read it, and as he did, he started to smile.

'Some good news, they want to publish an anthology of my poetry, a mix of old and new. They think it will help me re-establish my reputation.'

He looked up at Mary, a glimmer of hope in his eyes.

'That's wonderful, Alfred,' Mary exclaimed. 'you should include some of the poems you wrote in India, especially the ones about Ranikhet. I loved reading those.'

'And I will, but I'm going to need your help. My eyesight has deteriorated so much, and it feels like it's getting worse and worse,' Alfred admitted, his voice tinged with frustration.

'Of course, my dear,' Mary said, reaching out to take his hand.

'You choose the poems, and I'll copy them out and make up the manuscript. By the way, Henry Byett wants to see you tomorrow if possible. He's going to call in about five o'clock.'

'Good,' Alfred replied, 'I have some manuscripts I composed while I was away. I hope he can get them typed up and submitted for me.'

Mary hesitated for a moment before broaching another subject.

' The other thing we have to discuss is this cottage. You know we've been given notice to leave. The landlord wants to move in as soon as possible. But the good news is that he can't legally evict us until we've found a suitable alternative address.'

Alfred nodded.

'I've been thinking about this ever since you wrote to me about it in India, and I've decided that the best thing we can do is use the land we own at the Hook and build our own house on it.'

Mary looked at him, her brow furrowed with concern.

'But how are we going to do that, Alfred? We have no money.'

THE PALACE OF MY IMAGINATION

'Don't worry,' Alfred said, a determined look in his eyes.
'I have a plan.'

***

The next day, as the sun cast lengthening shadows over the fields, Henry Byett arrived at the cottage. He looked somewhat older, but his kindly countenance and ready smile were unchanged. Alfred greeted him warmly and led him into the sitting room.

'Henry, thank you for coming.'

'It's wonderful to see you again. But you look exhausted, Alfred.'

'And so I am, the trip back was less than ideal. I won't be signing up for any more long sea voyages.'

Mary arrived in the living room with tea and cake.

'Well, if there's anything you need, you only have to ask,' said Henry.

'There are a couple of things you could help with, Henry. I have a manuscript, one about the sea voyage out to India, and some articles about India which I wrote on the trip back.

'Given the state of my eyes at present, I'd be grateful if you'd consider getting them typed for me and then I can submit them to the appropriate places.'

'Of course, Alfred. I'd be happy to help. Have you seen anyone about your eyes?' Henry asked, taking the papers from Alfred.

'Not since India. But I think I'll have to get them checked, otherwise I won't be able to function.'

'I'm seeing Lou Robins tomorrow, I'm sure he'll have a recommendation for you—But what's this about building a house at the Hook? Mary mentioned something about it.'

Alfred explained.

'We own the land at the Hook. It's just sitting there unused. I think we can build a decent sized house on it. We can use some of my demob money to get started, and perhaps I can raise a mortgage on the value of the land through our solicitors. And there might be further income coming from my new anthology.'

Henry listened thoughtfully.

'It's ambitious, but it's certainly possible. The government have announced a subsidy to encourage building following the war. It's a significant amount; two hundred and forty pounds payable on completion and the receipt of a surveyor's report. So, the mortgage idea is a good one to get the house built. I know some people through the factory who might be willing to help with its construction.'

Mary looked between the two men, a mixture of hope and anxiety on her face.

'It sounds risky, but it might be a risk we have to take.'

Henry nodded.

'One thing I can offer right away, if you're up to it, is a lecture slot at the Mechanics institute in January. Everyone knows you've returned, and they want to hear from you. It's a four-guinea fee, and who knows it might lead to further similar opportunities? '

'I'll tell them about India.' said Alfred.

Alfred squeezed Mary's hand reassuringly.

'We'll make it work, love.'

THE PALACE OF MY IMAGINATION

Chapter 35

1920

The short and bitterly cold days at the beginning of the year did little to inspire Alfred to write. Not only that but he realised he no longer felt at home in Dryden cottage. They were living on borrowed time, and the landlord continued to insist on their finding alternative accommodation before the year was out. However, these were not the only reasons for the extinction of his creative flame.

He began the year with a heavy cold, and coughing prevented him from obtaining a good night's sleep. Insult was added to injury when a sudden lancinating pain originating in his weak eye radiated across his face into his jaw, making him cry out. He was also feverish and weak and took to his bed for five days near the end of the month. While the fever and the weakness abated, the crippling neuralgia did not, and his vision deteriorated further.

He had applied for a disability pension on Byett's recommendation, and was awaiting an appointment for a medical review, but the bureaucratic wheels ground very slowly as his application was passed through various departments.

Byett visited him at the beginning of February.

'Unfortunately, those articles I typed have been rejected by the Daily Mail, and by Duckworth. But I have some good news for you, you've been accepted for the lecture programme at the Mechanics institute in April.'

'I don't think I'll be fit enough, I can't see a newspaper clearly and I feel totally exhausted.'

'In which case I'll ask them to reschedule it. Lou Robins has suggested the eye hospital in Bath, if you wish I could write to them for you?'

'If you would be so kind, thank you'

'I have to say, you're not looking well Alfred, and Mary my dear you look exhausted. Are you eating enough?'

Henry's question was punctuated by silence, and Mary merely

stared at the floor, wearing a haunted look. Suddenly it all made sense to Henry. The room was cold, the furniture and carpets were threadbare, and Henry thought it unlikely that there was much in the way of food in the kitchen. He guessed that Alfred had received no income since his return three months previously and his capital must be diminishing quickly. He had never seen Mary look so crestfallen.

'You must allow me to help,' said Henry, 'I've been thinking about your situation and about your proposal to build a house at the Hook,' said Byett, as Mary entered the room.

'I've been fortunate to come into a legacy, and frankly, I have more money than I need at the moment, so I'd like to offer you a loan of £100, to get the ball rolling, as it were. You can pay me back if and when it suits you, and I won't ask for interest.'

Alfred looked at Mary.

Mary knew Alfred found it difficult to accept any form of charity or financial favour from anyone, and she wondered how he would react to this offer.

However, after a moment's thought Alfred said.

'If things were normal, I wouldn't accept this from you. But as you can see, our circumstances are somewhat dire. I can't see properly, my eye hurts. There's not enough food on the table—' Alfred's eyes moistened as he struggled to continue. The flow of tears seemed to irritate his damaged eye, and he winced slightly. Mary came over, took Alfred's hand and wrapped a reassuring arm around him as the depth of his depression became apparent.

'I just don't know what else I can do—'

After a few seconds, he had recovered enough to continue.

'As soon as the building is complete and the government subsidy comes through, you'll have the money back then.'

Henry studied Alfred for a moment, moved by his distress. He gave a small, sympathetic nod before responding.

'That's fine, Alfred,' he said, his voice softer than usual. 'I know how proud you are, how hard it is for you to accept financial help. But these aren't normal times, are they? If there's one thing I've learned, it's that sometimes, even the strongest of us need a hand.'

THE PALACE OF MY IMAGINATION

'I —We—can't thank you enough Henry.'

'It's a pleasure. Hopefully when all's done and dusted, you'll get back on track with your writing, and I'll be proud to boast that in some way I helped you to rediscover your talent.'

***

What Henry and Alfred could not know was that Mary was feeling haunted by a spirit from the past. Some weeks previously, when Alfred had been out surveying the land at the Hook, she had been walking back to South Marston after the Saturday market at Highworth. She had reached the outskirts of the village when a car pulled up immediately in front of her.

'Hello stranger,' said Adam Osney through a lowered window as Mary passed by the vehicle. It took a few seconds before Mary realised that the ruddy-faced, bearded features of the corpulent driver belonged to the boy she had once known all those years previously.

'Adam?' she said haltingly.

'Yes, it's me,' he replied with a grin, 'it's been a long time, Mary. How have you been?'

Mary felt a swirl of emotions— surprise, a degree of unease, and a tinge of vulnerability.

'I've been well, thank you. And you?—What brings you here?'

Adam chuckled.

'I've been doing very well. Business has been booming since the start of the war. I've been meaning to reconnect with old friends. Can I offer you a ride back to South Marston? We can talk about old times.'

Mary hesitated, glancing down the road. 'I don't know, Adam. It's been so long, and...'

'Nonsense,' he interrupted, opening the car door, 'just a short ride. It won't take long.'

Reluctantly, Mary got into the car, feeling a mix of alarm and apprehension. As they drove, Adam regaled her with tales of his success, his voice dripping with self-satisfaction. He spoke of his newfound wealth, his thriving business ventures, and his lifestyle changes. Mary listened, her thoughts drifting to the past and the simple life she now led with Alfred.

'Enough about me,' Adam said, finally pausing his monologue. 'Tell me about you. What have you been up to all these years?'

Mary took a deep breath, trying to find the right words. 'I suppose I've got God to thank that Alfred was returned to me despite the war. Alfred and I, we have—plans. We have some land at the Hook. We're going to build a house, and a market garden. It's going to be an uphill struggle, but it's what we want.'

Adam's eyes flickered with interest.

'And Alfred? Is he treating you well?'

'Yes,' Mary replied firmly, 'he's a good man.'

They continued talking, Adam probing subtly for weaknesses, trying to find a way back into her life. As they approached South Marston, he slowed the car and turned to her.

'Mary, I've never forgotten you. If you ever want more than just a quiet life, you know where to find me.'

Mary felt a chill run down her spine.

'Thank you for the ride, Adam,' she said, opening the door. 'But I'm happy where I am.'

As she walked away, she could feel Adam's eyes on her, the weight of his gaze pressing down on her back. She hurried home, her mind troubled by the encounter. And since that day, she had felt a lingering presence, as if Adam's shadow had latched onto her, a constant reminder of the past and the choices she had made.

Osney savoured the moment as he watched Mary walk into the distance. As he slowly accelerated through the village to the Stratton turn off, he realised how much he was going to enjoy this challenge.

Back in Dryden cottage, as Alfred and Henry continued their conversation, Mary glanced at the clock, the memories of her encounter with Adam stirring unease in her heart. She knew she had to confront these feelings, but she wasn't sure how or when. For now, she would keep this haunting secret to herself, hoping it would just fade in time.

***

As the summer sun cast long shadows over their flourishing

THE PALACE OF MY IMAGINATION

garden, Alfred stood by the potato patch, lost in thought. The vibrant green plants thrived under his care, yet he couldn't shake off the cloud of bitterness that hung over him. His once sharp eyes now strained even in the dim light, and bright sunlight drove him back in to the shade of their kitchen.

The neuralgic pain was a constant reminder of his physical limitations.

Byett arrived on that warm Sunday afternoon in late June, his concern for Alfred and Mary evident. He walked through the garden, admiring the rows of healthy plants and the abundance of produce. Alfred was busy preparing a large order of potatoes, but his frustration was palpable.

'This market gardening is a mean business,' Alfred muttered. 'I find it hard to deal with people who bicker and fuss to shave a penny or two off the price of a pound of potatoes. Sometimes I wish I was back at the forge.'

'You can't mean that, Alfred,' Mary interjected, her voice filled with concern, it nearly killed you. Surely, you've not forgotten that?'

'Yes, I remember that the work was obnoxious, but I recovered in my free time. The inspiration to write came so easily on those carefree weekends. Now I have nothing. No security, no inspiration. I can't even read.' said Alfred, his voice laden with despair.

'But you do have the lecture to look forward to next month,' Henry reminded him, 'people are looking forward to hearing you again after all these years. And if that goes well, you've got the prospect of similar events across the region.'

'Yes, there is that, I suppose,' Alfred acknowledged, though his tone remained despondent.

'Oh, by the way, I have a letter for you from your old patron, Lord Fitzmaurice, whom I recently met in Devizes,' said Henry, handing the letter to Alfred, who in turn passed it to Mary to read.

Mary opened the letter and studied it carefully. Gradually, her expression softened, and a smile spread across her face.

'How kind of Lord Fitzmaurice. He's aware of our problems.

JOHN CULLIMORE

He's contacted his own eye specialist, who urges you to visit him in Bath on any Tuesday morning. He's also sent a cheque for twenty-five pounds. Apparently, he applied successfully on your behalf to the Royal Literary Fund for a grant. So, it's not all gloom and doom, Alfred Williams!'

Mary squeezed his hand.

'And the first thing we must do is write and thank Lord Fitzmaurice for his help'

Alfred's eyes widened in surprise.

'The Royal Literary Fund, eh? That's incredible news. And to see an eye specialist who might help.'

Henry nodded enthusiastically.

'And with the lecture coming up, you have a chance to reconnect with your public and share your experience of India. Maybe that will inspire you?'

Alfred felt a flicker of hope ignite within himself.

***

The winter programme of lectures at the Mechanics' Institute in Swindon had become an established feature of the town's cultural life. The lectures were popular, and a large audience was guaranteed. The council spared no expense in attracting figures with national reputations and took pains to ensure that the programme of presentations would prove popular with the Swindonian audience. It was with these considerations in mind that Henry sought to prepare Alfred for his speech.

'It would be well worth you attending one or two of the lectures scheduled in November. That should help you to understand the audience and what goes down well with them. The talks tend to last about thirty minutes as a rule, and the best ones are given in an informal manner, with a little added humour, which can go a long way, I think. Do you have a title yet?'

'It will be about India. Why don't we say, '*The Religions of India*,' replied Alfred.

'I'll submit that to the committee as the title of your talk. They'll have to approve it. Another thing I wanted to suggest was illustrating your talk with lantern slides, which seems to be

THE PALACE OF MY IMAGINATION

particularly appreciated these days. The venue can provide all the projection equipment.'

'I'll bear all those things in mind,' said Alfred.

On the appointed evening, Reuben George, the Mayor, introduced Alfred to the audience, welcoming him back from his sojourns as a true son of Swindon. They applauded his return enthusiastically, keenly anticipating his delivery.

Alfred made a good start.

'Ladies and Gentlemen, as you know I've spent quite a lot of time in India during the war, and although I have now left it, it has not left me.'

The audience seemed to warm to him, and Henry felt some relief.

'India is a diverse and complex society, not least because it has several major religious traditions, and I wanted to explore these with you.'

So far so good, thought Henry, although Alfred's posture reminded Henry more of the parade ground than the lecture theatre. Alfred stood away from the central desk, perfectly erect, with his jacket tightly buttoned and his hands thrust deep into his pockets.

'I'm going to concentrate on the two most significant religions of India. That is to say, Hinduism, which about 70% of India's population identify with, and Mohammedism or Islam, with 20-25% of Indians being Muslims.

These two groups are further differentiated by language, geography, and culture. I'll say one thing about Christianity for comparative purposes, which is that less than one percent of Indians identifies with it.'

Henry continued to feel reassured but hoped that Alfred's venture into statistics would be limited. He also felt that Alfred's posture and demeanour were transmitting some anxiety to the audience.

'I think this is an important subject because there are significant Hindu-Muslim tensions. I also feel I should say that as a colony of our Empire, our actions and responsibilities as rulers have exacerbated these tensions through what I've seen as a deliberate policy of divide and rule.'

Henry was now feeling quite tense; he didn't feel Alfred should drift into politics, that wouldn't go down well. However, Alfred changed tack, but perhaps not in the way Henry had hoped he would.

'In simple terms, Hinduism is both polytheistic and monotheistic. It recognizes a multitude of deities while also affirming a single, supreme reality known as Brahman. On the other hand, Mohammedism or Islam, is strictly monotheistic, emphasizing the oneness of God – Allah - while stressing that Allah is entirely separate from His creation, and is not immanent or incarnate.

'Whereas we Christians have a monotheistic belief but believe in the Trinity—one God in three persons: and we accept that Jesus Christ is God incarnate.'

Alfred looked around the audience, expecting to see nodding heads and smiles greeting what he believed was a simplified analysis. But instead, he saw blankness, and some avoided his gaze.

Henry felt that in that moment, something had changed, and that the audience were beginning to tune out. The details continued from Alfred, although it was unfortunate that his forensic exposition of philosophical concepts, details of the various Hindu deities, and an explanation of the caste system now fell on deaf ears.

There was no humour and there were no slides to illustrate his points.

Henry was aware that the audience were becoming fidgety and increasingly bored. After forty-five minutes, a few began to leave, but Alfred was just hitting his stride and ploughed on, apparently unaware of the effect he was having. Henry tried to attract his attention, with somewhat exaggerated references to his pocket watch, but of course, he wondered if Alfred's vision was acute enough to register the gestures he was making.

Unfortunately, at this moment Alfred was not wearing the new

THE PALACE OF MY IMAGINATION

glasses prescribed by the eye specialist which reportedly had improved his sight markedly.

After a full hour and a quarter on his feet, Alfred suddenly stopped talking, with no sense of a summary or conclusion. There was some applause, although it seemed this was an expression of relief on behalf of the audience, mixed with some sympathy for the lecturer. A significant number had already left and thus the audience's verdict was clear.

Henry felt that Alfred would not be invited back to lecture at this or other venues, and thus the opportunity of a useful, regular source of income for the struggling writer was lost.

Henry walked with Alfred for some distance on his way homeward.

'I'm sorry Henry, I appreciate that the lecture wasn't a success. I've let you down. I didn't prepare in the way you'd suggested. I've been a bit preoccupied with other things.'

'But I've had some good news, about building the house at the Hook. The bank has agreed to loan me the money to build,' he said, with a twinkle in his eye.

***

JOHN CULLIMORE

Chapter 36

1921

It was late March and the days were lengthening. The weather had been settled for a week or so and the forecast was good. Alfred decided it was time to lay the foundations of his cottage. As he prepared his concrete mix, he thought back to the previous October when he and Mary had been walking around South Marston after Sunday lunch. They had noticed that at the junction of the road with the field path towards St. Margaret's Church, a derelict cottage was for sale. They had inspected the ruin and believed that much of the stone was salvageable and had the potential to form the walls of their new dwelling. Alfred wasted no time in negotiating a price with the agent, and it was his for the sum of twelve pounds.

Towards the end of the month, he and Mary began to demolish the remaining structure. It was hard physical work. Using simple tools, they loosened and loaded the stones into handcarts and then ferried them to the chosen site at the Hook. Once a reasonable quantity had been transferred, they chipped away the mortar clinging to the stones and sorted each one by size and condition. Alfred salvaged the old mortar with a view to recycling it later.

'Look at this stone,' said Mary, turning over a weighty rectangle of limestone with a date carved into it.

'Ah, 1671,' replied Alfred, inspecting the ancient stone, 'we'll use this one, so we'll be able to claim that the house dates back to the 17th century.'

'Do you think there's enough stone here for the whole house, Alfred?' asked Mary.

'There's certainly enough to form the external walls, but we'll need an inner course of brickwork, so that the walls are sufficiently strong and thick,' Alfred explained.

'And where will we get bricks from?' she asked.

'I've had some useful discussions with the canal company. There's a derelict lock near Longleaze Farm, and they're happy to

THE PALACE OF MY IMAGINATION

sell the bricks to us.'

'And how will we get them to the Hook?' asked Mary.

'Ah, there's the rub,' Alfred admitted, 'we'll have to do what we're doing here, and remove them piecemeal, bring them back to the Hook, and tidy them up.'

'Are we going to be able to do that, ourselves? It sounds like months of hard physical work,' said Mary.

'I see no way around it, Mary, but we can wait until the new year when this work will be finished, and we'll just take our time,' Alfred reassured her.

He had also ordered some new timber from the joinery in nearby Chiseldon and identified a carpenter and stonemason for the structural work.

'But is it all going to be worth it, Alfred?' asked Mary.

'Yes, I believe so. When the house is built, the government grant will pay for most of it, and then we'll have almost half an acre of land for planting. I think that's the way forward for us. And if I get my eyes sorted, having the market garden will dovetail well with being a writer. So yes, I'm confident this is right for us.'

He wrapped her in a reassuring embrace, his confidence radiating warmth and security. For the first time in some years, a glimmer of genuine happiness sparkled within her, and she felt excited about their future in the heart of the village.

By the end of February of the new year, they had successfully transferred a total of twelve thousand bricks from the old lock and carted them a mile and a half to the Hook. The villagers were bewildered by the constant coming and going of handcarts conveying the materials, and many of the village children joined in the activity of cleaning and storing the bricks.

They were averaging four return journeys a day, transferring two cartloads of material on each occasion. Alfred was pleased that the quality of many of the bricks would suffice for use in the quoins.

On days when the weather was mild, they worked until eleven p.m., then collapsed with exhaustion, their hands and wrists covered in cuts and their clothes filled with fine dust from the mortar. Alfred's already compromised eye had become further irritated by the dust.

JOHN CULLIMORE

Mary developed an infection in one of the cuts, but she struggled on in determined fashion. Fortunately, at this time the villagers, intrigued by the couple's dedication, began to offer more and more help. Some brought food and drinks to keep Alfred and Mary fuelled, while others took turns with the handcarts, lightening their load.

Mary was particularly grateful for the food contributions. She just hadn't the time to prepare meals for them, and Alfred had been keen to economise as much as possible. In fact, they'd been living on no more than a pound per week since early February.

One afternoon, as they were finishing up another load, old Mr. Thompson, the village blacksmith, approached them.

'You two are quite the talk of South Marston,' he said with a grin. 'I reckon half the children in the village are aspiring bricklayers now.'

Alfred chuckled. 'We're grateful for all the help. It's turning into a real community project.'

'Well, if you need a fire basket, a wood burning stove, or if there's any other metalwork you need, just let me know,' Thompson offered, 'I'd give you a very good price.'

'Thank you, Mr. Thompson,' Mary said, smiling warmly. 'We might just take you up on that.'

And now Alfred was ready to lay the foundations. The land was waterlogged and uneven. Aware that several new builds in the village had suffered from subsidence, he began by digging peripheral trenches from each corner and laid perforated pipes surrounded by gravel to redirect water away from the site. He then dug strip foundation trenches three feet deep, levelled the base, and compacted the soil to create a stable foundation. In total, he mixed twenty tons of concrete on-site using a simple hand-operated mixer, combining sand, cement, and coarse aggregate. He used wooden boards to line the trenches, keeping the concrete in place as it set. By the end of May, he had reached the stage where he needed to employ a stonemason.

***

The process of building the house had certainly worn Mary

THE PALACE OF MY IMAGINATION

down. But what Alfred didn't know was that she continued to be the focus of unwelcome attention from Osney.

The gossip within the village about the Williams' building project had spread beyond the margins of South Marston, and Adam had been fully briefed about what some of the more resentful locals considered the eccentricity and brazenness of the scheme.

He could hardly believe his ears when he was told that Mary was labouring like a navvy, making herself ill in the process. He raged at the arrogance of Williams in subjecting his wife to such indignity. He felt sure she would prefer to be cosseted and cherished, treated like a woman rather than as a slave.

Unable to control his anger, he threw his whisky glass at the wall, spreading amber liquid all over the farmhouse kitchen walls and frightening his dog so much that she ran yelping out of the kitchen. He decided he must act.

Having learned about the routine that Mary was subjected to, he decided to take matters into his own hands. The next day, he approached the disused lock and lay in wait for her to appear with her wheelbarrow.

And there she was, slowly approaching, a bandage wrapped around her left hand, and her hair spilling out from her hair clips. He thought she looked more beautiful than ever. Adam's heart pounded as he watched her struggle with the heavy load, a mixture of anger, concern and longing surging through him.

'Mary!' he called out, stepping from his hiding place. She was startled and nearly dropped the wheelbarrow, her eyes widening with surprise and fear.

'Adam? What are you doing here?' she asked, her voice trembling.

'I couldn't stay away,' he replied, his voice softening, 'I heard what that man is making you do. It's not right, Mary. You deserve better.'

She shook her head, looking away.

'It's not like that, Adam. I'm helping Alfred. We're re-building our life together.'

'At what cost?' he demanded, stepping closer. 'Look at you. You're hurt, exhausted. This isn't what you were meant for.'

Mary's eyes filled with tears, but she stood her ground.

'You don't understand, Adam. This is my choice. I want to be here. I love Alfred.'

Adam's expression hardened, his frustration boiling over.

'You call this love? Making you work yourself to the bone? He doesn't deserve you.'

'Stop it, Adam,' she pleaded. 'You don't know him. He's a good man. This is our dream.'

Adam took a deep breath, trying to calm himself.

'Well I'm sure it is *his* dream. But what about your dreams, Mary? You used to want so much more.'

Mary looked down at her bandaged hand, then back at him.

'Dreams change, Adam. People change.'

He stepped back, his anger mingling with a deep sadness.

'I just want you to be happy,' he said quietly.

'And I am,' she replied, though her voice wavered.

Adam watched as she resumed her task, her determination clear despite her weariness. He felt a pang of helplessness, knowing there was nothing he could do to sway her. As she walked away, he whispered.

'I'll always be here, Mary. If you ever need me.'

She didn't turn back, but he hoped she heard him. Adam stood there for a long while, watching her until she disappeared.

He headed off in his car, his anger and unresolved longing weighing heavily on him. He took the road into Swindon and made for the station and picked up a whore outside the Great Western Hotel. He took her up to Barbury Castle, his preferred rendezvous for such assignations.

Having agreed on the price and handed over the notes, he marched the woman into the woods, his anger and frustration mounting like a constricting cord around his chest. He pushed the woman to the ground, and despite her objections to his roughness, began his usual pre-coital routine of unbuttoning his trousers and forcing the girl's legs apart. As the girl's fear increased, she began

THE PALACE OF MY IMAGINATION

to wail and cry out.

'Shut up,' he cried, as he fumbled for his penis and covered the girl's mouth with his other hand. But for some reason, his usually reliable tumescence had deserted him. As his anger reached a crescendo, he punched the girl in the face, stood up, readjusted his clothing, and made his way back to his car without a second thought for the girl he had assaulted.

He drove back towards Swindon, his mind a storm of rage and self-loathing. He couldn't shake the image of Mary from his thoughts, her bandaged hand, her tired eyes, her unwavering determination. He pulled over to the side of the road, gripping the steering wheel until his knuckles turned white. Thus far, he had always been able to get what he wanted, to bend situations to his will.

Thinking of Mary rekindled his arousal, and his anger began to dissipate, replaced by a sly, inward smile. There was still another option open to him.

As he continued his drive through the countryside, his mind spun with possibilities. He realized that he didn't have to confront Mary directly or force his way into her life. There were subtler, more insidious methods to achieve what he wanted. He could leverage his newfound wealth and influence to create opportunities that would draw Mary away from Alfred, slowly, almost imperceptibly.

His thoughts turned to the village gossip he had overheard, the whispers of discontent about Alfred's building plans. If he could amplify those concerns, perhaps even fabricate a few strategic setbacks, he might sow seeds of doubt and frustration within Mary's already strained life. He knew some influential village residents well enough to pull a few strings, manipulate their opinions, and hopefully turn the tide against Alfred's project.

And then there was Mary herself. He could offer her small kindnesses and gifts, each one designed to remind her of the comforts and luxuries she was missing.

Adam's smile grew broader as his plan took shape. He didn't need brute force to win Mary back. He could wear down her resistance bit by bit, eroding her loyalty to Alfred and reminding her of the man to whom she was once betrothed.

It was a long game, but he had patience and resources on his side.

***

Byett was keen to see how the new build was progressing and called in on a sunny Saturday afternoon in early July. The weather had been relentlessly hot and sunny for the last three months. Upon arriving at the Hook, Byett was impressed that the construction of the walls had commenced. There was little sign of outside activity, but he heard noises coming from inside the new building and entered to find Alfred chiselling away at the surface of a block of stone.

'No rest for the wicked?' said Henry.

'I'm doing some of the little jobs,' replied Alfred. He appeared to be carving an inscription into the stone.

'What's "Ranik..." meant to mean?' asked Henry.

'It's going to be 'Ranikhet,' to remind me of the hill station where I was posted in India. This will be set above the front door, between the two first-floor windows—If it ever gets finished that is. '

'Is there a problem? it all appears to be progressing well,' said Byett.

'Well, it wasn't so bad until last week when the delightful Mr. Heath, our stonemason, walked out on us. I still can't believe it. He came in last Friday with a face like thunder saying the plans for the brickwork were substandard, and he wanted no part of it. We had a big argument about the thickness of the rear walls. He insists that the walls of the house must be eighteen inches thick, although the original plans say fourteen inches will suffice.

He said he had no alternative but to quit. Something must have happened, as afterwards I received notice from the parish council saying that building must stop, and further plans must be re-submitted to a full committee.

'It seems strange that this all happened so suddenly, I smell a rat somewhere amongst all this'

THE PALACE OF MY IMAGINATION

'You may be right Henry. It's a significant setback. The committee doesn't meet for three months, and our resources are already severely stretched.'

'So, for now work has effectively stopped.'

'Yes, it has. And if Mr. Heath is correct about the brickwork, Mary and I will have to spend even more money and take another two weeks to retrieve and clean another two thousand bricks from the lock.'

Alfred threw the chisel to the ground and stared vacantly into space.

'Anyway, Mary won't be able to help for some time. She's absolutely shattered and needs rest. She seems depressed and anxious, and she's withdrawn into herself. I suppose it's understandable.'

'Oh, I'm so sorry about that, Alfred, do give her my love,

'I feel bad because I recommended Heath to you. He was highly thought of in the Railway factory. But let me make some enquiries, this doesn't sound right. Is it possible that somebody has intimidated the stonemason to stop working for you, and provoked the intervention of the parish council? It all sounds very odd.'

'Well for the life of me I don't understand it,' said Alfred.

'I'll do some asking around. I know some of Joseph Heath's drinking acquaintances, and it might be worth me asking for minutes of the recent parish council meeting.'

***

As Alfred went out the following Monday morning to inspect the land he was cultivating, he had to acknowledge that his domestic situation was now becoming serious. The weather throughout the growing season had been capricious, and his garden at the rear of the Hook had yielded very little.

Late frosts in April and early May had damaged the blossoms, and heavy rains in June had blighted the fruits. Tomatoes and potatoes were afflicted by fungal diseases, their leaves mottled with black spots and their growth stunted. The relentless heat of July and August had only made matters worse, causing the few remaining unscathed vegetable plants to bolt and go to seed under the stress.

Alfred surveyed the withered plants with a sinking heart. They had barely enough garden produce for themselves, let alone any surplus to sell at the market. He had virtually no income coming in from book sales or royalties. To make matters worse, Mary seemed to have sunk into a well of depression and sadness.

As he walked back towards the cottage, he saw a car drawing up outside Dryden cottage. A few moments later the driver appeared, and he recognised Adam Osney, now noticeably older.

What on earth could he want, thought Alfred as he approached the house.

'You're Alfred Williams, if I'm not mistaken?' said Osney as Alfred approached, his tone casual, devoid of warmth, notably failing to offer his hand in greeting.

'Indeed. How can I help?' Alfred responded, his curiosity piqued.

'I thought I should come and introduce myself. I have the privilege of being your new landlord. I acquired some properties in the village about a month ago, so I'm taking the opportunity to meet my new tenants,' Osney said, his self-satisfied smile hinting at a sense of superiority.

'Would you like to come into the garden? I could offer you a glass of water,' offered Alfred, trying to maintain a veneer of hospitality.

'Er, thank you,' responded Osney, his eyes scanning the cottage and the gardens with an appraising look, 'but I have a very full diary today. I just wanted to confirm with you that you're planning to move out to a new property at some stage,' he continued.

'Yes, we are,' said Alfred, 'as soon as the building is complete.'

'And when might that be?' inquired Osney, his curiosity thinly veiled.

'I'm not absolutely sure, but I hope in about six months,' said Alfred.

'I see. Is it the property under construction at the Hook?' asked Osney, though he clearly already knew the answer.

'It is,' replied Alfred.

THE PALACE OF MY IMAGINATION

'Well, the best of luck with that. I just wanted to inform you that regrettably your monthly rent will be increasing from next month. I'm afraid inflation is playing havoc with prices, so there'll be an increase.'

This was certainly not news Alfred wanted to hear at such a sensitive time. 'I see,' he replied, trying to mask his dismay as Osney handed him a letter.

'This letter confirms the new rental terms,' said Osney with a wolfish grin, savouring Alfred's discomfort.

'By the way, I am interested in buying more land in the village, so if you ever have any wish to sell, do let me know.' Alfred remained silent and his expression neutral.

'Well, I'll be on my way now. Please give my regards to Mrs. Williams—I trust she is well?' he inquired disingenuously.

'She's a little run down. We've been working hard on the new house.' Alfred admitted.

'I'm sorry to hear that. Well, goodbye,' said Osney, turning on his heel and heading back to his vehicle.

Alfred watched him go, feeling a cold shiver run through his body and a profound sense of relief as Osney finally took his leave.

As Alfred entered Dryden cottage, he began to seriously entertain the thought of returning to the factory. Working in the GWR had been a monotonous grind, but it provided stable, dependable income. Literature had always been his passion, but passion didn't pay the bills or put food on the table. And he'd been trying hard to write, but for the first time he had found it difficult. The words didn't come as easily as they used to, and when they did, they seemed darker. Maybe it wasn't even worth trying to continue.

He opened the letter from his new landlord.

A twenty percent increase in monthly rent was the last thing he needed.

***

The church bells had just chimed three as Byett knocked on the door of Dryden Cottage. Aware of the couple's difficult circumstances, he was careful to time his visits so that Mary and

JOHN CULLIMORE

Alfred wouldn't feel compelled to offer him a meal.

Byett offered a deliberate smile as Mary opened the door, though he couldn't help but wonder if his concern for them showed on his face.

'How are you, Mary? I've heard you haven't been feeling well,' he asked as they exchanged a light embrace. He was startled by how frail and thin she appeared.

'My hand is almost back to normal after the infection, just a bit stiff around the thumb,' she responded, trying to put on a brave front, though Byett couldn't shake the sense that she looked haunted. He made his way to the kitchen, where he found Alfred reading the previous day's newspaper.

Alfred looked up from the paper as Byett entered, his face lighting up with a smile that didn't quite reach his eyes.

'Henry! Good to see you,' he said, setting the paper aside and rising from his chair. 'You've timed your visit well. The rain's been relentless all morning.'

Byett took a seat by the small kitchen table, glancing around the room. The once cosy cottage now seemed to have an air of neglect, as if the weight of recent struggles had seeped into the very walls. The curtains hung limp, their colours faded, and the kettle on the stove was dull and dented. He noticed the half-finished loaf of bread on the counter, barely enough to last them another day.

'Alfred,' Byett began, carefully selecting his words, 'I wanted to share what I've uncovered regarding your building project. I've come across some…interesting information.'

'I'm listening,' Alfred replied. Mary visibly tensed, her hands clasped tightly as she stared at the floor.

'I think I've figured out why your builder, Joseph Heath, walked away,' Byett continued.

'I spoke with one of his drinking companions, who later met with Heath and casually inquired about his work situation.' Byett paused, feeling the tension in the room rise.

'It seems someone persuaded him to leave. This individual, who also happens to be his landlord, encouraged him to object to your building project. That 'encouragement' came with thinly veiled

THE PALACE OF MY IMAGINATION

threats about his tenancy, along with promises of future construction work in the area.

'So, Joseph Heath chose the path of least resistance,' Byett added.

'He invented a plausible objection relating to the brickwork and decided to voice his concerns through the parish council.

'He was directed to your old acquaintance, Reverend McFadden, who, it turns out, is an old friend of your antagonist, and who was quite eager to listen, presumably having been primed in advance. And we all know what happened after that.' Alfred nodded in understanding.

'So, the mastermind behind this scheme is none other than Adam Osney.' said Alfred.

'Yes,' agreed Henry, 'he's been pulling the strings from behind the scenes.'

Alfred's face darkened, his jaw tightening as he processed the revelation.

'I should have known,' he muttered, his voice laced with frustration.

'Osney's never forgiven me for past events although I didn't think he'd stoop this low. He's obviously trying to starve us into submission by raising the rent, hoping that we'll run out of money and sell him the house and its land.'

'Presumably at what would be well below market price,' added Henry, recoiling at the mendacity of Osney's scheming.

Mary, still looking down at the floor, spoke softly, her voice trembling.

'He's obviously a dangerous man, Alfred. He won't stop until he gets what he wants.'

At this point, Mary simply lacked the courage to admit to Alfred and Henry that Osney's true aim was not just to undermine Alfred, but to claim her for himself. Overcome with guilt and a deep sense of hopelessness, silent tears began to stream down her face.

Alfred reached out to gently place a hand on her shoulder, attempting to offer some reassurance.

'We'll deal with him, Mary. We've faced worse.'

Byett watched the exchange, the weight of their predicament pressing down on him.

'Alfred, you need to be careful. Osney isn't just a landlord; he's a man with connections and influence. And Reverend McFadden—he has the ear of the parish. Together, they're a formidable force.'

'I know that,' Alfred replied, a steely resolve in his voice, 'but I won't be intimidated by Osney or anyone else. This project means everything to us. It's our future, and I won't let them take it away.'

Mary looked up, her eyes filled with worry.

'But what if they succeed, Alfred? What if they ruin everything we've worked for?'

'We'll find a way,' Alfred assured her, though his own uncertainty was evident. 'We always do.'

Byett hesitated before speaking again.

'Alfred, I'm with you on this, whatever you decide. But you need to approach this strategically, and you're going to need some help—from me. I know you've always prided yourselves on your independence, but this is a real crisis, and the only way through it is together.'

Alfred pondered Byett's words, the weight of the situation pressing heavily on him. After what felt like an eternity, he finally nodded.

'You're right. We can't fight this battle on our own.'

'Thank goodness,' Byett said, visibly relieved.

They sat quietly for a moment, the soft whistle of the kettle the only sound in the room. Byett couldn't help but notice how much Alfred had aged in recent months, the deepening lines on his face, his shoulders more hunched than ever. It was painful to see his friend, once so vibrant and full of life, now worn down by the unrelenting hardships they faced.

'Here's what I suggest we do—' said Byett, breaking the silence.

***

THE PALACE OF MY IMAGINATION

Chapter 37

1922

Three weeks later, on a Sunday morning in the middle of June, Byett called on Alfred after attending the parish church service.

'I'd expected to see you in the congregation, Alfred. I just wanted the chance to talk to you about the upcoming planning committee. Is all well?'

'Indeed, Let's go through to the garden,' said Alfred. 'we'll talk more there.'

Once seated, Alfred continued.

'As regards attending church, I don't plan on visiting it in future.'

Henry looked somewhat surprised.

'Well I do remember the vicar didn't exactly cover himself in glory when he burned one of your books in public, but I feel sure there must be more to it than that.' Henry wondered if recent events had completely soured his outlook.

'I just feel it would be hypocritical. Since returning from India, my views on religion have changed. I just wouldn't be able to recite the prayers with any sincerity. For me, the whole idea of God has altered,

'However, I don't want to cast doubt on your personal beliefs. So, we could just move on to discussing the planning issues.'

'Not at all, Alfred. I'd be most interested to hear what you have to say.'

Alfred took a deep breath.

'Well, since I've experienced other world faiths, I just find it impossible to remain an orthodox Christian,' said Alfred.

'But doesn't religion just give us a moral code, and isn't Christianity as good as any other religion? Surely, we all worship the same God at heart, even if we call Him by different names.' replied Henry.

'I agree. But Christianity preaches that salvation is only possible through Jesus Christ. It won't admit the validity of other faiths, and such intolerance has caused so much distress and division in the world.'

'True enough,' agreed Henry.

'I've met and admired many Muslims and Hindus,' said Alfred.

'But I've been particularly impressed by the Vedantic philosophy of the Hindus. It's quite a departure from our conventional views. The idea of God isn't limited to a specific image or doctrine. Instead, God is seen as a presence that lives within each of us.

'We just have to realise that God's purity and perfection is already within us. So rather than worshipping God as a being, we should really be in awe of the soul in our own bodies, and learn how to unlock its true potential.'

Byett continued to look puzzled.

'But we're all imperfect individuals. I just don't see how this kind of 'soul searching' you mention can correct our faults.'

'I know this is hard for you to accept. We see ourselves as separate individuals with discrete minds and bodies, but our true nature, our true 'self' is infact one with this infinite existence, at one with God.

'This 'self 'is never born and will never die. It continues after our earthly lives, and we may experience further lives on our path towards recognising our true potential. A single lifetime may be just one of the many steps in a soul's journey.'

'So now you believe in reincarnation as well?'

'Yes, I accept reincarnation, it's a vital principle of Vedantism.'

'The problem I have with all this is that everything I see and feel indicates that we are distinct and separate individuals,' replied Henry.

Byett was now convinced that the stress of Alfred's recent existence had caused him to completely lose his way, and he felt he ought to be bringing the conversation back to the stark reality of his current circumstances.

Alfred seemed to have reached a similar conclusion, but for a different reason.

'I see I may have overloaded you with ancient philosophical

THE PALACE OF MY IMAGINATION

concepts.

'So, let's have some tea and change the subject.'

With an air of relief, Henry went on to summarise what he had achieved since their previous meeting. Firstly, he had successfully transferred the planning application to the council's building committee, where the technical aspects could be properly assessed by those with the relevant expertise.

He had argued that while the parish council was the right place to raise general concerns about a local construction project, it was not the appropriate body to scrutinise detailed building plans. Henry continued.

'And this at least means that the local vicar will cease to have any influence. And the other good news is that we will have at least one ally on the committee—Reuben George. But the meeting won't take place for a couple of months, so nothing will happen soon.'

'And I've met with the draughtsman and asked him about adjusting the plans to ensure a uniform wall thickness of 18 inches, and he's confirmed that the foundations I've laid are more than capable of supporting the slight increase in wall width. I've paid him the necessary fees and he's resubmitting the revised plans later this week.'

'Alfred, that's excellent. I think all that remains for me to do now is identify the other voting members of the committee and try to anticipate any further objections that might arise. Whereas you and Mary just need to ride out the storm—On that subject, is everything all right?'

'We're coping, thank you. I've managed to get a post as Clerk to the local council, responsible for collecting rates. It's a considerable amount of clerical work and it's incredibly tedious, but it's keeping the wolf from the door.

'As regards writing, I've been brushing up some old manuscripts which I began working on before the war. You might remember the one about the Thames valley I began in nineteen fifteen. Infact this has unexpectedly produced two works.'

Henry Byett smiled, nodding approvingly, 'I'm glad to see you can rise above the stress you're under and still concentrate on some positive things.'

'For me, writing provides the best source of stress relief. Anyway, as I was saying, because I haven't been able to finish building the house, I've been spending my spare time cycling around the Thames villages. I made contact with people to get stories from them, which form the basis of the first book.'

'Alfred, you must've cycled hundreds of miles to get all that done.'

'Actually, if you count the journeys I've made since nineteen fifteen, I've probably racked up a few thousand miles.' Alfred said with a grin.

Henry couldn't help but chuckle.

'I met people in the evenings after work to speak with them at their leisure, so the local pub became the place to conduct their interviews. And there it became clear that their main source of entertainment was singing old folk songs to each other over a glass or two of beer. So, I started collecting all these old folk songs. Hence the second book!'

'That kind of dedication—surely it's about more than just getting another book published?' said Henry.

'Oh, definitely,' Alfred replied, 'it's been a welcome distraction, especially given everything that's happened here lately. But more than that, I've met some amazing people. Their stories and songs connect me to the past in ways I never could've imagined.

'Infact just last week, I met a ninety-four-year-old in Inglesham, Elijah Iles. He still sings in the local inn and he's a favourite of the villagers. Despite having no education, he can talk for hours about current affairs, what's going on in parliament, farming, and all with remarkable clarity.

'He's still very upright for his age, with a thick mane of snow-white hair down to his shoulders; makes him look quite distinguished. He worked until he was ninety, making baskets from materials he collected along the Thames.'

'He sounds positively superhuman,' said Henry.

'Indeed! As a boy, he worked on farms and heard stories firsthand from men who fought at the Battle of Trafalgar! He even

THE PALACE OF MY IMAGINATION

remembered songs his grandfather taught him, like one about the winter of 1788 when the Thames froze over for thirteen weeks. Listening to him was a real privilege. I can only hope I'll be like him when I'm that old.'

'And I have no doubt you will be, Alfred. From what you've just told me, it sounds like you're cut from the same cloth as that character.

'Well, it's good to see that you're not allowing the grass to grow under your feet, Alfred.'

'You know me, Henry, I have to keep busy. I've also decided to make a start on learning Sanskrit.'

'Sanskrit?' Henry asked, his eyebrows raised in amused astonishment.

'Yes, the ancient scriptural language of the Hindus, still used in ceremonial rites.'

'So, you're learning yet another ancient language?'

'Well since returning home I've read translations of the scriptures of the Hindus in something called the Vedas. We talked earlier about some of the religious aspects of the Vedanta, but there's much more to them than I expected.

'Within them are pearls of philosophical thought, the gems of ideas which appear much later in the philosophies of our world. I personally think the Vedas are superior to the writings of the Egyptians, the Greeks, Romans and the Bible, and they were written fifteen or sixteen centuries before Christ.

'Infact I think that people like Marcus Aurelius, Plato and Moreau were merely repeating ideas that had been written centuries before in the Vedas.'

'It's wonderful to hear you speak with such enthusiasm, but if you can read translations, why do you need to learn the language?' asked Henry.

'Because there's still an extensive untranslated literature on these issues which is just calling out for my attention.'

'That sounds very demanding.'

'It is, I've struggled to find a suitable textbook. I searched high and low in Oxford, but there was nothing. But I'm awaiting delivery of a reader from Harvard University in the United States'

'Well, I wish you all the best with that' Henry replied.

Henry was amazed that despite the depths of Alfred's current crisis, he still afforded new learning such priority. But then, he concluded, that was what had made Alfred a celebrated writer and Henry just an accountant.

THE PALACE OF MY IMAGINATION

Chapter 38

There is good living to be had, of every sort and kind
And, though you eat and stuff your fill, the womenfolk don't mind
But there's one fault about it all - should no one else oppose
One has to wage a constant war, with kinsmen for his foes
from Tales of the Panchatantra, Alfred Williams ,1930

The small committee room in Swindon's town hall buzzed with a quiet murmur of anticipation as Alfred and Henry settled into the seats reserved for members of the public. The polished wood of the long committee table gleamed under the lamps, casting a warm glow over the serious faces of the men seated around it. At the centre of the table, Reuben George, the Mayor and chairman of the meeting, shuffled his papers with the relaxed air of a man thoroughly versed in municipal proceedings.

Alfred clutched his copy of the plans, his fingers tracing the edges of the thick paper as he glanced nervously at Henry. Alfred was grateful for his friend's presence and had taken his advice and registered his interest in advance, prepared to speak if necessary. Now, as the meeting began, he took a deep breath and focused on the proceedings.

The mayor tapped the gavel lightly, calling the meeting to order.
'Good evening, gentlemen. I trust we all have the agenda before us. First, let us note the apologies for those unable to attend.' The usual committee formalities were quickly concluded, and Reuben George was keen to proceed. His deep voice commanded attention. 'We've been asked to consider a submission from Mr. Alfred Williams for the building work at the Hook in South Marston. The revised plans have been circulated beforehand. I believe the question raised was concerning the dimensions of the brickwork. Could I ask the Borough Surveyor for his comments?'

All eyes turned to the Borough Surveyor, a man of middle years with a stern expression softened slightly by the glasses perched on his nose. He leaned forward, adjusting the papers in front of him.

'Indeed, Mr. Chairman,' he began, his tone measured and precise.

'The original submission from Mr. Heath raised concerns about the structural integrity due to the proposed wall thickness. However, upon review of the revised plans, I am satisfied that Mr. Williams has addressed these concerns adequately. The increased wall thickness and the solid foundations should provide the necessary stability, and I find no further issues with this aspect of the proposal.'

Alfred felt a wave of relief wash over him as the Borough Surveyor's approval was noted. But before he could fully relax, one of the two men seated a few rows away from him, who had just been handed a note by his neighbour, cleared his throat and raised his hand.

'If I may, Mr. Chairman,' the man began, his voice edged with a deliberate tone of challenge, 'I would like to raise a concern regarding the land registry entry for the Hook. It appears to me that it is, in fact, owned by one Elisabeth Williams. Hence, we would challenge the contention that this land does not legally belong to Mr. Williams, and therefore, he cannot build on it.'

The unknown speaker then handed the document to the chairman.

In that instant, Henry recognised the speaker and looked sideways at Alfred, somewhat alarmed. However, Alfred appeared unruffled and stood up, signalling to the chairman that he would like to respond.

'I inherited the land from my mother, Elisabeth, after her death in 1917. Given the outbreak of war, probate was not granted until 1919, and I have a copy of the will here with me, along with a statement from the land registry. Could I draw the chairman's attention to the last sentence on the statement?'

Alfred handed over the paperwork to George, who, after donning his spectacles, proceeded to examine it. Silence reigned for two minutes.

'Yes, this seems to be in order,' George finally said, his voice

THE PALACE OF MY IMAGINATION

cutting through the tense silence.

'The crucial sentence reads, and I quote:'

'This document confirms Alfred Williams as the legal owner of the property at the Hook, South Marston. It is important that this document is retained, as the Great War has considerably retarded the updating of the registry.'

George paused for a moment, allowing the words to sink in.

'Well, if there are no other comments, I suggest that the committee approves these plans.'

No one spoke, but the mysterious individuals to Alfred's left stood up and immediately left the room. As they did, Henry turned and whispered in Alfred's ear,

'If I'm not mistaken, the older man who is leaving is Osney's solicitor and the younger one is his clerk!'

***

Alfred and Mary devoted the following week to purchasing and transporting another two thousand bricks from the lock. Two weeks later, Alfred secured a new stonemason, and construction resumed without further interruption.

On the final day of the year, the District Surveyor issued a certificate of satisfactory completion. After allowing three additional weeks for the house to dry out, Alfred and Mary finally crossed the threshold of their new home.

Ranikhet was more than just a house; it was the fulfillment of Alfred's dreams of India.

JOHN CULLIMORE

Chapter 39

Having caught the early train from Swindon, Alfred arrived in Covent Garden for his appointment with his publishers, Duckworth and Co. They had asked him to come up to London to discuss his plans for publishing new work, hoping to advise him on restoring his literary reputation after the war years had interrupted the flow of his creative efforts.

He had been asked to submit outlines of any work that was maturing and had decided to focus on his work on the Upper Thames region.

On the rail journey to London he recalled how before the war, as he recovered from the factory induced illness which led to his leaving, he had spent months researching, visiting small villages, within bicycling range and talking to the locals to gather authentic material. His notebooks were filled with snippets of conversations, lyrics of old songs, and descriptions of the picturesque landscapes and rural traditions. Indeed, some of his writings had already been serialised in the *Wiltshire and Gloucestershire standard* in 1915.

While there was still final editing to do, he hoped that his capturing of the essence of the Upper Thames would not only revive his literary career but also preserve the cultural heritage of the region.

As he approached the publishing house, he took a deep breath, feeling a mix of nervousness and excitement. The imposing building seemed to symbolize the gateway to his future. He was greeted warmly by the receptionist and soon ushered into a spacious office where Mr. Duckworth and another suited gentleman awaited.

'Ah, Alfred, welcome, welcome!' Gerald Duckworth said, rising from his chair to shake Alfred's hand, 'please, have a seat. We've been looking forward to this meeting.'

'Can I introduce my associate, Henry Maxwell? He has recently joined our editorial board and has a few questions for you. I should say that since the end of the war and all the economic challenges

THE PALACE OF MY IMAGINATION

that have followed in its wake, we're having to be more rigorous about what we offer to the market, so we're interviewing all our prospective authors in some detail about their latest works.'

'That's fine,' said Alfred, turning his attention to Maxwell, who picked up a slim folder, and while perusing its contents, proceeded to grill him, although avoiding any direct eye contact.

'I see that we've published two of your previous books that could be classified as covering folklore, rustic personalities and anecdotes, dialect, local conditions, topography etc. Those being *A Wiltshire Village* and *Villages of the White Horse*. The book you're working on at the moment, er... *Round About the Upper Thames*... seems essentially to be a third instalment of that genre in terms of its format. Or would you say there is something uniquely original to this work?'

Alfred thought for a few moments before replying.

'I would say that this book seems more pointedly to recognise that the rustic lifestyle is effectively dying out, and that with increasing mechanisation, and the passage of time, one no longer seems to encounter those notable characters, many of whom possessed exceptional strength and stamina, probably as a result of their outdoor physical lifestyle. Of course, the characters are all different—'

Maxwell scribbled a note and, without looking up, continued the interrogation.

'Can I ask about your definition of the Upper Thames as a distinctive region? I haven't previously heard that mentioned as a geographic entity.'

Alfred began to feel a little uncomfortable with the tone of Maxwell's questioning.

'You are right in the sense that this area is better defined geographically as border country, where four English counties meet near the origin of the river. But undoubtedly the dialect is, to my ear, homogeneous in this region and the lifestyle is almost exclusively agrarian.'

'I see, but in terms of the river, unless I'm wrong, it does not directly link these villages. Indeed, some of them are at quite a distance from its banks.'

Alfred was by now feeling a distinct lack of sympathy from Maxwell, and a slightly awkward silence followed, broken only by Duckworth's intervention.

'Henry, I think Alfred's focus on the Upper Thames as a cultural and historical region, rather than strictly geographical, is quite compelling. The blend of counties and their shared heritage is an intriguing angle.'

Maxwell glanced up, finally meeting Alfred's eyes.

'I understand. But Mr. Duckworth, we do need to ensure there is enough substance and novelty to capture our readers' interest.'

Alfred took a deep breath and continued.

'What I aim to do with this book is to capture the transitional phase of these communities. Yes, the 'Upper Thames' is also symbolic, a thread connecting the past and present. It documents a vanishing way of life before it's completely overshadowed by modernity. I believe this work will resonate deeply with readers who have a sense of nostalgia or a keen interest in cultural history.'

Duckworth nodded thoughtfully.

'Alfred, I think you're onto something important here. Henry's concerns are valid, and we must ensure the book is both engaging and informative. Perhaps we can include a map illustrating the regions and key locations you're referencing, to help readers visualize the Upper Thames area?'

'That's an excellent idea,' Alfred agreed, feeling a surge of optimism.

'And I'd like, if I may, to go on to explain my second work, *Folk Songs of the Upper Thames* , as this has emerged as a result of my researching the first. I became aware that folk singing was the prime means of entertainment for the inhabitants of the region, effectively defining their rural culture.

'I realised that there were several hundred songs recited in inns, at village festivals, during harvest homes, sometimes sung while the villagers were out working in the fields, but none of these songs were recorded in any way—they were all handed down through oral tradition.

THE PALACE OF MY IMAGINATION

'I also became aware that the elderly folk were the best repository of this knowledge. When one considers that with advancing time, the closure of village inns, the loss of village festivals, and the migration of the rural population into towns, this knowledge will be lost forever as the elderly population dies off, unless someone tries to preserve their words.'

Duckworth nodded while Maxwell scribbled more notes.

Alfred continued.

'What makes my work original is the way I drew these songs out of the villagers. I spent nineteen months cycling around the region—covering about 13,000 miles—getting to know the singers personally. This was often through encounters in village inns during winter evenings, as the village men were the chief exponents of folk song and they worked during the day, and their long hours extended well into the evenings in summertime.

'It was important to get to know them as they would only perform their songs once I had met them and won their trust. Hence, I feel that this work offers something distinctive and will serve as a lasting record of the song culture that entertained the villagers of the region.'

Duckworth leaned back in his chair, clearly impressed by Alfred's account, but keen for Maxwell to enter the discussion.

'And what are your thoughts, Henry?' asked Duckworth.

'I have some comments and some more questions. Mr. Williams. I believe what you have produced is unique—but I can't help but feel you might be missing an opportunity. Your work concerns folk songs of the region, but you haven't provided the musical background to them. After all, isn't what makes a song notable its special union of lyric and melody?

'I think it is a real pity not to include the music, especially in the context of providing a full record for future generations who may wish to go further and actually sing these songs.

'And you say in your preface that the singers had to sing the song to you, as they couldn't accurately reproduce the words just by saying them. Wouldn't the work be much stronger if you, or a musician colleague had actually notated the melodies?'

JOHN CULLIMORE

Alfred hesitated before replying. He was acutely sensitive to such criticism. His rather negative views on music had been previously recorded in interviews with the press, and he certainly had no ability in terms of musical notation. Maxwell certainly had a point.

'My wish is to preserve the words of these songs, for the historical record. I don't wish to promote them for their artistic or literary value,' Alfred replied, and he wondered if he might be coming across as rather stubborn.

Sensing this Maxwell continued his probing.

'The other thing that concerns me is that you admit in your preface that hardly any of these songs were composed in the Thames Valley, and that most were written in London and other large towns and cities. So, my question is, are you being honest enough with the reading public regarding the title of the work?'

'You are correct about their origins, but these songs are prevalent in the region, and very popular and seem to define the culture of this particular rural population.'

'But wouldn't it be more appropriate to call it *Folk songs of the English Countryside*?'

At this stage Duckworth, who had become slightly restless, intervened.

'I must say I find Alfred's title more appealing.'

Undaunted, Maxwell launched into another question.

'You admit that you've been very selective in your choice of song, in fact you seem to have censored songs which you classify as 'rough' or 'indelicate.'

'Indeed, there were songs offered to me that I believed to be immoral, and I would not be comfortable about sharing them in such a work.'

'But are you justified in suppressing these more 'down to earth' folk songs. After all, they entertain the villagers for all their rudeness. So, isn't this denying the real world? Is it just a sanitised record that you wish to preserve?'

An awkward silence followed.

However, Duckworth intervened, having made his decision.

THE PALACE OF MY IMAGINATION

'I think the fact that your discussion is so animated adds to the appeal of these works. I believe we can look forward to publishing them, if you'll take into consideration our comments. Would you be prepared to come back with a full draft of both?'

Alfred nodded, feeling a mix of relief and renewed purpose.

'Yes, I would be happy to.'

'Excellent,' Duckworth said, standing up and extending his hand. 'We look forward to seeing your completed work.'

JOHN CULLIMORE

Chapter 40

Osney saw Alfred walking into Swindon station on a freezing cold January morning and watched him board the nine-a.m. express to Paddington. Parked opposite the station, he paused to reflect on his strategy to undermine Alfred and had to admit to himself that it hadn't had the desired effect.

Somehow, Alfred had endured those extra months of hardship that he had precipitated, and now Williams was settled in his new home with Mary. Osney couldn't help but think of her. Taking another sip from his hip flask, he realised that Mary was now his primary concern. Perhaps it was time to raise the stakes even further.

As the train pulled out of the station, Osney's mind churned with possibilities. The thought of Mary stirred something dark in him. He had always harboured an unsettling fascination with her—her strength, her unwavering loyalty to Alfred, and the quiet grace with which she carried herself. She was everything that Osney's own life lacked: warmth, purpose, and genuine affection. But that admiration had twisted over time, warped by jealousy, lust and a burning desire to possess what Alfred had.

He imagined her now alone and vulnerable and sensed an opportunity. Osney gripped the steering wheel, the cold leather biting into his gloved hands. The engine of the Sunbeam purred as Osney started the car and drove away from the station.

Perhaps a visit to Ranikhet was now in order, a seemingly innocent gesture of goodwill. He would go now to Deacon's store in Old Town and buy her a gift on his way to South Marston. He would feign concern for Alfred.

Yes, he thought, that could work—and If Alfred wasn't around, then the opportunity would be even more perfect.

Osney took another swig from his flask, the neat malt whisky burning a path down his throat, fuelling his resolve—and his desire.

As he drove into the village, the sky turned a uniform grey, and

THE PALACE OF MY IMAGINATION

light snowflakes began to drift down from the heavens. Osney pulled up and parked his Sunbeam on a patch of land on the left of Vicarage Road, just before Ranikhet.

The temperature seemed to plummet as he stepped out of the car. The cold bit at his cheeks, and the snow underfoot was thin but treacherous, hiding patches of ice. As he approached Mary's home, his foot slid awkwardly on one of these hidden slicks, but he just managed to keep his balance, steadying himself with his cane.

Ranikhet, Alfred's new abode, stood quietly in the snowy landscape. The fire burning in the hearth cast a warm glow through the windows giving the house an inviting, almost serene appearance. But to Osney, it was a fortress—Alfred's fortress, the embodiment of all that had thwarted his schemes. He tipped his flask for another draught of whisky, only to realise with frustration that it was empty. A pity, as he had only filled it that morning. The warmth of the whisky had been a small comfort against the growing chill in his heart.

As he approached the gate, the village postman passed by, cheerfully calling out a hearty 'Good morning.' Osney merely raised an arm in response, keeping his head down, his face a mask of cold indifference. He had no intention of engaging in pleasantries, not today. He had come with a purpose, and he would not be deterred by the simple niceties of village life.

Reaching the front door, Osney rapped on it with his stick, the sound sharp and insistent in the stillness, the only noise in a world increasingly muffled by lying snow. After a moment, the door swung open, and there stood Mary, her expression shifting from curiosity to shock as she recognised him.

'Adam?' she stammered, her voice tinged with surprise and a hint of trepidation. She had not expected him, not here, not on this cold January morning.

'Mary,' Osney said, tipping his hat slightly in mock politeness. His eyes flicked over her, noting the way she clutched the door, her knuckles white against the wood.

'I hope I'm not intruding. I was just passing through the village and thought I might pay a visit.' His speech was obviously slurred and his eye movements occasionally erratic.

Mary hesitated, her mind racing, her fear increasing as she recalled the last time they had met and the conspiracy he had been conducting against Alfred. And now he was here, almost certainly inebriated.

'Alfred's not here,' she said quickly, as if that might dissuade him from whatever he intended.

'I'm not here for Alfred,' Osney replied smoothly, stepping past her as if he had already been invited in, 'actually, I wanted to speak with you.'

Mary's heart skipped a beat, but she forced herself to remain calm.

'Very well,' she said, stepping back to allow him inside.

THE PALACE OF MY IMAGINATION

Chapter 41

As Osney entered the warmth of Ranikhet, he glanced around, taking in the details of the house. It was modest but well-appointed, a place of comfort and care. The walls were lined with bookshelves overflowing with hardbacks, periodicals and Alfred's notebooks. The furniture was simple but sturdy, and a fire crackled in the hearth, filling the room with a pleasant heat. It was exactly the kind of home he had never known, and he hated it for that.

Mary led him into the sitting room and offered him a seat. She remained standing, her hands clasped nervously in front of her.

'What is it you wanted to speak to me about?' she asked, her voice steady despite her unease.

'I brought you a little housewarming gift—here you are.' said Osney and thrust a package at her.

'Open it,' he said, and decided he ought to sit down as the room began to spin slowly, the alcohol now clearly having an effect.

'Adam, I'm not sure this is appropriate,' said Mary.

In that instant his anger exploded.

'Open it now!' he shouted. Mary felt the fear mounting, her mouth became suddenly dry, and she looked at the floor, finding it increasingly difficult to move or meet his gaze.

She started to slowly unwrap the package, her hands trembling, hoping beyond hope that somebody—anybody— would come to the door and intervene. The paper crinkled under her fingers, each tear seeming to echo in the now suffocating silence of the room. She dared not look up at Osney, whose eyes bore into her with a wild intensity, his earlier charm now replaced by something darker, more dangerous.

The package was small, wrapped in plain brown paper with no markings or embellishments. It felt oddly heavy in her hands, and as she peeled away the final layer, the object within was revealed—a small, intricately carved wooden box.

Mary's breath caught in her throat as she recognised it as an old jewellery box, probably early Victorian, the kind she had seen once in a market in Bath, back when her father had taken her there as a child. She had admired it from afar, but they had never been able to afford such a luxury.

'What, what is this?' she stammered, her voice barely above a whisper.

'Open the box,' Osney commanded, his voice cold and menacing.

Mary lifted the lid. Inside, nestled on a bed of deep red velvet, was a necklace - an antique piece, with a large, blood-red ruby set in a delicate gold chain. The stone glimmered ominously in the light, its deep hue almost hypnotic. Mary's heart sank as she realised the implication. This was not just a gift; it was a symbol, a message.

'I thought it would suit you,' Osney said, his voice low and slurred, the alcohol fully taking hold. He stood up unsteadily, swaying slightly as he moved closer to her.

'A beautiful necklace for a beautiful woman. Doesn't it feel right, Mary?'

She recoiled, the box slipping from her hands and clattering to the floor. The necklace spilled out, the ruby gleaming darkly against the wooden boards.

'Adam, please,' Mary said, her voice cracking with fear, 'you need to leave.' Osney's expression contorted into a sneer.

'Leave?—You think you can defy me? You think you can just throw me aside as if I don't matter?'

The room seemed to shrink around her, the walls closing in as Osney's fury filled the space. Mary's heart pounded in her chest as she silently prayed for Alfred to arrive, for anyone to come and save her from this terrifying moment.

Just as she thought the situation couldn't get any worse, the door creaked open. For a brief moment, hope surged within her—perhaps it was Alfred, the postman, or a neighbour. But instead, a cold gust of wind swept into the room, bringing with it the stark realisation that she was utterly alone with this man, and no one was there to hear her should she scream.

Osney lunged at her, his hands gripping her arms with a brutal

THE PALACE OF MY IMAGINATION

force.

'You don't get to say no to me!' he shouted, his face inches from hers, his breath heavy with the stench of whisky.

Mary tried to pull away, but his hold only tightened, his fingers digging into her skin. Pain and distress surged through her, and she struggled desperately, her breaths coming in ragged gasps as she began to wail in terror.

Osney's response was swift and cruel—a sharp slap across her face that left her stunned.

'You're coming with me, now,' he growled, and without another word, he began dragging her toward the door.

As they stepped through the front door, it became evident that the weather had taken a turn for the worse. The snowfall had grown heavier, blanketing the front garden and the path with a thick layer of white. The world outside seemed unnaturally quiet, the snow muffling all sound, even Mary's frantic cries for help.

Desperately, Mary scanned her surroundings, hoping to spot someone, anyone, who could come to her aid. But the village was eerily empty, and the falling snow veiled any hope of rescue. Osney had timed his visit perfectly, and his grip on her arm tightened as he guided her forcefully towards his car.

The cold bit into Mary's skin, and she shivered uncontrollably, her thin dress offering no protection against the biting wind. She hadn't been given a chance to grab a coat before being forced out of the house, and now the icy air seeped through her, chilling her to the bone.

As they neared the car, Mary's foot slipped on a patch of ice, causing her to stumble. Panic surged within her as she lost her balance, but Osney, driven by his growing rage and desperation, didn't give her a moment to recover. His anger flared, and without hesitation, he began dragging her the remaining distance along the snow-covered ground, pulling her by the arm with a cruel intensity.

Mary's heart pounded in her chest as she was bundled into his car, the hopelessness of her situation pressing down on her like the thick snow blanketing the earth. The cold metal of the car seat bit through her dress, and she shivered, not just from the severe cold but from the fear that gripped her. Osney, reeking of whisky and rage, slammed the door shut, sealing her inside the dark, confined space.

The engine of the Sunbeam roared to life with a throaty growl, and the car lurched forward, tyres spinning and skidding on the icy road. The vehicle surged down Vicarage Road, fishtailing as Osney's heavy foot pressed on the accelerator, his hands gripping the wheel with drunken determination.

Mary's thoughts were a blur. Where was he taking her? What did he plan to do? The questions tumbled through her mind, each one more terrifying than the last. She could see the intersection with Oxford Road up ahead, familiar landmarks passing by in a blur. The village remained unsettlingly quiet, the snowfall muting all sound, making it feel as though they were the only two people left in the world.

Osney's eyes were fixed on the road, but there was a wildness in them, a glint that Mary had never seen before. He muttered under his breath, curses and threats that she couldn't fully make out, his fury simmering just beneath the surface. He was a man possessed, and she was at his mercy.

***

After a successful meeting with his publisher, Alfred returned to Swindon by train, arriving just as the clock struck six p.m. Noticing the onset of steady snowfall since the train passed Reading, he observed that the pavements were now blanketed in four inches of soft snow. Stepping out of the station, he was relieved to see Henry waiting for him in his new car. Henry reassured him that the main roads to South Marston were still passable despite the weather, and they set off cautiously through the town.

The main road eastward was relatively clear, but as they turned left onto Thornhill Road, the snow was less disturbed, and they proceeded even more carefully. As they neared Chapel Lane, Alfred noticed something that made his heart sink—Ranikhet was shrouded in darkness, an unusual sight that immediately set off

THE PALACE OF MY IMAGINATION

alarms in his mind. He wondered if Mary had gone out, but that didn't explain why the garden gate was ajar. She would never have left it open.

As they approached the house, Alfred's unease deepened. The freshly fallen snow revealed sets of footprints, mostly leading away from the house and into the lane. His concern turned to dread when he found the front door unlocked. Pushing it open, he stepped inside, his voice trembling as he called out,

'Mary?'

The silence that greeted him was unnerving, and as he walked through the entrance hall, a sense of foreboding settled over him. Something was terribly wrong.

Alfred switched on the hall lights, the sudden brightness doing little to dispel the unease that had settled deep in his chest. Henry moved ahead of him into the living room, the remnants of a once-roaring fire now just glowing embers in the hearth. As Henry stepped forward, he stumbled on something lying on the floor.

'What on earth is this?' he muttered, bending down to retrieve a small, ornamental box that had been carelessly discarded. Next to it, something caught his eye—a necklace, its gold chain glinting ominously in the dim light.

'I don't understand this, but it's very worrying,' Alfred said, his voice tight with concern. The scene felt wrong, disturbingly so. He needed answers, and fast.

'I'll go next door to the Ockwell's, see if they've noticed anything unusual.'

He hurried over, his steps quickened by the rising fear gnawing at him. The door was answered by his Aunt Miriam, her face a picture of calm concern.

'Have you seen Mary today?' Alfred asked, unable to keep the tremor out of his voice.

'No, I haven't, I'm afraid. Is everything all right?' Miriam responded, her brow furrowing as she noticed the distress in his eyes.

'She's disappeared. I'm worried,' Alfred admitted, the words tumbling out before he could stop them. Just then, one of Miriam's daughters appeared at the door, having overheard the conversation.

'I saw her getting into a car around lunchtime,' she offered. 'There was a man. I think I've seen his car here before.'

Alfred felt a cold shiver run through him as he pieced it together. The small clues, the scattered items in the living room, the unlocked door—they all pointed to one person.

'It must have been Osney,' he said, turning to Henry, his voice barely above a whisper, but filled with a grim certainty.

***

The car pulled off the Oxford Road into the yard of Osney's farm at Lower Hill, the headlights cutting through the thick curtain of falling snow. The yard was blanketed in more than six inches of undisturbed snow, and the heavy flakes continued to fall, muffling all sound.

As Osney brought the car to a stop, Mary glanced around, her heart sinking further at the sight of the isolated farmhouse. The farm looked as though it hadn't seen a soul in days, with no sign of life except the faint glow coming from the windows of the main house.

Osney got out of the car, his boots crunching loudly in the snow. He walked around to Mary's side and yanked the door open, his face a mask of grim determination. Mary, shivering uncontrollably, stepped out into the freezing night, her breath coming in quick, visible puffs. Her teeth chattered as she wrapped her arms around herself in a futile attempt to ward off the biting cold. She could barely feel her fingers, and the wind seemed to slice right through her thin dress.

Osney, seeming not to notice or care about her discomfort, led her towards the farmhouse. Although the place appeared deserted, the housekeeper had prepared the fire in the main living room and left the lights on in the kitchen before leaving for her cottage further up the farm track. Tomorrow was her day off, and Osney knew he had no reason to worry about being disturbed over the next couple of days.

Once inside the farmhouse, Mary's body ached from the cold,

THE PALACE OF MY IMAGINATION

and she instinctively moved towards the reassuring warmth of the range in the kitchen. The heat seeped into her bones, slowly bringing her back to life, though the fear that gripped her heart remained as strong as ever.

Osney, sensing her desperate need for warmth, tossed her one of his coats from a hanger. It was heavy, and it smelled faintly of the outdoors and tobacco, but she didn't care. She pulled it around her shoulders, grateful for any warmth it could provide. Osney then poured two glasses of brandy, the liquid sloshing slightly as his hand trembled. He thrust one glass towards her.

'Drink this if you're cold,' he ordered, his voice gruff and devoid of any concern.

Mary hesitated but knew she needed something to steady her nerves. She took the glass and sipped the brandy, the fiery liquid burning her throat as it went down. The warmth began to spread through her, and after a few minutes, her shivering settled, though the cold in her heart remained.

Gathering what courage she could muster, Mary spoke, her voice trembling slightly but trying to remain calm.

'Why have you brought me here, Adam?' she asked, her eyes searching his face for any sign of reason, of the man she once thought she knew.

Osney's expression darkened, and for a moment, she feared he wouldn't answer, that his anger might flare again. But instead, he leaned against the counter, his eyes narrowed, and his jaw clenched.

'Why?' he echoed, his voice low and dangerous, 'because you didn't leave me any choice, Mary. You made your bed with that fool Alfred, and now you'll lie in it, but on my terms.'

His words sent a shiver down her spine, one that had nothing to do with the cold. She could see the madness in his eyes, the obsession that had brought him to this point. She had to think quickly, to find a way out of this nightmare, but for now, all she could do was try to keep him talking, to buy herself time.

'Adam, please,' she said, trying to keep her voice steady, 'whatever you're thinking, this isn't the way. You're only making things worse.'

Osney let out a bitter laugh, the sound harsh and grating.

'Worse? You think this is bad? No, Mary, this is just the beginning. You're going to learn that no one crosses me and gets away with it. Not you—not Alfred— no one.'

Mary's mind raced as she tried to think of something, anything, that might calm him, that might turn this situation in her favour. But all she could see was the impenetrable wall of his anger, the darkness that had consumed him.

The farmhouse was silent except for the crackling of the fire and the howling wind outside. The isolation pressed in on her, making her feel even more trapped. But she knew she couldn't give up, not now. She had to survive, to find a way to escape, even if it seemed impossible. The night would be long, and she knew that her only hope was to stay alert, to wait for the moment when she could make her move.

Mary knew she had to act carefully, choosing her words and actions with precision. She decided that if she could gain even a small measure of control, it might give her a chance to change the course of this terrifying night.

'Would you like me to prepare some food for you?' she asked, her voice as steady as she could make it, though her pulse was still racing. Osney stopped pacing and turned to look at her, his eyes narrowing. For a moment, she feared he would see through her attempt to shift the dynamics. But then, something in his gaze softened. Perhaps he saw this as a sign that she was surrendering to the reality he wanted, that she was accepting her place in his twisted world. The idea of her working in his kitchen, like a dutiful wife, seemed to appeal to him. His aggression subsided, and a small, almost contented smile curled at the corner of his mouth.

'Yes, Mary,' he said, his voice calmer now, though still laced with possessiveness, 'go ahead and make us something. This is how it should have been all along.'

Mary swallowed the lump in her throat and moved towards the larder, her hands trembling slightly as she opened the door. She had no idea what she would make or how much time this would

THE PALACE OF MY IMAGINATION

buy her, but she had to keep him placated. The kitchen was stocked with basic provisions—bread, eggs, some cold meats. She decided on something simple, something that would require time and keep him occupied.

She set to work, her mind racing with possibilities. She could try to slip something into his food to make him drowsy, but she had no idea if the pantry held anything that could help. She could attempt to escape while he was eating, but the heavy snow and isolation of the farmhouse made that seem almost impossible.

As she cracked the eggs into a bowl, she glanced at Osney, who had settled himself into a chair by the fire, watching her with a mix of satisfaction and expectation. He seemed content for now to let her play the role he wanted. But she knew this calm could shatter at any moment if he sensed any deception.

She moved about the kitchen with a deliberate calmness, setting the table as if this were any ordinary night. All the while, she kept one ear tuned to the wind outside, hoping against hope that someone—anyone—might come by, though she knew it was unlikely.

Finally, she placed the food on the table, and Osney motioned for her to sit across from him. He poured them each another glass of brandy, his eyes gleaming with a dark satisfaction.

'You see, Mary,' he said, raising his glass, 'this is what it could be like. You and me, away from everything and everyone, just the two of us.'

Mary forced a tight smile and lifted her glass, though she barely sipped the brandy.

'Yes, Adam,' she replied, her voice betraying none of the turmoil she felt inside, 'just the two of us.'

Osney ate the hearty meal of bacon, eggs, and fried potatoes with the relish of a man who felt he had won, while Mary had no appetite but took the opportunity to drink a large glass of water. She noticed that every time she topped up his brandy glass, it seemed to amuse him. He raised it to her with a self-satisfied grin. Though he wasn't totally inebriated yet, she thought that might be something to aim for.

JOHN CULLIMORE

As she cleared the plates and put the kettle on to boil, she began washing the dishes.

'You don't have to do that,' Osney said, watching her with a mix of curiosity and satisfaction.

'But we can't leave the kitchen in a mess,' she retorted, her voice steady despite the tension that still hung in the air.

Osney seemed to relax a little more, leaning back in his chair, the earlier anger ebbing away. He was lulled by the domesticity of the scene—the warm kitchen, the smell of food still lingering in the air, and Mary moving about as if she belonged there. But while his anger subsided, it was replaced by another emotion. Now that he was in control of the situation, he started to feel a pleasant sensation of arousal as he tracked her every movement.

He moved towards her as she worked at the kitchen sink and standing behind her wrapped his arms around her waist and pulled her gently back towards him, lightly kissing her neck.

The fear was almost paralysing, but beneath it, she sensed a glimmer of hope. His arousal might be her only chance to manipulate the situation. She forced herself to remain calm, to think clearly despite the terror gripping her.

'Not here Adam, let me go upstairs.'

She felt him hesitate for a moment before he released her. His eyes bore into hers, filled with a dark desire that made her skin crawl.

'The door on the right at the top of the stairs,' he repeated, his voice low and heavy with expectation.

Mary managed a faint smile; one she hoped conveyed a willingness she did not feel.

'Give me a few minutes,' she said softly, as she topped up his glass with the last of the brandy, her voice steady despite the fear gnawing at her insides.

'Finish your drink.'

She walked slowly, deliberately, towards the stairs, aware of his gaze following her every step. Each creak of the wooden steps under her feet sounded louder than the last, echoing in the silence of the farmhouse.

THE PALACE OF MY IMAGINATION

When she reached the top, she glanced back briefly, seeing him still standing at the bottom, his eyes glazed with anticipation. She opened the door he had indicated and slipped inside, closing it softly behind her.

The room was dimly lit by a single lamp on the nightstand. Mary quickly scanned her surroundings—a large bed, a wardrobe, a small chair in the corner. No obvious means of escape. Her heart raced as she crossed to the window, hoping for some way out. But the heavy snowfall outside had piled high against the glass, and the drop to the ground was too far.

But then she saw a car moving slowly along the Oxford Road in the direction of Shrivenham. She waved vigorously at it, but it seemed to continue on the road and was soon out of sight.

Mary's heart sank as the car disappeared into the distance, its taillights fading into the snowy night. She let out a shuddering breath, fighting back the rising panic.

Turning away from the window, she tried to think quickly. The wardrobe—perhaps there was something inside she could use. She yanked the doors open, rifling through the clothing and spare linens, but found nothing useful. Her eyes darted to the bed, and she considered hiding under it, but dismissed the thought almost immediately—Osney would find her in seconds.

As she racked her brain for options, she heard the floorboards creak beneath her. Footsteps were moving closer, ascending the stairs. Osney was coming. Her pulse raced, her mind desperately searching for an idea—any idea—that might save her.

In a sudden flash of inspiration, she remembered the wardrobe. If she couldn't use it to hide, maybe she could use it as a barrier. She quickly pulled it away from the wall, the heavy piece of furniture scraping against the floor as she struggled to position it near the door. It wouldn't hold him for long, but it might buy her a few precious seconds.

The doorknob rattled as Osney reached the top of the stairs. Mary's breath caught in her throat as she braced herself against the wardrobe, using all her weight to push it just a little further, wedging it against the door.

'Mary?' Osney's voice slurred slightly, filled with drunken impatience.

'Open the door.'

She didn't answer, pressing her back against the wardrobe, every muscle tense. The door rattled again, this time harder, as he tried to force it open.

'Mary!' His tone shifted, anger seeping back in.

A few seconds later, the door cracked open, Osney's brute strength finally overcoming her feeble barricade. The wardrobe toppled forward with a crash, and he stumbled into the room, eyes blazing with fury, and Mary screamed.

***

'There's only one place he could have taken her,' Alfred said, his voice tight with urgency as he and Henry sprinted toward the car. They jumped in, and Henry quickly steered onto the Oxford Road, heading east. The main road was passable, with flattened snow packed down by the day's traffic, but icy patches still made the drive treacherous.

As they drove, Alfred's mind raced alongside the car. He kept his eyes on the road ahead, scanning for any sign of Mary or Osney. The tension in the car was palpable, both men acutely aware of the stakes.

A tractor with a snowplough attachment appeared on the opposite side of the road, slowly clearing the way for oncoming vehicles. The sight was a small comfort, a reminder that despite the storm, the world outside was still moving. But Alfred's world had shrunk to the narrow stretch of road in front of them and the farmhouse that lay ahead.

As they neared the junction for Shrivenham, Alfred's heart pounded in his chest. They could see the entrance to Lower Field Farm, the driveway leading up to the house where he was certain Osney had taken Mary. The farmhouse itself loomed in the distance, its outline just visible through the swirling snow. The downstairs windows glowed with light, but it was the lamp in the upper-storey bedroom that caught Alfred's attention.

'Slow down,' Alfred urged as they approached the gate leading

THE PALACE OF MY IMAGINATION

into the farm's yard. Henry complied, easing off the accelerator. As they passed by, Alfred's eyes were drawn to a figure moving in the window. His breath caught in his throat. It was Mary.

'Stop the car! Let me out,' Alfred shouted, his voice laced with desperation. Henry slammed on the brakes, the car skidding slightly on the icy road before coming to a halt.

Without waiting, Alfred threw open the door and bolted toward the house, slipping slightly on the snow-covered ground but never losing his momentum. Behind him, he heard Henry call out,

'I'm heading to Shrivenham to get the police!'

The sound of the car's engine revving up again barely registered as Alfred's focus was solely on Mary.

She was there, in the window, a shadowy figure backlit by the dim light inside. Alfred's heart raced as he sprinted up the driveway, praying he wasn't too late.

***

As Alfred burst into the kitchen, a sharp crack echoed through the house, followed by a piercing scream. His heart pounded in his chest, every instinct telling him to hurry. Spotting a heavy brass candlestick on the kitchen table, he grabbed it without a second thought and sprinted up the stairs, the sounds from the bedroom on the right guiding him like a beacon.

He reached the doorway just in time to see Osney forcing Mary onto the large bed, his intentions unmistakable and vile. Rage and adrenaline surged through Alfred as he charged forward. Without hesitating, he swung his arm back, gripping the candlestick tightly, and brought it crashing down on the back of Osney's head with all the force he could muster.

The impact was sickening, the dull thud reverberating through the room. Osney crumpled onto the bed, stunned. Mary scrambled away, her eyes wide with terror and shock, and Alfred raised the candlestick again.

'No!' Mary cried out, her voice desperate, 'just Get me out of here!'

Her words jolted Alfred back to reality. Dropping the candlestick, he grabbed Mary's hand, and together they bolted out of the room, down the stairs, and out of the house into the freezing night.

***

A couple of minutes passed, and Osney began to stir, groaning as he tried to shake off the pain throbbing in the back of his head. The initial shock wore off, replaced by a burning fury as he realised what had just happened. His eyes narrowed, and with a growl of primal rage, he staggered to his feet, determined to hunt them down. The chase was on.

Osney noticed the kitchen door slightly open, a clear sign of their hurried escape. His eyes followed the fresh footprints in the snow, leading across the yard and veering toward the road in the direction of Swindon. His pulse quickened with a mixture of anger and grim resolve. He retraced his steps to the farmhouse, his mind focused on one thing: catching them.

He climbed into his car, the engine sputtering to life as he turned the key. A momentary bout of blurred vision caused him to hesitate, his grip tightening on the steering wheel as he blinked furiously, willing the fog to clear. Finally, his vision sharpened, and with a growl of frustration, he slammed the car into gear.

Turning right out of the farm, Osney flicked on his full headlights, the beams cutting through the falling snow like knives. The car's engine roared as he gradually increased speed, eyes scanning the darkened road ahead for any sign of Mary—or the man who had struck him, whom he was certain was Williams.

He couldn't believe they had gone far. His frustration mounted as the empty road ahead mocked him, devoid of any retreating forms. But instead of easing his pace, his desperation to catch them only fuelled his urge to accelerate. He pushed the pedal harder, the car surging forward as the trees on his left blurred into streaks of dark green and white.

Then, a flicker in his rearview mirror caught his attention—headlights, about two hundred yards behind him. The distant wail of a siren followed, cutting through the night and confirming his worst fear: he was being pursued. Panic surged within him, and he pressed down even harder on the accelerator, the engine roaring as

THE PALACE OF MY IMAGINATION

he sped along the icy road.

But as he rounded a bend, his heart sank. Up ahead, no more than four hundred yards away, a wall of headlights blocked his path, stretching across the entire width of the road. A roadblock. He could feel the noose tightening around him.

Instinctively, he eased off the accelerator, but stopping in time was out of the question. He slammed on the brakes, the tyres screeching in protest as the car skidded uncontrollably. The vehicle veered to the left, leaving the road's surface entirely as it plummeted down the steep embankment.

Time seemed to slow as he saw the frozen canal ahead, its ice-covered surface gleaming ominously in the headlights. The solid form of the lock at Longleaze loomed closer, and with gut-wrenching inevitability, the car crashed into it. The impact was deafening, the force throwing him against the steering wheel as metal crumpled and glass shattered. The last thing he saw before darkness consumed him was the icy water rising rapidly around the vehicle.

JOHN CULLIMORE

Chapter 42

June 1926

Byett arrived for his visit, carrying a basket of freshly baked bread and some homemade jam, hoping to lift Alfred's spirits. He had heard that they were again struggling financially, and on a previous visit a week earlier, he had noticed that the larder was looking distinctly empty.

As soon as Alfred opened the door, Byett noticed the stark change in his friend's appearance. Alfred's clothes were shabby and worn, his face was pale, and his eyes lacked their usual spark.

'Alfred, good to see you,' Byett greeted, masking his concern with a warm smile. 'How are you faring?'

Alfred attempted a weak smile in return.

'Hello, Henry. Come in, let's talk in the garden,' Alfred said, leading his friend through the familiar hallway. They settled into the worn chairs in the garden, the early summer sun casting a warm, gentle light over the neglected flowerbeds and bird-pecked strawberries.

Henry looked at Alfred, concern etched on his face. 'Alfred, you don't look well. Is everything all right?'

Alfred let out a deep sigh, his eyes wandering over the overgrown plants.

'It's been tough, Henry. The last few years have been... well, they've been a real struggle. I've written five manuscripts, and every single one has been rejected. The latest book on the Thames—I had such high hopes for it, but they turned it down because my 'Folk Songs' book didn't sell well. And the garden; it's been nothing but trouble - the weather, the birds devouring the fruit—it feels like I'm losing on every front.'

Henry listened attentively, his heart heavy for his old friend.

'I had no idea things were this bad. I thought you had some success earlier this year when your poetry anthology was published?'

Alfred nodded, a heavy weight of melancholy pressing down on

THE PALACE OF MY IMAGINATION

him.

'It did sell well at first, especially after those good reviews. But I had to pay the publishers sixty-five pounds just to get it out there, and whatever financial benefits there were have long since dried up. I fear the public has forgotten about me.'

'Sometimes I wonder if I made the wrong choice, staying here. I should have relocated to India after the war and taken Mary with me. I must be such a disappointment to her.'

His admission felt like a blow, and he felt the crushing weight of his own words. All his recent thoughts were clouded with reflections on his hardships and a deep-seated sense of failure, particularly regarding his career as a writer.

He knew he had returned to South Marston a changed man. The experiences he had gathered from his travels, the fresh inspirations, the intellectual freedom and the rich tapestry of the world beyond his small village, had had all left an indelible mark on him. Those three tumultuous years of war had transformed his life in ways he could never have imagined.

Yet, despite all that, he couldn't shake the feeling that he had clung too tightly to the familiar, to the images and themes of a bucolic past. Perhaps he had underestimated his audience's desire for something new, something different.

Still, he had made his choices, and he knew it was futile to dwell on them now. The despair gnawing at him served no purpose, and he knew he had to suppress it.

Henry, sitting quietly beside him, noticed the turmoil etched on Alfred's face. His heart ached for his friend and the burdens he and Mary had borne. He leaned in closer, his tone gentle and reassuring.

'I think you're being too hard on yourself, Alfred. Mary's stood by you through everything. How is she holding up?'

A shadow crossed Alfred's face.

'Not much has changed. She still hasn't fully recovered from that ordeal with Osney.'

The weight of the memory settled between them, unspoken yet palpable. Henry realised they had never really confronted what had happened that night. Perhaps now was the time.

'May I ask... did she suffer any physical harm?' Henry inquired cautiously.

'Nothing serious,' Alfred replied, though his voice was heavy with unspoken pain, 'but he tormented her for months before the kidnapping, and I didn't realise what was happening. I feel so guilty about that and she regrets not confronting it sooner.'

'That's easier said than done, especially under those circumstances,' Henry pointed out.

'You're right,' Alfred agreed.

'And that night,' Henry continued, 'when you fled the farm, how did you manage to escape him?'

'It wasn't as hard as you might think,' Alfred explained. 'The snow made it tough, and we knew he'd come after us in his car. But we veered off the road onto a footpath that leads under the railway aqueduct about half a mile from his farm. From there, we made our way back to South Marston through the fields.'

'So, your knowledge of the countryside likely saved your lives,' Henry said with a small smile.

'I suppose that's one way to see it,' Alfred responded.

A heavy silence followed, and Henry could sense that Alfred wasn't eager to delve further into those painful memories.

'So, what's keeping you busy now, Alfred?'

'What's been keeping me afloat, mentally at least, is my work with Sanskrit. I've made great strides in my studies and translations. It's the one thing that gives me hope. I've really enjoyed completing translations from an ancient work called the Panchatantra—a series of fables that teach worldly wisdom using animal characters. Not dissimilar to Aesop's fables, maybe pre-dating them.

'And of course, my attachment to the Vedas and their underlying philosophy has grown ever stronger.'

Byett recalled their previous discussion about Vedanta and was curious to learn how Alfred's views had evolved.

'So, have you made any further progress with Hindu philosophy?' he asked. 'Having re-read some of your early poetry

THE PALACE OF MY IMAGINATION

I think it's fascinating that there were clear similarities with Hinduism , even before you encountered India or the Vedanta.'

Alfred nodded.

'Yes, I always had an instinctive feeling that aligned with Vedantic ideas, but immersing myself in Vedanta completely transformed my view of the universe.'

Byett leaned in, his interest piqued.

'And what specifically caused this shift?'

Alfred paused, gathering his thoughts.

'It was the realisation that the only true reality is infinite, unchanging, and eternal consciousness—what Vedanta calls 'Brahman'. That concept was a revelation for me.

'But there's a consequence of this understanding that might be hard for you to accept: the perception of an objective universe is an illusion. It's just a manifestation of Brahman and it has no independent existence. Realising this truth is essential for attaining liberation.'

Byett was taken aback by Alfred's assertion that the universe was somehow unreal.

'I find it hard to believe that everything I see, and feel is just an illusion.'

'But it only exists in our consciousness,' Alfred replied, 'when we lose consciousness, the universe, as we perceive it, ceases to exist.'

'Sure,' Henry said, considering Alfred's words, 'if I lost consciousness, the universe would cease to exist for me. But it would still exist for everyone else.'

Alfred nodded thoughtfully.

'That's a common perspective, Henry. But Vedanta suggests that what we perceive as the universe is merely a projection of our minds, like a dream. When you're dreaming, the dream world seems real, but when you wake up, you realize it was all an illusion.

'Our waking state is not so different. The universe, as we know it, is a construct of our mind and senses. We just happen to share the same construct.'

JOHN CULLIMORE

Henry shook his head, still wrestling with the concept.

'So, you're saying that everything we experience—our entire reality—is just a product of our imagination?'

'In a sense, yes,' Alfred replied.

'The physical world is transient and ever-changing, while the true reality, Brahman, is eternal and unchanging. Our senses and mind create a veil that conceals this truth from us. The goal of Vedanta is to pierce that veil and realise our true 'Self'—our oneness with Brahman.'

Byett raised an eyebrow.

'So, have you made any progress in identifying *your* true Self?'

Alfred smiled wryly.

'Certainly not,' he admitted.

Byett was puzzled. 'But you seem to understand it so well.'

'Yes, I've gained some theoretical knowledge of Vedanta,' Alfred explained.

'But that's not enough to truly know my inner Self. That knowledge will only be revealed to me if my mind reaches a state of inner peace, and I'm far from that right now.

'I also need to let go of the longings I have for comfort and contentment. You might think that strange, but unless I make those changes, I'll never see my true Self, and after my days I'll just continue the cycle of birth and death.'

'Are you talking about reincarnation?' Byett asked, incredulous, 'you don't really believe in that—do you?'

Alfred looked him in the eye and replied calmly, 'Yes... and ... yes.'

Byett looked uncomfortable and was clearly unconvinced by Alfred's views, however he felt tremendous sympathy for him, believing that Alfred's current difficulties and previous traumas had not surprisingly made him susceptible to these exotic abstractions and created a negative state of mind.

Sensing some tension in Henry, Alfred attempted to lighten the mood.

'You know Shakespeare was in line with Vedantic teaching. Do you recall the famous passage from 'The Tempest?'

THE PALACE OF MY IMAGINATION

'I don't,' smiled Henry, 'but I'm sure you're about to remind me.'

'*The solemn temples, the great globe itself; all which it inherit shall dissolve. And, like this unsubstantial pageant faded, leave not a rack behind. We are such stuff as dreams are made of, and our little life is rounded with a sleep*,' Alfred quoted with a smile.

'It's a poetic way of saying that our reality is not as solid as we think.'

Henry managed a small smile in return.

'I may not fully grasp or agree with everything you say, but you certainly give me a lot to think about, Alfred.'

JOHN CULLIMORE

PART 7: TRAGEDY

Chapter 43

Whate'er I prized, in that you took delight-
Beauty and Truth; lived happy in my sight
Smiled through your tears upon Life's rugged way,
And loved the pleasant tale and fable gay
Dedication to Mary Williams, in Tales of the Panchatantra, 1930

February 1930.

As Alfred mounted his bicycle outside the hospital, he reflected that the year could not have got off to a worse start. His manuscript of the Panchatantra fables had been rejected by Duckworth, but far worse than this, Mary had been admitted to hospital after experiencing unremitting abdominal pain.

After exploratory surgery, she had been diagnosed with incurable cancer.

For the last ten days, he had been cycling in from South Marston to Old Town twice daily to visit her, and he had been devastated to note how ill Mary looked today. She was in pain, appeared pale and wasted, with grossly swollen legs, making it impossible for her to move around. He had brought some snowdrops and early daffodils and a bottle of port wine, which she seemed to appreciate. But now he felt totally exhausted and could not face the prospect of cycling back to South Marston to the cold empty shell of Ranikhet.

As he pedalled slowly through the grey, wintry streets, Alfred's thoughts drifted back to better times. The small house they called Ranikhet, named after a place in India, that had captured his imagination, had once been filled with laughter and love. Now, it was just a reminder of his failures and the impending loss of the one person who had always believed in him.

He stopped by the side of the road, resting his bicycle against a

THE PALACE OF MY IMAGINATION

tree, and sat down on a nearby bench. The cold air bit through his thin coat, but he barely noticed. He felt numb, not just from the physical exhaustion but from the relentless emotional toll of the past few weeks. The rejection of his manuscript was a blow, but it paled in comparison to the agony of watching Mary suffer.

He remembered how Mary had smiled when he handed her the flowers earlier that day. Despite her pain, she had tried to comfort him, squeezing his hand and whispering words of encouragement. She was the strong one, always had been. Her strength gave him a small measure of solace, but it also broke his heart.

He realised at this stage that he could cycle no further. The exhaustion was too much, and the emotional weight too heavy. It was almost dark on this dull January afternoon, and he decided to visit Henry. His friend's house was conveniently located at the bottom of Victoria Hill, on his way home.

Light snowfall began as Alfred descended the hill from Old Town towards New Swindon. The snowflakes fell gently, dusting the streets and giving the bleak evening a quiet, almost serene quality. As he neared Henry's house, his heart lifted slightly when he saw the warm glow of light coming from the living room window. The light offered a small beacon of comfort, a signal that a friend awaited within, ready with a listening ear and a place to rest.

Alfred dismounted his bicycle, his legs shaking from both cold and fatigue, and walked the remaining distance to Henry's front door. The familiar creak of the gate and the crunch of snow underfoot seemed to echo in the stillness of the evening. He paused for a moment, gathering his thoughts and trying to push aside the overwhelming sadness that had been his constant companion.

Knocking on the door, Alfred knew Henry would understand the depth of his despair without the need for too many words. The door opened almost immediately, and Henry stood there, a look of concern quickly replacing his initial expression of surprise.

'Alfred, come in, come in,' Henry said, 'You look frozen. Let's get you warmed up.' Henry said, stepping aside to allow him entry.

Henry asked Alfred to stay for dinner, but Alfred refused on the grounds of having no appetite. However, he did accept a cup of tea. As he sipped the warm beverage, Alfred brought Henry up to date with Mary's condition. Through tears, he added.

'Without her, everything seems pointless, valueless. I'm not sure I wish to continue.'

Henry felt helpless, knowing there was little he could say or do apart from resting his hand lightly on Alfred's shoulder, a subtle gesture of sympathy.

'For fifteen years, I have been fooled by promises that I would succeed, and I believed them. See the result—failure. And now my dearest has to go the hard way to death without seeing our hopes realised,' Alfred said.

'But I must be going. Thank you for listening and for the tea,' he added, attempting to rise.

'You're not going anywhere in this weather, Alfred. You'll stay here tonight, and you can borrow a spare pair of my pyjamas,' replied Henry firmly. Alfred was too tired and forlorn to resist.

'This may not be the ideal time to say this, Alfred, but I've heard from a publisher in Oxford—Blackwells'. I met Basil Blackwell at a dinner recently and told him about your book of Sanskrit fables. He'd like you to go up to Oxford to meet him when it's convenient for you,' Henry said, opening his briefcase to extract a letter.

'And the other thing is, you are being considered for inclusion in the national roll of honour, for services to Literature. The documents are with the Prime Minister, Ramsay MacDonald, and he is due to sign things off next week. That means you'll get a Civil list pension—you'll not need to worry about money—I'm just sorry it's taken so long....'

Henry looked up from the letter to see that Alfred had fallen deeply asleep.

Henry sighed softly, placing the letter back in his briefcase. He carefully draped a blanket over Alfred and stoked the fire, hoping to offer a small measure of comfort to his friend in such a troubled time.

***

The next morning, Alfred awoke feeling more refreshed than he

THE PALACE OF MY IMAGINATION

had in weeks, despite having slept upright in an armchair for ten hours. However, as soon as he was fully awake, the weight of his situation fell upon him. Even after Henry reminded him of the encouraging news from Blackwell's and the prospect of the pension award, Alfred could not shake off the gloom that enveloped him.

'Well, whatever honour may be attached to me being awarded this grant pales into insignificance in the light of the circumstances,' Alfred said, his voice heavy with sorrow.

Despite his sombre mood, Alfred was grateful to share a hearty breakfast with Henry. The warmth of the food and the companionship provided a brief respite from his worries. After breakfast, Alfred prepared to visit Mary at the hospital.

'I'll visit Mary first,' he told Henry, 'and if time allows it, I'll telegraph Oxford to arrange a meeting with Blackwell.'

Henry nodded; concern etched on his face.

'Take your time, Alfred. And remember, I'm here if you need anything.' Saying this, Henry thrust a few pound notes into his hand.

Alfred thanked Henry and set off, the early morning air crisp and cold. As he cycled towards the hospital, he tried to focus on the small glimmers of hope Henry had offered.

When he arrived at the Victoria hospital, Mary was sleeping. He didn't have the heart to wake her. He gently caressed the back of her hand, taken aback at how cold it felt. He carefully replaced it under the blanket and told the ward Sister that he would return later. The Sister nodded sympathetically, understanding the strain Alfred was under.

Alfred stood by Mary's bedside for a moment longer, watching the rise and fall of her chest. The rhythmic sound of her breathing was both comforting and heart-wrenching. He whispered a silent prayer for her, then turned to leave, his steps heavy with sorrow.

As he walked out of the hospital, the chilly wind bit at his cheeks, mirroring the coldness he felt inside. He mounted his bicycle and headed for the Post Office on Victoria Hill.

JOHN CULLIMORE

Chapter 44

April 1930
'O son of Kunti, whatever one is absorbed in at the time of death, is the state one attains in the next life'
Extract from Bhagavad Gita. Chapter VIII, verse 6

Alfred pedalled the remaining yards into the entrance at Ranikhet, having just returned from his meeting with Blackwell in Oxford. With luck, he would be able to pick up some port wine from the larder and cycle to the hospital for five o'clock visiting. As he dismounted his bicycle, he was surprised to see two village children approaching, clutching a bouquet of flowers.

'These are for Mrs. Williams. We hope she'll be home soon,' one of them said.

'Thank you,' said Alfred, recognising two of the Ockwell brood, his adjacent neighbours, 'I know she'll appreciate them. Give my regards to your mother.'

'Mummy said if you'd like to have Sunday lunch with us, you're very welcome,' the other child chimed in.

'Thank you, thank you,' Alfred replied, touched by their kindness. 'I'd appreciate that very much.'

As the children scampered away, Alfred felt a warmth in his heart, a brief respite from the constant worry and sadness that had enveloped him. He made his way inside and quickly retrieved the port from the larder, then set off for the hospital.

Arriving just in time for visiting hours, Alfred hurried to Mary's room. She was asleep, her face a mask of fatigue and suffering. He quietly sat by her side, not wanting to disturb her rest. After a few moments, Mary stirred, her eyes slowly opening. She stared quizzically at Alfred, not seeming to recognise him at first.

'Look what I brought,' he said gently, showing her the bottle of port and the bouquet. 'And these lovely flowers are from the Ockwell children.'

Mary's face suddenly tensed as she reached out to touch the

THE PALACE OF MY IMAGINATION

flowers, and she emitted a shallow cry of pain. Alarmed, Alfred quickly went to fetch the nurse. After checking the bedside charts, the nurse confirmed it was time for Mary to receive some more morphine.

'I'll be right back,' the nurse said, hurrying off to get the medication. Alfred sat back down, holding Mary's hand, feeling helpless as he watched her struggle.

'It's all right, my love,' he whispered, brushing a stray lock of hair from her forehead, 'help is coming.'

The nurse returned promptly, administering the morphine with smooth dexterity. Mary's tense features gradually relaxed as the medication took effect, and she sighed with relief.

'Thank you,' she murmured weakly, her eyes fluttering open to meet Alfred's gaze. This time, there was recognition in her eyes, a flicker of the Mary he knew and loved.

'Don't mention it,' Alfred said, squeezing her hand gently, 'just rest now.'

As Mary drifted back into a more comfortable sleep, Alfred decided it was time to cycle home.

He realised he hadn't eaten all day and had been feeling slightly nauseated. As he turned off the Oxford Road towards South Marston, this nausea intensified, and he began to feel a tightness across his chest. He was just about to pass the Carpenter's Arms and was forced to stop. In doing so, the pain lessened to a degree. He was also sweating profusely but felt very cold.

He remounted his bicycle and gingerly recommenced his journey into the centre of the village. He knew that he had been overdoing it and resolved to take some aspirin and brandy. He was nearly home. Finally, Ranikhet came into view, and the slight downhill incline meant that he could stop pedalling, which was fortunate as the pain seemed to have returned.

He noticed that the sun now seemed to be shining directly on the front of the house, brightly illuminating the carved letters of Ranikhet in the stone above the front door. He felt sad as he thought how he would have loved to have shown Mary the beautiful hill station that had been such an important part of his life, realising this could now never be.

He went into his house, pausing only to pick up some post off the floor. Setting it down he went to find aspirin from the tin in the larder and some linament to rub on his chest.

He headed for his bedroom, exhausted. He lay down on his bed, too tired to remove his boots, and the pain was almost intolerable. He opened the packet of aspirin and stood up to fetch a glass of water from the bathroom.

Then the pain really exploded in his chest, and everything went black.

***

The next morning, his neighbour Miriam Ockwell noticed that Alfred's bicycle was still parked outside the house and the post from the morning deliveries had accumulated in the letter box. Concerned, she knocked but received no response. The front door was not locked so she entered and called out for Alfred.

'Mr. Williams? Alfred?' she called, her voice echoing through the silent house. She moved cautiously towards the bedroom, a sense of dread growing within her. As she entered the room, she saw him lying across the bed, motionless.

'Alfred!' she cried out, rushing to his side. She felt for a pulse but found none. Tears welled up in her eyes as she realised he was dead. She stood there for a moment, gathering her composure before hurrying back to the village to get help.

The postmortem confirmed that Alfred had suffered a massive heart attack.

***

THE PALACE OF MY IMAGINATION

Chapter 45

Mid-April 1930.
The Offices of Blackwell Publishing

In his office in the centre of Oxford, on a morning when the promise of Spring seemed to be more than fulfilled, Basil Blackwell had just finished opening the morning's correspondence when his secretary appeared at his office door.

'There's a Mr. Byett to see you.'

'I don't know of anyone called Byett. I'm expecting Alfred Williams,' he replied.

'I believe Mr. Byett is here on his behalf,' replied the secretary quizzically.

'Why then, show him in.'

Henry Byett entered the office and shook hands with the publisher.

'Thank you for seeing me. I realise that my friend Alfred was due to see you today to present his revised manuscript. However, I'm deeply saddened to have to bring you the news that he died suddenly last week, from a fatal heart attack.'

'I'm so sorry to hear that,' responded Blackwell. 'Please take a seat.'

'He was here only a couple of weeks ago. I was most impressed with him. As soon as he entered the room, I was aware that I was in the presence of a rare spirit.

'He seemed to radiate serenity and a gentleness that was most arresting. Our discussion about the book of fables was very straightforward. He promised to revise his typescript according to my suggestions, and bring it to Oxford again to meet our illustrator here, and to complete the preliminary plans for publication.'

'I'm not sure if you are aware of the tragic situation; his wife is also seriously ill,' said Henry.

'Indeed, I am. On the day we met, Alfred courteously excused himself from lunching with me, for he was anxious to be getting home. I asked him which train he was catching? But then he told me he had cycled here from Swindon!'

'I thought that a pause to eat a meal in between two rides of twenty-seven miles could hardly be amiss, but let it go at that, and proposed yesterday for this meeting.

'A look of pain came into Williams' eye as he asked me, very gently, if the day after would be equally convenient, for his wife had just undergone surgery of doubtful value, and the day I had offered was that on which he was to bring her home from hospital. So, today was agreed, and Williams went on his way.'

'That's so typical of Alfred,' said Henry. 'His wife is still alive but is terminally ill and now back at their home in South Marston. She is very keen that his final book be published posthumously, and she also wishes to donate Alfred's library of Sanskrit literature to Oxford University. She has asked if you would be able to assist in this matter.'

'This is indeed tragic,' said Blackwell, 'and I will try to help in any way I can.'

Henry was clearly overcome with emotion, and after a brief pause to collect himself, he continued.

'I apologize, Mr. Blackwell, but this has affected me deeply. I've known Alfred for 35 years. I've always supported his artistic endeavours, but he struggled to gain the recognition he deserved.

'Ironically, on the day he died, the Prime Minister's office confirmed his admission to the Civil List. He would have received a pension which would have seen the couple comfortably into the future. In fact, the letter conforming this from Ten Downing Street was found in Alfred's house—unopened.

'Recently, Alfred had hit rock bottom. He had received hardly any earnings in the last eighteen months. And since Christmas, they seemed to have survived on no more than five shillings a week.

'The death certificate mentioned a heart attack, but I believe starvation must have played a part. I believe he was denying himself food so that he could bring little comforts to his wife in the hospital. We found a pound note pinned to a piece of paper.

THE PALACE OF MY IMAGINATION

On it, he'd written 'For Port Wine for Mary.'

Blackwell was silent for a moment, deeply moved by Henry's account.

'I will do everything in my power to ensure Alfred's work is published and his wife's wishes are honoured.'

***

A week later, Blackwell arrived at Ranikhet and was welcomed in by Henry.

'Thank you for coming. If it's agreeable, Alfred's wife, Mary, would like to talk to you briefly, but I should warn you that she is very ill and has little time left.'

Blackwell nodded, steeling himself for the encounter.

'Of course, I understand,' he said, his voice filled with empathy.

Before proceeding upstairs, Henry showed Blackwell the extent of Alfred's Sanskrit library. A mere ten books propped up on otherwise empty bookshelves.

'Alfred sold his entire library of Greek and Latin classics in order to buy these Sanskrit texts,' Henry explained, a touch of sadness in his voice.

Blackwell examined the books with reverence.

'You can reassure Mrs. Williams that they will be relocated into the Bodleian Library,' he said softly, understanding the depth of Alfred's sacrifice.

Henry led Blackwell upstairs to Mary's room. The air was laden with the scent of roses, which filled a vase next to the bed, and the muted light of the afternoon filtered through the half-drawn curtains.

Mary lay in bed, her frail form barely making an impression on the mattress. Her pale, yellowish skin was drawn tightly over her withered face, and only her eyes moved. She smiled at Blackwell and pointed to a case on the floor next to the bed.

Henry opened this to reveal the revised typescript of the *Tales of the Panchatantra*. He handed it to Blackwell, who smiled reassuringly at Mary.

'I promise you that your husband's Sanskrit texts will be well bestowed, and I will lose no time in producing this book,'

Blackwell said earnestly.

Mary responded with another smile and extended a withered hand to Blackwell. He gently took her hand in his, feeling the fragility of her condition. It was clear that the effort expended by Mary was taking its toll on her, and the time had come for him to leave.

'I will always remember meeting with your husband,' said Blackwell softly, 'for he was one of those who left you a better man than he found you.'

Mary's eyes glistened with tears as she nodded slightly, her strength waning. Henry and Blackwell exchanged a sombre glance, understanding the depth of the moment. Blackwell squeezed Mary's hand one last time before releasing it and standing up.

'Thank you,' Mary whispered, her voice barely audible. 'Alfred would have been so grateful.'

'It is I who am grateful, Mrs. Williams,' Blackwell replied. 'Rest assured, his legacy will endure.'

THE PALACE OF MY IMAGINATION

Chapter 46

On the day of Alfred's funeral, Byett stood at the edge of the gathering, his thoughts torn between sorrow for his friend and anger at the injustice of it all.

His first thoughts the day before had been for Mary. She knew her time was short, and though she couldn't be present in person he had made sure that she was able to observe the slow procession to the churchyard from her bedroom window. He had spoken to her earlier, her voice barely above a whisper, as she expressed her gratitude for being able to witness Alfred's final journey. Now her frail silhouette was just visible from the church gates, and he hoped sincerely that the view from Ranikhet offered her some small comfort.

Henry, meanwhile, was lost in memories.

The night before, he'd sat by Alfred's still form, unable to reconcile the lifeless body with the vibrant man he once knew. Alfred's blue eyes had always sparkled with enthusiasm, and his voice, so full of life and expression, redolent with melodic variations of light and shade, had always been a joy to listen to. Now, the man who had charmed so many with his wit and intellect lay cold, his drawn face showing the pinch of starvation, a victim of circumstances that seemed too cruel to accept.

As Henry joined the funeral procession walking directly in front of the coffin down Church Lane, his anger simmered. The injustice of it all gnawed at him. If only Alfred had been granted the Civil List Pension a few months earlier, he thought bitterly, things could have been different. Alfred might still be alive, after all he'd only lived fifty-three years and he should have looked forward to at least another decade or two of working, writing, and sharing his unique gift with the world.

Henry's bitterness only deepened as he recognised faces in the crowd—some belonging to those who had refused to buy Alfred's books, those who had dismissed his work as irrelevant, and those who had scoffed at his passion for literature.

JOHN CULLIMORE

The chairman of the Swindon Education Committee was there, the very man who had told Alfred he was wasting his time studying literature and languages, and that he should focus on practical skills if he wanted to succeed at the GWR factory. And there, too, were representatives from the factory itself, men who had criticised Alfred's work publicly and swore he would never again be employed under their roof.

The hypocrisy of it all sickened Henry. Here they were, gathered to pay their respects, to offer hollow words of praise for a man they had neglected and scorned. It was as if they were turning Alfred's tragic death into some grotesque spectacle, eulogising him as a hero while conveniently forgetting the part they played in his downfall.

The words of the old adages echoed in Henry's mind—prophets are always without honour in their own country, and genius is often recognised only after death. Never had those sentiments felt truer than today, as he stood among a crowd that had failed his friend in life but now sought to immortalise him in death.

Yet, just as his anger threatened to overwhelm him, Henry paused. This wasn't what Alfred would have wanted. The past was beyond reach, and no amount of bitterness could change what had happened. With a deep breath, Henry let go of his resentment, choosing instead to honour Alfred's memory by remembering the joy and brilliance he had brought to those who truly knew him.

Alfred's story, Henry knew, wasn't just one of tragedy and neglect. It was one of passion, creativity, and a love for the written word that no amount of hardship could ever fully extinguish.

Two weeks after Alfred's funeral, Mary passed away peacefully at Ranikhet.

THE PALACE OF MY IMAGINATION

EPILOGUE

Chapter 47

9th April 1930. Doon Valley, Northern India

At midnight, in the delivery ward of the maternity hospital in Dehradun, Rosa Milne gave birth to a healthy son. Her husband, Peter, a British army officer, was away on manoeuvres in the Northwest Frontier Province. They had previously decided on a shortlist of names, and Rosa felt that Adrian suited him best, and it recalled the name of her Anglo-Indian father.

The infant thrived in their home in Dehradun, a small town nestled in the foothills of the Himalayas. Rosa took great joy in caring for Adrian, her days filled with the gentle rhythm of feeding, bathing, and rocking her son to sleep. The serene landscape of Dehradun, with its rolling hills and lush greenery, provided a peaceful backdrop and Adrian's childhood was filled with the natural beauty and tranquility of the sub-Himalayan landscape. The family lived in a charming colonial-style bungalow surrounded by lush gardens.

At the age of five, Adrian was enrolled in St. Thomas' School, a prestigious day school catering to children of British and Anglo-Indian families. The school, located in an elegant building with high, arching windows, offered sweeping views of the surrounding hills, lending the institution an air of both tradition and serenity. The curriculum followed the British educational system, with a strong emphasis on both academic excellence and character formation, fostering an environment where Adrian's intellectual curiosity could flourish.

Adrian thrived in this setting. He quickly developed a strong affinity for literature and history, two subjects that seemed to captivate his ever-curious mind. His teachers often remarked on his eagerness to learn, encouraging him to delve deeper into topics that went beyond the curriculum. The school's library soon became his favourite refuge, a sanctuary where he could lose

JOHN CULLIMORE

himself in books that transported him to distant lands and times. During school holidays, his passion for reading persisted.

One memorable summer, when the family rented a house near Mussoorie, Adrian made a thrilling discovery: a small, cool room at the back of the house that housed a tall bookcase packed with novels and reference books. While his father eagerly tried to engage him in activities like fishing, tennis or cricket at the local club, Adrian was increasingly drawn to the worlds found within the pages of Dickens, the Brontë sisters, and even the Bible.

That summer, he devoured books, his favourite discovery being Shakespeare's *Hamlet*. Its themes of murder, love, and unchecked revenge captivated his young imagination.

His growing love for literature paved the way for his next big step. Just after his thirteenth birthday, Adrian was awarded a scholarship to a prestigious public school in Shimla. The transition to the new school was seamless, and Adrian flourished there.

His intellectual growth was rapid, particularly in literature, where his passion only deepened. Volunteering to manage the school library, Adrian took it upon himself to read as much as he could, developing what one of his teachers described as an almost encyclopaedic knowledge of the great authors and their works. His command of language and his ability to articulate his thoughts matured, enabling him to win the school essay prize two years in a row.

For his sixteenth birthday, Adrian asked his parents for a gift that signalled the beginning of his serious writing aspirations: a second-hand typewriter he had spotted in the window of a curio shop in Dehradun.

When it was finally his, he set to work, starting with stories inspired by the very world he knew best—his school. These early stories captured the camaraderie and mischief he shared with his classmates, and the pranks they pulled on unsuspecting teachers.

Adrian sent his early efforts to various Indian magazines. Although most responses were polite rejections, his persistence paid off when one of his stories was accepted for publication shortly before his seventeenth birthday, earning him the modest

THE PALACE OF MY IMAGINATION

sum of five rupees.

However, just as his writing ambitions were beginning to take flight, tragedy struck. It was a few days before the end of the summer term of his first year in the sixth form when Adrian was called to the office of his housemaster, Mr. Bevis.

With a grave expression, Bevis had to deliver heartbreaking news that would change the course of Adrian's life forever.

It was lunchtime and Bevis knew Adrian could be found in the school library. He thought it wise to have the school nurse accompany him.

Adrian's heart skipped a beat as he saw the sombre expressions on the faces of his housemaster, Mr. Bevis, and the school nurse, Miss Whitfield. He carefully marked his place in *Robinson Crusoe* and set the book down, feeling a sense of dread wash over him.

'Adrian,' Mr. Bevis began gently, 'I'm afraid we have some difficult news.'

Adrian's mind raced, trying to prepare himself for whatever they were about to say. Miss Whitfield stepped forward, her eyes filled with empathy.'

It's about your mother, Rosa,' she said softly.

There was an awkward silence and then Bevis said.

'The Good Lord has called her back to Him.'

Adrian looked perplexed.

'Called her back. Why, what does that mean?'

'I'm afraid you mother has died,' said Miss Whitfield.

Rosa had collapsed at home and despite being rushed to hospital, was dead on arrival. The doctors later confirmed that she had had a fatal brain haemorrhage.

Adrian was immediately sent home where his grandmother was waiting to console him. His world had been turned upside down. He had loved his mother deeply. Rosa had ensured that his upbringing was well-rounded, and she had taught him about his Indian heritage and the importance of family values.

She had made an important contribution to his love of books. Evenings at home were often spent reading together, with Adrian eagerly listening to tales from both Western literature and Indian folklore.

Adrian's grief was overwhelming in the days following his mother's sudden death. The vibrant, nurturing presence of Rosa, which had filled their home with warmth and love, was now a painful void. The funeral was a bleak and serious occasion, attended by family and friends, all sharing in the sorrow of losing such a cherished soul. Adrian stood next to his father, Peter, feeling the weight of his loss pressing down on him like never before.

After the funeral, Peter, recognising his son's distress and knowing that he would have to return to the barracks in the Punjab within a week or two, decided it was best for Adrian to spend the summer with his grandmother, Teresa.

Teresa's bungalow was nestled further up the valley, on the borders of the forest, and offered a change of scenery and a refuge from Adrian's recent painful memories.

During these weeks of grieving, Adrian had not been able to displace Rosa from his mind. Although he had always been somewhat self-reliant, having spent some years at boarding school, he now really craved the need for solitude and privacy.

To achieve this, he began to venture outdoors regularly. He started to wander around Dehradun - the bazaar, the fish market, the railway station, the police station, the tea estates, the clock tower, the temples and mosques. He walked everywhere, not really thinking, believing somehow that he was being led by his mother on an affectionate journey through places which would have been familiar to her.

When he grew tired, he ventured into the cinema. He saw the 'Wizard of Oz' and he entertained the notion that the monsoon rains, soon to come, might sweep him off to a fantastical place where he could be with his mother again. The thought brought bittersweet comfort, helping him to start to process his loss while sensing her presence beside him.

After a week or so at his grandmother's house, he had asked to sleep in the bedroom his mother had as a child.

Here, he was surrounded by her cherished possessions, faded

THE PALACE OF MY IMAGINATION

photographs of her youth, and the remnants of a small library. Like Adrian, his mother had a penchant for reading, and it was clear from her books that poetry was her particular passion. He found solace in the familiar scent of these aged books. The bedroom became his sanctuary.

Among the volumes that caught Adrian's attention were anthologies of poetry—dog-eared pages marked with his mother's delicate handwriting in the margins, where she had underlined her favourite verses or scribbled poignant reflections.

But there was one in particular that captivated him. Its title was *Selected Poems* by Alfred Williams. What made it especially fascinating was the inclusion of a whole section of Indian poetry, some of which had been written in places where his father had been stationed—and where he had visited him; Cawnpore, and Ranikhet amongst them.

One of the poems about Ranikhet especially caught his interest and he decided to copy it. Noticing that his mother had marked the page with a peacock feather, he carefully transcribed the verses into his journal. As he wrote, a strange shiver ran down his spine.

'Where burns the tiger, fiercely vext,
The panther, crouching in his den,
And rugged lion, leaping next,
To rend the ruby hearts of men.'

Sitting on the terrace, he continued his perusal of the Williams' book of poetry. As the sun began its descent on an early summer day at the edge of the forest above Dehradun, the atmosphere was imbued with a tranquil yet vivid beauty. The sky transformed into a canvas of warm hues, blending shades of amber, rose, and gold that gradually deepened into twilight blues and purples. The fading light cast long, soft shadows through the trees, their leaves rustling gently in the evening breeze.

His grandmother emerged onto the terrace bearing a tray carrying a selection of food. Warm, fragrant pakoras, delicately spiced samosas, a bowl of tamarind chutney and a small dish of cooling raita. There was also a plate of freshly cut mangoes, his particular favourite, their golden flesh glistening in the fading light. She asked him to retrieve a thermos of steaming chai from the kitchen, where the aroma of cardamom and ginger wafted through the air.

They observed the last rays of sunlight dipping below the horizon, enjoying the comforting presence of each other and the simple yet delicious food.

The air became filled with the rich, earthy scent of pine needles mingled with the faint sweetness of blooming wildflowers. The fragrance of the forest floor, damp from the day's heat, rose up, carrying with it the subtle hints of moss and fern.

As darkness took hold, the forest came alive with sounds that echoed through the stillness. The rhythmic chirping of crickets began to dominate the air, creating a soothing symphony that seemed to blend with the soft whisper of the wind through the branches.

In the distance, the low, mournful hoot of an owl echoed through the trees, while the rustling of small creatures in the underbrush hinted at nocturnal life beginning to stir. The sound of a nearby stream, gently flowing over rocks, provided a calming background, its steady murmur a reminder of the forest's timeless rhythm.

Fireflies started to appear, their tiny lights flickering like stars scattered amongst the trees, adding a touch of magic to the gathering darkness. The forest seemed to be wrapped in a serene embrace as the last light of day slipped away.

Adrian felt a sudden weariness, and his eyes closed involuntarily.

'It's time you went to bed, young man.' said Teresa, as she stood to clear away the dishes.

'Thank you, Dadi,' Adrian murmured affectionately, 'I'll see you in the morning.'

Teresa smiled warmly at her grandson, her eyes reflecting the tender affection she felt for him.

'Goodnight, my dear. Sweet dreams.'

THE PALACE OF MY IMAGINATION

Within seconds of his head touching the pillow, Adrian was asleep.

The next thing he knew, the scene had changed dramatically. He found himself seated high up amidst the forking branches of a tree projecting over the edge of a steep ravine.

Looking down, he saw a thirty-foot drop below him. He was clutching a rifle, his feet supported on a network of ropes slung between branches. He was dressed in a khaki uniform, and squinted as the sun crested the ridge ahead, its bright rays briefly blinding him, prompting him to adjust the brim of his hat for shade.

Peering into the depths of the ravine where the valley flattened out, he sensed movement. His heart raced as he spotted an animal, moving lithely and fearlessly yet almost noiselessly through the undergrowth. It was a magnificent tiger, its muscles rippling beneath a coat of burnished orange and black stripes, leading back to a tail that flicked powerfully. The tiger began its ascent of the ravine with graceful, confident strides.

Suddenly, a shot rang out from the high branches of a tree on his left. Although the shot did no more than graze the tiger, the animal halted, looked to its right, and then changed its course, heading straight for the tree in which he was seated. Another shot came from the left, but still the tiger's approach was unimpeded. As the tiger sprang, it let out a great roar that reverberated through the ravine.

In panic, he dropped his rifle and covered his eyes. He could hear the rustle of leaves and feel the vibrations of the tiger's powerful leap. The roar grew louder, filling his ears and drowning out all other sounds. As he sensed the tiger's breath on his clasped hands, hot and moist, Adrian's fear peaked.

He braced himself, waiting for the inevitable, when, suddenly, there was silence.

His heart was hammering in his chest as he slowly opened his eyes. To his astonishment, he was no longer in the tree. Instead, he found himself back in his bed, drenched in sweat, the morning light streaming through the window.

JOHN CULLIMORE

The dream lingered in his mind, leaving him both awed and unsettled by the apparent reality of the experience. But gradually, he was engulfed by a feeling of peace and understanding.

He felt sure that his mother's spirit had at that moment moved on but in doing so had left him with with another feeling - a clear sense of his purpose in life.

He knew now where his destiny lay. Picking up the photograph of his mother as a young woman, he kissed it gently and murmured a soft thank you.

He would become a writer—a faithful recorder of the events and emotions, the victories and failures, the joys and the horrors of life.

Deep within him, something assured him that he had made the right choice.

John Cullimore   November 2024

THE PALACE OF MY IMAGINATION

Afterword and Historical note

Alfred Williams was a real-life poet and writer, born in the village of South Marston, Wiltshire. He was celebrated as a poet and author during the second and third decades of the 20th century, but tragically died prematurely aged 53, ending his life in poverty and hardship.

I first became aware of him when I moved to Swindon in 1992. As I delved into Swindon's heritage, I discovered Alfred's remarkable story. Despite his limited formal education, he experienced a life-changing intellectual awakening while working at the forges of the Great Western Railway Factory in Swindon. His extraordinary efforts at self-education led to the creation of his poetry and prose, which garnered significant recognition in the media of his time and cemented his status as an artist.

Reading his works, I was captivated not only by his creative output but also by the way he lived his life and the challenges he overcame. Many share the view that "His greatest work was his life" [1,2]. His dedication to achieving his artistic goals under such challenging circumstances is what made him exceptional. Yet, in Swindon today, there is little apparent to commemorate his life, and aside from his seminal work, *Life in a Railway Factory*, much of his writing is no longer in print.

In telling Alfred's story in the form of a novel, I have adhered to the broad strokes of his life while making some adjustments for narrative purposes. To maintain the story's flow, I have applied some time compression, particularly to the early years of his life, meaning that the dates do not align exactly with historical records.

The characters of Alfred, his wife Mary, George Ockwell, Henry Byett, Reuben George, Lou Robins, and Sir Basil Blackwell were real and significant enough to merit inclusion in this fictionalised account.

This novel gave me a valuable opportunity to delve into Mary's character. The biographies offer little insight into the true nature of Alfred's life partner. In Clark's biography, she isn't even mentioned in the index, and nearly all references to her are superficial, apart from the account of their courtship.

She is depicted as a silent, dutiful figure—essentially voiceless and without opinions. However, the reality must have been far more complex. I enjoyed reimagining her character, giving her both strengths and vulnerabilities that not only brought her to life but also helped drive the plot forward.

The other characters in the novel are fictional. There were some notable exceptions who were modifications of true characters including the vicar in South Marston who publicly burned Alfred's books, and a known but unidentified individual, likely to have been a prominent farmer, who harassed and abused Mary Williams. This latter person inspired the character of Osney, one of Alfred's principal antagonists in the novel. This incident was mentioned, though not detailed, in Byett's biography of Alfred [3].

Another of Alfred's key antagonists, the factory foreman, was well-documented in real life, though his name was never revealed. Readers seeking further information may find the two major biographies of Alfred Williams [2,3] particularly enlightening.

All the dialogue in the novel is fictional with the exception of a few italicised quotes and some of Sir Basil Blackwell's sentences are reasonably accurate renderings.

As a child, Alfred once lay down on the railway tracks as a long luggage train passed over him. While this may sound perilous, it was apparently less dangerous than one might imagine in the era of broad-gauge railways and before the introduction of standard gauge track and transversely placed railway sleepers. However, the experience frightened Alfred sufficiently that he never repeated it!

Alfred visited all the places mentioned in the novel.

While there is no evidence that he directly confronted German troops, his long sea voyage and his training as a gunner inspired me to imagine an action sequence off the coast of Madeira.

Similarly, though he did not take part in a tiger hunt, his diaries describe encounters with a diverse array of wildlife, including

THE PALACE OF MY IMAGINATION

tigers, in the areas he explored throughout the subcontinent. They also confirm the presence of a man-eating tiger near Ranikhet during his stay, providing a dramatic context for this part of the novel.

He did attend a séance in Durban, though the full extent of the medium's predictions remains unknown. Nevertheless, her comments deeply unsettled him.

I chose to write a novel about Alfred because his story is both exciting and tragic, worthy of being recounted at a time when his memory is rapidly fading in his hometown. In a novel, I could bring Alfred and his world back to life within its pages. I could explore his attitudes, beliefs, and decisions through imagined conversations and interactions with other characters. This allowed me to delve into his emotional depths in a way that biographies often cannot.

Ultimately, the challenge—and the joy—of writing a novel about Alfred has been to convey an uplifting message about an extraordinary life. I hope I have succeeded and that his story will continue to be celebrated far beyond the limits of his origins.

Acknowledgements

I would like to acknowledge all the help I have received in writing this novel. First and foremost, my thanks go to Caroline Ockwell, the Chair of 'The Friends of Alfred Williams.' As far as I know, this is the only remaining group dedicated to preserving Alfred's memory, with an ever-diminishing membership. Caroline, a lifelong resident of Swindon, possesses extensive knowledge of the local history and geography of Swindon and Alfred's corner of North Wiltshire. More significantly, her family originates from South Marston and her great-grandparents lived next-door to Alfred whilst he lived in Cambria Cottage. In the novel, Uncle George is based on her great-grandfather. His son, Charlie was Alfred's childhood friend and featured in two of Alfred's poems. Caroline's lifelong passion for Alfred's legacy has driven her efforts to campaign for the preservation of Alfred's

JOHN CULLIMORE

house, Ranikhet, ensuring it remains intact for future generations to appreciate.

I would also like to thank Harini Narayan, one of my former colleagues from Swindon, she hails from Bangalore. Her insights into the historical, philosophical, and religious aspects relating to the Indian subcontinent were invaluable to this project.

In 2009, I co-wrote a musical play about Alfred entitled *The Hammerman* with my schoolfriend John Moorhouse, a teacher and playwright. My contributions included composing the songs and orchestrations, while John crafted the libretto. Supported by the Heritage Lottery Fund, the musical was performed in 2010 and 2012. John's work demonstrated the popular appeal of Alfred's story and was imbued with his characteristic gentle humour. John's passing in 2023 was a profound loss, and I remain deeply grateful for his role in maintaining my interest in Alfred.

Finally, I must extend my gratitude to the staff at the Swindon and Wiltshire History Centre in Chippenham and at the Swindon Central Library. Their assistance in granting me access to archives, including Alfred's diaries, correspondence, and original works, was invaluable. These materials remain available for public viewing by appointment.

For further information, please visit my website: https://johncullimore.wordpress.com.

Further reading

1. David McKie, 'A life of hard graft and great craft', Guardian, 17th May 1995, p. 15
2. Leonard Clark, 'Alfred Williams. His life and Work. David and Charles, 1969
3. Henry Byett, 'Alfred Williams. Ploughboy, Hammerman, Poet and Author. The Swindon Press, 1933

Printed in Great Britain
by Amazon